"You broke your captain's jaw," the woman said to Worf, "and three ribs."

Worf shrugged. "It is not my fault if he had weak bones."

"Why did you come to this planet? To Sindikash?"

"I like the architecture."

The woman's mouth pursed a bit. "You're absent without leave. There's an assault charge pending."

"How interesting." Worf's words were calm, but inside, his Klingon spirit was raging. This woman had turned many strong Klingons into little more than *P'tak*—dishonorable slaves who did their evil masters' bidding with no thought of honor. And now he must pretend to be just another one of her conquests. Would his warrior's heritage let him act as a Klingon with no honor at all?

STAR TREK
THE NEXT GENERATION®

ANCIENT BLOOD

DAY OF HONOR

BOOK ONE OF FOUR

1

DIANE CAREY

POCKET BOOKS
New York London Toronto Sydney Tokyo Singapore

An *Original* Publication of POCKET BOOKS

POCKET BOOKS, a division of Simon & Schuster Inc.
1230 Avenue of the Americas, New York, NY 10020

ISBN: 0-671-00238-4

First Pocket Books printing September 1997

10 9 8 7 6 5 4 3 2 1

Printed in the U.S.A.

Dedicated to our great-aunt Katie Simon, who, by not retiring until the age of 89, taught us and our kids all about hard work and its wonderful rewards.

ANCIENT BLOOD

Chapter One

"CAPTAIN PICARD, MY MISSION is urgent. If it fails, six star systems and ten Federation colonies are going to fall under the influence of the most nefarious planet in this sector. I can't give you any more details than I have already. All I can say is we're picking up two key witnesses on whom our entire plan depends."

Interesting words.

Strange.

Evasive, yet somehow revealing.

"Commissioner . . . you're asking me to use my starship to delay a legal transport in authorized spacelanes."

"That's right, Captain."

"So you can arrest two of the passengers?"

"Arrest is a little harsh. Take them into protective custody is how I'd put it."

"Very well. If it's so vital, let's go get it done."

Jean-Luc Picard hadn't bothered to sit down in his ready room just off the ship's bridge. The commissioner followed him out, and Picard felt the other man's eyes all the way.

His first officer and security chief were waiting on the

bridge. They were the only bridge crew who looked at him. The others—ops, helm, science station, tactical, engineering—were all fixed on their duties. Lieutenant Commander Data, in his elementally android manner, concentrated on his console and on the dominating main viewscreen at the fore of the bridge, which showed a docile vision of an oncoming ship.

"Transport on the screen, Captain," William Riker reported. "Roughly ten kilotons, carrying cargo and thirty-two life-forms."

"Pull them over, Number One." Picard turned then to the security officer. "Mr. Worf, prepare to go aboard and take two persons into custody. We'll be remanding them to Commissioner Toledano."

The Klingon officer nodded once. "Aye, sir."

At Picard's side, the commissioner leaned close and murmured, "Must've been hard for you, getting used to having a Klingon on the bridge of a Federation starship."

Will Riker—a bit taller than the Klingon though not as brawny—came down the port ramp, his eyes fixed on the transport as they drew nearer. "Hail them, Mr. Worf."

"Aye, sir," Worf responded, and played the glossy console before him to open hailing frequencies. Then he spoke into the com receptors. "This is the U.S.S. *Enterprise.* Stop your engines and prepare to be boarded."

"Do our—passengers—know we're coming?" Picard asked.

"No," Toledano replied. "It was too risky to tell anyone. There are two people on that ship who have to be isolated and protected. There's no place safer than a starship. Then, we'll rendezvous with another starship, which will take them to an unspecified starbase. Even I don't know the ship or base. Not yet anyway."

"We're in the vicinity of the Vaughn-Creighton system, aren't we?"

"Uh, yes."

"Does this have anything to do with the planet Sindikash?"

"I can't talk to you about that yet."

"Yes, you said that."

"Sir, they are not reducing speed." Commander Data's android face remained typically expressionless.

"No answer to our hail, sir," Worf added from the upper aft bridge, his bass voice like low thunder.

Picard deliberately said nothing. There was a certain art to captaincy, and that involved not doing his crewmen's jobs for them.

"Tractor beams," Riker decided.

Data looked at his board and worked it. "Tractor beams engaging, sir. Sir . . . their engines are still not reducing power. There is no response at all. They have not raised shields."

"Prepare to beam aboard immediately," Picard injected. "We'll shut those engines off ourselves, or they'll overload."

"Why wouldn't they respond?" Toledano asked as he, Picard, and Worf headed for the turbolift. "Aren't they required to answer you?"

"Could be any number of problems," Picard said as Worf stepped aside to let him board the lift first.

Despite not wanting to talk to him "yet," Toledano had already told him a great deal. Two witnesses were involved in a tentacled network of espionage and were willing to speak to the Federation in exchange for sanctuary. Their information probably had something to do with Sindikash, the only habitable planet in the Vaughn-Creighton system, a colony of the Federation inhabited by Earth people from . . . Asia? No . . . Bulgaria? Something like that.

He felt Riker's questioning eyes follow them into the lift. The first officer should know what was going on, and there was a subtle chastisement in that trailing gaze.

A twinge of resentment boiled up in Picard as the lift doors closed. Not at Riker, but at Toledano. If the Federation had briefed him, told him what was going on, had followed procedure for covert missions, he'd have known whether he was dealing with Romulans or Orions or lizards or insects by now. He'd have reviewed the situation and informed his officers. Certainly no information could funnel off the ship without their knowing about it, and those witnesses would've been just as safe. Might it be asking so much for the Federation to trust its captains as much as the captains trusted their officers?

Instantly in his head he heard the arguments both ways, and pressed his lips rather than voice the thought to Commissioner Toledano, who would eagerly detail the Federation's side. Picard would be obliged to counter with the captains' side, and since he was already hearing it all in his mind, why hear it again in the lift?

"Mr. Worf, have you notified your security team?" he asked, determined to change his mind's subject.

"Four guards will meet us in the transporter room, sir," the big Klingon rumbled. "Also, one engineering technician, who will shut down the transport's engines, if they are not shut down already."

"Very good. Commissioner, I would appreciate some idea of exactly why I'm sending guards to my transporter room."

Toledano, a middle-aged man who had once been handsome and was now a somewhat silver-haired echo of that, sighed. "Captain, I can't talk to you about this yet."

"Regardless, I have to be able to give my team some idea of what they're looking for, or they won't be able to do their jobs. They won't be able to protect anybody if they don't know what they're protecting against."

The commissioner frowned, tried to add that up, and sighed a second time.

"These two people are witnesses to an event that could tie an interstellar espionage network to a person we haven't been able to implicate," he said. "No one on that transport knows who those two people are. When we get on board, the witnesses will disclose their identities to us, and we'll take them into custody. That's all there is to it, really."

"Mmm," Picard responded, and thought very little else. He fixed his eyes on the lift doors before them.

"No one on board this transport knows who the witnesses are?"

"Except the witnesses themselves," the commissioner said.

"Of course."

"They did all this themselves. They contacted us, they

arranged transport, they didn't purchase tickets or book passage until the last possible second—we don't even know what they look like."

Worf's comm badge beeped then, and he tapped it. "Lieutenant Worf."

"Security, sir. Transporter Room One is under repair. The molecular stabilizers are off-line."

"Very well. Divert to Transporter Room Three. Worf out." The Klingon touched the controls. "Diverting to Room Three, sir."

"Very well," Picard said. Another forty-five seconds in the lift.

"Hopefully, by the time we reach the transporter room, Mr. Riker will have pulled that transport over and be holding it. We should be able to beam directly on board and isolate your two witnesses straightaway."

"I'll breathe a sigh of relief then, Captain," the commissioner told him.

In the transporter room they came upon Worf's four security guards and Ensign Jensen, a new transferee barely out of Starfleet Academy but one who Worf had high hopes for. Since the *Enterprise* was so far away from central Federation space, the young man had been on two starships, two transports, and four Starfleet supply ships just to get out to the *Enterprise.* He was twitching with anticipation to actually beam out in the captain's company.

Picard could tell—he'd seen the look. And Jensen's eyes never once left him. As if the commissioner's jolly attention weren't altogether plenty.

"Ready, sir," the transporter officer said as they walked in. "The transport is stabilized. Mr. Data linked into their computer and managed to reduce their engine power by about forty-eight percent so far. He'll keep trying, but the rest'll most likely have to be done on board."

"I'm ready, sir!" Jensen piped.

Picard nodded. "Very good, gentlemen. Still no response from the crew?"

"No response, sir," the transporter officer answered. "But there are some scrambled emissions coming from over there, and Mr. Data thinks it might be an on-board mechanical malfunction. They might be trying to answer. They may be trying to shut down their engines, too."

"Understood." He turned to Toledano as he accepted a standard issue handphaser from Worf. "Let's take care not to startle them. Mr. Warren, energize as soon as we're in position."

He motioned the boarding party to the raised transporter platform, where each took a place on one of the clear disks as the transporter officer replied, "Aye, sir."

"Energizing, sir," Warren informed, and the familiar faint buzzing began.

In an unnoticeable minute, Picard's surroundings had changed to the chalky walls of the transport's docking bay. That moment of mental fog when the surroundings changed was shunted quickly aside. This place smelled like a slaughterhouse.

This place was also crushingly silent. Not even the throb of engines anymore. Data must have succeeded in shutting them down by remote.

But that smell—

"All hands, stand by . . . security alert." The sound of his own voice startled him.

Jensen moved into the captain's periphery. "Sir, permission to confirm engine shutdown?"

"Negative. Stand by."

"Ah . . . aye, sir."

Picard stepped across the small loading bay toward the passenger entrance, which was recessed downward about three inches and carpeted. A few paces beyond the step was the door to the seating coach. Worf stepped behind him, without requesting permission. Evidently he wasn't going to allow Picard to open that door without guard cover, and Picard did him the courtesy of not pointing out his defying the stand by order.

Together they descended the single step onto the carpet. Picard looked down, suddenly feeling as if he'd stepped into a soaked sponge and gone down to the ankle.

Behind him, someone gasped.

His foot and Worf's were down into the nap of the carpet,

which was indeed soaked through. A ring of glossy liquid cuffed his boot and Worf's. Only now did he realize that the burgundy color had nothing to do with the carpet itself. He had no idea what color it once had been.

Now it was the color of blood.

"Oh . . . God . . ." Commissioner Toledano's voice quavered with subdued violence. He drew a breath, but couldn't choke out another word.

His jagged face severe, Worf stepped past Picard to the door. He put his hand on the controls, then turned and motioned his four guards forward onto the gore-soaked carpet. He glanced at Picard. "Captain, if you would please step aside."

Though he summoned his voice, Picard also found it in the same state as Toledano's, and cut it back before some choked squawk came out. He nodded and stepped to one side, instantly nauseated by the pull of sticky suction on his boot.

How many life-forms had someone said were here?

Thirty?

He had started adding that up in gallons when the door sloshed open.

Worf went in first. Another security man flanked him, and together they aimed their phasers sharply in two directions. Then the three other guards splashed in, crouched, and took over the aim.

Leading the way into the coach, Worf's stiff posture wavered in a way that could only be described as shock. The other guards each reacted subtly, but they reacted. A shiver. A drooping phaser. A stumble down to one knee on the soaked carpet. Picard's alarm doubled as he followed them inside.

The coach was engulfed in the syrupy odor of corruption, blood, slaughter. To his left was the forward part of the cabin, to his right the aft. The rows of seats were all occupied, but with corpses.

All human or humanoid, he noticed first off, one head, two arms, two legs—except that the first ten or so rows of seats were occupied by people whose torsos were drenched from the necks down with bodily fluids. Their faces stretched upward, sideward, mouths aghast, eyes tight or wide, all staring in that last moment's frozen horror.

Under the astounded eyes of his captain, the stunned security men, the frozen commissioner, and poor Engineer Jensen, who still hadn't quite made it through the doorway, Worf took one confirming step toward the nearest couple of rows, then squished his way back to Picard.

"Sir," he rasped, "their arms . . . are missing."

"How many . . . like that?"

"Twenty-one, sir. Arms forcibly avulsed at the shoulder. Two of those have had their eyes gouged out. The remaining passengers' throats have been cut."

Standing near the entry, unable to move, Commissioner Toledano gulped, "What's 'avulsed'?"

Worf glanced at the commissioner, then at Picard, then the Commissioner again. "Torn off, sir."

Not cut. Not phasered. Torn.

Sheer force.

"The blood splatters on the bulkheads," Worf went on, "suggest the torture was done in this area. Then the victims were dumped back into their seats."

The lieutenant of the security squad, pale with revulsion, came back from his reconnaissance of the rest of the ship and the cockpit. He swallowed a couple of times. "Sir . . . captain and copilot are both . . . the arms are the same. The steward's over there, behind that serving cart. Guess he tried to hide. Didn't help, though. Engine room's pretty bad, too. Both engineers had their throats cut."

"Some with throats cut," Picard murmured, "some with arms pulled off."

He squinted at the rows of seats, a hideous procession of gore from fore to aft, and he walked along the rows, now desensitized to the squish of his boots on the blood-soaked carpet. The first two people's facial expressions were relaxed, almost as if they could look up and say, "Hello." Only the indelible stare of their eyes and the paper whiteness of their drained faces gave away their true condition, give or take the tunic of blood each wore. The second, third, fourth row . . . muscles frozen in perpetual astonishment, brows drawn, teeth bared, eyes wide. And it went that way, all the way to midships.

"These," Worf said, "saw those in front being killed. Their faces are mottled, as if flushed with panic before being drained by hemorrhage. The murderers started up there and worked their way aft, forcing these people to watch. Then . . . here," he said, stepping aft past several bodies who still possessed their arms; he paused at two corpses who were missing arms.

Picard noticed what he was getting at—those in front had their arms ripped off, then some didn't, then two did.

"Then these two spoke up," Worf suggested, as if relating the details of an ancient battle. "The attackers found what they wanted and came back here. And these two paid by having their living eyes gouged out before their arms were taken off."

The two pathetic corpses, a man and a woman, slumped in their ghastly final throes. The woman's head rested upon what was left of the man's shoulder, her hair matted with his blood and muscle tissues.

"Commissioner," Picard said, turning, "let me introduce you to your two witnesses."

Poor Toledano picked his way through faint impressions of the other men's footprints in a vain attempt to avoid the unavoidable blood soaking the carpet. "Do you really think so?"

"Our medical and forensic departments will confirm all these people's identities in comparison with the ship's manifest and the departure records. Assuming that *someone* knows who your witnesses were, I'll bet these two are the ones."

"Because their eyes are . . ."

"Yes, partly. They were obviously punished more than the others, with the intent that the message of this should get back to someone. Perhaps a lot of someones."

"How?"

"I don't know. Word does tend to escape in these kinds of events. A memo here, a whisper there, a security officer's spouse—it gets out. Whoever did this was counting on that, or they wouldn't have resorted to such theatrics. They didn't know who the two witnesses were, so they tortured everyone until the witnesses spoke up. They were brave people, hoping to save others by giving themselves up. Unfortunately, it failed. After the attackers found and tortured the witnesses, they took care of these others with some dispatch."

He looked sadly at the remaining passengers, whose throats had been cut.

"Those were the lucky ones," he added as his heart twisted in empathy. Innocent passengers, on a safe, well-traveled spacelane.

Worf splashed toward them, his legs bloody to the knees now. "Forensics will be making a complete investigation, but so far tricorders have failed to pick up any physical clues. There may be some dusty residue of skin tissue, but it will take some time to sort those out and do DNA identification." The Klingon stepped a little closer, and spoke more intimately than Picard had ever remembered him doing. "Sir, whoever did this . . . we are dealing with people who have no honor at all."

The weight of that was evident in the tenor of his voice, which seemed somehow deeper than Picard had ever heard it. Worf was deeply disturbed, and there was enough of his upbringing among humans left in him to let his feelings show.

Toledano turned a shade greener and sidled closer to Picard. "I'm sorry to say, I have a pretty good idea who did this."

Picard glanced at Worf, then frowned at Toledano. "Well, speak up, Commissioner, now's the time."

The nauseated Federation official steeled himself visibly. "We're pretty sure . . . it was a band of Klingons."

Worf stiffened. "Impossible!"

"I'm sorry," Toledano said again, but he seemed certain.

Suddenly furious, Worf confronted both Picard and the commissioner so powerfully that even Picard felt the threat in that posture. "Klingons do not arbitrarily torture anyone! Klingons will kill—but not like this!"

Toledano gathered his voice. "You know more about Klingons than I do, obviously, but . . . I'm sorry, but that's what I think we've got here."

"We'll discuss it back on the *Enterprise,"* Picard interrupted, seeing where this was going.

"Klingons do *not* behave this way!" Worf continued.

Picard shot him a warning look. "I said *later,* Mister Worf."

Clamping his mouth shut, Worf blew his fury out his nostrils.

"At the moment," Picard said, "we have a few more troubling questions. For instance," he went on tightly, "where are the arms?"

His crew and the commissioner glanced about, as if expecting to see a pile of ripped-off limbs in some corner. Such a presence would be dreadful. Its absence was somehow more so.

As the stink of the slaughter suffused the air around them, and Engineer Jensen shuddered in the doorway, driven mute by the horror of his first boarding-party mission, Commissioner Toledano managed the two steps to bring him to Picard's side. Pale as the thirty-plus victims, visibly holding down his supper, he lowered his gaze briefly to the bloody carpet, then raised it to Picard.

"Captain . . . I think we'd better talk."

In that posture, [illegible] instantly [illegible] anyone [illegible] will [illegible]

[illegible] more about [illegible] I'm sorry, but that's what I [illegible]

[illegible]

Maybe [illegible] don't have [illegible]," Worf commented.

[illegible]

Clenching his jaw [illegible] his [illegible]

"[illegible] the moment," [illegible] said. "[illegible] a few [illegible] questions. For instance, [illegible]"

[illegible] crew and [illegible] glanced [illegible] as if expecting [illegible] in some corner [illegible]

As the [illegible] of the situation [illegible] [illegible] Picard [illegible]

[illegible]

The true danger is when liberty is nibbled away, for expediency, and by parts.

Edmund Burke

Chapter Two

"Now you understand the kind of people we're dealing with. We have the specter of Sindikash, an entire planet, becoming a planet of criminals, a haven for the worst the galaxy has to offer. They'll take the whole sector down. We're right on the edge."

Federation Commissioner Perry Toledano crushed his hands into each other over and over, as if to wipe off the blood with which they had all been so thoroughly saturated. How surreal it had been, to board the *Enterprise* again and hurry off to separate quarters, to change clothing before many of the crew had to be exposed to the stink of uniforms saturated to the knees with blood. What a strange thing for a captain to have to consider.

"Why did you say that the Klingon Empire was involved in this?" Picard asked.

"I didn't say the Empire was involved," Toledano explained. "I said there were Klingons involved."

Worf smoldered so hotly it seemed his chair could have melted out from under him. "And *I* told you Klingons do not behave in that way."

"These Klingons do." Toledano offered a sympathetic but unforgiving shrug. "They're not working for the Empire. They're working for the ringleader of this crime network. I'm telling you, it's true."

"Commissioner," Picard interrupted, trying to pacify both men, "what Mr. Worf means is that Klingons are hardwired to react emotionally and violently. Because of that, they could never have survived as a culture unless they developed certain restraints."

"Restraints? Like what?"

"Like shame," Worf boiled over. "Klingons do not slaughter innocent people who have no weapons with which to fight back."

"It's a matter of honor," Picard added. "They even celebrate it. The Day of Honor is coming up next week, isn't it, Mr. Worf?"

Worf glared at Toledano. "Thursday. It could *not* have been Klingons."

"Okay," Toledano attempted, "but it was."

"Wait a minute," Riker interrupted. "I don't understand something. The criminal organization on this planet is no secret. Are you telling me that the ringleader is a secret?"

"No," Toledano said. "We know who it is. But we can't find any witnesses. You saw what happened to those who dared try to speak out. According to the laws of Sindikash, two witnesses are required to speak against a capital crime. Two, not just one. Two."

"This situation has been going on for nearly fifty years," Riker continued, "on a planet that was colonized well over a hundred years ago. What's the rush?"

Toledano bobbed his brows as if to indicate the validity of the question. "The rush is that they're about to hold a referendum—a special election. We've only got ten days. The election will do two things—one, it will select the new governor. The current governor is lying in a sickbed, in a coma, with an assassin's wound to his brain."

"Assassin? What kind of wound?"

"A projectile weapon."

"You mean like a bullet?"

"Something like that. When the colony was set up, they outlawed energy weapons for everyone except law enforcement officials. But there's a loophole—a lot of people started carrying propellant weapons and old style pistols, mostly for protecting their herds from predators. They found out they liked having those weapons, and a lot of people there even collect antique weapons. One of those struck the governor in the side of his head. Local doctors took the projectile out, but he's in a coma. Federation physicians were refused. We're not sure who refused them, but we have a pretty good idea."

"I can understand that," Riker commented. "A planet tends to trust its own, after all."

"We *are* 'its own,' Commander," Toledano told him. "These people are humans, settlers from Earth. They're directly descended from Earth people, and some of them are right from Earth. It's not like we were offering human physicians to work on Cardassians."

Worf shifted his legs impatiently. "What is the second thing the election will do, other than decide who the governor is?"

The commissioner met his eyes. "The second referendum is to decide whether the planet should secede from the Federation. Both candidates are promising to support withdrawal if that's what the people want. Sindikash will be just outside Federation jurisdiction, but *inside* the sphere of Starfleet patrol space. That'll throw all our jurisdictional laws into a gray area. What can we stop and what can't we?"

Riker nodded. "It's only happened five times in the whole of Federation history, and four of those were disasters. Surely the Sindikashians know that. Or Sindians. Or Kashites—what do they call themselves?"

"Seniards, Commander," Toledano corrected. "They call themselves Seniards."

"Why?" Worf asked.

The commissioner shrugged weakly. "I don't know—why are people from France called 'French' instead of 'Francians'?"

Riker shifted his long legs self-consciously. "Beats me,"

he mumbled, and glanced at Picard as if they had an inside joke.

Toledano looked ten years older than he had ten hours ago. His Federation agency suit was gone now, the crisp, gray, blood-stained suit now replaced by a more casual shirt and pants that didn't match. His face was creased with the memory of what he had seen aboard that ravaged transport. "That's why we chose the *Enterprise* for this mission. We need a Klingon." The commissioner looked nervously at Worf.

"There's a group of Klingon expatriates on Sindikash," the commissioner continued. "We can trace several instances of this kind of action—well, maybe not *this* bad, but bad—right back to them. They're not giving the orders, though. We need to get the person who is. So, Mr. Worf, this is a voluntary mission. You don't have to take it. Once you take it, though, you'll have to consider yourself committed, because we can't do it twice. And you can be sure that any lingering suspicions about whether your loyalties are to the Federation or the Klingon Empire will certainly disappear."

Worf felt all his body hairs go suddenly prickly and his eyes widen. He looked at the audaciously affable man, then at Picard, then back at the commissioner.

"Sir," he said sharply, "I will do this because it is my mission and my duty to do so. I will do it *because* I am a Klingon. If Klingons are doing these things, then I am the one to go."

Toledano seemed completely shocked at Worf's tone of voice. As his lips fell open, he glanced at Picard for explanation.

"You're insulting him, Mr. Toledano," Picard said. "You're lucky it's Worf you said that to, or *you* might be missing an arm."

"I'm . . . I didn't mean anything—"

"You implied," Worf said, "that I would have to be bribed to do my duty, sir."

Only willing to be apologetic to a degree, the commissioner nodded. "I don't think I exactly meant that. But it *will* look good on your record. It's not like Starfleet has a lot of

Klingons. Accept the apology and call me names after I leave. I don't really care. This problem is in my lap, and I've got to handle it the best way I know how. Right now, you're the best way."

To his credit, the commissioner stopped talking and let his words sink in. He was at once a troubled man, friendly, both certain and uncertain of himself, but he seemed to believe in what he was doing.

Worf allowed him that. "I understand."

"Thanks," Toledano replied gracefully. "If we can get two witnesses against the person we've targeted, we can make an arrest. The lieutenant governor's been acting as leader, but he's under constant attack by the other person on the ballot. That other person is the one we believe is the undisclosed kingpin of this network of crime webbing out into the sector. No—we don't *believe* it. We *know* it. We just can't secure evidence. You saw what happens when they feel threatened—"

"And that's why we're so interested in this election, isn't it?" Picard noted. A queasy feeling rose in his stomach. "If we can make an arrest, there can't be an election at all."

"That's right. Colonial law. You need both candidates, or no election."

"So your main objective is not to dissolve a criminal organization, but subvert an election process."

Toledano frowned. "You're making it sound bad. When the evidence is gathered, we want official Starfleet personnel to make the arrest. That way the trial can be held off-world, and be completely objective. That's not what I'd call subversive. Since there happens to be no *in absentia* clause in Seniard law, it'll be at least a year before another election can be organized. We have to arrest this candidate before the election, and have witnesses who'll testify that the organization leads right back to its source."

"And who is this candidate, Commissioner?"

"Her name is Odette Khanty. Captain, she's the injured governor's wife."

"The lieutenant governor and I have legitimate disagreements, and I'll address those, but not these tawdry allegations contrived for political gain. There's simply

no evidence to support any of these frivolous accusations against me."

Mrs. Khanty was quoted two days ago in the Ozero Square in Burkal City, where she spoke to Early News's Dushan Smith about the possible indictments against her and her staff.

"There will always be bad people. I can't know what's in the hearts of others. I only want what my husband wanted. I want what's best for the working people of Sindikash. Yes, I know there are risks. An assassin's attack has cost my husband a normal life. I know they'll get me eventually. All I can hope for is to live long enough to help the colony achieve independence from the United Federation of Planets. If that costs me my life . . . so be it. My husband has nearly given his life. I can do the same."

In the background, the gathered crowd launched into applause and cheers, and some chanted, "O-DETTE! O-DETTE!"

"Mind-boggling."

The captain's unhappy comment settled over the disturbing images of politics at work.

Nearby, William Riker leaned forward and manually clicked off the viewscreen. "It's as if she's speaking to six-year-olds."

From a chair set off to one side, as if in its own universe, Lieutenant Worf watched the captain, but said nothing. The idea that Klingons had done the torture on that transport still burned deep in him. He had not been able to eat or rest since Commissioner Toledano had first made that claim. If he could jump out of the starship and descend to that planet on the power of his outrage, he would do it.

He knew his own thoughts, but wanted to know Picard's. The captain would be Worf's barometer of action, for he could no longer trust himself.

The captain leaned back in the chair behind his desk. Picard's quiet presence always dominated any room.

As Worf watched Jean-Luc Picard now, he saw the

captain as he often did—more scholar than warrior. Yet Worf knew Picard as a strong man who would fight fiercely when he felt the time was right. It was clear that Odette Khanty's pseudo-philosophy troubled Picard. He seemed disturbed that the intellect of deceit was gaining an upper hand, and a Federation planet was slipping away in the grease of artful deception.

"You'll notice the media didn't challenge Mrs. Khanty at all," Commissioner Toledano pointed out, sitting on the other side of Riker. "She controls most of them, but there are still some who speak up against her. They just get shouted down. How can the people of Sindikash make an educated choice if they only see one side of anything?"

Riker, sitting near Worf in front of the captain's desk, added, "After the governor got shot, Odette Khanty's approval rating was higher than the lieutenant governor's, but now that's starting to wear off. They're about fifty-fifty."

Toledano nodded. "She's risen to popularity not on her own ability, but on sympathy for her husband. Any criticism is met with portrayals of her as a devoted wife being harassed by her husband's enemies. The people know Sindikash is degenerating into the local center of criminal action, but Mrs. Khanty has been claiming the Federation refuses to do anything about it. What gall! It's *her* criminal action!"

Despite the challenges of the mission, Worf's attitude was flagging. He could not muster much concern for a planet full of people who would swallow such tripe. His hands clenched and unclenched so hard that his fingernails cut into his palms with every grip. Anchoring himself on the pain, he burned to get going on this mission, to sweep up the filthy rumors of Klingons indulging in frivolous torture.

There had to be some other explanation, some key fact that had gone undiscovered.

He wanted to go there, turn Sindikash inside out until the molten core of the planet froze solid in the cold of space, and uncover those cursed facts.

Then he wanted to cram them in Commissioner Toledano's nostrils until his eardrums popped.

"This is a bizarre situation," Riker admitted, "but I've

got to tell you, I'm uneasy about intruding into a free election, even on a Federation colony."

Toledano shrugged impolitely. "What's your solution, then? Walk away from Federation citizens and let them be terrorized by criminals because you're 'uncomfortable' about interfering? Do we sit by and allow a group of thugs to spread to other planets? You're a pretty cold man if you can forget the blood we walked through just a little while ago."

The captain gazed in new admiration at the commissioner, and noted the annoyed glares of Worf and Riker. Toledano had more guts than he had first seemed to possess.

"Sindikash is still a Federation establishment," Picard told them. "The colony's been enriched, the standard of living has shot up, mortality rate's dropped, and the market for their goods is now quadrant-wide. It's always difficult to know how tightly to hang on when a colony wants independence. These things occur so rarely.Dozens of planets are petitioning to become part of the United Federation of Planets; it's suspicious when a planet tries to break off—especially when they'll still be within our sphere of protection."

"And they darn well know that," Toledano rushed in.

"Won't be easy," Riker pointed out. "Local power can be a monster to push aside. If she can manipulate the next judicial appointments alone, she'll be shielded from all kinds of charges. I hate when this sort of thing happens. The guidelines are always so vague."

"It *is* vague," Picard agreed.

Riker turned to him. "Sir, don't you think the people of Sindikash should choose their own leaders?"

Picard nodded forthrightly. "Yes, I do. However, we certainly should assure they have legitimate, honest leaders to choose from. If I were a citizen of Sindikash, I'd look to the Federation to help assure that."

"Mrs. Khanty is far from honest, sir," Worf said with undisguised contempt. "There are bogus trials and frequent executions, maimings in the name of justice, nighttime kidnappings, and mysterious deaths of key persons."

"Mmm," Picard intoned, obviously troubled. "She's only

in position to take over the governorship because her husband's in a coma."

"That's right. If he were dead," Toledano said, "the election would already have taken place. If he were conscious, there wouldn't have to be an election. With him in a coma, Odette Khanty's merrily sculpting public opinion in her favor. She'd never even be a candidate if this hadn't happened to him. She was running this illegal network, but she wasn't anywhere near planetary power. Now she's one election away from it. If we can find a way to arrest her, we can postpone the election. Then we'll have time to convince the colony not to secede."

Riker raised a brow. "You mean, time to pressure them."

The commissioner looked at the captain with grudging respect. "You're very blunt, Mr. Riker."

"His job is to be blunt," Picard spoke up. "And he's right. The Federation wants time to cut the favored-trade status, let the Seniards know what it's like to be out there alone, threaten to withdraw protection—"

"Look, we're not the brutes here!" Toledano said sharply, offended. "We're not going in with battleships like the Cardassians do!"

"No," Riker agreed, "but you'll cut trade, hit their goods with tariffs, withdraw patrols, frighten them, and you know very well that Starfleet won't stop patrolling this space."

Toledano waved his arms. "If this were the Klingons, you think they'd let any of their colonies go? Or the Romulans? Or the Cardassians? If Sindikash votes to secede, we won't go in with force."

Picard nodded. "But we certainly have a right to convince them otherwise, after the huge investment we've made. Let's face it—Odette Khanty knows the Federation'll still stick its neck out for Sindikash."

"And *you'll* be the ones doing it, Captain," the commissioner added. "You and the rest of Starfleet. Your job is to find a reason to arrest Mrs. Khanty. Not to frame her, but a legitimate charge—from her own records, a !rime with witnesses, or a recorded confession. She's not forthright enough to ever admit having done anything wrong, so that leaves us the other two options. It took years for her to create this criminal structure, and it'll take time to bring it down, but with this secession vote we're running out of time. We're in a race to make Odette Khanty a criminal before she becomes a governor."

Riker settled back in his chair, still troubled. "The people of Sindikash have the right to make a bad decision, Commissioner."

"You've made that point," Picard told him. "But don't forget—almost fifty percent of the population still wants to be part of the Federation. They've got rights to protection, too. If delaying this election process is the only way to ensure those rights, then we're willing to chance it."

Toledano pointed at Picard, but looked at Riker. "We don't want to *affect* the election. We just want to *postpone* it."

Now that all the conflicting points had butted antlers, the ready room fell suddenly quiet.

Picard sat in the midst of that silence for several seconds, running over in his mind all that had been said. He knew the decision was essentially his, even though this sounded like orders for a mission. He knew he could object if he believed he should when it came to something that was internal to a planetary government.

After a time, he sighed. "This is like opening a diplomatic pouch, gentlemen. We *can* do it, but we had better find illicit goods inside."

"So you'll do it?" Toledano pushed.

As he felt the eyes of Riker and Worf, each pulling in his own direction, Picard stood up. "We'll do it."

Chapter Three

"Is he here yet?" Alexander asked impatiently.

"Not yet. I asked you to wait in our quarters, Alexander."

"I couldn't wait. I never thought Uncle Ross would come onto the ship! I'm going to show him everything! Can I take him into main engineering?"

"Probably." Looking down at his son as they both waited in the transporter room, Worf realized that he had rarely seen such joy of anticipation in Alexander's face. A visit from a close family friend, almost a relative—no, such events did not occur often in starship life. Ross Grant had been very close to Alexander when he was living with K'Ehleyr, his now-deceased mother. How friendly Ross had been with K'Ehleyr was something Worf had no desire to learn, especially since Ross Grant had many times provided Worf with information that aided one investigation or another, and Worf had learned that Ross was excellent at his job, a reliable friend and, for a human, surprisingly driven by honor.

Alexander had not seen Grant in years. What else was Worf depriving his son of experiencing? Life on the starship had once seemed a good option. There were a few other children on board, though as tensions increased on the Romulan and Cardassian borders, such practice had become less and less popular with ship's crewmen.

Should I find another way? Would he be happier with relatives, on a planet, on Earth with his grandparents, rather than on a starship with his father? How much is a father worth? Should I ask him?

He turned to Alexander, opened his mouth to speak, and was driven silent by the boy's anxious twitching. Alexander looked at the transporter pad as if he could will the machine to start buzzing, then glanced at the console and the young transporter trainee adjusting the controls.

How much is a father worth who can barely summon the will to ask a simple question?

Worf cursed himself, and faced the pad again.

This business of being a parent . . . he had not planned for anything like that in his life, never anticipated these critical minutes. He had been shut out of Alexander's early childhood, but suddenly found himself responsible for the boy's youth. An important time for any boy, but especially a Klingon boy.

Now what?

He was rescued by the first signal beep of the transporter console, signalling that the person to be transported was ready on the other end. The other end was a Starfleet supply ship bringing necessaries to the starship, as well as serving as a transport for any persons who might be shifting assignments. Or visitors.

But Ross Grant was not a visitor today—he was on assignment from the United Federation of Planets Intelligence Agency, assigned to Worf's mission.

"Here he comes!" Alexander yelped, and rushed toward the transporter pads, to be stopped by his father's quick grab.

"Wait until he materializes," Worf admonished.

The transporter whined happily, singing the song of its job, and a pillar of lights appeared at the center right of the platform. A fog-faint sizzle of electrical action touched

Worf's face and told him the transport process was finishing up. That surge of power was a long-familiar clue.

"Uncle Ross!" Alexander called, unable to control himself until the process finished.

The lights swirled around a solidifying form, then washed the form in one last sparkle and dissolved, leaving a human of average height and build standing in the chamber, wearing a bright yellow plastic hat with a conical top and a wide brim in the back and a flat plate on the front.

"Uncle Ross!" Alexander charged the platform.

"Lex! Look at the size of this boy!" Ross Grant dropped his duffel bag and jumped down from the platform, where he met Alexander with an encompassing hug. The boy's lanky frame came right off the deck. The yellow plastic hat tumbled off Grant's head and fell on its conical top on the deck. "Yike! Dropped your present."

"A present?" The boy broke the embrace and dove for the hat.

"It's a helmet," Grant said. "Firefighter's helmet. It's over almost 180 years old. Belonged to my great-great-great uncle. He was a fireman in Seattle. See? Engine Company 9. I come from a whole long line of firemen and rescue workers. 'Course, then there's me, the computer wimp."

"You're not a wimp." Alexander swept the yellow helmet off the deck and turned it over and over in his hands. "It's for me? You mean it? Your family helmet?"

"Sure, I mean it. After all, you're the closest thing to a son I've got." Grant folded an arm around the boy. "That makes us family. So who's better to have it than you? It's your Day of Honor present. Your grandparents told me all about the whole deal, and I couldn't just let a commemoration go sliding by, could I? Kinda like Christmas. Now, don't forget to leave me milk and cookies tonight!"

"I won't!" Alexander beamed at him and slipped on the helmet. "How does it look?"

"Like it was made for you, buck. Now, clear out of the way and let me say hi to this mutant gorilla over here. Hey, Wuff! We're finally going to work together on a mission! Is this great?"

Worf reached out and caught the hand offered by their old

friend. "Very great," he offered. "It gives me reassurance to have you along."

"Liar," Grant laughed. "You're nervous as hell. You shouldn't have recommended me for this if you didn't want an old pal along."

"Grant," Worf moaned, knowing this would come up, "I did not recommend you."

Grant's smile didn't fade. "You didn't? Come on! What're the odds!"

"Evidently better than we expected." Worf stepped past him and picked up the duffel bag. "This is a complete coincidence. As impossible as it is to believe, you actually possess the skills this mission needs."

"Whoa—zing! Right in the heart. Don't play games now—you need me this time as much as during the Preficon II incident." Grant coiled his arm around Alexander again and struck a heroic pose. "I'm still putting out fires, just like all the Seattle Grants before me, except I put 'em out with brains instead of retardants."

"I'll carry that," Alexander announced, and took the duffel bag from his father.

"Oh—just a critical-mass second, buck," Grant said, and made him put down the bag. He opened it and pulled out a package. "Here you go, Lex. It's your Day of Honor present."

"But you gave me the helmet."

"The helmet's from me. This one's from your grandparents. It's a holodeck program. Journals from one of your Earth ancestors. They thought that since you're having a Klingon rite of passage, you ought to have something from your human side, too. I thought it was a nice idea. They're always thinking of you, punk."

"Thanks . . ." Alexander looked up at Worf. "Can I go see what's in it?"

Worf nodded. "You may scan the content, but do not use the holodeck without supervision. Understand?"

"Can you do it with me, then?"

The innocent question sent a lance of regret through Worf as he felt the answer tighten his throat. "I have a mission on a planet."

"On Sindikash?" Alexander anticipated.

"How do you know about that?"

"News gets around. The whole crew's talking about what happened on that transport."

"So much for security," Grant chuckled. He smiled and jabbed Worf in the chest. "Isn't that your job, big guy? Got no poker face at all, do you?"

"I had nothing to do with it."

"Yeah, yeah."

"Can I go scan the tape?" Alexander asked.

"Sure," Grant pushed in. "I'll get my gear squared away, and we'll go get some chow. It'll be like old times at your grandma's table. Big slabs of homemade bread, baklava, lamb chops—"

"We have replicator food on board the starship, Grant," Worf pointed out.

"Well, we can pretend, can't we? I'll see you later, Lex. Dibs on the biggest slice of ultra-super-replicator double-dollop slow death by melted caramel, deal?"

"Deal!"

With one last warm hug, Grant gave Alexander a little shove and sent the delighted boy dodging out of the transporter room.

Worf watched his son leave and fought to control a terrible grumble of regret. He could never remember hugging Alexander. Did the boy want to be hugged? Worf's foster parents on Earth were warm and friendly people, but they had held back in their demonstrations, wisely knowing that some day he would have to survive as a Klingon, and heavy emotions would have to be masked. He had assumed they were right, and taken the same course with Alexander.

But he and the boy lived on a ship full of humans. Did that mean Worf was the only person holding back in the boy's presence? Did his son see him as a cold island in a sea of warmth? Grant's free-flowing affection blanketed Worf with sudden self-reproach, and he didn't know what to do about that.

And Grant complicated matters when he turned to Worf and slung an arm around him—as best he could, given that he was a head shorter than Worf and half as wide.

"I can't believe I'm here!" he bubbled, and waved to the transporter trainee. "Hey, hi there."

"Afternoon, sir," the young officer responded, a little ill at ease with the chief of security right here.

"Like the job?" Grant asked.

"Yes, sir, I do. I've just started here."

"You married?"

"Grant," Worf snapped, pulling his old friend toward the door panels. "Back to work, Ensign Escobar."

"Yes, sir." The young officer averted his gaze instantly.

Worf scooped up the duffel bag that Alexander had frivolously forgotten now that its secrets were out, and steered Grant out into the corridor.

"What a great ship!" Grant gushed. "I couldn't keep my eyes off it as we were coming around to the docking port. Man, it's big. Ship's big, you're big . . . everything but me is big!"

As some of the tension of the past few days flowed away, Worf sighed. "You can stay in our quarters. After your gear is stowed, I can brief you on the mission."

"I know most of it," Grant said. "I heard about the . . . y'know . . . the . . ." He pointed at his shoulder and made a ripping motion.

"The arms." Worf sighed again, and more of that tension let go of him. He was no longer alone in this task before him. There was someone here who had a common background, if not common heritage, someone who knew him better than anyone else on board, and who was not intimidated or ill at ease around him.

Ross Grant wasn't ill at ease around anyone, and somehow that helped.

Grant lowered his voice. "Do you really think it was Klingons? Torture like that? People without any way of defending themselves? I mean, flash-and-burn is one thing, but torture . . . that's something else."

"The Federation suspects a band of Klingons on Sindikash. I intend to find out. Klingons would not consider those kinds of actions honorable. If the rumor is true, I want to know what kind of Klingon could do those things."

"Oooh, hot button," Grant cooed. "Not taking this

personally or anything, are we? Even if it's Klingons doing this stuff, how is it your fault?"

"Not my fault," Worf told him. "Somehow my responsibility."

"You're nuts. If humans are doing it, it sure isn't my fault. You always screwed yourself to the wall with that kind of thinking, and you're still doing it. This is a mission. You've got a job to do. That's all it is. We'll go down there, I'll work my magic, you'll break some heads, we'll crack the crime network, and leave a silver bullet behind as we ride into the sunset. You, me, a couple of white horses—you know the drill."

"I know."

Leading the way into the turbolift, Worf gripped the duffel bag as if it were some kind of lifeline, and he met Grant's easy expression and friendly eyes.

"For Alexander's sake," Worf said quietly, "your presence is a good comfort. He needs to see some elements of family from time to time."

"Well, he's got you, doesn't he? You're his dad. What else does any kid need?"

"More," Worf told him candidly. "Especially now, as he gets older."

Grant laughed. "You're so hardwired! Don't worry. I can see right through you, just like I always could. You just get a nice steel rod to chew on, tell me all about this graft on Sindikash, we'll go down and clear the field, then we'll come back to this crate and have a family reunion that'll shake the bulkheads."

As the lift doors opened on the deck where Worf lived with his son, he stepped out into the corridor, then paused. He tried to feel better about what was ahead of them, and in some ways he did, yet nagging anticipation kept him from being pleased that he and Ross Grant would now get the chance to blend their dissimilar abilities.

"Such an event," he said, "will be much more pleasant after this mission is over. I hope it ends soon."

With a nod, Grant chuckled again. "And you'll break its legs if it doesn't, right?"

* * *

"And that guy over there . . . a ferret." Grant was speaking quickly, clearly nervous.

"What?" Worf felt nervous as well. It was not fear of battle or conflict that was bothering him. It was the fear that Toledano had been right, that Klingons were involved in these dishonorable acts.

"You know. An Earth ferret."

"That is a human, not a . . . ferret."

"Oh, come on. Get involved, will you?"

Sitting in a public square watching passersby and trying to decide which animal they were in a previous life did not strike Worf as a pleasant way to pass the time. Grant's insistence on this activity was on a par with other eccentricities Grant had shown over the years, all of which amounted to speaking when there was nothing to say, or when speech was a detriment to their plans. But his flawless record had shown Worf that his sometimes strange behaviour was worth the price of his involvement.

"Oh, look at that guy over there. Elephant. No doubt about it. Ouch—and he's walking with a peacock!"

Worf grunted.

"An earth peacock, I mean. Oh—right there. Guy with the hat. Some kind of lizard, for sure. You can tell by the way he walks that he's got that kind of personality. And look at that mouth!"

"He is not a lizard. I have fought lizards."

"You always did have a concrete imagination. You shipboarders ought to unclench once in a while . . . chihuahua . . . panther . . . slime devil . . . hey, you're not eating. Aren't you hungry?"

"No."

"You didn't eat much when we had dinner with Alexander, either. It's the honor thing, right? Klingons shouldn't act like that. Y'know, I sure hated to say good-bye to Alexander so soon. I hope we can wrap this up fast. Will you relax? Why are you so nervous? You checked the schedule, didn't you? She's coming eventually, right?"

"Yes, she is coming."

"Vulture . . . mugatu . . . tribble . . . you can get me inside, can't you?"

"We shall see very soon."

"Because if you can, then I can find the trail. I've cracked criminal organizations on fifteen planets so far. You know how?"

"You talk too much, Grant. You always talk too much."

"Because I understand how technology helps criminals, that's why. They *have* to keep records. Any organization bigger than three people nowadays has to keep records."

"You have explained this before."

Grant continued without a break. ". . . They steal huge amounts of wealth and they have to keep track of it. And that track leaves prints. The riches flow back and point. And that's how you bring 'em down. You just get me to a computer inside the governor's private square. I can sniff out—hey! Hey! Look—there she is! She's coming!"

"Grant! Do not turn that way! Pretend you do not see her."

"Don't see her? How can anybody miss her? She's surrounded by guards."

"I *see* that."

"Man, they're ugly. They're coming this way! We're gonna be face to face with Odette Khanty! Do you think her husband's really in a coma?"

"Quiet! Get up very casually and walk to the side of the square. Move into the crowd. Leave me to deal with them."

"Forget it. This is my mission, too. I'm not leaving you here all by yourself. Even a gorilla like you needs a little backup."

"Then sit still. Sit very still. Whatever happens, do not be moved."

He felt the eyes of Odette Khanty and her guards. The Cafe D'Atraq was in the middle of the city square, and he knew she would not notice him as long as he and Grant did not get up. All the natives were clearing a path, tightening into the sides of the square to allow her and her elite team of Klingon guards to pass through.

This place, this planet and its townships, was a tapestry woven of the Oriental Express and the American Old West. With a transplanted populace of Greeks, Turks, Lebanese,

Armenians, Assyrians, Tuscans, and Moors, Sindikash bore a decidedly Gothic atmosphere. The planet's buildings were frontierish, its prevailing spirit exotic, and Worf and Grant were two outworlders in a place that knew its identity.

Watching Mrs. Khanty and her hooded guards move toward them under the tiled arches of the mosquelike square, Worf and Grant were now alone in a deserted cafe, while dozens of people eyed them from the sides of the square. All others had moved politely aside.

The woman touched the front of her pink suit to make sure it was perfectly presentable, then fingered the silk Paisley scarf neatly pinned at her neck. Her dark blond hair had been put perfectly in place, though it appeared to be casual; straight but thick, curved under slightly at the bottom, just above her shoulders. Just right. Feminine, yet efficient. Worf knew about her—she was not born to the place with which she had become so unbreakably associated. She saw herself as having earned her position.

Anger bled into Worf's heart as the eyes of the guards, the Rogues, fixed upon him and he felt their animosity.

Klingons. They really were Klingons! Every one of them was a *Klingon!*

Khanty nodded to her vanguard to keep moving forward in spite of Worf blocking their path.

Klingons. Klingons in service to a human. A human woman. A woman criminal.

What kind of Klingons . . .

He knew Commissioner Toledano wasn't lying, and Worf had expected Klingons, yet until this moment he had been hoping that the perpetrators of such atrocities were not *just* Klingons. Perhaps dregs had been dug up from all sorts of cultures across space, and Starfleet Intelligence had mentioned only the Klingons because Klingons were so visibly different from most humanoids. Perhaps that.

But now, as he looked at Mrs. Khanty's Rogues, as they were known on Sindikash, he saw that this was a pack of Klingons and only Klingons, a pack who had simply rejected anything Klingons are supposed to think about right and wrong, not here because of any sense of honorable conquest, duty, family loyalty, or anything else Klingons might be motivated by. These had just thrown all that away, cast off centuries of attachment to the things that held a culture together. These Klingons were destructively pursuing personal power, rather than acting in some way that would hold society, even Klingon society, together. Profit and gain could be pursued in a way that strengthened culture, but these Klingons wanted to go around those rules and achieve through the basest acts of brutality and opportunism.

Scum. Nothing. He was looking at empty hoods. Empty!

"Ugulan." Mrs. Khanty's voice sounded in the quiet square as she spoke quietly to the sergeant of her guard. "The Klingon."

"Yes, Mrs. Khanty." As if he didn't notice that he himself was Klingon and so were all his men, Ugulan motioned for his men to halt, but they remained in formation around her.

Then Ugulan himself stepped forward, his face deeply shaded by the purple hood. He moved through the empty tables to the one where Worf sat defiantly. With his purple hood and the dagger at his belt, he was effectively threatening.

"You will stand aside for Mrs. Odette Khanty to pass through," he said.

Grant looked at Worf, but said nothing.

Worf sipped his drink, took a long, considered swallow, then said, "I will not be moved."

"All citizens must stand aside when a public official comes through," Ugulan insisted. His tone implied this would be the last polite suggestion.

Worf looked up at him. "I am not a Seniard. Therefore I do not move."

"Therefore," Ugulan responded, pulling his dagger, "your friend is arrested."

Springing to his feet, Grant gasped, "What? Hey! I'm just visiting!"

The dagger swung upward as if to be its own exclamation point, and was on the downward arc when Worf came to life. Ah! At last! His move was extremely simple and not particularly inspired, a basic block of Ugulan's arm, but Worf imagined he had Ugulan nearly figured out already and could afford to not be creative.

He was right. Ugulan was thrown off, and clattered into a stand of empty iron chairs. The chairs went over, clanging like gongs against the brickwork street, and Ugulan went down among them. By the time he had scrambled to one knee, Worf was squared off between Ugulan and Grant, standing ground like a living portcullis.

One of the other Rogues clasped Mrs. Khanty's arm to draw her away from the developing trouble, but she resisted.

Worf didn't wait for Ugulan to get entirely to his feet, but freely charged the guard and drove him into a parqueted wall, knocking a stenciled sign from its hook. Ugulan's hood fell from his head, revealing his spinelike brow ridge and showing clearly that he, too, was a Klingon, as if there had been a bit of doubt.

Worf had clung to that silly doubt, but now his rage drove down his illogic.

Angry now, Ugulan reached into his jacket and drew his government phaser.

Worf didn't back off. "So," he said, "the Rogue Force of Sindikash uses women's weapons."

Evidently one of the universe's classic simpletons, Ugulan allowed himself to be goaded. He thrust himself to his feet and accommodated his opponent by holstering the phaser and bringing the dagger forward again.

Guarding Mrs. Khanty, the other Rogues were furious, too. Any guard who had his phaser out now put it away.

"You're so predictable, boys," the woman commented.

"Let us!" one demanded.

Would they make no move without her permission? Were Klingons not Klingons?

"Go, Genzsha," she said.

Two of the Rogues stayed with her, but the forward four rushed to Ugulan's side, and all squared off against Worf.

The big contenders circled slowly against the square's buildings. By appearance, Klingons fit well among the medieval dye colors of Sindikash—earthy, moody, deep and stirring colors that gave an impression of permanent autumn, flickering with gilded designs crafted from the planet's micalike ores. Even the brickwork imitated the woven texture of the Persian-style carpets the colony was famous for.

It also made a mean surface to knock against. Hitting a wall on Sindikash was entirely different from hitting a wall anywhere else. The walls here had exposed dentils of brick to smash against, and the newcomer made good use of that. Careful not to let Ugulan get a grip on him, Worf shoved Ugulan and two other Rogues into the same wall so hard that the impact set a stained glass window rattling. They all came up again, but came up bruised and gashed from the ragged brickwork. If only all planets cooperated so well.

Holographers who had been following Mrs. Khanty and the Rogues sprang forward now and began recording the moment. Some even dared skirt the onlookers or dodge through the grappling Klingons so they could get images of Mrs. Khanty standing there, watching calmly.

A silk wall covering shivered as Worf blew past, with two Rogues in his grip. The cafe became a blur of kicks, spins, elbows, and grunts. Stacks of etched clay urns dissolved and skittered across the brick, matched instantly by the audible crack of a limb. Worf almost stopped to make sure the limb wasn't his—then decided a broken arm would only make him angrier and that might help.

An instant later, though, one of the Rogues went down groaning. Genzsha moved forward to drag his fallen comrade from the arena, but did not join the fight himself.

Worf decided he would have to do without a broken arm, and therefore crammed his elbow into the face of a second Rogue and knocked him silly. Two down.

He knew he might be giving himself away—certainly, if they paid any attention they would see the Starfleet training involved in his movements. Not just the systematic moves of a schooled Klingon, but uneven elements of surprise, attack, feint, never letting his timing or style be mapped. Just when he was expected to block a punch, he would let it through, but dodge it, ripping every tendon in his attacker's arm. The two remaining Rogues were still fighting, but they were also dizzy and grunting.

Driven by the personal insult these men were to him,

Worf took on both at once, not allowing them to divide the attack as they attempted. He took a vicious blow from one, but, instead of swinging back, he reached out to the other and dragged them together before him.

Then, with physical control that surprised even himself, Worf lowered his arms and stood very still. His shoulders went slack. His stance changed. He stopped fighting.

Since he had stopped, the two remaining Rogues could no longer be justified in attacking him again. Like wolves twitching around a stag who refused to run, they blinked, gaped, shifted, and glanced back at Mrs. Khanty, but they didn't know what to do. Boiling with frustration, Ugulan burped a command in Klingon, and then the Rogues grappled the newcomer.

Their eyes rolled with contempt, for he had humiliated them by stopping. Clearly, they knew, Worf hadn't had to let himself be arrested.

His plan was a success. Odette Khanty was intrigued.

She moved between her battered guards and stood before the only Klingon in the square who didn't work for her.

"Why did you let yourself be taken?" she asked.

Worf controlled his breathing enough to imply that he wasn't even winded. He could breathe later.

"Because you have to maintain order," he said, too quietly for the people watching to hear. "If your men are not feared, you will not have order."

"Then why did you fight in the first place?"

"To demonstrate that I did not have to be moved if I did not want to be."

"If you had just let yourself be stunned, you'd have just woken up later on the street. Now they're going to have to beat you."

"Fine."

"And after making your point, you'll let yourself be beaten?"

"That's right."

"You'd have done very well during the Middle Ages. On Earth, I mean. Where did you learn to fight?"

He felt his dark face flush bronze. "I tried to join Starfleet."

"Why?"

"Some Klingons claimed that Starfleet is the place to be. That they were trying to get in. I spit on them all."

"On Starfleet?"

"Daily."

"Why do you spit on a force you tried to join?"

"I spit on their insistence that lessers should be able to tell me what to do. That I should be subservient to people I knew were not my equals. They do not allow men who disagree to settle it like men."

"So what happened? They kicked you out? Why?"

"I disciplined my commanding officer."

Odette Khanty grinned. She seemed to find that idea appealing, considering Starfleet's buttoned-up manners.

"Well, you're going to be taken into custody for a while for disturbing the peace. What's your name?"

Worf said nothing.

The woman continued to gaze at him, refusing to ask again.

Finally he shifted and answered, "My name is Worf."

"All right, Worf. I'll probably speak to you later."

Odette Khanty looked through the groaning guards to Ugulan, who was glaring through his own wounded ego at Worf.

"Detain him in the capitol prison. Hold his friend, too."

"On what charge?" Ugulan asked.

"The same. And check out his story about Starfleet."

"Yes, Mrs. Khanty."

"Well, here we are. In jail."

Grant seemed untroubled by their predicament, Worf thought.

"Obviously." Stating the obvious was another of Grant's habits that Worf found hard to bear. Then again, what was obvious to Grant might not be obvious to others. An observation Grant had made on Garlath IV had saved ten people's lives.

"Not bad, as jails go. I mean, they got carpets, y'know?"

As vital as Grant's obsevations might be, Worf could not force himself to listen. Grant's voice faded into the background as he reflected on what his oath to Starfleet and his own honor had forced him into: He had lost a battle on purpose, which was difficult enough. But to lose it to warriors who had forsaken their code of honor!

But by his action, Worf had gotten this powerful woman's personal attention. For good or otherwise? Worf refused to judge yet but clung to the statement the woman had made about talking to him later. He knew he had managed to tickle her interest in him, and that she preferred using Klingons as her personal security team. She had shown definite curiosity about him when he'd proven that he was more clever, if not stronger, than any of her current Rogues.

How the other Rogues would feel if he joined them—he would deal with that when the time came.

"Somebody's coming!" Grant said suddenly.

Worf sat up, listened to the faint thud of several footsteps on the stone outside this dugout holding area, then carefully eased back and tried to look as if he didn't care about much.

Under the soft lights of the cellblock corridor, Ugulan and two of his guards strode in, with Odette Khanty in their midst. She was a poised woman who struck Worf as efficient but cold, colder in person than her carefully crafted public image. She approached the cell bars as if they weren't even there.

She looked directly at Worf, ignoring Grant entirely. "It's even worse than you said. You broke your commanding officer's jaw and three ribs."

Worf offered only a limited shrug. "It is not my fault if he had weak bones."

"Why did you come to Sindikash?"

"I like the architecture."

Mrs. Khanty's mouth pursed a bit, rounding her cheeks. "You came because Starfleet has so little authority here at the moment. You came because we're in a state of flux between Federation membership and autonomy. You weren't kicked out of Starfleet. You're absent without leave. There's a pending assault charge."

"How interesting."

"Why didn't you go back to Q'onos?"

Sudden silence fell between them. They looked at each other, dueling.

"Same problems there, hm?" Mrs. Khanty eventually said.

Worf scowled. "Many Klingons no longer understand the need for authority. They made a treaty with the Federation."

"I understand that sort of feeling."

"It is not a feeling. It is fact."

"Yes, of course." She watched him for a moment. "You beat my Rogues. How did you do that?"

Worf clenched his fists to keep from spitting on her. Here was a woman who had found a way to make Klingons turn from their honor. They were nothing but low-life murderers, souring the reputation of Klingons all around. Could he pretend to be a Klingon with no honor?

"Klingons are ethnocentric," he said. "They have a tendency, more than most, to think they are superior in every way. They do not see the strength in others. That is why we could not, for so long, beat back the Federation. But I have grown beyond such constraints. I see the strength of rigorous rationality in Vulcans. I see the stubbornness of humans. There is strength in patience. There is strength in calmness. I remained calm and stubborn in the face of your Rogues, and I beat them."

"By understanding those who would be your enemies, yes," she said. "I see that. Very good. I like that. You beat Klingons by understanding the weakness of Klingons."

Stung by this woman's approval, Worf forced a nod of thanks. He saw in her eyes an incredible coldness that seemed to compensate for her inability to wield a weapon. Oh—it burned to be admired by such a person! He was embarrassed for himself because he had to gain her approval at all, but embarrassed also for the Rogues, who were for some reason ruled by this person.

"I have an offer for you. As you noticed, I have a special security team of Klingons. They call themselves the Rogues. That's their own name for themselves. I need them, because I can't trust anyone else. Not until my husband recovers and can take his governorship again. My husband wants us to establish our independence. I stand by that."

"Sindikash is a Federation colony."

"Was. Was a colony. We stand on our own now. We're frontiersmen, we Seniards. We're all expatriates from Earth, mostly from middle and eastern Europe. We're very tough people; we want our own identity. The lieutenant governor doesn't want us to have that chance. With the governor ill, I have to stand alone against those who would destroy my husband's dream."

"You think the lieutenant governor arranged the assassination attempt on your husband?"

The woman paused. "You're very blunt, aren't you?"

"Yes."

"I appreciate that. Within the next two hours, you should decide whether you might like to be part of the Rogue Force. If so, I can offer you protection from Starfleet."

"Can I have this human as my assistant?"

"Why would you want a human assistant?"

"He saved my life once. I owe him."

Khanty seemed to appreciate that on some level or other. "I guess you can have whatever you want. The Rogues are very independent. We appreciate independence here. But be clear on this: I need loyalty. Things happen to those who betray me or don't keep their agreements. The rewards of loyalty are equally bountiful."

Worf eyed her. "And what if you fail to keep your part of the agreement?"

The woman looked at him, and she was suddenly as cool as the wall.

"Then you may kill me," she said. "That's the deal."

The ship took it up as she tugged at her
tether,
Brace, footrope, and halyard all singin'
together;
So did the seagulls which round us did call,
But, O, my heart sang it the strongest of all!

Chapter Four

BEFORE WORF LEFT FOR SINDIKASH, there was a favor he had had to ask of his captain.

"Captain . . ."

"Mr. Worf? Something else?"

Worf stepped inside the captain's ready room through a haze of uncertainty, feeling as if he were stepping into a tunnel.

When the captain's muted voice bid him enter, he did. The cloying glances of his shipmates on the bridge gave way to the steady gaze of Captain Picard, and now Worf once again stood before the glossy black desk.

"I have . . ."

"Yes?"

"A request, sir."

The captain put down the padd he was working on, some ship's business or other, and asked, "Something about your mission you don't understand or approve of?"

"No, sir, nothing like that."

"Is everything all right with Ross Grant? Have you explained the mission to him?"

"He already understood much of it, sir," Worf said. "He enjoys this kind of thing."

"Oh, I don't blame him. He's had noted success on several planets. He's quite innovative with computer trails." The captain paused, and his voice turned mellow. "And I'm glad you're able to spend time with a family friend. I hope you'll be an effective team."

Feeling oddly small on the smooth, utilitarian carpet of the captain's office, Worf shifted his feet and nodded in silent agreement to that, then forced himself to move forward on why he was really here.

"Sir, I have a personal request."

Picard tilted his head. "Yes?"

"Next week is the Klingon Day of Honor."

"Oh, yes. Thursday."

Clearing a roughening throat, Worf nodded again. "The actual observation period is roughly four days."

The captain leaned forward and pressed an elbow to his desktop, instantly understanding. "And, of course, you won't be here."

Relieved, Worf let his shoulders sag a bit, and even shrugged. "This is Alexander's first real exposure to the Day of Honor as more than a time set aside to tell stories. He is now twelve years old. That means he must begin to study the history of the Day of Honor, and to understand the full meaning of honor and respect for an enemy's honor."

"The Klingon meaning of honor, or the human meaning of honor, Worf?"

"I beg your pardon, sir?" Worf paused, bandied a few things about in his mind, then decided to take a stab at his own answer. "There is only one honor."

Picard offered a somewhat rare smile. "Oh, no. No, not at all. How often have you heard the term 'Klingon honor'?"

"But I was not raised Klingon. My foster parents did their best to keep me close to my natural culture, but I've found many discrepancies in the actual practice of . . . being Klingon. Alexander has not really been raised Klingon, either, though I have tried. I would like him to at least be familiar with the rites of passage."

The captain leaned back again. "That doesn't really answer my question, but what is your request?"

Worf hesitated, and shuddered down a plaguing doubt. Was this a mistake? Was he overstepping his privileges as much as he thought?

Could it be that having Ross Grant on board had made him assume his other crewmates, even his captain, could be put upon as friends at any moment of inconvenience?

Blood flushed hot in his cheeks and behind his eyes.

"Perhaps this was ill-considered," he struggled. "If you will excuse me—"

"No, I will not excuse you," Picard objected. "State your request."

Curse me for a weakling. He knows me too well.

Knowing he was caught, Worf knotted his fists, battled with himself—and lost. All right, there was no way out.

He drew a breath.

"Since you know more about Klingon culture than most others aboard, since you have been so associated with the structure of Klingon government and know something of our history, I . . ."

"Yes?"

"I would like . . ."

Picard offered a reserved smile, and Worf nearly melted with embarrassment.

The captain pocketed the smile. "You'd like me to usher Alexander through the Day of Honor."

Feeling a wince cross his spine, Worf managed to smother his inner storm long enough to grind out, "Yes, sir."

Jean-Luc Picard pushed to his feet. Striding before the panorama of open space as it showed through the tall viewports behind his desk, he gazed out for a moment, looking in the direction of Sindikash. The planet shone on the star horizon as only a shimmering dot. Even its sun was barely visible from this far away, obscured by several nebulae and a belt of asteroid pebbles.

"You're quite right about me, Mr. Worf," he said many

seconds later. "I *am* uneasy around children. They seem as alien a life-form to me as any I've met. A child's first Day of Honor celebration is akin to a bar mitzvah or some other such rite of passage. It's really your place as the boy's father to give him the proper exercise, to make sure he's truly a changed person when it's over."

Feeling the muscles in his legs tighten, Worf worked past the pressure of his choice. "I know that, sir. I would prefer to be here with him, but not at the cost of honest government for Sindikash. If these atrocities are being carried out by Klingons, I have a primary responsibility. I made a commitment, and I must follow it through."

"Yes, you must. Mr. Worf, this is one of those times when we realize how clumsy a situation we've made for ourselves by having families aboard starships. It divides the attention of personnel who need very much to concentrate. It also seems to enhance our awareness of our own mortality, and the cost if we risk our lives. We *must* risk our lives. It's endemic to our duty here."

"And I will, sir," Worf croaked, "willingly."

The captain nodded, seeming to understand the layers of the situation.

"And I'll do all I can for Alexander," he promised. "But keep in mind that you're quite right—I'm not the best person to handle a child's pivotal moments. Yes, I have a few intimacies with Klingon culture, but I'm not sure it'll help as much as you hope."

Worf's whole life had been a series of choices, each chased by doubt. Both he and his captain were uneasy now, and things had not begun that way. "Do your best with your mission, Mr. Worf," the captain finished, "and be assured, I shall do my best with mine."

"Alexander, this is entirely unacceptable!"

"But you said I could pick!"

"I assumed you would pick Klingon history! Not human history!"

"You said I could pick from any historical period in my ancestry. And I'm one-quarter human!"

"But the American Revolutionary War?"

"That's when my ancestor was alive! You said I had to pick one of my own ancestors."

"Yes, I know what I said . . ."

"My grandparents sent me this program for my first Day of Honor. It was my mother's, they got it from her human relatives on Earth."

"But why a human experience?" Picard had to shout over the cannonfire. "It's a Klingon holiday!"

"I know that," the boy shouted back. "Since it was Captain James T. Kirk and Dahar Master Kor working together who founded the Day of Honor, and I've got both human and Klingon blood in me, I think I should be able to choose either one."

Picard ducked a lashing line. "Yes, well—"

The boy grasped his arm. "You're not going to freeze it, are you? Just because of some ship attacking?"

"Not the attack, per se . . . but this particular holoprogram is very old and doesn't comply with the safety controls as well as the more up-to-date programs."

"It's not my fault. My Mother's great-aunt has this journal made into a holoprogram over fifty years ago. She got it from her great-grandmother. The journal's been in the family since—"

"Yes, I know. Since 1777!"

"You said I could choose! You *said!*"

"I said."

Jean-Luc Picard found himself grappling an old style ship's pin rail, his hands entangled in coiled sisal ropes hanging from belaying pins, wondering how children survived at all with so concrete a sense of right and wrong, and what had been once said that could never later be altered.

He *had* said. He had told Alexander to select an ancestor's struggle with honor, and prepare to study that. He had expected the boy to select a Klingon ancestor, something relatively recent, with which Picard had some familiarity.

An officer in a blue jacket charged past him and hurried

along the amidships deck, calling, "Reload and run 'em out! Try a ranging shot, please, Mr. Nightingale! Ready on the heads'l sheets! Ready on the braces! MacCrimmon, cross on the weather side, you idiot! Wollard, that main brace is fouled, lee side! Up the shrouds with you!"

"Aye, sir!"

"All hands, wear ship!"

Picard looked up as three men scrambled up the supporting cables of the middle mast—the main. He'd played at this part of history, sailing ships and all, but the holoprograms made up for people of his age had built-in foolproofs. He could give an order to wear the ship then pull the wrong line, and the pretend ship would somehow compensate.

This wasn't one of those foolproof programs. This was a journal of the real thing, and he found it even smelled different from a made-for-entertainment holoprogram.

Smoke spun like Spanish dancers through the infernal din of cannonfire. The boy at his side had proved more clever than Picard expected.

Instead of examining his Klingon heritage for a Klingon holiday, he had chosen a relative from his deeply buried human heritage and provided Picard with these holotapes, long ago dramatized from the diaries of that ancestor.

Now here they were, huddled on the bow of a ship of war, with canvas rattling above and the boom of battle drumming at close range.

He didn't even know which battle this was. The year—1777. The American Revolutionary War.

"Not my best period," he muttered. His voice was snatched away by a tail of cannon smoke. "Couldn't you have had a Napoleonic relative?"

"What?" Alexander huddled at his side, wincing at the sound of heavy artillery. The Klingon boy was incongruous here among the scrambling human crew. But this was a computer program, and the crew would see him as a human youth.

"Why did you choose this program?" Picard asked again. "The Day of Honor is a Klingon exercise."

"I've been hearing about Klingon honor all my life," Alexander said. "Stand your ground, choose strong enemies, fight forward, and die in battle. There has to be more to it. I wanted to see what's in my human background. Maybe we can find something."

"Maybe." Picard grasped the lines nearest his head and pulled himself to his feet, then leaned over the ship's varnished rail and peered downward. The letters on the nameplate were carved and painted—*Justina.*

He looked up then, into the rigging, to seek the skittering ensigns flying at the mastheads. There, whipping eccentrically with the staggered motions of the ship, was the unmistakable arrangement of white lines, blue background, and red bands. The H.M.S. *Justina.*

He scanned the deck. Seemed to be a ship of about a hundred fifty feet, at least two decks above the waterline—not particularly large, even for this era. And there were three masts. Not a brig. Some kind of frigate, perhaps.

Which battle was this? A critical encounter? The battle of Long Island, perhaps?

He cursed himself for not knowing enough about naval battles of the Revolutionary War, and almost called a pause to the program so he could go off and study.

Then again, this wasn't grade school, nor was it a lesson even meant for him.

Only the lowermost sails, the biggest ones, were flying, and at the front of the ship there were three triangular sails reaching out to the bowsprit. He thought there could be more, but wasn't certain.

Soot-stained and glazed with sweat, crewmen scrambled like insects all over the ship, each tending to a particular job, mostly involving the row of cannons on the port side, facing that enemy ship. On the stepped-up aft deck—that would be the quarterdeck—at least two officers surveyed the battle and siphoned orders to the gun crews and the helm. Lined up on the quarterdeck and the main deck were a whole other set of men who weren't working any part of the ship. These wore red jackets and worked with long-muzzled rifles. They were firing independently, taking aim in almost leisurely fashion, picking off men on the other ship, then going through the many steps of the reloading process.

"Marines," Picard murmured. "Sharpshooters . . . how interesting. I've rarely seen that."

Often he'd just had members of his own crew stand in as the "crew" of the holoship, for the fun of it. He'd had the holodeck provide the ship and the sea, and taken it from there.

This program, however, had its own crew, its own weapons, its own grit of reality. Whoever had designed the program had done an excellent job, and had clearly fleshed the journal entries out with historical sources and references. To the extent possible, this was what really happened on this date centuries ago.

Alexander peeked over the port rail at the other ship and gasped. "That ship's shooting at us with noise!"

Picard looked, not understanding.

The other ship was smaller than the vessel they were on, but seemed to have more maneuverability, twisting in the bright gray-blue water as if turning on a corkscrew. It charged toward them, swinging about to put its fresh guns abeam, and it was very close now, hardly more than fifteen yards or so. Dangerously close.

POK BOOM—a puff of smoke appeared near the forward quarter.

"That isn't just noise," he said. "Those are cannons. They're shooting—"

Puff. The rectangular sail over their heads imploded, wagged, then struggled to take the shape of the breeze again, but now there was a shivering two-foot rip in it.

"Cannonballs," Picard finished. How to explain? "Heavy iron balls fired from . . . from heavy iron tubes."

"What would those do?" Alexander screwed up his face. "Just hit the ship? Put a hole in those blankets up there?"

"A great deal, if I recall correctly." Picard glanced around. "They can smash the wood, tear the lines, or crush the men. And those blankets are sails."

He felt movement of the ship beneath him, and crouched

closer to the pin rail as crewmen dashed back and forth across the forward deck. Some were shouting, others concentrating on the process that would reload the run-out cannons. Some had to climb overboard to do that. The stench of the last discharge rolled over Picard and the boy, setting them both hacking until their chests ached.

A gust of fresh breeze relieved their stinging lungs and eyes somewhat, and Picard opened his eyes in time to see what he thought was the swinging boom—a heavy wooden shaft to which one of the headsails was attached. Then, as if the giant shaft had stabbed his very chest, he realized he was really seeing the bowsprit of the attacking colonial ship swinging inboard over the *Justina*'s port rail!

"Good God!" he choked.

His own voice barely sounded over the devilish scratch of the other ship's dolphin striker and chains knocking against the rail and bulwarks. They'd collided!

For Picard, a starship captain, "near" was hundreds of thousands of kilometers. Not here, though. "Near" now translated into mere inches as the two battling ships jutted hard against each other, heaving sickeningly, then jockeyed for position. Without engines, there was no way to reverse the course of the attacking ship and back out of the *Justina*'s shrouds.

A terrible series of popping noises sounded from the other ship, and several of the marines on Picard's ship suddenly fell dead or dying. The other ship had sharpshooters, too!

"Stay down, Alexander!" he called.

"But they can't hurt us," the boy protested. "It's just a holoprogram."

"I'm not certain of that. Do as I say."

The sea beneath them heaved unevenly, putting the *Justina* down into a trough and raising the other ship up on a swell. The other ship's bow was magnified a thousand times in Picard's eyes as it rose, as if it meant to climb over the rail and crawl onto *Justina*'s foredeck. The hull was narrow-beamed and shallow, the bow sharp, masts raked at an angle that made the ship look as if it were going ten knots standing still. It was rigged differently from this vessel—the sails were not square and set perpendicular to the body of the ship, but were fewer, larger in proportion to the body of the ship, and flew, streamlined with the hull, from fore to aft.

Picard recognized it—the early rig of the American schooner. It would someday become famous for its simplicity and speed. At this point, the word "schooner" didn't even exist.

The enemy's nameplate crawled upward and tipped high behind *Justina*'s mast supports—what were those called?—and Picard suddenly had an identity on the attackers. *Chincoteague.*

An American ship. In 1777, those would be colonists who had declared themselves independent and were now fighting a war for the final decision.

The *Chincoteague*'s fifteen-foot bowsprit bashed fitfully into one of *Justina*'s masts and both ships staggered. The colony ship's bow grated against *Justina*'s side, gouging off layers of paint and wood. The paralyzingly loud cannonfire fell momentarily silent, other than one or two pops from the stern of the British ship. The American ship couldn't fire because none of its cannon could aim at its enemy now, with its bow pressing against the side of the *Justina,* and evidently it had no bow guns. That would've been acceptable—except that they would grind each other into sawdust if this colliding was allowed to continue.

"Well, this can't go on, can it?" Picard shoved himself upward, climbing first onto the rail, then farther up into the vertical cables and horizontal footropes and wrapped one leg well into them. Then he grasped the other ship's chains with both hands and hauled for all he was worth.

He found himself attempting to push over a mountain with his bare hands. The bodies of the two ships grated against each other with unimaginable power. The other ship's bowsprit grated hard against the mast again, turned as if nauseated, as if it meant to disengage itself from its own bow, and rolled away down the deck of the *Justina.* Picard kept hauling.

"What are you doing, Captain?" Alexander cried from the deck.

"Better not call me 'captain,'" Picard told him. "We're not sure what rank I am."

"Oh . . ." The boy glanced around, trying to decide just how real a holoprogram could be.

Picard knew from experience—bad ones—that the quirky holograms as old as this one were much less manageable and more subject to participation than current technology, and that things could go wrong.

He rearranged his leg and kept hauling on the chains. Suddenly the *Chincoteague* surged back a good two meters. He grabbed a different part of the chain and hauled again.

"Hands off, redcoat!"

Startled, Picard glanced over his shoulder. On the bow of the colonial ship, a rough-looking sailor aimed a flintlock pistol at his face. Rough, yes, but under the layer of dare and contempt, he was only about twenty years old.

Picard kept pulling. "We have to get these ships apart, or we'll maul each other into the sea! Is that what you want?" Without waiting for an answer, he reached down, snatched a coil of line from one of the pins, and tossed it at the colonist. "Now, haul away, boy! We have to change the angle of this ship!"

The line was made fast to its pin, and stayed fast as the sailor paled a shade, belted his pistol, and did as he was told. He braced both feet on the bow rail of that ship and hauled back.

"When this is over," the sailor called, "I'll be shooting you, sir!"

"Better than drowning," Picard drawled back.

Sir. Well, he was *some* kind of officer. He hadn't even bothered to look at what kind of jacket he was wearing.

"Captain?" Alexander's knobby head appeared below.

"Stay down. And don't call me 'captain.'" Picard kept the pressure on the bowsprit chains, though his arms were shuddering now. But the ship—the *Chincoteague* was moving!

Or perhaps the *Justina* was moving beneath him, under the combined force of his actions and the pulling of the other ship's sailor on the line. The *Justina* began sluggishly swinging around, putting the ships more side by side than bow to beam. That allowed the bowsprit of *Chincoteague* to release its dance with the *Justina*'s foremast and bob freely in the rigging.

With the cooperation of the swells and a slacking breeze, the colonial ship's bowsprit moved outboard another yard. It stalled, then began moving again, and this time floated completely out. In a surreal motion, the other ship continued moving away. Its hull turned abeam and the cannons began roaring once again.

True to his promise, the colonial sailor dumped the line joining the ships, fumbled off the rail, jumped down to the deck, and drew his pistol again. He aimed it as squarely at Picard as the bobbing of *Chincoteague* would allow, but *Chincoteague* drifted backward and was swallowed by a dense shroud of cannon smoke just as the sailor tried to take aim. He made a wild shot, but it was far off.

"Shrouds! That's it!" Picard shouted victoriously and grasped the cables that supported the masts from side to side. Then he grasped the horizontally tied footropes. "And ratlines! Yes, of course. Ah, these were the days! Sometimes I wish we had things like this aboard the *Enterprise!*"

Ridiculous. What a thought.

"Why don't we have them?" Alexander asked, appearing at his side.

"Because we don't have masts to support. If you look up at these, you can see what they do."

Alexander craned his neck to look up at the maze of lines and pullies. "This boat has too many things on it. Do you know what all this does?"

"No, not all of it," Picard admitted. "I've played at the era, but I've never actually *worked* at it. I've paid more attention to tactics of these types of battles than the details of sail handling. Perhaps this is a good time to—"

His words were blasted apart by a half dozen cannonshots at stunningly close range. The *Chincoteague*'s brief dance with *Justina* had allowed both ships time to reload and run out their guns again. Now both ships had opened fire again.

Instinctively, Picard ducked and pushed Alexander down as the ship beneath them shuddered from hits on her hull. The sound of cracking wood was as disgusting as bones breaking, and was punctuated by the screams of dying men on the gundeck below.

Alexander pushed out from under Picard's arm and looked along the deck, then suddenly drew a sharp breath and trembled. Not five steps away, a crewman lay shuddering and gasping, dying. He raised his head pathetically and looked at his own body, now a field of jagged splinters from the broken bulwark. A cannonball had come through the body of the ship between the deck and rail, skewered this poor man with dozens of sharp stakes, then plunged across the deck and out another passage it had carved for itself in the opposite bulwark. Picard still heard the water hissing where the hot ball struck, and there was a column of steam out there in the water.

Alexander struggled to breathe as he watched the poor man die like that, full of splinters. This was a boy who came from an age of cauterizing weapons and distance fighting. Yes, he was born of a culture that prized hand-to-hand fighting, but Klingon stories and Klingon day-to-day life were two different things. There really wasn't that much blood drawn anymore.

There was blood drawn today, plenty of it. The dying man turned his eyes to Alexander in a ghastly, final plea that Picard felt bolting through the boy.

"Barbaric . . ." Picard waved at the sulfurous smoke rising from the *Justina*'s own cannons, and peered through the gray clouds at the other ship.

The hull was cracked in several places above the waterline. The top half of the foremast was broken like a twig, bent over to one side, caught in the rigging. But with that fore-and-aft rig, the colonial ship didn't have as many lines tangling the space above her decks, and the broken mast was being cleared quickly away by men smeared with soot and blood.

This was all very close and immediate—very personal. Not like a battle aboard a starship, where the enemy was half a solar system off. Hologram or not, this program was based on detailed diaries of someone who had been here and seen this, on this day, in 1777, who could still taste the gore and sweat as he wrote his journal.

Where was that person? Where was Alexander's ancestor?

One of the gun crew? An officer? One of that line of redcoated marines who were now taking aim with rifles?

At his side, Alexander flinched hard as the marines fired their volley, all at once, with cold organization. Withering fire rained across the other ship. Screams rose from the deck, and the *Chincoteague* fell off her attack stance. Even from here, Picard could see the wheel spinning. The helmsman had been mown down, and so had anyone near enough to take his place.

Letting out a moan of empathy, Picard stuffed down a ridiculous urge to jump over there and help steer the other ship.

Suddenly a commotion on the main deck caught his eye—three men in officers' dark blue coats were joining the gun crew in a supreme task—one of the huge ship's cannons had tipped over on its side, guntruck and all, and the fabulous weight of the iron monster would take several men to heave up.

Those must be the command officers. Yet Picard saw in their effort the long years they had spent on board ship. They didn't look at all as he had when he had played at historical programs before. Their uniforms were tattered and smutty with gunpowder and splinter dust, and the wool strained around their muscles as they threw their weight onto the cannon with force matching the effort of the deckhands. Slowly the big gun began to shift.

The cannon was enormous—what did that thing weigh? A thousand pounds? Beneath the deadweight maw of iron, a jagged scream erupted. Some poor crushed soul was still alive under there!

The deckhands and officers got the cannon up a foot or so, but the effort took all the men in that area of the ship. There was no one who dared let go long enough to pull the injured man out. For a moment, the team floundered as the unfortunate sailor screamed and tried to claw his way out of the man-made trap.

"I can pull him out!" Alexander piped, and slipped past Picard.

But a man from another gun crew waved a copper knife with one hand and grasped Alexander's arm with the other.

"Y'ain't headin' for the main deck, is you, swab?" the man barked, spinning Alexander around and giving him a sturdy shove. "Y'know the rules. Niver go within a boathook's length of d'captain. Got that, boy?"

Alexander managed a nod, then looked at Picard. Pretty clear message—should he stay a boathook's length from Picard? And what the devil was a boathook?

"Sergeant!" one of the uniformed men at the cannon gasped, straining horribly to keep the cannon's bulk up.

Instantly a tall young soldier appeared from behind the mast—he wore a red jacket over his sailor's shirt, and he took a moment to put down a black-muzzled rifle. A marine sharpshooter. A sergeant.

The marine sergeant dropped to the deck and crawled under the cannon. Unthinkable!

"Oh, my," Picard murmured with admiration.

"He's going to get crushed!" Alexander said. "He just went right under that thing!"

"And it would've been you being crushed if you hadn't been stopped."

"I'm not afraid!"

"That's commendable, but you're also not strong enough to pull that injured man out of there. You have to use common sense. Sometimes you're of more help staying out the way."

"Doesn't sound very good," the boy complained. He fell

silent and watched as the marine sergeant squirmed under the massive cannon, then reappeared with his arms around the half-crushed sailor. Blood drained from the sailor's mouth.

Picard winced. He knew a lost cause when he saw one.

A slice of empathy rushed through his chest. Holoprogram or not, this incident had really happened, and those men had really died, or lay moaning in agony until they finally died. Medical science in colonial times couldn't hope to snatch many back from the maw of death in battle.

"He did it!" Alexander jumped in victory as the Marine shimmied the sailor out from under the cannon.

An instant later, the officers and deckhands gratefully let the cannon dump to the deck. The *boom* of its weight on the planks sent a shudder up and down the entire ship.

The officers instantly dispersed to other parts of the ship, undistracted by the good deed they had just done.

Alexander, Picard noticed, continued watching the marine sergeant.

The marine was crouched on the bloody deck, holding the crushed sailor as if cradling a child, and he continued to do so, speaking softly and inaudibly over the din of gunfire, until the sailor's grasping hands fell limp and his frightened eyes glazed over.

Alexander continued to watch, deeply moved by what he saw.

"Starboard gun crews ready?" someone called.

"Ready!" the answer came.

"Hands to the fore course braces!" The shout came from the main deck, somewhere amidships, not far from the discarded cannon. At first Picard didn't pay attention, but then the same voice shouted, "Mr. Picard, fore braces! Aren't you paying attention?"

Well, so much for a simple lesson.

He shot a stare in that direction, and saw one of the officers waving at him.

For a terrible instant he glanced around at all the lines, in a panic that he couldn't remember what a fore brace was and how to work it; then he forced himself to think. The officer had said "Mister" Picard.

And Picard was wearing a blue jacket of the same type as that man. The deckhands were wearing striped shirts, or no shirts at all, dark bell-bottom trousers, and most had bare feet. Picard's breeches were white, not bell-bottom, and he had shoes on.

Inhaling sharply, he looked toward the nearest bunch of sailors, who were scrambling to ditch some wreckage overboard and secure a cannon truck, and he shouted, "Hands to the fore braces, gentlemen!"

Two of those men jumped forward to the area where Picard and Alexander were standing. "Aye, sir!" one of them responded, then they separated.

They snatched at two lines made fast to belaying pins on opposite sides of the ship. Picard followed those lines up into the sky, into the rigging, and discovered that they were attached to the ends of the long yard from which the biggest forward sail hung.

"The fore . . . main," he muttered. "No . . . the fore tops'l—topgallant . . ."

No use. He didn't remember what that sail was called. It had a specific name, but he couldn't scrape it up. He could tell that those lines would turn the sail, and could probably turn it almost perpendicular to the body of the ship if necessary. The yard, a long spoke of wood that looked very heavy, wasn't attached to the mast, but moved freely on its own lines.

The men unmade the lines from the pins, took hold of them, then turned to Picard for orders.

He looked aft. Nobody was paying any attention. Was he supposed to do something?

"Uh . . . stand by," he said to the men.

"Standing by, sir," one responded.

"Prepare to come about!" somebody called—that same officer from amidships.

Picard looked at the men. Oh, well. "Prepare to come about," he repeated.

"Ready, sir," the port side sailor acknowledged, and he and his crewmate looked up, then tugged or released the brace lines until the sail lay across the body of the ship without favoring either side.

As the wind changed, Picard heard a new voice carried to him, a slightly deeper voice, but quieter. "Wear ship," the voice said.

Amidships, the officer called, "Helm alee!"

From the wheel, a third voice called back, "Helm's alee!"

Lee . . . lee side . . . windward was where the wind was coming from, so lee was where it was going. Wear ship—turn so the breeze was at their stern. He knew that.

Sure enough, the ship bobbled on the surging water and began swinging about into the direction the breeze was blowing. The ship set into a troubled roll, not up, not down, not side to side, not fore and aft, but somehow all of those at the same time. Up, side, pitch, aft, roll, side, down, down more—ghastly! Why was there so much romance about this way of life?

The sails sagged, fluttered, whipped as if confused, then—*whap, whap,* SNAP—the air socked into them and the ship sluggishly moved toward the other vessel.

Only now did Picard notice they were just a kilometer or two from land! A vast stretch of green hills flickered under the warm sun. He wondered where they were. Coastal United States, likely, but where? Off Florida? Maine?

The brand-new United States, declared so by its defiant founders only a year before this. Now there was a war, a great test of resolve, because it was surely not one of resource.

He knew how the Revolutionary War would come out, but he still shivered with excitement at seeing this. The brilliant technology of his own time was allowing him and Alexander to see the technologies upon which it was built. And even more, the attitudes that built it.

"Adjust that sail to the new heading, gentlemen," he said, trying to sound as if he knew what in hell he was talking about.

But they did it. One of them let out his line, and the other drew his line in. They watched the sail the whole time, and soon it matched the angle of the sail in the middle of the ship and the one on the third mast. Mizzen. Mizzenmast.

"Simple enough," he said aloud. "Well, I'm recalling a few things at least."

"That's well!" the officer amidships called. "Make fast, all hands. Starboard gun crews, stand by! Mr. Picard, the bedamned heads'ls, if you please! Captain Sobel wants the ship brought about some time today!"

"Oh—" Picard swung around and looked at the triangular sails running from the bowsprit, but hadn't any idea what to do with them. Then, as he forced himself to think, he realized that the headsails were filled from the wind coming from the port side, but were still tied to pins on the starboard side of the ship. "Gentlemen, take care of these immediately."

He tried to be noncommittal, because he wanted to see whether or not he had guessed right.

Sure enough, the men bounced to the lines holding the free corners of the sails, unfastened them from the pins, then ran to the same lines on the other side and drew them tight. So the headsails had to be shifted from one side to the other, depending upon where the wind came from.

Now the *Justina* had come all the way around and had her bow to the land. The *Chincoteague* now lay off the British ship's starboard side, the side with the loaded and ready guns. Those marines who were still standing now picked their way across the wreckage-littered deck, through the blood and over the bodies of fallen men, and took up position on the starboard side.

All seemed to relax some and watch as the sailors and ship's officers struggled to clear the decks of wreckage and bodies, and to find the wounded.

Picard looked at Alexander, but the boy was fascinated by the actions of the one marine sergeant who had impressed him before, by not letting that poor crushed gunner die alone.

"Are those men in red going to shoot those weapons again?" Alexander asked.

"I think they're out of range," Picard told him. "I don't believe they had rifled muskets yet . . . but I'm not sure about that. It means the inside of the barrel has a kind of twisted ridge that makes the bullet—ah, the ball—spin as it comes shooting out."

"What would that do?"

"Improves range and accuracy. But I don't believe they have that—well, they might."

"Mmm," Alexander uttered. "Phasers are better."

"Yes, but with every invention comes a countermeasure. With bullets came kevlar vests. With phasers, we came up with shields. Every age has its challenges."

"Fire as you bear starboard, Mr. Pennington," the deep voice from aft filtered on the wind, and with a sudden flicker of awareness Picard realized he was hearing the captain's voice. Captain Sobel was his name, wasn't it?

Pennington, the officer at amidships, ordered, "Starboard guns as you bear . . . fire!"

The ship was still moving, coming slowly around until most of her guns could focus on the *Chincoteague,* but, given the curved shape of the ship's side, not all the guns could aim at the same time. There were four . . . yes, four cannons on each side of the main deck. How many were below, on the gun deck? Ten? That would make this ship an eighteen-gunner.

"Formidable," Picard muttered. He looked across the glinting water at the other ship. *Chincoteague,* as he now counted her gunports, seemed to have about half that, with only guns on the main deck. But she was more maneuverable and quicker, turning brilliantly out there on hardly a puffing breeze.

If her gunners were more skilled, or just more determined, or more desperate—

FFFFOOOM! The deck beneath him shuddered bodily with the paralyzing report of bow and midship cannons. A few seconds later, as *Justina* jolted on a swell, the midship to aft cannons pounded the sea's surface. Guntrucks thundered on the deck planks as the cannons jolted backward with the power of their own percussion, to be yanked to awkward halts by strong retaining ropes. Amazing—the cannons probably weighed fifteen hundred or two thousand pounds each.

Any standard-issue hand phaser was a million times more deadly, but somehow at this moment Picard couldn't muster any more respect for that delicate weapon than for these monoliths, which took such cooperation to make, board, and use.

Puffs of smoke and fire appeared on *Chincoteague*'s black side. Impact tremors disturbed the swells. Screams of wounded men pierced the clear day, even more disturbing than the thunder of cannons.

The *Chincoteague*'s sails fluttered and the ship briefly staggered, then the bow swung out of sight in a pall of cannon smoke and Picard couldn't judge what was happening out there.

But there was fire on the other ship.

He was sure of that.

"She's bearing off!" someone shouted, and the crew—those still standing—broke into cheers.

"Shameful," Picard commented, "to cheer the defeat of an enemy."

Alexander looked up at him. "Why is it shameful?"

"Could just as easily have been us. It's not polite."

"But we beat them. Why shouldn't we celebrate?"

"It's not my taste to do so."

The boy looked at the retreating colonial ship. "It's mine," he admitted, and he stood up and started cheering with the rest of the crew.

Picard stared at the boy, caught by the child's disrespect for the opinion of his mentor, but also by his defiant sense of self. Hadn't quite expected that . . .

"Alexander," he began, "Alexander, pay attention. We have to be somewhat careful. This holoprogram is over seventy-five years old, and was written by historians, not technicians. Things can happen."

The boy divided his attention between Picard and the retreating *Chincoteague.* "Bad things?"

"Yes. This program is only barely compatible with the ship's modern systems. The safeties may not work properly. I have no way to know whether or not that sailor's pistol would actually have hurt me."

"We're not quitting, are we?"

"No, no."

"We're going to stay and look for my ancestor, aren't we?"

"Yes, I'm sure he's here somewhere."

"Then what should we do about the safeties?"

"Until we know," Picard said, "I suggest we duck."

Chapter Five

"Attention, Cargo Sindikash four-zero-five, this is Commander William Riker aboard the Starfleet scout Jackson Taylor. *Shut your engines down immediately and prepare to be boarded."*

The words sounded familiar. Similar words had triggered the entire mission Worf was on, and he couldn't shake the sensation of having been through this before.

The odor of blood by the gallon still wafted in Worf's nostrils. Such a visceral reaction boiled inside him that he could barely keep from challenging every last Rogue here and now. Bitter embarrassment electrified him—he had defended the indefensible. Commissioner Toledano had been right about the grim murders on that transport.

He was among Klingons, and he should feel at ease, yet he did not. He must pretend to be their comrade, yet he could barely make himself do it.

Yet I must.

The vision of the thirty-some dead innocents, the mutilated witnesses who were not even spared their own eyes, and the sorrowful disillusionment in Captain Picard's face haunted him more with every minute.

And all the arms were still missing.

"Starfleet!" Ugulan choked out from the pilot's seat at Worf's side. "I *told* you someone was spying on us!"

"They patrol this space," Worf fiercely shot back, despising himself for even speaking to such a being. "We took our chances. Chance went against us."

"It was probably you!"

"You never had a mission fail before I came?"

"Curse your skull! Put the automatic defenses on! We have to try to outrun them!"

"Ridiculous. We have to fight them."

"That is Starfleet!"

"So it is. And you are a frightened woman in man's armor."

Nettled by shame and broiling inner fury, Worf poured all his frustration into goading Ugulan. He had to control himself—restrain himself from driving his knuckles into Ugulan's mouth and out the back of his neck. Not yet . . . not yet . . .

He concentrated on the screen.

The air in the cockpit was hot. He was sweating under his Rogue uniform. He hated the uniform. He hated the screen. He hated everything.

What had made these Klingons become what they were? What had driven them from their loyalty and honor to the strengths that made the Empire survive? He had managed to fight them and win in the square in Burkal City, and that gave him a clue. Were they simply inadequate? Had battle training been too rigid for them? How had someone like Ugulan ended up doing the bidding of a human woman?

The answer might be here, now. Ugulan wanted to escape at the sight of one Starfleet shuttle. Where were his parents? Who was his family, and were they ashamed? Was their name ever spoken in their own land anymore?

He thought back to the names of the dishonored families whose power in Klingon society had been lost, and wondered—was he flying with their sons? With the fathers of disgraced Klingon boys who would pay all their lives for the dishonor here?

His hands played on the controls with a hunger so deep that his fingers hurt. The shame of pretending to be one of them boiled beneath his skin. Mission or not, he could not banish the nausea of humiliation.

On the cargo ship's forward screen—the only screen that could pull up a view of outside—the Starfleet scout angled toward them, its small, tight body gleaming in the light of the nearby sun.

Piloted by Ugulan and the other Rogues, the freighter was old and underteched, the perfect kind of ship to be completely ignored by Starfleet or anybody else. Odette Khanty had counted on that. Worf knew this shipment was organized by the governor's wife, and that it was a shipment of something illegal according to Federation interstellar trade regulations, but Grant had been able to find no shred of recorded evidence that led back to her.

Odette Khanty was ahead in the polls, but only slightly, and she wanted an edge. Her husband's injury had pushed her ahead for a while, but now sympathy was beginning to wear off. She needed to boost public opinion in her favor again, and Worf was riding in her way of doing that.

This freighter was Odette Khanty's latest plan. It was loaded with illegal goods and headed for Cardassian space, but it was never intended to arrive there. It was supposed to be "captured" by Sindikash patrols. By then, the Rogues would have abandoned the freighter, and left in it only the name and the identity codes, not of Odette Khanty, but of the lieutenant governor. This was a giant warp-powered frame-up.

And here I am, volunteering for this delivery, without even knowing what I am delivering. I wish I could deliver a foot into the throat of each Klingon here.

Forcing himself to stop dreaming, he shook himself back to the action of the moment. Now a Starfleet scout had spotted them and veered in at high warp, and Ugulan was panicking. The other six Rogues on board were agitated, but waiting for Ugulan to make a decision.

Pathetic invertebrate cowards . . .

The freighter belonged to the lieutenant governor's brother, and this morning the Rogues had stolen it and loaded it with unmarked crates. Worf, as the new Rogue, had been careful not to ask questions, for surely that would be a signal. Once the cargo of illicit goods was discovered, Odette Khanty's plan was for the freighter's ownership to be revealed, and the lieutenant governor implicated—at least in enough people's suspicions to tilt the election handily.

Begrudgingly, Worf admired the craft of the plan, but still his hands grew cold in spite of the heat in the cockpit. This was not his kind of mission. He was the wrong man for espionage.

"Betrayed! Betrayed . . ." Ugulan frantically worked the controls as the ten-man Starfleet scout closed in on them. He barked at his men, who negotiated the ship around a dust belt and between two asteroids, but there was no universe in which a loaded freighter could outmaneuver or certainly outrun a Starfleet pack.

"Attention Cargo Sindikash," Riker's voice came again, more forceful this time, angry. *"Heave to or we will fire on you. Do you copy? This is your last warning. Stop forward propulsion immediately."*

"We have to do it," the Rogue named Goric said. "They'll cut us to shreds."

"Do it, Ugulan!" another Rogue demanded.

Ugulan snarled, "We are supposed to destroy ourselves before ever giving up."

"For her?" Goric charged. "I have no wish to die for that woman!"

Worf turned and sneered at him, and for a moment he could be himself. "What *will* you die for?"

Goric gaped back at him, caught briefly in the magnetism of underlying meaning.

A strained silence, bizarre stillness, folded over the cockpit.

What are you and how did you come to this?

"That was the oath we made to her," Ugulan reminded them, but not with enthusiasm. "We swore on our honor we would never allow ourselves to be captured as evidence against her. She has not violated her agreement with us."

"You are all cowards," Worf snarled. "You swear an oath that swallows your honor, then you betray even that."

On that, Goric spun again to Ugulan. "It does me no good if she wins and we are all dead!"

Ugulan growled, looked at the other Rogues, deciphering their agreement with Goric, and decided whether or not he wanted to self-destruct for Odette Khanty's purity of position. "If we fail her, we'll be hunted down."

"Better dead tomorrow than today," Goric declared.

The other Rogues grumbled their agreement.

Worf held his breath, prepared to circumvent disaster if he had to, for he indeed did not intend to die for Khanty, but that turned out not to be necessary. Ugulan pounded the helm console, slowed the ship down, and prepared to comply.

All around Worf, the Rogues' faces were pasted with bloody-minded anger as they realized their acrimony would get them nowhere. Worf scrutinized them as if their pasts would rise in print on their foreheads if he looked hard enough. Were their plans for power and influence eroding before their eyes? Were they angry that all they could do now was be angry?

His stomach twisting with disgust, Worf found a certain sorrow in watching the wreckage of Klingons thinking there was nothing to do but give up.

Give up! Curse you all into the dirt!

Worf plunged in between Ugulan and the helm and slammed the thrusters back on again, and doubled the freighter's speed under them.

"What are you doing!" Ugulan demanded. "We can never outrun them!"

"Then we should do something else!" Worf bellowed back.

Ugulan came halfway out of his chair. "We are not stupid! That is Starfleet!"

Worf cast him a glare. "Frightened children!"

Mortash, the nearest Klingon behind Ugulan, shouted, "A penal institution is better than dead!"

"How would *you* know?" Worf tossed over his shoulder. He shoved Ugulan away from the helm and took it himself. "Filth!"

Instantly Ugulan came to his feet again, and his phaser pressed into Worf's cheek. "I command this ship," he said.

On the same breath, the Starfleet patrol vessel blew a direct phaser shot in what might have been a crippling attack had Worf not tilted the freighter and caused the blow to glance. The Klingons shuddered, but everyone stayed upright.

"Under your command, the ship is dead and so are we." Worf went on piloting as if Ugulan's weapon were nothing but a stick pressing his face. "I can force that ship's shields to flutter."

Ugulan changed his stance to accommodate the slight tilt of the deck. "How can you?"

"I know the Starfleet prefix codes."

"How can you know that?"

Worf piloted the freighter in a clumsy elliptical course back toward the underbelly of the Starfleet patroller. "I stole them before I left."

Ugulan stared at him and growled, "You can make the shields drop?"

"Not drop. But I can make them shift. Long enough to drive one shot in. Sit down here and fly directly at it."

His mind obviously boggled, Ugulan glanced at Goric, Mortash, Gern and the other slime. Worf saw a bizarre anxiety crawl through their expressions, as though only now realizing they might not be forced to the wall after all. Hair-raising excitement charged them all suddenly.

Ugulan's phaser fell away. "You had better leave no traces, lunatic! I will not pay your price for you!"

The head Rogue made a quick motion, and Worf gave him the helm, then shifted to the weapons and tactical board to do what he said he could do.

"They are firing!" Mortash shouted, and his words were eaten in a pounding uproar from outside.

Malignant electricity bolted through the freighter, its plates shrieking, funnels of lubricants and gases spitting from a dozen places in the inner frame. Suddenly the whole cabin was twenty degrees hotter. Worf felt his uniform become an oven as he furiously played the controls, tapping in the complex codes. On the screen, the Starfleet patroller no longer looked small. They were on collision course, and the freighter was making no return shots.

Mortash clutched his console and shouted, "Veer off!"

He plunged forward and swiped Worf's head with his armored cuff.

Worf's brain wobbled, and for a few moments his eyesight blurred. He felt blood drain down the back of his neck, but before he could lash out, Ugulan did it for him.

"Down, maniac! A chance is a chance!" the Rogue leader smashed Mortash back, and Worf was free to clear his head and continue feeding the codes.

"Stay on course," he ordered, and Ugulan resentfully complied, maintaining the collision heading. "Ready . . . ready . . ."

From the sensor grid console, Goric shouted, "Their shields are shifting! Now! Now!"

With his left fist, Worf hammered the firing controls. Half-power defense-only phasers bolted from the body of the freighter—nothing near the power of Starfleet phasers, but formidable enough if they could be fired on a ship without shields.

"This is Commander Riker! Cease fire immediately or we will target your engines!"

"Did it get through?" Ugulan gasped, staring at the screen. "We are still on collision! They did not explode! Did the shot get through?"

"They are not dead, are they?" Mortash roared from behind Worf. "Do you see them dying?" He pointed at Worf. "This one has killed us! We are damaged! Veer off!"

"Shields are stabilizing," Gern called over the crackle of their own damage. "Starfleet's, not ours."

Ugulan shot a piercing glare at Worf. "I will cut your throat myself just to hear the sound!"

"Do it while you steer!" Worf spat back. *Animals, pathetic animals!*

Ugulan leaned hard to one side, and the ship moved with him, heeling up onto its starboard warp package, leaving barely enough passing space under the hull for the Starfleet vessel to shoot by, so close that the hullplates rattled with the force of the other ship's engine wash.

"You have seconds before they come about," Mortash mourned. "We should both cut his throat before they slaughter us!"

Casting a fearless glower, Worf bit his tongue. *Why not just pull out their arms?*

Luckily, he kept it to himself.

"They are coming about!" one of the Rogues shouted from the aft panels.

On the main screen, sensors were following the Starfleet ship as it arched around, its top hullplates gleaming and showing off the rectangular body shape of the vessel and the glowing red phaser ports. It was coming around to finish them.

"What is it doing?" Mortash shuddered then. "It is—slowing down!"

"Why would it?" Ugulan struggled with the half-frozen helm, trying to bring the bulky freighter around so they could pretend to go down fighting.

One by one the Rogues moved through the noxious stink of damage and gathered around the main screen, crowding up behind Worf and Ugulan. Together they watched the small Starfleet scout come around to kill them. It was slowing down to draw out its own victory and to shame them, so they thought.

Worf watched it, barely breathing. His quaking hands on the console nearly gave away his bitter delight.

The patroller was indeed slowing.

Then, in a shocking change, it pitched to one side and spun half a turn.

"Look!" Ugulan pointed at the screen.

The patroller's back was broken by a sudden explosion from inside its aft topdeck, blowing the impulse engine across space. The sparks washed back and engulfed the Starfleet scout.

Mortash grabbed for the sensor grid readouts. "It is hulled! It is hulled! Our shot got through! We hulled it!"

He stumbled back to the main screen, just in time to see

the Starfleet ship spark, crackle, then turn itself inside out, its skin peeling back an instant before the warp engines blew themselves into solar balls.

Worf clamped his mouth shut, determined to hold back his grunt of victory. If they showed no restraint, then he would show all of his.

The ignoble crowd erupted into a cheer, and less than a full second later the freighter rocked upward violently on an impact wave and half of them were thrown to the deck. They clawed back to their feet, staring at the screen.

A puff of blue residue twisted where moments ago a Starfleet ship had hovered.

Gone.

"Commander Riker!" Ugulan bolted. "Hah!"

Then he spat on the deck, hitting Worf's boot with his comment.

Chapter Six

"THAT'S DONE. DAMNED REBELS."

The officer from midships, Mr. Pennington, was probably the first officer, Picard now figured. There were other men in blue jackets, too, who would be other lieutenants of various tenure, and midshipmen. They each seemed to have a particular assignment. One tended the main deck gun crews. Another monitored sail handling. There must be more of those men below decks, taking care of other aspects of the ship's business now that the fight with *Chincoteague* was over.

"Not so different from the way a starship is run," he murmured, mostly to himself.

"Is this an important battle?" Alexander asked quietly.

"I don't know yet," Picard told him as they enjoyed a moment of fresh breeze pressing through the lingering gunsmoke. "There were thousands of skirmishes between 1776 and 1787. It was a long war."

"Why don't you take over the ship and find out?"

"Well, this isn't like a holonovel, you know. This is real history. I've been on pretend ships, but this one was real."

"What difference does that make?"

A little embarrassed, Picard hesitated, then plunged ahead. "There's a difference between a passive interest and a way of life. It's one thing to enjoy naval history, and quite another to actually be on board an historic ship and make it go. No one likes to admit he hasn't the faintest idea of what he's doing, but here I am. Let's just listen and see what we can learn."

The boy stared at him for a moment of awakening, then simply nodded.

Picard and Alexander kept their mouths shut and listened as the crew muttered about whether or not the captain would decide to pursue the colonial ship or to go on with their mission, whatever that mission was. Where had they been heading when the attack came under the clear afternoon sun?

Why had the colonist attacked in broad daylight, when the larger ship had a decided advantage? What had they been trying to protect?

Picard took a moment to look at the land. Was something there worth protecting—with a valuable ship, costly guns and ammunition, and the lives of men, at great risk under a noon sun, with the wind on the enemy's other side?

"Mr. Picard!"

Pennington. This was a bulky man, but quick at picking his way through the dead and wounded and all the splinters and chunks of smashed wood. He came through the maze of clutter as if he'd spent his life doing it. Probably had.

"What are you going to do?" Alexander asked.

Picard glanced down. "Answer him." He looked up at the officer and called, "Yes?"

Instantly he realized he should've said "sir." Fact was, he wasn't used to saying that to anyone on board his own ship. He was used to having it said to him.

"Mr. Picard, are you injured?"

"Oh . . . no, sir, I'm not injured."

"Perhaps you should see to your duties then."

"Yes, of course. I will."

Pennington immediately about-faced and headed aft again, barking at the crew and surveying the damage.

"Well, there's something," Picard said. "Apparently I'm in charge of the foredeck."

"What's your rank?"

"Lieutenant, I'd say. A second or third officer. Or fourth. Let's see if they'll do what I say, shall we?"

He moved toward the nearest clutch of men, a gun crew and sail handlers, who were standing at the starboard rail, watching the retreat of the colonial ship, its sides still boiling smoke. That was a busy crew over there.

His crew should be busy, too. Picard glanced about, assessed what he saw, and simply said, "Gentlemen, let's clear away this wreckage and secure the guns. And coil those . . . those . . ."

"Aye, sir!" two of the men chimed, and others muttered the same. They were all sweat-drenched, blackened with cannon soot and shot grease, and their horny hands were bloody, but they seemed to know exactly what he meant.

Good thing, because he didn't. He wouldn't have known himself how to secure the guns, or which part of this wreckage had to be salvaged and which cast overboard.

"Salvage what you can," he said pointlessly, just as a test.

"Yes, sir," one of the Englishmen said.

"Take the wounded below," Picard threw in after glancing again at the litter of wounded men, and particularly the man who had been slaughtered by splinters. "And see to the dead."

One of the sailors stood up and stepped to him. "Sir, the wounded on the orlop deck?"

"Uh, yes," Picard agreed, "the orlop deck."

"And the dead?"

Alexander was looking at him.

Picard hesitated. "The hold."

"Very good, sir." The sailor turned to his mates and told them what to do.

"Well," Picard sighed to Alexander, "that seems to be some of my job."

"Can we help them?" Alexander said.

Clapping the boy on the shoulder, Picard smiled. "Exactly what I had in mind. You help those men shove off the wreckage. I'll triage the wounded."

"But you're not a doctor!" the boy protested.

"I'll just do my best. Promise me you'll do yours."

"I will."

"And don't throw anything overboard without asking."

"I won't."

Picard drew a breath to steel himself, and was instantly assaulted by the overpowering odor of blood and sweat, but mostly blood. It had a hot, salty, cloying presence as he moved into the litter of wreckage and wounded. He knelt immediately beside a groaning sailor whose leg had been shattered at the thigh by hurling wood. A blown-apart piece of line served well enough as a tourniquet, but the leg was clearly destroyed. This man would probably die, given this technology, and it would be a long, tortuous passing. Giving the delirious man a sorry pat on the shoulder, Picard moved on.

He knew, of course, that this was a vision of something that had happened in the distant past, and he couldn't really save a life, but there was a certain stinging reality in the fact that this *had* happened. As he had told the boy, this was not a holonovel. It was true history. These men had fallen on this ship, they had bled into its planks, they had driven back the desperate colonial ship, and men had died there, too. This suffering beneath his hands was very real, a taste of a witnessed event without need of imaginary embellishment, and it was his responsibility, as the posterity this program had been created for, to appreciate what he was seeing for the truths it displayed.

But it was time for him to get some rest, and then command his starship again. Picard found himself oddly disappointed to return to the twenty-fourth century. It was a transition he would have to make several times in the next few days, and it never ceased to be disconcerting.

The next evening, Picard and Alexander returned to the ship, the program waiting patiently for their return to the 1700s.

Until the sun sank into the milky sky, they cleaned the ship and sorted the dead from the dying from the might-live. Picard and Alexander both engaged in a crash course of squaring away a ship after a battle. The cannons had to be lashed down and cleaned. The wounded had to be tended with the eighteenth-century version of voodoo they called medicine, and, though appalling, it involved more common sense than Picard would've expected. He knew he had been guilty of disparaging the past as primitive, but they weren't really primitive. They simply hadn't the advantage of several more centuries of brilliant shoulders upon which to prop themselves. They were far more on their own than he had ever been, and he gained respect for them as this battered ship and crew saw to themselves without the advantage of retreating to a starbase for repairs and treatment. Whatever happened to them, they *had* to handle it.

He and Alexander became intimately part of that, and were learning very fast. Inevitably, the moment came when Picard, officer or not, helped carry a wounded man below.

What a heart-punching experience—he grimaced as his fingers sank into the blood-drenched flesh of the agonized sailor. The deck beneath his feet was gritty with a stew of powder grains, splinters, and blood. He fought to keep from retching.

Every "old" sailing vessel or museum ship he had ever visited had been clean as newspun cotton and had no particular odor. The cotton, oakum, and pitch once used to caulk decks had ages ago been replaced by epoxy and some kind of synthetic that looked the same, but wasn't as messy.

This ship was different. It wasn't a replica, or even a museum preservation. It was the real thing, in full function.

The moment his head went under the deck supports of the companionway hatch, his innards heaved under the assault of fumes of sulfur, tar, pitch, coal, bilge water, blood, oil-soaked sisal ropes, and the slimy excuse for drinking water. Eternal dampness pervaded the stenchy darkness, and for several minutes he could barely stay conscious. Every breath brought a wash of nausea. He was glad Alexander was up on the deck. Some things a boy should not have to endure. No lesson was worth this.

Even as he entertained that revelation, two boys younger than Alexander dashed past with lanterns, heading down the gloomy, stinking orlop deck, crunching on the sand-coated deck. Powder monkeys.

Children aboard a fighting ship . . .

If he had cherished any fantasies about living this way, they now faded fast.

Four hours later, the main deck was cleared of wreckage and wounded, the cannons were cooling, the ship's carpenters were shoring up the holes blown in *Justina* by iron balls, crew were scrubbing the blood from the decks—and so, by the way, was Alexander—and there was talk of rowing ashore to pick out a tree that could replace part of a topmast that had been shattered.

Order was slowly and deliberately returning, with a remarkably steady sobriety. No one complained. Even the wounded resisted their moans. It was a sight to behold.

Picard was indulging in a moment of admiration when a young man in a uniform jacket approached him, a fellow who at second glance couldn't have been more than sixteen years old. But wearing an officer's uniform. A yeoman?

"Mr. Picard, sir," the young man began, "Mr. Pennington's regards, and would you please assign two men to assist the afterdeck brace splicing."

"Regards to Mr. Pennington, and you may select any two men who are not right in the middle of something else."

"Very good, sir."

"Oh, and Mister—I'm sorry, my boy, what's your name again?"

The young, dark-haired fellow's brow furrowed, as if he thought Picard must have got a knock on the head. "Nightingale, sir. Midshipman Edward Nightingale."

"Oh, yes—I'm sorry. Must be the smoke."

"Aye, sir."

"When you've discharged your current duty, report back to me, please."

"I will, sir."

The young man was skinny and long-legged, as tall as Picard but half the weight. He hadn't gained his late-teenage meat yet, though there were signs of that coming.

"And, Mr. Nightingale, bring that boy over there with you when you come back."

"The swab? Oh, aye, sir."

He watched Nightingale hurry back across the scrubbed

deck, and once again scanned the working crew. Which of these men was Alexander's ancestor? Was he lying wounded below, perhaps? How many days of this program would they have to endure before singling him out?

Alexander's relatives, who had saved this diary program and passed it along to him, had never specified the ancestor's name. They thought part of the exercise was for Alexander to find the man.

But Picard had a ship to run, and a tinderbox situation on the planet of Sindikash to handle. Riker would interrupt the holodeck experience if necessary, however, and the ship was hovering just outside Sindikash's sensor range, waiting for Worf's reports.

Beyond that, the ship would run itself. Like the captain of this frigate, he also had lieutenants whose job it was to mind specific decks and departments. No point hovering about, micromanaging. He wasn't actually inclined to do so, though he felt the tug of other responsibilities. He had learned better many years ago, when he himself was officer of the watch.

Standing here on this old-fashioned deck, with the sunset of the past glowing on his face and neck, he felt as custodial about this British frigate as he did about his own ship, for in many ways this small vessel needed him more.

At least, today it did.

Today, the H.M.S. *Justina* was in hostile waters, thousands of miles from a friendly port, defending what her captain, officers, crew, and king believed was right.

And he had a boy's idea of honor to tend. He mustn't forget that.

A week ago, he might've huffed off the concept that a twelve-year-old child's view of the universe would be important to him. Something was different, now that Worf had made this request of him. The universe had gotten a little smaller.

Ah, here came the boys.

Alexander's white shirt was drenched from the chest down with blood-streaked water. Behind him came Mr. Nightingale, expectantly looking at Picard.

"Mr. Nightingale," Picard began, "I'd like to have you

give this lad a quick lesson in the structure of this ship and its rigging."

The midshipman blinked, confused. "Sir?"

"You heard me," Picard said, clasping his hands behind him. "It's an exercise for you both. Please begin."

"Oh . . ." Nightingale paled somewhat, as if afraid he were being tested, as Picard had carefully implied. "Yes, sir. Here, swab, pay attention."

Alexander frowned at the nickname, and Picard wondered if there were indeed some powder monkey on this ship who had been given that nickname. Just as he himself had been given the position of a lieutenant who probably did exist, Alexander seemed to be taking the place of a boy who had really been here.

"That's the bow and bowsprit," Nightingale began, quite obviously uneasy with this simplistic, even weird, assignment. "The rigging from there to the masts are called stays. The sails running on the forestays are heads'ls. The supports athwartships are the shrouds, which come down to deadeyes and lanyards, and are affixed to the chainwales on the outer hull. We have three masts, fore, main, and mizzen, and raise five sails on the fore and main, which would be the course, the lower and upper tops'ls, then the t'gallants and royals. The mizzen is rigged with a fore-and-aft spanker and a tops'l . . ."

Leaning toward Alexander, Picard muttered, "Sounds like Mr. Data and Engineer LaForge having a technical debate in the engine room, doesn't it?"

Alexander grinned conspiratorially and nodded.

Midshipman Nightingale paused, glanced at Picard to judge whether or not this lesson were too entirely idiotic to believe, but since he got no disapproval from his senior, the young man struggled on.

"We carry twenty-four guns and a squadron of marines. Uh . . . the fore and mains'ls are squares, and they're suspended from yards, and the painted part on the ends are the yardarms. The sails are lowered and hoisted by halyards, swung about with brace lines, furled with clews and bunts, adjusted by sheets, um, which are all called running rigging, on account of they're moving about—"

"All right, enough," Picard interrupted, letting him off the hook. "Well done, Mr. Nightingale. Alexander, you will be quizzed later."

Both boys stared at him as if he'd grown—well, hair.

Satisfied, he nodded and glanced up at the rigging, hoping it wasn't obvious that he was, in fact, stapling all those cursory details into his mind. Running rigging, standing rigging, clew bunt somethings, main, fore, so on. All right, so he'd missed a bit. Some of the tangle of lines and cables was beginning to make sense enough that he needn't embarrass himself. There was a certain amount of cooperation any holoprogram required of its user. If he failed to do his part to understand and fit in, the computer program would twist itself into knots, and Alexander's lesson would go wanting.

Or take weeks.

As the sun set, the heat went out of the day. Now the breeze was almost chilly. Picard decided they must be somewhere north of the mid-United States. No farther south than Chesapeake Bay—

"Chesapeake Bay!" he uttered. "The *Chincoteague!* Of course. I should've realized."

"Pardon, sir?" Midshipman Nightingale asked.

Picard parted his lips to fumble out an explanation but was drowned out when a cannon was fired off their stern.

Nightingale spun around, scanned the water, and shouted, "Spider catchers! My God! Spider catchers!"

He lunged for the ship's bell and rang it viciously.

"Spider catchers!" he shouted again.

Pulling Alexander away from the ship's rail, Picard peeked over and scanned the water. Against the darkness he made out the forms of three small boats, about the size of whaleboats, perhaps twenty or twenty-five feet long, approaching the stern. Just as he looked, one of the boats flashed with a cannon shot directly on its bow. He saw the gun move independently of the body of the boat, and realized that at least one of these small attackers was armed with a swivel gun. Something that small could be reloaded much faster than the ship's cannons.

"All hands!" he called out. "All hands on deck!"

What the hell—somebody had to.

By now much of the crew had heard the bell, and with his shout they began pouring out of the hatches and companionways. The captain appeared on the afterdeck, with Pennington and two other officers. The captain of the marines appeared, only half-dressed, and peered over the side, then rushed below again to muster his sharpshooters.

In the raiding boats, the colonists were faster. About ten to a boat, they maneuvered their craft along the sides of *Justina* and opened fire with hand pistols and rifles.

On the ship's deck, several men stumbled and fell even as they scrambled to run out a gun or two. At least two cried out in pain.

The captain stooped to his left, and for a bad instant Picard thought he'd been struck, but, in fact, he was reaching to help Mr. Pennington, who had staggered to one knee. The first officer—hit!

The spider catcher flotilla skulled about in the ship's own shadow, almost invisible against the dark water. Picard peered over at them, trying to gauge their movements, but the complete lack of light was dumbfounding. The sun was a memory now and there was no moon, no stars through a descending cloud cover. Briefly he thought about lighting lanterns on deck, but wouldn't that provide excellent target practice for the assaulting flotilla?

Mr. Nightingale appeared beside him again. "They must be desperate, sir!"

"Desperate for what, Mr. Nightingale? What are they defending?"

"The Delaware Station Boatyard, wouldn't it be, sir?"

"Oh . . . yes, quite likely."

He was about to say, "Is that all?" but remembered that installations like boat-building operations, docks, supply stores, and anything else that mobilized the enemy was always a target in wartime. Military installations were few in colonial America, for there was little formal military, no navy to speak of. A few shabby fortifications here and there, and a loose militia of untrained colonists, but that was all.

The captain came to midships, where he could see what was happening, assessed the problem, and turned to one of the other officers. Then that officer turned to the foredeck and said, "Raise heads'ls, Mr. Picard."

"Aye, sir," Picard responded, and turned to the nearest bunch of crewmen. "Hands to the heads'ls, please."

Five . . . seven . . . nine, ten crewmen came rushing to the bow of the ship, and he met them there. They busily unmade eight coils, and three men unfurled the headsails, though that meant climbing out onto the bowsprit and possibly becoming targets. They were single-minded despite the booming of pistol shots and the response from Marine Captain Newton's sharpshooters, who had rushed out onto the deck. There were cries from wounded men every few moments as shots hit home on the spider catchers, and also from them to the deck of the British ship.

"Ready on the jib halyards, sir," one of the foredeck crew gulped.

"Acknowledged," Picard responded numbly. "Haul away."

They did, and the triangular jibs ran up the stays, popped full of the offshore breeze and tightened to life, giving the ship some steerage way. The bow began swinging inward toward the land, turning the broadside of the ship toward the spider catchers who had been hiding in the ship's aft quarter shadow. He felt the connection between the hull and the water, the sails and the wind, and even through his boots felt the rudder bite deep. By golly, there *was* some fun to this.

And he saw the logic to it. The spider catchers were on the port side, using their swivel gun to blow damage into the ship's sides every few minutes, and trying to pick off the sailors with hand weapons. Now that the ship was turning on the breeze from offshore, she was putting her stern to the small attacking boats and slowly bringing her starboard side around—her starboard side, where men had been quickly loading the main deck midships guns.

"Fire, Mr. Simon."

Foom! The first gun went off at the captain's steady direction, and its response was a clap of water only inches from the stern of the nearest spider catcher.

"Next gun, please. Fire."

The second gun went off.

Instantly, the spider catchers' boat broke in half, spilling its men into the sea. Those still alive swam frantically toward another boat, whose oarsmen were quickly drawing away from *Justina.*

"Are they giving up?" Alexander asked.

Their oars dashing the water white, the spider catchers coordinated their efforts and stroked hard to put distance between themselves and the deadly bite of the marines' rifles, not to mention the starboard cannons.

Still . . . something was odd about this. Why would they come all the way out here, only to quit so soon? That wasn't the nature of rebels. If the British won this war, the colonists would remain colonists, and the price of their audacity would be high and brutal.

Just as the last few marines fired off considered shots into the dark night, Picard felt a sickening lurch come up through his feet and legs, and he was thrown sideways into Nightingale, and both drove into the ship's rail.

Right through the deck he felt the consistency of the sandy bottom—soft, mushy, gritty, but plenty hard enough to stall the ship.

He realized instantly what had happened. The *Justina* had been duped by these men who knew these waters, teased into turning inward toward shore. Although there appeared to be water for another quarter mile, indeed it was shallow water. They were aground.

Aground, and under attack!

Chapter Seven

"OH, BEAUTIFUL! COME HERE, PRECIOUS, right up here on my lap. You, too, honey. There we go. Isn't this nice?"

Holographers, cameras, video equipment, sensor broadcasters, and every manner of recording device available on Sindikash hummed merrily as the governor's wife gathered several handicapped children against her, drawing two of them up onto her lap.

The governor's mansion was decorated for the holiday of the founding of Sindikash, which would come in three weeks. Traditional colors were gold, purple, and black, so banners and ribbons of those danced about the halls, and wreaths of grape vines with fake plastic grapes were hung on every window and over the mansion's massive stone hearths, which were virtually symbols of Sindikash themselves. Most homes had these chunky hearths, or at least a mock version, and they were traditional in the lobbies of most public buildings. Sindikash liked its traditions.

Worf was getting tired of tradition. He wanted to be on the ship, with his son, celebrating his own tradition, but instead he was here, standing beside the entrance, standing guard over somebody else's.

Back in the quarters he and Grant shared now that they were Rogues, Grant was pecking away at an old style computer terminal, trying to find the track he spoke of, the trail that would tie Odette Khanty to her seedy network.

Worf, Ugulan, and the other Rogues had just come back from space, limping back on the freighter they had failed to "deliver" to Sindikash authorities on the Cardassian border. Worf hoped his message would get through to Picard that the trick had come off as planned. The heavily coded message had been sent along very thin civilian lines, through several trading packets and one drunken lightship keeper. Might take four or five days.

Could he keep Grant safe for five days? The election was ticking closer with each day. They barely had a week left.

He and Grant were completely isolated on Sindikash. Communication with the ship was rare, costly, slow, and dangerous. Any quicker method would attract attention or trip signals. The two were on their own, and that meant Grant's life was in Worf's hands.

He started to wonder if teaming up with a close friend might not be a ghastly mistake.

With some effort, he managed to stuff down those thoughts. Again.

One room beyond the executive office, the comatose governor lay in his sickbed, hooked up to several machines that were monitored by doctors in a small in-house clinic one floor below this. The door to the governor's room was open, and the end of the bed visible, with the unconscious man's feet creating an uneven bulge in the red blanket.

Worf watched Odette Khanty with the children, hugging and smiling, letting them tug at her hair, as the image of her with them was teleported all over the planet, into the perception of the Sindikash public.

"So wonderful," she murmured, then laughed. "All right! Let's just send all of you down to the mezzanine to have ice cream and mints!"

The children cheered and clapped, and she clapped with

them. Then a gaggle of aides and parents helped the children out of the room and down the wide carpeted hall, leaving only the media with their recording equipment and lights.

Mrs. Khanty stood up, still aglow with the adoration of the children, and held her hands out graciously to the reporters. "Anything else I can do for you today, anyone?"

From the back of the small crowd, a reporter asked, "Mrs. Khanty, what about allegations tying you to the explosion at the Lowelli Granary in the Great Eastern Territory? And about the Sindikash One-Four Transport? Rumors say there were two witnesses about your involvement with that explosion aboard Sindikash One-Four. Is that true?"

Mrs. Khanty controlled her expression masterfully, putting forth a beaming face of sympathy for the reporter. "I understand your feeling obligated to ask those kinds of questions, and all I can say is that there's no evidence linking me or anyone around me with any such event. There's simply no evidence. And I can't help it if some people are so consumed by greed and hate that they say evil things about us. We simply have to rise above all that."

"Thank you, ladies and gentlemen," Paul Stefan, Mrs. Khanty's assistant said, interrupting gracefully. The boyish-faced young man motioned them toward the door. "Mrs. Khanty has had a very busy morning. Don't forget tomorrow morning at ten—we're going to allow several of you to film Mrs. Khanty as she tends the governor. Those will be the first public viewings of the governor since the assassination attempt."

The reporters and cameramen murmured their thanks, but no one threw any more questions back.

"If you'll excuse us now," Stefan continued, "see you in the morning, Nick . . . thank you, Max, nice to see you . . . Celia, thank you for coming . . . Louisa, you lost weight!"

Mrs. Khanty nodded and chatted with a few reporters who cooed with the thrill of being so close to her. Their obsequiousness gave Worf a twisting stomach.

Finally, Stefan managed to herd them all out, and he went with them to make sure none "strayed."

He closed the office door behind him.

"Scan," Mrs. Khanty said instantly to Ugulan.

While Ugulan took out his old style tricorder and scanned the room for any devices that may have been left behind, Mrs. Khanty went to the sink in the kitchenette and ostentatiously washed her hands, making sure to scrub between the fingers and halfway up her arms.

"Dirty urchins," she grumbled out loud with a visible shudder. "Their fingers are always sticky. Why can't their parents keep them clean? Filthy, smelly embryos. Why do people have children? Ugulan!"

She came back into the outer reception room, her face flushed now, her expression thoroughly different than that which had met the cameras.

"Ugulan, get your pack of swine in here, you beetle-headed cur!"

"Yes, Mrs. Khanty." Ugulan put down his tricorder and whipped out a communicator, quickly signaling the Rogues without a word. Since they were just outside, guarding the hallway, they arrived in seconds and came crowding through the marquetry doorway.

By then, Mrs. Khanty had finished drying her hands and was standing with her face to a wall, her shoulders tense and her head slightly bowed.

Worf sharpened to some kind of attention. Disgust rolled through his stomach as the Rogues filed in, silent as statues, and one by one took positions along the wall, and even behind furniture, if possible.

How he hated to be in their company! To be dressed as they were, to be counted as one of them, to walk through the streets, assumed to be a Rogue! He watched the procession with uneasy curiosity and roiling animosity, and the moment slowly became surreal.

Seven Klingon warriors, fully armored, fully armed, holding the only energy handweapons allowed on the planet, other than law enforcement officers. They stood with their shoulders pinned to the walls and their eyes unfixed. Some of the toughest warriors in the quadrant now steeled themselves to face a single human female.

I am not one of them, yet I drown in their shame. When can I finish this?

The antique clock on the mantel ticked passively, its pendulum ushering in a creeping dread. The single window, with its leaded glass panels and stone frame, made Worf long to be anywhere but here.

"Luck."

Odette Khanty's first word was as soft as dripping rain. Worf had to strain to hear it.

She was still facing the desk. Across from Worf, against the far wall, Ugulan's face was forward but his eyes were on the woman. His fists clenched and unclenched repeatedly.

"Nothing but luck. Certainly brains weren't involved."

Mrs. Khanty seemed to be speaking to herself, as if reading something on the desk before her.

"Or loyalty."

Slowly she turned now, eyes down to the woven carpet's bundled flowers and Paisley scrolls. Her arms remained at her sides, her hands fanned out somewhat, as if she meant somehow to steady herself.

"Endangered my plans for this planet . . . a mission worth more than all your lives and all your mothers' lives. A chance to slander our opposition and get everything we want in one sweeping blow. And you couldn't follow through. Couldn't do one thing right. Wouldn't follow through on the promises you made. How can I ever trust any of you again? What am I going to do *now?*"

The word "now" came out like a slap. She suddenly raised her head so sharply that her hair bounced in punctuation.

Her face had changed. This one—Worf had never seen this face before. Her dark-smudge brows were flat, tight, the grooves around her lips suddenly defined, and her eyes were severe as dry ice. In them were both contempt and pure rage, as if she were dressing down a demure protégée who had unexpectedly said a bad word.

Worf's face turned hot from bitterness and embarrassment for the whole Klingon race. He had tried all his life to be an individual, to resist taking the course of this group or that faction, or even this or that culture, but today he was a clutching mass of Klingon, both aggravated that a human woman was dressing down those who should be warriors, and yet pleased that Ugulan and these low-lifes had to endure being chastised like children.

They deserved it!

Step by step, Odette Khanty strode slowly down the middle of the office area, not looking any Rogue in the face, her eyes instead fixed on the carpet. None looked at her.

"Do you have any idea . . . what I could arrange to have done to you?"

She passed the last Rogue, turned around, and slowly strode back. She looked at none of them. Her eyes fixed upon the wall at the opposite side of the room.

"Do you comprehend how far," she went on, "you would have to run?"

The clock clicked, then bonged. *One, two, three . . .*

"The sewers you would have to hide in?"

Five, six.

"There's only one real man among you. If not for him," she said with a sharp gesture at Worf, "where would I be?"

Worf stiffened and held his breath. *Marvelous! To be a superior weed among a field of chaff! What am I now?*

As its heavy knob clacked, the office entrance door brushed open against the thick carpet. One of the teenaged pages stepped in, carrying a bundle of wood for the fireplace's evening fire. Fire was completely symbolic on Sindikash, a custom to have most nights. A warmth of spirit and connection with the difficult past.

But not tonight.

The page stopped, stared, realized what was happening, found himself skewered on Odette Khanty's glare, and ducked out without even turning around. The heavy door clunked shut, and two of the Rogues winced at the sound.

Mrs. Khanty glared at the door, frozen in her fury.

Then she turned to the Rogues, and started looking them in the eyes, one by one.

In the next minutes, hell itself found voice.

Chapter Eight

"MRS. KHANTY . . . YOU SENT FOR ME."

"Worf. Yes, I sent for you. One moment, please . . . all right, now . . . you were the one who kept the freighter from being captured by Starfleet."

"How do you know?"

"I know. Why did you do that?"

"Because . . . I would rather not specify."

The private office smelled of the wood fire burning at the other end of the room. Wood fires were popular on Sindikash, though unnecessary as of fifty or so years ago. Worf stood before Odette Khanty, who sat passively behind her carved 18th century barrister's desk. He felt strangely small. Somehow the comforting smells and old-fashioned decor made him aware of how out of place he was. Every fiber of the carpet was another twist in the tightrope he walked.

She was wearing a thick velvet robe of some kind with brocade sleeves and a satin collar, posing Worf with an image of casual royalty. The robe must have possessed some kind of sentimental value, for the end of one sleeve was a bit frayed and no one had repaired it.

Worf was in privileged quarters here, for he was upstairs from the governor's recovery suite, and no one—no one—came up here without personal and confirmed request by Mrs. Khanty and without jumping four or five hoops of security clearance. The fact that he was here, without any other guards, came as a message to him, direct from her.

"Then I'll specify for you," the woman said steadily, unintimidated by his presence or his size. "Because Ugulan and the other Rogues were going to let themselves be captured instead of destroying themselves as they swore to me they would. You didn't want to be captured. But you also didn't want to die. Isn't that right?"

"True." Straightening his back, Worf looked over Mrs. Khanty's head at the sculpture of a hawk on a wall shelf and allowed himself to be honest for one flashing second. "I am not a man who will die easily."

The governor's wife leaned back in her chair, which with its drape of embroidered fabric looked more like a throne—and she knew that. Her neatly done hair fingered her shoulders. Her cheekbones caught the pale light.

"But you didn't let yourself be captured either," she said.

At her candid tone, Worf relaxed his stance and looked her in the eyes. For the first time, he felt as if he could speak as something of an equal.

"That would have been bad for both of us, Mrs. Khanty," he said. "I am absent without leave from Starfleet, and you . . ."

He deliberately paused, but continued sparring with that firm gaze. He told her with that gaze that he knew what she was.

"Yes," she murmured. "This was my chance to suck twenty percentage points away from the lieutenant governor. I could've handily won the election. Now, it'll be close. I don't like 'close.' I'm down to three days now. What can I do in three days? Do you know what will happen to you and all the Rogues if I lose?"

Several possible answers of varied degrees of intensity ran through his mind. Finally he plucked one. "The lieutenant governor will take action against us."

Mrs. Khanty did not smile, nor did she in any way offer tacit approval.

"No," she said. "I will."

He stood before her in the amber aura of the imitation gaslights that pervaded the compound, and said nothing.

"I have an assignment for you," she went on, "which is going to put you over the line into my complete trust. The Rogues have to pay for their cowardice."

Worf frowned in protest, abruptly defensive about Klingons and cowardice fielding the same sentence. Right through his sudden distaste at defending the Rogues, he said, "It was not their fault that the Starfleet scout picked up the freighter."

"Not that part," Mrs. Khanty agreed. "It's this other part. We had a pact. They swear allegiance to me, stay on my planet, enjoy expatriate status here, be my elite guard, gain influence and power, and in return they swore they would self-immolate before letting themselves be caught, which would cast me under suspicion. They didn't hold up to that pact. They understand there's a price. They will have to pay it. I want you to be the collector."

The heat from a burning log snapping in the fireplace pressed against the back of Worf's neck. Mrs. Khanty was completely unreadable. There was no inflection in her words, no evil gleam in her eye, no conniving enjoyment, no sultry threat. She might as well have been speaking to a chef while arranging a banquet menu.

"Choose any one of them. Make sure you don't leave any flotsam," she added, without waiting for him to accept the assignment. "I can't have this kind of thing happening again."

She paused then, and folded her hands on her lap, and crossed her legs. And waited.

He stood before her and simply could not think of a single thing to say. How did one accept a job to kill someone else just to make a point?

Since he first heard Commissioner Toledano's claim that Klingons had inflicted torture and callous murder, he had wanted to kill. His gut had churned since that moment until this moment, and now he felt as if his innards had been pulled out. He was being handed a chance to kill a dishonorable Klingon. He could do it in the line of duty. He *could* do it . . .

"One question," Worf said. "You have not asked me for my oath of allegiance. May I ask why?"

"Because I wouldn't get it, would I?"

"No."

Mrs. Khanty was evidently not interested in his oath or too used to no one's ever defying her. She seemed perfectly comfortable with the situation.

She nodded, once.

"With or without an oath, don't betray me, Worf," she said. "It's not a good idea."

"You should've whipped out your badge and arrested her! This is great! We've got her! She just asked a Starfleet officer to go out and assassinate somebody so she could get her revenge and keep her hoods in line!"

Ross Grant spread his arms in victory, not taking it personally that he hadn't been the one to "crack" Odette Khanty's pretty cover. He spun about the room like wind, amazed at the audacity of their opponent.

Inwardly grateful for his friend's generosity, Worf sadly shook his head. "She said it was an 'assignment.' Someone had to 'pay the price.' She told me to be 'the collector.' She was very careful. She said nothing that might not be taken in some innocent way, given some other context. And you know how skillful she is at twisting facts."

"Do I!"

"Also, she made sure we were alone. There were no other witnesses. Sindikash law requires two, not one."

Grant started to say something, paused, then shook his head. "Yeah, right, well . . . yeah, I know that, I know . . . damn."

Glad not to have to make that point again, Worf sat down to adjust his boot. As he watched his fingers work down there, all he saw was those two knarled hands, strong and trained, closing around a Klingon throat.

"The larger problem still remains. She wants me to kill

one of the Rogues as an example. If I do it, then she will trust me."

"Oh, you bet," Grant uttered. "She wants to kill two birds with—well, you know what I mean."

"Yes," Worf sighed, "and if I fail to do it, we could lose our chance to get you 'inside.'"

"Hell, don't do that! Whatever happens, we can't let that happen. I'm the only thing she can't be careful against."

Worf buckled his boot again and sat straight. His eyes ached from all these hard thoughts. "Yes . . . and in order to keep her trust, I must earn it by completely incriminating myself. She and I will be obligated to each other."

Grant shrugged. "Standard mob procedure. Make your henchmen do something they definitely don't want to get caught doing, make sure all the right people know it was done, so you're not the only one committing crimes. Then they gotta stick with you. Oldest story in the book. Seen it a dozen times."

Frustrated, Worf only nodded.

"Y'know," Grant added, "this is a big step you've taken here. From what I've been finding out, she used to give these special jobs to Ugly-an. Now he's out and you're in. You watch out for that guy, bud. I don't want you coming back without arms."

"I intend to keep my arms," Worf assured, and stood up. He drew a choppy breath, held it briefly, let it out, then headed for the doorway. "Be sure to lock yourself in."

"Hey!" Grant called. "Where're you going? You shouldn't be going out alone. You want me to go with you?"

"Not this time." Worf yanked the door open, squared his shoulders, and forced himself not to look back. "I have a Klingon to kill."

The midnight sky lay upon the domes of the city complex. Gothic spires toyed with low-lying clouds. The scent of wet grass and steamy wool rode an inbound breeze from the herd of American bison grazing passively in the valley just outside of town.

Cafes and clubs murmured with laughter and music, from

the twange of mandolins to the whistle of clarinets. Sindikash was a comfortable place with a great deal to lose.

Mud. Rain had come lately, but briefly. The cobblestones were greased, hard to walk upon. His boots slipped as he moved, and each slip injected him with a tremble of insecurity. This was not a good place to be.

In the darkness of the alley between a church and a post office, he could see nothing.

Not even his own hands.

He should not have come alone. No one alone was safe on Sindikash.

Since he was a child he had a sense of when there was someone else around. His father had been the same way. Suspicious.

Everything made him suspicious. The shivering wind. The click and whistle of music. The pale flickering lights from the street beyond, which caused a bizarre doorway of silver fog in the distance. That was the end of the alley. He wished to be there, so his spine would cease its quaking. This was a bad time to go alone.

As his hunger for the angled light at the end of the alley grew, he realized he was already halfway through. Now he could not turn back safely. He would have to go all the way through. How many steps had brought him to this point? How many were left? Usually he counted his steps. Tonight he had forgotten.

A buffalo mooed in the deep night. He longed to be among them, where the jab of a blade or the lance of a phaser might be blocked by a quick dive behind a furry body. Protection, protection . . .

The mouth of the alley glowed like battle before him. He wanted to be there. His own heartbeat pounded from his hips to his head with a drum that blinded him to all but the far light and its tinsel curtain of mist.

Step, step, mud, slip, feel absurd, balance, step again—

Suddenly his left knee buckled and shot out from beneath him. His spine screamed as it slammed to the mud-slicked cobblestones. One of them struck the back of his skull, dazing him abruptly and blurring the vision overhead of the tops of the buildings and the gauzy sky.

Then hands—fists—at his throat, dragging him to his feet—he struggled to react, but his hands were tingling from the fall and for a critical instant he couldn't even find them.

Dizziness spun through his skull and his equilibrium snagged as someone hauled him to his feet—and no one could do that but another Klingon.

In an instant of panic, he clamped his numb arms to his chest, clumsily hoping to protect his vital organs from the blade bite he knew was coming—

But none came.

"Walking alone in the city," a voice rumbled before his blurred eyes. "Not very wise, Genzha."

"Worf! You!"

Genzha pressed back against the brick church, wildly thinking that he might be able to use the wall as a brace, but before he could raise hand or knee, or find his own dagger with these numb fingers, his arms were pinioned behind him and clasped with some kind of strap.

Unbidden fear dashed through him as he realized that he was being held down by a professional, trained soldier—a Starfleet-trained soldier.

Surprised that he wasn't dead yet, Genzha gasped, "But Ugulan is the one! I was watching out for Ugulan! She chose you to do this instead of him?"

"She chose me. A strange universe we live in, where nothing is certain for long."

"What do you want? I sicken of your gloating!"

"I want you to remain very quiet." Worf's breath was hot against Genzha's ear. "Walk before me, and we'll talk about who lives until morning, and who dies."

"Transporter room to Riker."

"Riker here. Data, what are you doing in the transporter room?"

"The trainee requested that I come here to handle a situation. I am, in turn, requesting your advice."

"What've you got?"

"We accepted a parcel from Mr. Worf, sir, transported from an asteroid breaker, which picked it up from a Torkezzi fuel

ship, which evidently received it from a container vessel out of Sindikash."

"Okay, what's in the parcel?"

"A very angry Klingon, sir."

"A Klingon!"

"Yes, sir. Evidently he was drugged until seven hours ago, when he awakened on board the breaker and let his dissatisfaction be known."

"Did he hurt anybody?"

"Negative, sir, his wrists and ankles were manacled. However he is very loud and no one could get close enough to gag him."

"Have you got him under control?"

"I succeeded in gagging him, sir."

"I guess there are advantages to being an android. Why would Worf send us a hogtied Klingon?"

"No idea, sir. We have only a request from Worf that the Klingon be detained in secrecy for an as yet undetermined period of time."

"Hmmm . . . all right, we'll do that, if he wants."

"Where would you like me to detain the Klingon, sir?"

"The brig. He'll be fine. Our brig is nicer than most."

"But the charges, sir? He can be detained only twenty-four hours without logging charges."

"I'll think about that. Just lock him up for now. Make him comfortable."

"Yes, sir."

"Data?"

"Yes, sir?"

"Not too comfortable."

"Understood, sir."

"Riker out."

"He's late. What has he got to do that makes him late for a meal? He has no assignment, he has no duty, he has no reason to be absent from a Rogue supper."

Worf listened to Ugulan's trumpeting with a touch of amusement and said nothing. He sat at the far end of a long table laid out nightly with Klingon food for the Rogues.

They were expected to eat together. It was the only way they could interact. Or keep an eye on each other.

But Genzha was breaking the pact. He was not here in time for supper.

According to the agreement between themselves, they could not begin eating until all were accounted for.

And Worf was hungry. Hungry and satisfied. He'd had a chance to kill, and he had found his reserve. He wished Alexander had been there to see it. He wished Picard had been. He wanted somebody to know.

And why not? What good was control unless he could gloat over it a little?

He glanced around at his ready-made audience. In a minute, they would all be afraid of him. He liked that.

"Genzha," he said, "will not be joining us."

Ugulan's eyes widened and he rounded on Worf. "What do you know? Where is he?"

Worf leaned a casual elbow upon the table and picked up a stick of rolled meat. "He will no longer be with us. That is what I know."

The other Rogues—Mortash, Tyro, all—suddenly turned stiff with realization, stared at Worf, then glanced at each other. None seemed to know what to say.

Also staring at Worf, Ugulan seemed the most shocked of all—Worf had just stolen his job.

Worf punctuated his point by taking a bite of the rolled meat stick.

Then, quite unexpectedly, Mortash broke out in a bar-room laugh that rolled along the carpet-hung walls. He scooped up his tankard, raised his glass to Worf, and indulged in a deep swig. Tyro and Kev laughed then too, and soon Tyro and the other Rogues nodded in satisfaction and plunged into their food.

Momentary confusion gripped Worf as he tried to figure out what was happening. Why were they laughing?

These were not just guards—they were Klingon guards. Expatriates or not, Klingons needed structure. That was the reason for the supper together ever day, for their pact with Odette Khanty, and their agreements between themselves. Evidently, it was no mystery to them that one of their own had disappeared. Worf expected them to take revenge upon him for his actions against another Klingon, and his legs were tense for the fight he thought had been coming.

Yet they weren't reacting that way at all.

Suddenly he understood what was going on. What he saw around him, this bizarre cheerfulness—except for Ugulan—was pure relief! They knew one of them was destined to "pay" for the freighter incident, and now that debt had been fulfilled. And each Klingon was glad it wasn't paid with his blood. He realized with some loss that these were not only not particularly good Klingons, but not particularly good people.

They were cowards! Shameful!

His appetite withered. He put down the meat stick. All he did now was watch the others wolfing down their dinner.

They ate their meal with the joviality of water purging over a dam, gushing merrily past a blockade that had minutes ago seemed insurmountable. They talked and gulped, back-slapped, chewed and laughed in some kind of purging, and even seemed to be enjoying each other's company.

All but Worf, and Ugulan. The two rivals sat in silence.

And they watched each other.

Chapter Nine

IF WORF HAD NOT BELIEVED in witchcraft, he did now. She had spun a spell of underlying fear that could not be lightly banished.

Worf felt the lingering heat of that spell. He was sustained only by the thought of the starship backing him up and the fact that he did not have to stay here much longer.

Amazing! She had made Klingons afraid!

There must be something more to her than meets the eye, he thought, cherishing his shoulder sockets and appreciating possession of his elbows. He quickened his pace as he crossed the brightly tiled Burkal City Central Courtyard to the onion-domed Rogue apartments. Sindikash posed a stirring Orient-express sensation, and Worf found the escape from Mrs. Khanty's domination to be a relief.

So much shame, he thought. *To want refuge from an enemy I could lift with one arm. I must be getting old.*

He hurried into his quarters, glancing around as he ducked behind the curtain of wooden beads and through the heavy oak arched doorway.

In the small chamber, utilitarian in spite of the warm

carpets on the walls and the stenciled ceilings, Grant hunched over a portable computer terminal whose screen cast a shifting glow upon his tired face.

"How are you doing?" Worf asked.

Ross Grant shook his head in strange admiration. "Captain Picard's plan worked great. You're in tight with her. She's dismissing two of Ugulan's choices from being her husband's private guard and installing you. Must've been some dilly of a cargo on that freighter."

"We are not even certain what the cargo was," Worf rumbled. "Can you find out?"

"I tried. Couldn't find it. Could be chemical poison for agricultural sabotage," Grant said. "She could strangle a whole planet by holding their crops hostage. She's into that lately."

"With her name involved?" Worf asked hopefully.

Grant shook his head and tapped at his computer. "Hell, no such luck! She's good. Damn, is she good. I never saw anybody with this much strata of coverage. We could only prosecute about halfway up to her. But look at this—one by one, everybody associated with her is being arrested. Her organization could crumble in ten minutes if we could find the one link tying her to all the stuff she's doing. It's weird, Worf—she's doing so *much* illegally that it's hard to get everything in your head that she's doing, but somehow that creates a tapestry that she just hides behind. She just shrugs and acts like she can't understand why anybody would be mean to her. But she's got this ruthless inner person—"

"I know," Worf commented. "She bolted the Rogues to the wall with words alone. She inflicted mortal fear into fully grown Klingon warriors. There is something more to her. They seemed in terror for their souls."

"They did? Wish I'd seen it! Bet it was a party."

Relaxing for the first time in hours, Worf sighed. "They were actually afraid of her."

"Why not? I sure am."

Grant leaned back, grimaced, stretched his arms and winced at the stiffness in his back and shoulders. Then he tapped his computer readout screen with one finger.

"I've got her whole organization in here. The Fed's

right—she's jockeying to take over the planet and break off from the Federation so she doesn't have to follow anybody's rules but her own. Sindikash'll be a fortress of crime, and its people will be trapped inside. I got it all. Mountains of it. But there's nothing to tie *her* to it. Without that one shred of evidence linking her to a major crime, something that can be prosecuted, something simple enough for the people to understand, the planetary authorities won't have dink to go on." He looked up at Worf, his eyes drawn and tired. "I don't know what else to do."

"Continue working," Worf said. "Be a Rogue. Do your job. Then . . . we'll be here when she makes a mistake."

Grant looked up at him. "She doesn't make any, ever!"

"Everyone does." Putting his hand on the precious computer console with its raft of criminal charges aching to be made, Worf fixed his gaze on Grant. "You and I are inside now. We will be here when she makes her mistake. Or we will arrange one."

Jean-Luc Picard watched the spider catchers from a deck tilted fifteen degrees, expecting them to turn back, now that *Justina* was aground, and make some different sort of assault.

But they didn't. They kept hauling on their oars, scooping their comrades from the water, and rowing out of range.

"Captain! Captain!"

It was the helmsman calling. Picard almost answered. Instead, he turned to his foredeck crew and said, "Gentlemen, let those heads'ls go loose. They're only serving to push us over onto the shoal."

"Aye, sir," several of the men responded. They seemed ready to do exactly that, so he'd apparently thought right.

Without taking the moment to pat himself on the back, he noticed that quite a bit of this sailing-ship business simply involved common sense and simple observation. Rationally, of course, he knew he could commonsense around for a year and still not know everything. Still, the crash course was operative.

"Officers midships, please."

Picard looked at Nightingale and Alexander. "Come with me, boys."

They thunked across the deck planks sixty feet or so to midships, and joined the captain, the captain of the marines, and the other lieutenants. Picard moved next to Mr. Pennington, who was clutching a bloody right arm.

"You all right, Mr. Pennington?" he asked sociably.

"Well enough," the first officer rasped, obviously grappling with considerable pain. "The ball missed the bone."

"Let me bind it up for you."

The bulky man leaned back on the ship's rail. "Thank you . . . thank you very much. Very kind."

Picard glanced around and was gratified to receive Nightingale's instant donation of a black neckerchief.

The captain appeared around the mainmast after observing the retreat of the spider catchers. "We're aground, gentlemen," he said simply. "We have to get off immediately. There's also damage to the rudder from that swivel gun. Mr. Simon and the carpenter's crew are about to go offboard to attempt repairs. We must be able to steer the ship, or we are lost. Clearly, the insurgents will be coming back now that we're foundering. We must act quickly. We'll have to warp her out."

Tying a sturdy bandage around Pennington's wound, Picard smiled and shook his head.

"Is something funny?" Pennington asked.

"Oh, no, no, sir," Picard demurred. "Just thought of something else. Sorry."

Alexander pulled on his sleeve and whispered, "He said warp! Do they have warp speed?"

"No, no . . . this is where the phrase came from. It's rather comforting how little some things change."

"Mr. Picard?" the captain said sharply, annoyed by the murmuring. "You have something to suggest?"

Picard faced him. "Well, yes, sir. I'd like to volunteer to lead the away team—the landing party."

"Very well. Take Mr. Nightingale and one other fellow, and go ashore with a hawser. Make fast to a tree, and we'll use the capstan to reel the ship off the bar. Once we've done that, you shall unmake the line, travel north on the shore, make fast to another tree, and we'll warp the ship up the coast until we find better bottom. Mr. Chappell, run all but four of the guns inboard and secure them until we get off the bar."

A young lieutenant nodded. "Very good, sir."

"Let's station Captain Newton's marines on deck as security until we can run the guns out again."

"Aye, sir."

"And make certain the hold is secure also. I thought I felt some shifting."

"Aye, aye, sir."

"Oh, and Mr. Picard—"

"Sir?"

"Take along a marine with you as your armed guard."

Picard nodded. "Thank you, sir."

He pressed back a smile. This business of taking orders was downright nostalgic, and easier than he'd remembered. Been a long time. He found some comfort in it, letting somebody else decide.

"Take that marine," Alexander suggested excitedly, pointing at the tall blond fellow who had caught their eye before.

The captain had started to walk away, but now turned back. "Yes, fine, take the sergeant with you. Mr. Pennington, where do you believe we're aground?"

"Where, sir?"

"Where on the hull."

"Oh—midships, sir. Midships to the stern, sir."

"I'd say that as well. Better run six of the guns on each aft deck up forward of midships. Shift the weight off the aft keel. Pay out a heavy warping line . . ."

He paused, looked down at the tilted deck, and seemed troubled.

"Perhaps a spring line, sir?" Pennington suggested.

The captain nodded. "I was thinking that, but as I consider it now, I believe we'd rather swing the bow about. Run the line out the forward cathead."

"Aye, aye, sir."

"Oh, and while we're at this, best we station a boat

midway between ourselves and Mr. Picard on the shore, to relay communication."

"Very good, sir."

Pennington summoned his resolve, mastered his pain, and hustled away, carrying all that on his shoulders, as the captain peered briefly at the shore, then also went aft.

Picard at once felt sympathy and admiration for these people, who had to come up with clever ways to do the simplest things, even communicating over short distance. In his time, he had only to push a button, and unthinkable technology allowed him to communicate through billions of kilometers of spatial vacuum. As he watched these officers try to work out their problems, he realized he was standing upon their accomplishments. Things were easier for him because things had been so hard for them.

On the other hand, they knew their enemy. The last man standing would be the winner. Picard never knew ahead of time whether the strange alien he encountered would befriend him, kill him, marry him, or eat him. In his universe, a person could step into a faulty transporter, and come out in the shape of a turnip.

Well, every generation had its burdens.

Short minutes later, he was in a row boat with Alexander, Nightingale, two deckhands who were acting as oarsmen, and the sergeant of the marine grenadiers, with his loaded rifle.

The sergeant wore a formal scarlet coat with white facings and brass buttons, but beneath that he wore a sailor's checked shirt and rather loose trousers, probably because he had been living aboard ship and the typical tight breeches and waistcoats were taxing in that environment. Picard had noticed that the grenadiers were usually indistinguishable from the sailors, except when engaged in battle. Then they put on their red coats and stiff-fronted yellow headgear with the embroidered letters GR—*George Rex.*

Of course. King George the Third.

The sergeant was a tall young man in his mid-twenties, perhaps a little over six feet, his hair as blond as Mr. Nightingale's was dark, and he possessed enviable cheekbones and a set of very Aryan blue eyes. He seemed a bit nervous, glancing at the dark shoreline, probably worried about snipers or a trap. He was not sitting, as the others all were. Instead he rested a knee on one of the slat seats, and balanced as well as possible there, with his rifle at the ready.

For a few precious minutes, while rowing toward the broccoli-bunch trees of the shoreline, there seemed to be peace in the bay. Behind them, a faint moon glowed through the haze, casting little light, but enough to make out the ghostly image of the ship against the gauzy night.

Picard paused for several minutes and just watched the ship, taking in the shape of the hull, the high transom, the heads'ls slapping loose, and the phantomish movement of dark, small men along her deck.

"It's so pretty . . ." Alexander was watching the frigate, too. As a child of space travel, he wasn't used to seeing the ships he lived upon except from the inside, and this was a whole different perception.

"There's the repair party," Picard said quietly, noticing a small boat with four men who appeared at the stern of the *Justina.*

"They're getting ready to fight again, aren't they?" the boy asked.

"Yes, repairing the damage to the rudder. The ship has to be able to maneuver or she's lost. The captain thinks another wave of attacks is coming."

"He thinks this is . . . a trap?"

"A wave of targeted attacks, yes. The colonists know they can't win against an armed frigate of Royal Navy seamen and soldiers with a direct attack. They have to weaken the enemy first."

Alexander scowled. "Doesn't seem honorable to me. They should come out in the open and fight."

"How would you fight against an enemy far larger, better trained, better armed, and well-financed? Come out and stand before him?"

"Isn't that better?" The boy turned to him. "Isn't that more honorable?"

So at least he hadn't forgotten why they were doing this.

Picard seized the moment. "Let's start with this—what do you think honor is, Alexander?"

At the bow, the grenadier sergeant snapped to look at him suddenly, and seemed about to say something, but Alexander spoke up without noticing that the sergeant's blue eyes were fixed on the two of them now.

"Honor," the boy began, "is winning."

Picard nodded, and gave him the courtesy of a pause. "But many win through dishonoring themselves. So there must be more to it."

The boy frowned, trying to visualize what he was talking about, and seemed to accept that things like that happened. He searched for another answer and finally decided to try one.

"Honor is . . . *how* you win, then."

"Mmm," Picard uttered, and glanced one more time at the ship. "I see I'll have to be more creative about this."

The Grenadier turned partly around, readjusting his stance in the shifting boat. "I'm sorry, sir, I do not know you. What is your name?"

"Picard."

"French?"

"Yes, as a matter of fact. Jean-Luc."

"But you sound quite British. And you serve the Royal Navy."

"Yes. I was educated at Oxford."

The marine puffed up a little, smiled with mischievous collegiate rivalry, and said, "Cambridge."

"You speak exceptional English," Picard observed, "but you're not English either, are you?"

The sergeant smiled. "My name is Alexander Leonfeld. I am Austrian. My father is the Fifth Duke of Leonfeld and my mother was born to the family of Gosch-Embourg."

Picard nodded as if he understood the significance. "Very nice."

And not really surprising. If Picard remembered his military history, marine sharpshooters were usually of high standing, even royal or peered birth. They were the most intelligent, the most educated, and were favored as choices if they came from respected, established families.

Mindful of his duty, Sergeant Leonfeld turned back toward the land and continued scanning for movement. He fitfully caressed his loaded rifle.

Alexander stared and stared at the sergeant, and finally he scooted closer to Picard in the stern of the boat.

"It's him!" the boy whispered.

"Pardon?"

"That's my ancestor!"

"How do you know?"

"Because his name is Alexander! I was named after him!"

Chapter Ten

WITH HER KEEL BALLASTED by new revelations, the small rowboat surged toward the land, heaved up on a new tide every few seconds by the oarsmens' pull.

Picard drew Alexander very close and put his lips to the boy's ear. "Any other clues?"

The boy nodded vigorously. "He wasn't American or English," he whispered back.

"Mmm," Picard murmured. "Good clue."

"Alexander" was not an uncommon name in these times, and the *Justina* was tightly packed with crew and soldiers. Still, the holoprogram would likely shove Picard and Alexander together with the person they were supposed to be meeting, in a kind of cyber-destiny.

How clever that Alexander's relatives hadn't told him the name of the ancestor, but made him hunt for the man. Rather than striking straight for their quarry, Picard and Alexander had spent considerable hours, and a notable adventure, learning to understand the lifestyle, rather than just sitting and listening. Far better.

And now, here the man knelt, in this little boat. Alexander was watching the other Alexander with new eyes, the eyes of a boy gazing upon legend embodied.

Picard grimaced as the boat's keel rasped against the stony bottom, and they were ashore. Embarrassed by the flinch, he noted how very real all this had become for him in the past few hours, and hoped Alexander—the boy—felt the same. Of course, he realized again, this *had* happened. It wasn't a story. In moments, he and Alexander would step out onto a shore with young men who had been here, in these very woods at this very moment, for this was Alexander Leonfeld's journal of his American experience.

That night these woods had held this cloying chill, left over from the day's humidity, still tacky beneath their wool uniforms. These were times far before the sweat-wicking fabrics of Picard's age. That night, the moon up there had hovered in its shroud of haze and looked down with unhelpful dimness upon the H.M.S. *Justina,* and it was the same moon Picard now looked up to see. The moon of Chesapeake Bay, sometime in the summer of 1777.

He waited until the two oarsmen jumped out and dragged the boat farther up onto the gravelly shoreline. Then he, Alexander, and the other Alexander climbed out and together they all dragged the rowboat to a stable position, then came around to its stern to haul up the four-inch-diameter braided hawser that had come along with them, strung all the way from the ship. In fact, it was a modified dockline—really three docklines fixed to each other with two carrick bends, making it long enough to reach the shore.

Picard assisted in hauling the line ashore and directed his men to walk it several yards north of the ship's bow; then he himself selected a tree. With a certain small vestige of pride, he threw the bitter end of the meaty line into a clove hitch around the trunk. As he surveyed his handiwork with some satisfaction, he regretted being one of several upperclassmen at Starfleet Academy who had petitioned to have the marlinspike seamanship course dropped from the requisites. After all, what good was knot-tying and simple line repair to a Starfleet serviceman?

What good, indeed?

Luckily, the petition had been denied and he had grimly taken the course.

"Not bad," he muttered. "Thank you, Commander Graves. And I do apologize." Then he turned to the rocky shoreline and looked out at a second rowboat that was holding position midway between the shore and *Justina.* He cupped his hands around his mouth and shouted, "Haul away!"

From the small boat, the order was relayed to the ship: "Haul away, all!"

A moment or two passed as the efforts of the crew were coordinated on the ship's capstan bars. The capstan was essentially a large winch, pushed around by men holding baseball-bat-sized spokes. Ordinarily such a contraption was used to raise the anchor, but as today witnessed, there were other uses.

Hovering just under the surface of the water, the hawser danced tenderly with the tides, disappeared below, then came up again and into the carved cathead at the ship's bow. As movement on deck became steadier, the line began bouncing on the surface, then lapping the top as it grew shorter and tighter, drawn inboard by the turning capstan.

This was slow business. Picard couldn't quell a twitch of impatience.

He took a moment to glance at Alexander, and true enough to Picard's suspicions, the "swab" was staring unremittingly at his human ancestor. Alexander Leonfeld was oblivious to the attention, but stood, looking rather majestic, on the shoreline, his youth and stature adding to that scarlet uniform jacket with its white facings and gold buttons, still somehow bright in spite of weeks at sea, and his white leggings, and his long musket . . . yes, quite a figure, compared with a midshipman, a couple of deck-hands, and a rather dour uncle-type whom the boy perceived only vaguely as a real ship's captain. Sergeant Leonfeld cut a statuesque form against the shimmering evening sea as he stood guard, his rifle ready, his eyes scanning the curving shoreline.

"It's up!" Nightingale rejoiced. Picard looked, and saw

that the line had finally cleared the water and was now wagging like a giant jump rope, barely over the surface. Glittering droplets of water poured from its soaked braids. Gradually, the line lost its drape and became straighter and straighter.

Finally, at the tree, the line began to strain and groan. The tree spat bark and squawked as the tourniquet tightened. Picard and his landing party watched the ship. The line grew straighter, and stiffer.

Mired on the shoal, *Justina*'s great bulk began to heel over, her keel biting into the shoal as her weight shifted. If she didn't come off, she'd either be stranded, or she'd turn on her side altogether. The captain was letting her go over very far, until Picard could see the deck almost as a wall, tilted at forty or more degrees. Each degree attested to the captain's determination to deny the enemy this prize if he could. What was the code of honor here? Would the captain destroy his own ship before letting her be taken? Picard didn't remember the habits of the British Royal Navy at this time, but he also knew that several colonial fighting ships, and other ships during other wars, were often refitted enemy ships that had been captured. A captain could conceivably survive a battle, lose a ship, gain a new command, and find himself firing on the very vessel he had once commanded.

"Stand back, gentlemen," Picard said as the line grew tight and hard as stone. If the line parted, or one of the knots came free, it would whip back and shear someone's head off. Given the tenuous nature of this old-tech program, he couldn't take a chance of that being himself or Alexander.

"Mr. Picard!" Edward Nightingale gulped as if holding down his dinner, and pointed frantically out onto the water beyond the ship. "Look! Sir, look!"

Two more ships were swinging out of an inlet! One was a single-masted ship with a fore-aft sail, large enough to deck perhaps a half dozen cannon, but the other was a two-masted ship of about eighty feet. Both that ship's masts were square-rigged.

"More spider catchers are with them!" one of the two oarsmen said. "We gotta get on back!"

He struck off toward the rowboat, but Alexander Leonfeld plunged from his guard stance, caught the frantic sailor, and roughly held him back. "Bennett! We'll be ambushed on the water!"

The brawny sailor swung around and wrenched his arm back. "You can't order me! You're not a Navy officer!"

"But I am," Picard said, stepping between them. "Stand down, Mr. Bennett."

Sergeant Leonfeld still didn't let go of the panicked sailor, and that mastery of the moment reflected itself almost comically in Alexander's face as Picard glanced at the boy. Leonfeld was ankle-deep in shore water, but seemed uncaring of that. He was determined that this man not be sacrificed to an impossible situation.

Helpless, the men and the boy watched in soul-sick frustration as two attacking ships and the spider catcher boats opened fire on the stranded *Justina.* The cannon blasts wakened the settling night with bright orange flashes and bits of flaming material. Red-hot bits rocketed through the darkness and sliced into *Justina*'s heads'ls, ripping them to shreds and leaving the shreds burning.

"Canister!" Nightingale choked. "Dear God, that brig's using hot shrapnel against us! Oh, how impolite!"

Now, *that* Picard knew about. Bits of metal, nails, broken glass, heated up and poured into canisters, then fired out of a cannon, to blast apart in midair, scatter, and rip up anything it struck. It would set fire to sails and wood, and shred flesh on contact. Not nice.

Then again, neither was an armed phaser bank.

The *Justina*'s headsails were on fire now, causing the crew to scramble to put out the flames, thereby keeping them from efficiently returning cannonfire. Picard wished he could see what was happening on the deck as it tilted more and more.

The line—should they cut the line joining the frigate to the land? Or were the capstan men still pushing the bars? Still trying to warp the ship off the shoal?

No one had called from the relay boat. So far there was no order. And if the captain wanted the line cut, he could just as easily sever it from the deck.

The quiet bay at once became a hornet's nest. Cannonfire was met with vicious and sporadic response from the *Justina* as the British ship's crew struggled to run out her guns quickly. Rifle fire, though, cracked every few seconds from *Justina*'s deck. The grenadiers.

Beside Picard, Alexander Leonfeld's whole body quaked with the same helplessness Bennett had expressed. Shuddering, the grenadier sergeant suddenly raised his own rifle and took a quickly considered shot at one of the spider catchers. *Snap-flash-CRACK.*

And an eddy of acrid gunsmoke. Now his flintlock was empty. He rushed to reload it, while Alexander the swab gazed in mute adoration from a few steps away.

"Hold your fire, Mr. Leonfeld," Picard said quietly.

The sergeant looked up sharply and demanded, "Why should I?"

"Because you could hit our own men in the other rowboat. Look—they're trying to get back to the ship. And you'll also draw attention to us. That'll serve no good."

Leonfeld quaked with hopelessness, continued to load his flintlock—which took quite a few steps—but did not fire again.

Alexander said, "Captain . . ."

Picard looked, and noticed the boy speaking to him but still staring not at the ship, not at the water or the battle, but at Sergeant Leonfeld. Picard instantly understood. Alexander wanted him to let this strapping young man, whom now the boy "possessed" as a relative, take action. Any action; but that would not be appropriate. Picard could only guess about his own participation in this scenario, but surmised what the officer whose place he was taking might have done. If the boy's hero worship fit poorly into that scheme, so be it.

The screams of their shipmates and their enemies alike splintered the night. *Justina*'s crew kept up a valiant fight, but the ship was lost. Surrounded. Either she would burn, or her captain would strike his flag, put out the fire, and surrender.

"Why are those boats so determined?" Alexander asked. "Why are they attacking us again and again!"

"They're defending the boatyard," Midshipman Nightingale told the boy. "They want to be sure the British assault fails. They must've known we were coming somehow."

"How would they know?"

"Spies, likely. Traitors."

Alexander shook his head, confused. "Why do the British want to attack a boatyard?"

Edward Nightingale peered with his youthful eyes through the trees at the battling ships, wincing each time a puff of cannon smoke burst into the moonlit haze, then pausing until seconds later, the accompanying *poom* would reach them. His soft English accent added a certain lilt to his sentences. "Delaware Station Boatyard specializes in converting working ships to fighting ships in mere weeks. American vessels are built low and narrow, without much room for provisions. After all, they rarely have to cross the ocean. They're built—"

Suddenly hell's gates opened before them as *Justina*'s port broadside cannons lit off all at once, instantly shattering one of the spider catcher boats, but completely missing the single-masted ship that quickly dodged around her stern and fired a raking shot.

Nightingale winced and swallowed hard, then spoke with a terrible struggle. "American ships are built primarily . . . primarily for coastal trade or fishing. As such, they're considerably faster and more maneuverable than . . . ours."

Alexander prodded, "What does it take to make one into a fighting ship? What's the difference?"

Picard almost spoke up to say the differences were essentially the same as in their time, but Nightingale was still clinging to the conversation, even as his hands trembled on the branches he clutched. "The bulwarks must be pierced with gun ports, certainly, and the decks reinforced for the weight of cannon. Shot lockers and an antifire magazine must be built, and the crew quarters enlarged, because a fighting crew is so many more men than a cargo crew. Such alterations convert a beast of burden into a fighting rig . . ."

The midshipman's voice trickled off as he paused, deeply disturbed by what he saw out on the water.

"Interrupt holoprogram, code Riker Zero One."

Around Picard and Alexander, the old-style holoprogram slowed to a crawl, but this time, due to its partial incompatibility with the modern holosystem, didn't entirely freeze. A cannon puff from out on the water groaned toward the *Justina,* its flash of fire and violence slowed to a long bright yellow slash, and there it seemed to stay.

To their right, the door to the holodeck appeared, opened, and William Riker strode through.

"Sorry to interrupt, Captain."

"Mr. Riker," Picard sighed heavily, shaking himself back to his other world. "Are you dead yet?"

"Yes, sir, I'm dead. Everything went as you planned. The patroller trick was a good one, sir."

"Thank you. Alexander, why don't you go get lunch while I speak to Mr. Riker."

Alexander glanced furtively out at the ship and the battle, clicking along very, very slowly,then shrugged and nodded. He started to leave, but hesitated one last moment to gaze fondly at the paused form of Alexander Leonfeld, the man whose name he carried. The boy seemed unwilling to leave his new hero in such a state. Only the silent eyes of Picard and Riker eventually drove him off the holodeck and on toward lunch.

After he was gone, Riker looked around at the nearly still men from the past and said, "Heck of a lesson plan, sir."

"Yes, I'm rather enjoying myself, more than I expected to. But you can see this technology isn't completely compatible with ours. It's still moving along. The computer can't completely stop it unless I authorize a complete shutdown. Interesting."

"Yes, it is." Riker peered out over the slowly flickering waters at the stranded frigate. "Lose your ship?"

"Not mine," Picard said peevishly. "Well? What's going on?"

"Oh, sorry. Worf destroyed the drone ship with his usual panache." Riker offered a canny grin. "The freighter had to turn back to Sindikash, so I assume that happened because Worf successfully sabotaged it and kept that shipment from reaching Romulan space. The Rogues didn't make a very good showing for themselves. They're supposed to throw themselves on their swords for Odette Khanty, and they didn't. I guess she wasn't worth dying for."

"So she failed to frame the lieutenant governor."

"Right. And Worf made it look as if they almost got caught, so now she's not very happy with her Rogue force. That can work in our favor."

"Yes. It'll make her desperate," Picard observed. He looked out at the *Justina,* a template for desperation.

Riker nodded. "And now Worf's a hero in Khanty's eyes, because he kept the freighter and the Rogues from being arrested. If she had any doubts about him, she won't anymore."

"Perfect. Very good—*very* good. What was in that shipment, Mr. Riker?"

Riker retired an itch on one ear and said, "We aren't sure, sir. Tainted seed, bogus pharmaceuticals, chemical adulterants—Odette Khanty's done 'em all. Things would've looked bad for the lieutenant governor, to be attached to a cargo like that. Even Worf couldn't find out what was in that ship, but whatever it was, I'll bet we're glad it didn't get through."

Picard nodded and peered out over the barely frozen bay and said, "Poor luck often forces men to fail at their missions. I'm glad to hear Mr. Worf is having better fortunes. Has Mr. Worf been able to maneuver Mr. Grant into an inside position?"

"I don't think so. Worf's last communication came through several relays, but he indicated that he is gaining the trust of Mrs. Khanty. He'll find a way to get Grant inside. Even if the Rogues don't particularly like him, they certainly trust him now. He's slowly wheedling his way to the upper levels of security at the governor's mansion, and he's taking Grant right along with him—"

The door section, hanging independently in the middle of the forest, parted again. Commander Data strode in, his pale golden face shining in the moonlight of Chesapeake Bay. His catlike android eyes flickered a bit as he spotted them in the trees and picked his way through to the bay shore.

"Sir," he said cordially to Riker, then looked at Picard. "Captain."

"Yes, Mr. Data?" Picard acknowledged.

"I have scanned and reviewed all available information about arms shipments, distributions, contraband, or disposals in the sector, and found no caches of weapons numbering between ten and forty. I am sorry, sir."

Picard felt his brow draw, and saw that Riker had the same expression. "Weapons, Mr. Data? I don't recall a need to check records of weapons shipments or disposals—"

"The weapons belonging to the passengers of the transport who were killed, sir," Data said, with his innocent manner of reporting facts as he saw them.

His amber eyes flicked to Riker, then back to Picard. When neither seemed to know what he was talking about, he pointedly added, "The arms, sir."

Riker's eyes got big and his lips pressed flat.

"Oh . . . the *arms* . . ." Picard rubbed a hand over his own mouth to wipe down the gallows grin.

Data nodded. "Yes, sir. You said they were missing."

Will Riker developed a cough, folded his arms around his chest, and nurtured a sudden fascination with Sergeant Leonfeld's scarlet tunic and white breeches.

"Nice uniform," he muttered.

Data's childlike face tilted. "Is there some problem, sir? Did I misunderstand? The murdered passengers were disarmed, correct?"

Picard looked at Riker and found no help from a man whose knuckles were pressed to his tightening lips.

"Eh, yes," Picard began, "they . . . were disarmed. Em . . . Mr. Data, cancel that search for now. I'll give you more specific orders later regarding that . . . Mr. Riker, do you concur?"

"Mmmhmm." Riker's back was to them, his arms still folded, one hip cocked. The moonlight silhouetted his head and shoulders. Picard raised his chin. "Carry on, Mr. Data."

"Very well, sir." The android turned and strode back through the freestanding doorway.

Picard cleared his throat and squeezed his eyes shut for a moment, contemplating the vagaries of linguistic communication.

Still hugging his rib cage, Riker sidled toward him, eyes a little wide and one brow a little up.

"Maybe you'd . . . like some lunch now, sir?" he suggested.

"Lunch?" Picard tossed back. "Lunch, Mr. Riker? While my ship is out there being captured? I'm surprised at you, man. Such ideas. I've a mind to disarm you."

Riker smiled and nodded. "Have a nice stranding, sir."

"See? Right here. The governor was leaning toward independence, but he wanted strong ties to the Federation and eventual readmittance as a full-fledged member planet. Mrs. Khanty wanted no more ties at all. She was careful about it, though. I can only find one time when she slipped and mentioned it while she was talking to a women's club. Let me change this—there."

"Play it."

Worf peered over Grant's shoulder in the privacy of their Rogue quarters, where they had set up their computer access terminal. Grant had spent every off-duty hour, including some he should've spent sleeping, digging into the government computer links, trying to find his way to Odette Khanty's private holdings, that "track" he spoke of.

On the tiny screen, Odette Khanty came to life, speaking to a group of women.

"*—valiant type, aren't we? We're frontier stock. Seniards don't like being told what to do from way over there somewhere. The Federation wants to levy controls on us about how we ship our ores. We* know *how to ship ore!*"

"Frontier stock! She's never been within transporter distance of a real frontier in her whole—"

"Be silent, Grant."

"My husband is a great statesman who only wants the best for Sindikash. No one outside of Sindikash should say what the best is. Our families, our children are more important to us than to anyone else. I mourn the fact that my husband and I never had the chance to have our own children. Perhaps when he recovers from his terrible injuries, and I have great hopes for this, we will be able to begin that spirited enterprise of raising a baby."

"Incredible!" Grant reached forward and used the keyboard to pause the computer playout of Mrs. Khanty addressing the women's club.

Worf leaned back and fixed his eyes on the frozen image of the woman. "Which part?"

"The way she gets away with this chopped fodder! You know how she feels about kids. And I think she likes her husband a whole lot better now that he's unconscious. Now that the governor's in a coma, Mrs. Khanty's maneuvering her little pink self into power on the planet. But she's doing it in this innocent, sweet-me way. Makes me gag."

"This mission is getting under our skin," Worf said with worry. "It makes me burn, pretending to be one of these people. I still feel saddled with the actions of the Rogues, no matter how I try to remember that I am *nothing* like them. I hear the captain's voice in my head, telling me not to take all this so personally, but it *is* personal! It *is."*

Shrugging with an endearing sense of himself, Grant nodded and muttered, "Eh, it's our flaw. That's what makes us such a great team. We take things personally. Now look at her face. See how she keeps her eyebrows just a little bit up? That's a body language thing. And her chin only goes up when she's talking about Sindikash as a whole unit. When she talks about herself, she tucks her chin and gives her head a little tilt, like a shy person does. And she nods real slow in agreement with herself. I'll bet she practices in front of a mirror. Hitler used to do that, y'know. The Seniards like to think they're ferociously independent, but they follow her like sheep if she appeals to them as a group. She uses their independent spirit to steer them to her course. She's a marketing genius. Especially when you consider she's selling an empty pot."

"The pot has a great deal in it," Worf corrected, more loudly than he intended. "All corrupt!"

"I know. There are dozens of incidents where hundreds of people die—mishandling of ore during shipments that cause load-shifting . . . extortion . . . bribery . . . jury tampering . . . cutting corners that shouldn't be cut . . . she's setting this planet up to be the platform for her organization, and the people are swallowing it."

Troubled by the caginess of their adversary, Worf glowered until his eyes hurt. Was there some way to just handle this clever woman with a phaser or *bat'telh* or a club? Challenge her to a warp equation?

"Public perception can be steered," Worf commented, trying to keep distance. "If the election can be postponed, there might be a chance to clean things up."

"Yeah, but wow!" Grant leaned back and stretched his aching arms. He slumped again and waved his hand at the computer. "The trail of bodies and indictments and convictions behind her goes back as far as the eye can see. Her former associates are all dead or in jail! And she gets up and rails about independence and how they need to make their planet pure from dirty outside influence. It's like Al Capone complaining that there's too much crime! How does she keep anybody's loyalty?"

"Fear," Worf told him. "Desperation for some, and for others, greed. Like the Rogues. They hope to have influence all the way back to the Empire. Most powerful enticement for expatriate Klingons."

Grant looked up and smiled. "Like you, huh, toughy?"

"In another life." Worf took the seat next to his partner and concentrated now more on Grant than on the screen.

"Can't help it." Grant scratched at the Rogue uniform as if to communicate its inappropriateness for him. "This is a woman who pulls people's arms out, and I can't find the trail! Can you imagine what it must be like to have your arms pulled out?"

Worf did his best to calm his friend, although he felt little calm himself. "You will find the trail. As you did on Pasha IX." Worf almost smiled. "In your way, you are a warrior. The hand of Kahless will guide you."

Grant smiled briefly, then turned back to his work.

His guts curling in frustration, Worf wished Captain Picard were here to deal with this wily woman. He felt patently not clever enough for such an adversary.

"Play the rest of it," he said, feeling his throat go raw.

Grant grimaced, and started the computer again.

"We must protect the identity of our planet, the integrity of our economy, and the individuality of our people. We do that by circling our wagons against those who would have a say in our way of life. We need independence to stretch our wings—"

Huffing once again, Grant pounded the keyboard until the image stopped again. Worf almost stopped him, but couldn't find it in his soul to disturb the wave of emotion surging in Grant's eyes.

"By the time they realize what's happened, she'll have chains on those wings," Grant said. "What she doesn't tell them about is the den of thieves the planet will attract without any Federation presence. She can turn the place into a clearing house for any lowlife who wants to work outside the law. And she'll get a cut of everything, from non-replicables to slavery. All I can think of is all the little Alexanders running around this planet who'll have a crummy life because I can't find one simple link."

Grant shook his head, overwhelmed by the frozen image of Mrs. Khanty speaking at a time when she didn't think she was being recorded. After several long seconds, Grant's silence betrayed to Worf just how deeply his partner had been moved by what had begun as a simple computer search.

"I've got it all here," Grant mourned. "Just nothing to tie

her to all this illegal stuff. The bees swarm around this dragon lady, and none of them ever stings her. She's just never *quite* close enough to anything bad that happens. She has these things done by the Rogues or by her gardener's wife's jester's grandmother." He slumped further and crushed his hand over his weary face. "Ooooh, I just gotta get something . . . folks are dying."

Worf pushed up from the chair. "You need rest."

"Mmm, can't. Gotta keep picking. And you gotta go, too. You're on duty in the governor's corridor in fifteen minutes. If you don't show up, you could end up on her bad side. And believe me, pal, we don't want to get on this dame's bad side. Don't worry. I'm okay. I'm just . . ."

"Frustrated," Worf filled in. "As am I. This is not my kind of enemy."

"Heck, I know," Grant chuckled. "No live grenades for you to fall on, then try not to grunt when they go off. Nah, she's more in my line of work, anyway, Wuff. After all, they sent you here for a whole other reason than they sent me. You're here to get attention and beat people up and growl and make Ugulan look like a U-gu-rangutan." Pointing at the computer, Grant said. "*This* is me. I just gotta get *inside* somehow, to some source of private records. A terminal inside the shielded area."

"There must be a way," Worf said. "I will contact you. Be ready."

Standing over his old friend, Worf saw a man who often seemed a clownish, uninteresting computer technician with a rather simple assignment. Indeed, Worf often found him quite annoying. Yet he was a man in whose heart beat a code of honor as strong as any Klingon's. Much stronger than the *P'taks* who served with Khanty, and feared her for reasons Worf could not understand.

If Worf had found this mission unsatisfying, it suddenly bored itself deeply into his mind and heart. If he had been shamed by the actions of the Rogues, he now took those shames personally. He wanted a good end to this, not for the people of Sindikash or the integrity of the Federation, but to redeem Klingon honor, to wipe the stain of the

Rogue Klingons actions from the galaxy, to make certain that Alexander, just now learning the meaning of honor, would have no reason to feel ashamed of his Klingon heritage.

He ran over and over again in his mind things he should say to Grant. Mission partners should be able to offer each other sustenance. Old friends, even more.

As inadequacy plagued him, Worf found his thoughts straying to Alexander. Was he nurturing his son, or only raising him? Hadn't he seen the same expression in Alexander's face as he just saw in Grant's? A search for elusive peace of the soul?

"I will get you inside, Grant," he said. "I promise you that."

The corridor provided sanctuary and distraction. The colors were like the streets and buildings of Sindikash. Earthy, moody. The walls were hung with carpet-woven tapestries rich with deep colors—beet, plum, copper, wedding cake white, mustard, otter brown. Mosquelike doorways to other offices and tiled moldings offered a prevailing spirit of the exotic. Elaborately colored stencils mapped the walls. The bushy brown skins of bison served as rugs and chair coverings.

In Worf's time here, he had found the Seniards to be generally enthusiastic and decent, charitable and honest. Unfortunately, a significant percentage of them failed to see that others were not so noble, and that they were being led around by their noses. Soon they would suffocate.

The offices were deserted. The mansion was in nighttime repose. The aides and pages had gone home or retired to their quarters. Mrs. Khanty was down the corridor, in her own private chambers.

Worf was here, guarding the executive suite, where Odette Khanty had chewed the heads off the Rogues, and where the governor lay, as he had for many weeks now, in the silence of his coma, monitored from the clinic upstairs.

The quiet was enraging.

Still, Worf forced himself not to be lulled into complacency. He stood guard until almost midnight before pressing the private signal in his subcutaneous transponder.

Across the courtyard, the other transponder, embedded in Grant's forearm, would be vibrating softly. *Come now.*

Those minutes waiting for Grant to arrive were far worse than Worf expected. Was he losing control of himself? Was he becoming too personally involved in this mission? Was he rushing things in order to hurry back to the ship and take over as Alexander's mentor?

"Hey! I'm here." Grant appeared at the end of the corridor, speaking in a quick whisper. "Can I . . ." He pointed to the suite door.

Worf nodded, keeping his gaze on the corridor beyond Grant as his partner hurried toward him. Quickly he unlocked the door and let Grant inside. "The computer terminal is in the kitchenette. Work quietly. There may be listening devices inside."

"Right," Grant murmured, his eyes wide. He was tense as a cable. "This is our big chance. No more picking up bits by hacking from outside. Everything's got to be on her private—"

"Go, Grant, go." Worf shoved him in and pulled the door shut again.

Now the fire was lit. If anyone came, there would be no getting Grant out in time.

He scanned and scanned the corridor, his head constantly swiveling. Imitation candles in sconces cast a softening glow upon the corridor, offering the eerie sensation of a castle in twilight, and casting shadows that seemed sometimes to move. He wished he could be like Data, divorcing himself from his emotional core and his imagination.

What was that?

Had he heard something? Had the outside door just creaked?

He took a step to his right, toward the lobby.

Before his second step he swung around and froze, listening. Voices? Was someone coming from the stairway? Or the elevator? Mrs. Khanty?

His spine felt as if it were twisting. There seemed to be

nothing to fear from this single, small woman—how was she so effective? How did she control Klingon warriors? What kind of enemy was this?

His hands were cold, his fingers aching. He flexed them fitfully, and thought of those who no longer had fingers. Or lives.

He listened, watched, turned, listened again, but no one came. The corridors were still as rocks. He hoped Grant could make good use of the time on the private terminal. Something, anything, to end this mission.

Worf chided himself for such feelings. This mission could not be rushed. Then he angrily reminded himself that Klingons were not Vulcans, and his feelings were valuable possessions that could drive his resolve. He was a Klingon, raised as a Klingon, but by humans, and he had found his adoptive parents' interpretation of being Klingon to be sketchy and not always serviceable. Sometimes he was too Klingon, sometimes too human, and sometimes, other things.

Troubled, Worf tried to shake off his worries, to tell himself that he was isolated, and this was why he felt so troubled. Things were much clearer on board a starship, his duties delineated, and his role as Alexander's father somewhat easier. Somehow, that job got harder whenever he was separated from Alexander. What kind of man would his son become, living with a foot in two cultures so unlike each other?

The corridor whispered back at him, its lemony sconces passively imitating gaslights, though without the sense of warmth. Worf found himself chilled, but from within. He was trying not to focus on problems insurmountable from the hallway, when the silence was abruptly ruptured by the thunderous howl of an alarm. The red emergency lights were flashing!

Bolting away from the doorway, he stared for that first uncontrolled instant at a looping red light above the door to the governor's chamber. The alarm was deafening, furious, like the exaggerated barking of a terrorized seal.

Before Worf could so much as flex a leg, two distant doors flew open and the entrance to a stairway thundered with pounding feet; suddenly, the corridor was filled with medical personnel. And four Rogues! Ugulan, Mortash, Goric, Tyro—

The alarm was from the governor's life-support system.

As the doctors and police plunged into the private doorway, Worf plunged for the office entrance and yanked the door open.

The inner rooms were chaotic. Alarms all over the medical equipment squealed and flashed. Grant backed slowly out of the recovery room as the medical staff flooded in. All Worf saw was the back of Grant, his tensed shoulders, his clenched fists.

The governor's legs twitched convulsively beneath the linen cover, and just as Worf entered the room the legs stiffened and went still. The swarming doctors, nurses, and technicians went into clinical emergency treatment, but as Worf slowly moved to stand beside Grant, a sense of desperation shivered across their actions.

The other Rogues pressed back from the action as the medical personnel swarmed over the bed. One doctor crawled up onto the bed and pounded the governor's chest.

"It was poison!" Grant belted out, gasping. "You've got to find out what she put in there!"

"What who put in where?" the doctor on the bed demanded.

"Mrs. Khanty!" Grant pointed desperately at a tube leading into the governor's left arm. "She came in through that door over there and she put something into that tube! Then everything went crazy! She poisoned him! You've got to find out what she gave him!"

Stunned, the doctor plucked at the tube. More medics rushed to the bedside with intubation devices and syringes. As Grant stared at the doctors, Worf at Grant, and the Rogues at both of them, the doctors and technicians worked to decipher what had happened. They took a quick blood sample and slipped it into a portable analyzer. Sure enough, the doctor confirmed Grant: "He's right. Neurotoxin. Get a neutralizer in here!"

"It's too late," another doctor said cryptically. He stood back, and all the others paused ever so slightly as, with a final twitch of one important knee, Governor Khanty slipped beyond reach.

Then they tried to keep working, but there was no more hope on their faces.

One of the medical technicians backed away from the bed with the same horrified expression as Grant's. A nurse pushed him farther back, and checked a machine. Then she paused, sighed, and her shoulders went slack as the inevitable set in. She turned, and watched.

"Grant," Worf pressed. He took Grant's arm. "What happened?"

Breathing only in the most uneven huffs, Grant stared into the chamber at the event he had been unable to stop.

"She did it," he choked, shivering. "Mrs. Khanty did it. She came in here. She didn't see me . . . she didn't know I was here."

Ugulan, Goric, and three medics turned sharply and looked at Grant and Worf.

"The governor was alive," Grant said. "He was stable. She came in . . . and now he's dead. And I let her be in there with him."

He looked at Worf, and suddenly it was as if the two were alone on an island.

"She did something to make him die," Grant struggled. "And it's my fault."

All despotism is bad, but the worst is that which works with the machinery of freedom.

Junius

Chapter Eleven

"LIAR!" UGULAN SHOVED A FINGER at Grant's chest. "You're covering the fact that you murdered the governor!"

"Keep your dishonorable mouth shut, Ugulan!" Worf had managed to hold himself in check until he heard that. He crashed forward past Grant and landed the heel of his hand on Ugulan's chin, driving the Rogue back a step. "I will brand your face with your own words!"

The Rogues couldn't have stopped him, but when two of the medics got between him and Ugulan, Worf stopped his forward surge. What good would it do to peel Ugulan's skin off?

"If I poisoned him," Grant shouted at Ugulan, "why would I tell them what was wrong so they'd have a chance to save him?"

"Quiet, human!" Ugulan turned sharply to Goric and said, "Contact Paul Stefan."

"Begin an investigation," the doctor said, looking at his own staff. "Time of death is 12:41 a.m. Coastal Standard Time. Get a statement from Mrs. Khanty about her whereabouts in the last fifteen minutes." He turned again to Grant.

"I don't want you to speak to anyone until the investigation can be officially started. Is that clear?"

Grant tried to say something, then only nodded.

"You, too," the doctor told Worf. "You were on duty here, too, weren't you?"

"Yes!" Worf blurted. He stepped back to Grant's side, hoping everyone here would take that as a vote of support. What a smell this situation put off!

"Don't say anything more, any of you." The doctor turned to Ugulan and said, "Seal off these rooms. Put these two men in isolation until we figure out what happened here."

"Yes, Doctor," Ugulan said, and his gray eyes gleamed with the idea of setting Worf away from the other Rogues.

Worf bristled instantly. What would happen if Ugulan managed to isolate him and Grant?

"No!" he challenged quickly. "I will confine both of us to our quarters. Until there are charges made, if any, you have no precedent for jailing us!"

Another Rogue, a comparatively short-statured Klingon whose name was Tyro, rose unexpectedly to Worf's defense. "Confine them to quarters, Ugulan. There are no charges yet."

"Do not defend me, coward!" Worf shouted, raising a fist to Tyro. He knew in a cold flash that Tyro's help came not from his status as a fellow Klingon, a fellow Rogue, or any other kind of fellow. Tyro only wanted to avoid setting a more threatening precedent—that the Rogues could imprison each other at all without charges.

Ugulan drew his dagger—because phasers weren't allowed in the mansion—and swung on Tyro. "I will decide!" Instantly, he swung back to Worf and gestured toward the hall door. "Out!"

The hunger of that dagger pricked at Worf's angry mind as he led the way out of the executive suite, with Grant right behind him. The twists of this mission were maddening! If only he could just roar out all the truths!

After them, the Rogues filed out, too, leaving behind a corpse and its doctors. Through the doorway and down the corridor which barely accommodated their wide shoulders, the ghastly queue walked. Two Klingons—even if there *were* two real Klingons here—could not easily walk abreast in this corridor, and Worf felt as if his clothing were crawling around on his skin. Why did this corridor need to be so cursed long? Who had built this stupid, foolish, ugly building!

The tiled lobby approached slowly, as if detached, and in his mind Worf saw the stone veranda outside, the long, curving flagstone stairways leading to the tiled courtyard and the expanse of ground they would have to cover in order to survive.

Grant let out a startled grunt behind him.

Like a trigger snapping, Worf swung around, yanked Grant past him, then raised a foot and slammed it into Ugulan's chest.

"Back away!" he snarled, jamming his fist into Ugulan's throat. Ugulan's arms flared, and sure enough, that dagger had been forward, toward Grant's spine. Another few seconds—

No one was carrying a phaser today—a sour bit of luck having something to do with regulations during certain hours. It didn't matter—it gave Worf an advantage. He held Grant protectively away, positioning himself between his partner and the other Rogues, most of whom were still corralled in the hallway.

"Stay away from him!" he snarled.

"Protecting a human?" Ugulan accused. "And a liar?"

Worf gritted his teeth. "He is not lying."

"Did you see what he saw?" Goric blistered from behind Ugulan, and pushed his way forward.

"I will not speak to any of you sniveling weaklings!" Worf spat. "I will make my statements to the City Police."

Ugulan surged forward, unintimidated by Worf's dagger. Clearly, the Rogues believed Grant about what Mrs. Khanty had done, and they meant to silence him or anyone else who could endanger the ruthless woman they had come to fear, their last line to power and influence.

Worf shoved Grant back and deflected Ugulan's blade

with his own, making a ghastly *scratch* that echoed under the domed ceiling fresco and made the crystal chandelier tinkle with sympathetic vibration. It felt good, finally, to kick and shove!

"Run, Grant!" he shouted as the Rogues crowded toward him. Battle honor went to the wind—he knew they would gladly gang up on him, but Ugulan was blocking their way.

"I don't want to leave you!" Grant protested as he scrambled for maneuvering room.

Worf feinted backward toward the main door and swung around long enough to blast it open with his boot. Then he twisted back in time to rake his blade across Ugulan's chest, driving the head Rogue back a step.

"Out!" he shouted to Grant. "Run! Get to the police!"

"Oh, damn—" Grant looked around frantically, glanced upward and saw something, then clasped a heavy brass vase from a cloisonné table.

Using both hands and every excuse for a muscle he owned, he heaved the vase into the air toward the ceiling. It sailed in an arc, its own weight soon compromising the flight, and tumbled end-first as if Grant had cast a bowling pin. At the apex of its flight it slashed through the giant crystal chandelier. The thousand bangles of cut glass barely affected the vase, but the glass was blasted to bits. With a harplike chime, the chandelier dissolved. Needles of glass rained down upon the startled Rogues, who never even had time to raise their arms to cover their faces. Glass scalpels rocketed downward, slicing their cheeks, scalps, and eyes, embedding in their hands, popping through the fabric of their Rogue uniforms to impale their arms and shoulders.

Worf made a maniacal leap toward Grant and the open main door. In midair he felt a dozen glass shards drive into his left hip and leg, but his head was clear.

And Grant was clear!

The two of them skidded to the brick deck of the veranda and crashed into an iron table and chair set. The chairs clanged on the veranda's circular brick rail and tumbled over, but the table stayed up and Grant landed under it.

Worf's pelvis and leg were gripped by pain, and he felt

blood drain down his leggings. He shoved himself to his good foot and hauled Grant out from under the table.

"See? You are a true warrior," he complimented as he hauled Grant down the curved stairs toward the courtyard. A blotchy trail of amethyst-colored blood smeared the steps behind him.

He glanced back at the veranda. Goric staggered out, clawing at his right eye. Blood covered his face and he was completely disoriented, gasping with pain and fear. After him came Gern, then Tyro, both picking at blades of glass embedded in their heads and arms. Ugulan staggered out, staring viciously, with the central tine of the chandelier protruding from his shoulder. He balled his fists around a dagger in one hand and a large spear of glass in the other, and roared with fury.

"Uh-oh," Grant gulped. "Think we made him mad?"

"I hope we made him insane! Come!" Worf urged and pulled Grant into the tiled expanse of the courtyard.

Each step sent blistering pain up and down his left side as the shards of glass continued to drill into skin and muscle. Grant dodged under Worf's arm and gave him some support, but on the veranda Ugulan, Mortash, and the other Rogues were overcoming their own injuries, or at least becoming insensitive in the blur of their fury and insult. Their future was shuffling away across the courtyard, and they meant to throw a rope on it.

If that meant dying on the tile, so be it!

"They're coming," Grant gasped. "They're halfway down the stairs . . . they're making it onto the tiles . . . oh, man, we're gonna be butchered—"

"You go," Worf choked. "Run for the police."

Struggling with Worf's considerable weight, Grant glanced behind them again. "No chance, bub. We go, we go together."

"You cannot fight Klingons!" Worf spat out his contempt. "Not even *those* Klingons!"

"Wish I had a flare gun or something—"

"Grant, they will not kill me. Klingons do not attack fallen Klingons."

Now who was lying?

But Grant, unfortunately, was not fooled. "Oh, not *those* Klingons! What's with you? Competing with Mrs. Khanty for Flimflam of the Month? They'll kill you and eat you!"

"Too gristly," Worf grunted as he slipped to one knee.

Hauling Worf to his feet, Grant heaved. "Don't try to snow me anymore, will ya? We just gotta make the outer gatehouse." He cast another nervous glance at the staggering Rogues, who were closing the distance between them, slowly becoming numb to their own pain, blinded by the trouble they were in if Worf and Grant made it out.

Worf leaned heavily on Grant and forced his throbbing leg to move. There were more lives at stake than their own—all those doctors and medics and nurses who had heard Grant's claim about Mrs. Khanty. Those people were all dead if Worf and Grant were brought down here. The bodies would disappear, the courtyard would be scrubbed of the blood, and Odette Khanty would implicate the "missing" conspirators in the murder.

Aggravated that he and Grant might just have handed Mrs. Khanty her alibi, Worf drove furiously for the ornate stone gatehouse. His chest pounded. His pulse roared in his ears. Through the iron gates he saw people milling about in the public square. If they could reach the square—

His leg folded under him again. The dozen glass shards were impaling more and more muscle with every flex, working their way deeper through his clothing. The pain was crippling, searing his body as he struggled forward, scraping across the tiles, clinging to Grant, who didn't have the power to carry a man the size of Worf.

They scraped across the tiles, driven by the clack of Ugulan's boots and those of the other Rogues who were still able to see and move. The main gate began to swirl before Worf's eyes. He was losing blood. Shock was setting in, blurring his vision. Desperation began to take over, just as rage was driving the Rogues in spite of their injuries. He had to reach the gate, he had to get Grant to the City Police. They could not be caught here!

Suddenly, Grant choked and grimaced hard, arching his spine as he staggered. He dropped Worf and dropped to one knee. As he fell, Worf shivered at the sight of Ugulan's dagger embedded in the fleshy part of Grant's back, just under the shoulder blade.

"Aw!" Gasping in pain, Grant coiled his convulsing arm against his body and braced himself on the tiled floor with his other hand. His eyes crimped tight. "Crap! Aw, crap, we're all done now! Iced by gorillas!"

"Get up!" Worf snapped. "Up! Use your legs!"

He shoved himself upright, damning agony down his leg and halfway up his side, and scooped Grant up with his good arm.

"Move! Move!"

He could hear Ugulan's footsteps and those of the other Rogues, getting closer and closer, clapping on the tiles unevenly. The Rogues were all hurt and staggering, but the distance between them was shrinking. Worf harbored no doubts that if that space closed, Ugulan and the others would find the strength for one more slaughter.

"Oh, God . . ." Grant sank against him.

"Move!" Worf demanded again.

"She won . . ."

"She did not win!"

"We're beat, Worf, she beat us—"

"Not yet! Move!"

"You never listen to me."

"Walk!"

Yard by yard they slogged toward the gate, but Ugulan's very breath was chasing them now. Mere inches separated them from the bloody hands of the head Rogue and the bite of Mortash's extended dagger.

Worf willed the blurring iron gates open before them, and the gates began to shudder with movement. The might of his determination caused the gates to part and swing inward toward them—magic! The gates were opening!

As effort drained him and once again dragged Grant to one knee at his side, Worf grieved at the steps between them and the opening gates. Just steps—

"Hold it! Stop!"

He raised his sagging head at the shout that came from the gate.

"City Police!"

A dozen officers of the law surged into the courtyard, weapons drawn on the stunned Rogues and on Worf and Grant, though it was plain who was chasing and who was being chased.

"Hold it, all of you! City Police!"

A stocky police officer, with thick hair that was silvering prematurely, got between Worf and Ugulan. The Rogues had no choice but to back off, faced down by the police weapons that would have cut their daggers out of their hands. The policemen surrounded the Rogues and divested them of their blades.

The lead officer, the one who had barked the desist order, approached Worf and Grant.

"I'm Lieutenant Stoner. You're the two who witnessed the governor's death?"

"Yes!" Grant gasped, spittle flying from the corner of his mouth.

Trying not to lean on Grant, Worf squinted through the blur. "How do you know?"

"The doctors notified us."

Grant pointed back at the Rogues. "They're gonna kill us to cover it up!"

Ugulan shot out an accusing finger. "They're spies, infiltrating the governor's mansion! You cannot keep us from our rightful revenge! We are Klingons!"

Worf took a faltering step toward him. "How would *you* know what it is to be Klingon!" he shouted in Klingon. He could no longer hold back. "What is it," he shouted at Ugulan, "that makes you cower like a beaten slave before that woman? That you obey her orders no matter how much shame you bring to yourself, to the Empire, to all Klingons?"

Ugulan stepped close, so only Worf could hear him. "She has our oath," he said quietly, sadness replacing his fury. "She has our Oath of Sto-vo-kor. It was the only way she would grant us sanctuary on this world."

Worf had been prepared for any answer except that. Sto-vo-kor was the Klingon Valhalla, the place all warriors went when they died. The Oath of Sto–vo–kor was no mere oath of allegiance. It gave a commander the power to decide a warrior's fate after death. These Rogue Klingons feared for their very souls, which, at a word from Khanty, would have been sent to oblivion.

Worf's anger flowed out of him. He faced Ugulan proudly. "I pity you," Worf said.

As he spoke, three policemen held him back. And it took all three of them.

"Quiet, quiet," Stoner said. "Everybody just hold your lunch," he said evenly. "We'll sort it all out. You're all under arrest until we do. Your 'rightful revenge' will have to wait."

"You can't hold us!" Grant protested. "They'll get to us if you do!"

Stoner looked at him, then looked at Ugulan. "Mmm, yeah," he uttered.

Incredible—he understood! A flicker of hope shot up through Worf's pain as he watched the police lieutenant's amicable face. The shock that he wasn't alone anymore struck him with the power of a phaser stun.

"They cannot circumvent the law!" Ugulan protested. "They have to be held!"

"I said, quiet, and I asked nicely, didn't I?" Stoner told him. "You Rogues think you run the whole planet. Nobody's going to get to anybody. We'll put all of you in custody until we know what's going on. Okay, boys, take the Rogues away. Medium security till we figure out who to charge."

"This is criminal!" Mortash argued.

"We'll see," Stoner said, unimpressed. "Bye. Those Rogues, they're just so noble, you know?"

"Oh, man . . ." Grant sagged against the police officer who was holding him up.

Stoner watched the Rogues until they disappeared, flanked by other officers, through the gate and down the street toward the City Police Central Station.

"Okay, gentlemen," Stoner said with a sigh. "What's your story?"

"He's a Starfleet officer," Grant said. "I'm a Federation agent, and we're investigating certain shipments of contraband through open spacelanes."

"Hmm . . . well, I'm sorry your welcome to Sindikash couldn't be any better, but I don't have any more reason to believe you than to believe them. Do I? Are you carrying any I.D.?"

"Obviously not," Worf grumbled.

"But . . ." Stoner pushed back his maroon police hat. "But the doctors did contact me and tell me you were in trouble, so somebody believes you, so . . . I'll confine you to quarters under guard until I can sort out your identity. Can you give me a contact code or something I can use to verify who you are?"

"Yes," Worf snarled. "You can contact my ship."

"What's your ship?"

"The *Enterprise.*"

"Wow . . ." Stoner's blue eyes widened. "Wait'll I tell my kids. My son built models of the first two *Enterprises* for a school project, with individual hull plates."

"I shall arrange a tour of the real thing," Worf offered, "assuming we survive."

"Yeah," Stoner uttered sympathetically. He kept his voice down from the curious crowd that had gathered near the gates. "I know what you mean. Let's get you guys some treatment. Then I have to confine you till I clear this up. We'll see what happens."

"Sit down, Grant," Worf instructed. "You'll have no feet left if you continue to pace. It hardly serves you to be walking around on stumps."

"I can't sit," Grant shuddered, his whole body shaking as he twisted like a wind sock. His shoulder was bandaged and he rubbed his arm fitfully. "She killed him. She killed her own husband! I told you she didn't like him! That's what always happens to people who get in her way. It was all because that freighter didn't go the way she wanted it to. She couldn't frame the lieutenant governor, and she needed public opinion to go her way. This was the one thing she *had* to do herself. She's trying to get that public sympathy back."

"I know."

Grant paused. "Then you believe me?"

Shifting his injured leg, Worf offered a nod and wished the two of them had taken a day off to reminisce before embarking on this mission.

"Yes, of course I believe you. However, I did not see her enter the governor's suite."

He settled back into the big overstuffed buffalo-hide chair and tried to get Grant to relax by example.

Oblivious to Worf's effort, Grant hugged his own body tightly and swung about, pacing in front of the flagstone fireplace. "I should've stopped her the second I knew she was in there. I just froze. She didn't see me, and I just couldn't make myself move. I let her kill him."

"Nonsense," Worf told him evenly. His voice was like a deep drum beneath the frantic tight-throated choke of Grant's panic, and he clung to the sound of his own words. "The governor might've died anyway."

"But he didn't just die. He was stable! The blood is on her hands this time. Her own, personal hands. Grant, please try to avoid obsessing."

"I can't believe this fell into our laps!" Grant blustered on. "We're turning ourselves inside out to get proof of her activities, and she does this right in front of me! But if it's just me saying it . . ."

Suddenly his entire expression changed. He swung around, his legs braced.

"Worf! You believe me, right?"

"Yes, of course I do."

"You know she killed the governor to make sure the independence referendum takes place on schedule, right? She must know the Federation's got a stake in postponing it, right?"

Uneasily, Worf nodded. "Yes, both also right."

Grant rushed to Worf's chair and knelt beside it, gripping the thick buffalo fur on the chair's arm with both hands.

"According to Sindikash law, they need two witnesses for

a capital crime! You haven't made your statement yet!" He pounded the buffalo hide and leveled a finger at Worf. "You gotta back me up! You gotta say you were in there, too! You gotta say you saw her in there at the same time I did!"

Worf sat up straight, his legs and arms suddenly tight. Had he heard right?

"You want me to lie under oath?"

"Oh, what lie? You know she did it!"

"Yes . . . I know she did it."

"If there aren't two witnesses, then she can't even be charged or held in custody pending an investigation. She'll be free to do—" Grant stopped, his throat knotting again, and made a gesture with one hand toward the other arm—a ripping gesture.

Shoving to his feet, Worf put a few steps between them, as if to stride away from the whole idea of what Grant was asking of him. A sudden jolt of hope—one stretch of the truth. That was all, to free Grant and bring down this corrupt organization before it became interstellar.

"We can get you off the planet," he attempted. "The captain will make sure—"

"No!" Grant stood up and braced his legs. "Forget it. I'm not leaving. This is our chance to stop this woman from all these things she's been doing. And it's a chance to save a lot of lives she's got in her sights. The whole planet'll go down the sink if we don't hold our ground." He put his hands on his chest and grimaced. "I can't be the one to let that happen. I couldn't live with myself, y'know?"

After a moment Grant held out a beseeching hand as the small fire crackled behind him.

A friend . . . a fellow warrior despite his oddities . . . and as close to a godfather as his son possessed. . . .

Grant's voice was a crackle of strain. "You've got to say you were inside, Worf, in the room. You know what the truth is. All you have to do is *say* that it is!"

His whole body suddenly numb, Worf wanted from the pit of his being to give the answer Grant so desperately needed—and deserved.

Yes, deserved!

Why could he find no voice?

Though his response was bogged down in hesitation, he knew his face told clearly what he was deliberately not saying.

He knew, because of the way Grant was staring at him.

"You're . . ." Grant's jaw slackened in astonishment and his face went painfully white. "You're not gonna back me up, are you? Oh, my God . . . you're not going to back me up!"

Feeling his face crumple, Worf forced himself to speak. "I cannot perjure myself for you. I have my honor to consider."

Grant looked as if his chest were collapsing. "Honor? You've got to be kidding! We've got a whole planet and a fifth of the sector to think about here! You talk about law? There have to be two witnesses—that's the excuse for law on this godforsaken rock! She made sure of that! You think she wasn't setting that up for just this kind of incident? She pushed that law through to protect herself, not to protect the people of the planet! And it's working! And you're gonna let it?"

The last few words stuck in Grant's throat, yet his meaning came across as clearly as subspace beacons.

The sudden silence nearly broke Worf's legs beneath him. Ten thousand answers surged and receded in his mind before he mouthed the only one he could push out.

"I am sorry . . ."

Instantly, Grant gasped. "Sorry? We're partners!"

"Partners in *law,"* Worf said on a raw breath. "Not in dishonor."

How hollow the words sounded. How fleeting, weightless.

Grant shook his head, his eyes narrowing to pain-ridden slits. He shuddered and turned cold as a blade in winter. Sweat broke out on his face, and his whole body seemed to steam. He leaned forward over a rug-covered table and clutched at the rug until it bunched in his hands.

Quaking as if old age had rushed up on him, he shivered and gagged. "She'll turn my skin inside out . . ."

Gripped with empathy, Worf moved to Grant's side,

hoping to provide some physical support. "We can get you off the planet, Grant. Mrs. Khanty—"

"I told you, I'm not leaving." Grant shook his head emphatically. "I'm gonna stick up for what I know."

Fraught with his burden, he turned, pressing his legs up against the table, and gripped Worf's Rogue uniform collar with gnarled fingers.

Worf gritted his teeth, suddenly light-headed and possessing no more substance than a useless bit of paper. He felt as if he were fading away where he stood. Fading to nothing. He was nothing—he could do nothing . . .

"You've got to stick up for it, too," Grant rasped. "It's the truth, and you know it. You can make the truth happen if you just say what you know! You've gotta do it!"

His fingers twisted tighter, his brows knitted, and Grant took one breath and held it until finally it came bursting out.

"For God's sake . . . *lie!*"

"We'll get you off the planet. And all this will be sorted out according to the law."

The ghastly decision had been made, and now lay in stone at the bottom of Worf's stomach. A half hour had crept by.

Grant no longer argued about getting off Sindikash and into the protective shell of the *Enterprise,* where Odette Khanty's tentacles could not reach.

Instead, Grant sat on a kilim ottoman, staring at the carpet, not looking up.

"Lie," he croaked.

Worf struggled to his feet and forced his swollen leg and hip to move. He dared not let his body stiffen up, so he paced behind Grant, as Grant had before him. "Another team can come here from Starfleet and continue the work. Mrs. Khanty is beginning to make errors."

"We've got her *now,*" Grant pleaded. "Lie. Do it."

"Killing her husband herself was a major step toward distrust of everyone around her. She can enshroud herself only so long, taking things into her own hands this way."

"I'd do it for you."

Worf looked at the back of Grant's head, haloed by imitation candlelight from a stained glass sconce. Grant did not turn to meet his eyes.

The rejection sizzled on his skin.

Could he blame Grant, who could see no other course? A chance was a chance. Their last.

A knock at the heavy oak door broke his thoughts, but not his concerns. He limped across the carpet, nearly tripping on the fringe, and opened the door only two inches to see who was there.

"Hi, sir, it's Ted Stoner."

"Lieutenant," Worf said with notable relief. "Come in."

The police officer stepped inside with another officer, then nodded to three other police guards to stay out in the entryway, then removed his hat and unbuttoned his thick maroon jacket.

"This is Officer Zared," Stoner said.

Worf nodded. "Officer."

"Sir," the policeman responded, and clasped his hands as he stood by the door as formally as a Starfleet yeoman.

"Well," Stoner began, "we checked out your story and everything clicked. You're a Starfleet officer from the *Enterprise.* We've got confirmation from a Jean-Luc Picard."

"Captain Picard," Worf corrected, more amused than he would have expected to be.

"Oh . . . sorry."

"Forgiven."

Stoner offered an easy shrug. "Anyway, I can't hold you. You're being remanded to Starfleet custody. They've agreed not to remove you from the sector until the preliminary investigation is wrapped up. But Mr. Grant," he said, turning, "has to stay here. He's a Federation operative, but he's also a civilian, and Sindikash law requires we hold him on the planet for further review of his case."

"No!" Worf protested. "He will be killed!"

"What d'you care?" Grant moaned.

As his chest tightened, Worf swung to face him. "Never say that again!"

With a sigh and a nod, Stoner said, "I don't blame you for

worrying about that. I know how things are here. I'll hold him in protective custody under my own recognizance until there are charges filed. By then, I think I can get Starfleet fully involved, and you guys can protect him yourself."

"You expect me to leave him on this planet?" Worf challenged, stinging with Grant's loss of faith in him.

The lieutenant's round face tilted in understanding. "You don't have a choice. There's been an injunction issued to evict you from the planet, and, unfortunately, I can't let Mr. Grant go yet. I think the judge is afraid that if we let you both go, we'll never see Starfleet again, and some of us really want to see Starfleet again, if you get what I mean. And I've got some . . . well, let's just say I've got some other people to protect. Everything's a trade-off around here, I'm sorry to say."

"We were hoping to change that," Worf commented bitterly, suddenly caught up in the officer's candidness.

"I got that idea," Stoner said, careful not to commit. "Officer Zared is here to escort you to the City Spaceport and see that you're put on a transport out of Sindikash space. I've arranged a security passage, so you'll be safe till you reach your ship, but I can't authorize any weapons. Meantime, I'll take care of Mr. Grant. You can count on that."

As Worf gazed into Ted Stoner's eyes, he saw the problems of the planet suddenly borne by a young law officer whose burden should not have been so overwhelming. He saw an honest man in the middle of a corrupt web, and he empathized deeply. After all, sooner or later, Worf and Grant would leave this place. Ted Stoner and his other honest comrades would still be here.

Perhaps Worf could arrange for Sindikash to be a better place, if he held the course. Yet his sense of loss was growing heavier by the moment, especially as he looked at the crushed shell of a being who had been his partner and friend.

In every fiber of his posture, Grant communicated a sad slippage of trust between them.

Worf looked at Stoner, desperate for some glimmer of hope, but there was no other course. Not now.

Finally, Worf limped around in front of Grant, but no power on the planet could make Grant look up at him and see the friend he had seen just a day ago.

"Grant," Worf began, "Lieutenant Stoner will see to your safety. He will protect you. And I'll be back. Grant? Do you hear me? I *will* be back."

Chapter Twelve

"I NEVER IMAGINED THEY COULD take a Royal Navy frigate . . . never, never . . ."

Midshipman Edward Nightingale stared out onto the open water of Chesapeake Bay. Picard watched him, deeply sympathizing with the shocked young sailor.

Here they were, huddled in landed exile as their ship was attacked from all quarters. The cannonfire on *Justina* had ceased now. The captain was surrendering rather than lose the ship and crew in a futile battle.

"We have to get out of here," Picard said sharply. "They've seen the warp line and they know there was a landing party. They'll come ashore to find us."

Nightingale turned to him. "But the ship—"

"The ship is captured," Picard snapped, making sure to destroy any thoughts of heroic insanity. "Its crew will be prisoners of war. We must see to ourselves, or we'll be the same."

"Yes, sir . . . but where should we go?" Nightingale asked. "Where can Royal Navy men find safe haven in the colonies?"

"I know," Grenadier Leonfeld said. "I have family here. In Delaware Station."

Worry creased his brow. He was embarrassed to have relatives in the colonies.

"Who are they?" Picard asked.

"My cousin and his family, sir. He was born in England and came here a few years ago. He is a Tory, loyal to the Crown. By trade he's a master weaver. I wrote to him and told him I was coming to the colonies."

"What was his response?"

"I received no response before the ship set sail." His voice grew soft as he added, "I hope he is still . . . alive."

"Alive? Why wouldn't he be?" Picard asked, then instantly regretted that. People died of the lowest, commonest germs in these times, of simple wounds and infections, of childhood diseases that no one in Picard's time even knew about anymore.

"There was a fever, sir," Leonfeld said. "He wrote to tell me his mother had died of it. That was the last time I heard from him."

For the first time in a while, Alexander actually spoke up—and, indeed, Picard noticed this was *the* first time the boy had spoken to his ancestor. "Were you very close, Sergeant?" he asked.

Leonfeld sighed, but it was more of a shudder. His eyes tightened again. "We were more brothers than cousins. We lived in the same house for all our childhood summers. When I came of university age, I went to England and lived with him while attending Cambridge. He wanted me to go into business with him. In point of fact, he wanted me to come here with him. But I wanted a military future. Thus I became a grenadier, and he became an American."

Anticipation blended with fear as Leonfeld gazed down the bay beyond the movement of those ships, and unconcealed emotion clutched his eyes. "If Jeremiah is still here, he will shield us for a while."

Picard clarified. "You say he's loyal?"

"Oh, yes," Leonfeld said sharply. "A proud servant of the Crown. Jeremiah knows well his own blood."

"Is his name Leonfeld also?"

The sergeant looked at him, as if somehow this cast more doubt on their situation, then he peered again through the trees.

"Coverman," he said. "Jeremiah Coverman."

A faint breeze floated down from the night sky and embraced the name of the man they needed to find. Just as Picard braced to rise and step forward, the men around him went suddenly glassy-eyed and began to slow down.

"Oh—" Picard glanced at Alexander and stood up. As they turned, looking for the holodeck entrance, it appeared and opened right in front of a magnificent four-foot diameter oak tree.

"Captain?" Riker came through the entry, but didn't see them right away in the darkness.

"Here, Mr. Riker." Picard pushed his way through the bushes.

"Sir," Riker began, and strode toward them over the mossy roots. "Worf just contacted us from an approaching Sindikash trader. He'll be here in about four hours. They released him when you confirmed his identity. And we have another problem.

"Which is?"

"Evidently, Ross Grant witnessed Odette Khanty's presence in her husband's hospital room seconds before the man unexpectedly died of some kind of aneurysm caused by toxin."

"He was poisoned? Is that confirmed?"

"Yes, it's confirmed. His condition was improving, and he did have a large quantity of two toxic substances in his system, and he sure didn't give them to himself. Grant says he saw Mrs. Khanty put something into the IV tube."

"And Mr. Grant's the only witness?"

"Yes, sir. Sindikash planetary law requires—"

"At least two witnesses for capital crime conviction. I know."

"But Worf hasn't made a statement yet," Riker explained. "His cover's blown, by the way. That's the only way he got off the planet. Grant's in protective custody with the City Police as a material witness."

Picard frowned, irritated at this turn of events. "Well, this is very troublesome, Mr. Riker."

"It's worse than that, sir. Worf knows Grant isn't lying. We know the kind of crimes this woman's engineered, and there's no doubt in my mind or Worf's—"

"Or mine, very definitely. I would certainly find it satisfying to discover some way to convict this individual for the things she's done."

A voice out of the trees behind him caused a tug between Picard's two current realities.

"Is my father in trouble, Captain?"

The captain turned. "Oh—Alexander. No, not in the way you mean. He'll be here shortly. It's Mr. Grant who's in trouble."

"Uncle Ross?" Alexander came forward out of the trees. "He's in trouble? He's practically family." The boy looked at Picard, then at Riker. "I really care about him."

Riker put a hand on Alexander's shoulder. "We'll all do our best to make sure that nothing happens to him."

"You won't let anything happen to him, will you?"

"No, son, no."

"My father won't let anything happen to Uncle Ross, will he?" Suddenly the boy picked up on a bit of expression that Riker allowed to slip through, and Alexander swung back to Picard. "You should at least tell me what's happening. I deserve that. I'm a member of the crew, you know!"

Up to that moment, Picard would have happily deceived the boy into the candy-land of partial realities that children certainly deserved, but something about that declaration stopped him. Where Alexander got this perception of membership in the crew he had no idea, but that was perhaps part of the ballast of living on board a ship—there was no dividing of social structure here. There were no sailors and civilians, no adults and children. They all lived together on this dangerous island. Somehow the ship's sense of inclusion had infected the boy, and now he wielded it with an altogether proper embrace. Alexander saw himself as eligible for the truth.

And when had Picard heard anything so utterly pure and enheartening as that?

Picard looked at Riker. "He's right. He deserves to know."

Dubious, Riker shifted from one foot to the other, and his blue eyes carried a spike of doubt. "There's been a murder, Alexander. The governor of the planet has been assassinated, and your father believes the man's wife did it."

"Mrs. Khanty?" the boy filled in instantly.

"How do you know?" Picard asked sharply.

"I checked. When my father and Uncle Ross headed for that planet, I had Mr. Data show me the files. I read all the headlines and letters. A lot of people don't like her, but a lot of other people think she's practically an angel."

Frowning away his disapproval, Picard said, "Mmm . . . angels are always fodder for street brawls."

"She's no angel," Riker said.

"I know," the boy answered. "Uncle Ross is too nice to go up against somebody like her. He's not a Klingon, like me or my father."

Mouths of babes again, Picard thought with a sigh. True enough. He gazed into the boy's clear and decisive eyes, and could not bring himself to mollify that courage and concern.

"He's a witness to Mrs. Khanty's presence in the room just moments before the governor suddenly died, and apparently she assisted the dying somewhat."

Riker nodded. "Mr. Grant needs corroboration for what he saw, according to Sindikash law, and even though Worf absolutely believes what happened, he can't truthfully *say* he witnessed it."

"Has Worf made his official deposition yet?" Picard asked.

"No, sir, not yet. Worf thinks Grant could be in danger if Mrs. Khanty isn't charged. She'll be able to consolidate her power almost instantly if public opinion goes her way."

"What?" Alexander pulled on Picard's arm. "You mean, if my father doesn't back Uncle Ross up, he could get hurt?"

Both men looked down at the boy, weighing need to know against the right to know.

"You've got to tell me!" Alexander insisted. "I've heard things!"

Picard paused, but realized he'd already crossed that bridge and, like the fleeting of youth, there was no turning back.

"Your father didn't see the woman hurt her husband, Alexander. He can't say he did."

Alexander backed away a step and squared off in a position where he could look at both officers. "Why can't he?"

The simplicity of youth was still effecting a cost despite all the rites of passage. Picard gazed into the boy's determined eyes, but there was little assurance to be given.

"If he knows the truth happened," Alexander persisted, "why can't he *say* it happened?"

Picard drew his brows tight. "It's a matter of honor, Alexander. For your father, it is."

The boy looked at him, struggling. "But honor and truth are supposed to be the same, aren't they? They go together, don't they?"

"Number One, I've faced some of the most challenging adversaries in the galaxy. I've come up against the Borg, the Q, the Cardassians, Romulans, Orions, the Klingons, and even my own holodeck gone hog-wild, yet never have I been so paralyzed as I was five minutes ago, staring down at a boy with one damnably simple question."

As the two men strode down the ship's corridor toward the captain's office, Commander Riker replied, "Sometimes facing the simple logic of a kid's mind can be pretty daunting, sir."

"It's not the child. It's the question."

A work crew doing repairs on the bridge jumped out Picard's way as he and Riker headed for the Ready Room. Picard chuckled inwardly at himself, thinking in terms of the *Justina* and not crowding the captain on the command deck. He stared briefly at the working ensigns, then his own knees, seeing beyond the Starfleet uniform to the 1777 Royal Navy breeches and jacket that now felt somehow as natural. He wished he were still wearing them. He felt as if he'd abandoned something, and ached to go back.

"Why didn't I have an answer for Alexander?" he mourned. "Poor boy, he certainly deserved one."

"Yes," Riker said, settling down in the chair at one end of the couch. He smiled and his eyes sparkled devilishly. "After all, he's a member of the crew."

"Well, yes, he is," Picard said, brushing away Riker's attempt at a joke. "Everyone subject to the fate of any vessel over any stretch of time is a member of its crew. Alexander has a sense of self. He doesn't just feel he's part of the crew because of his father. He thinks that because of himself and his loyalties. He's quite a young man."

Riker smiled again. "Learning more than history, are we, sir?"

"On two fronts, I'm afraid," the captain admitted as he watched two ensigns attempt to dislodge a heavy climate-control unit from the ceiling panels. "When I first began the program I never imagined either would take on this much substance. And this Odette Khanty is a poisonous creature." Picard leaned back thoughtfully. "If Worf doesn't back Grant up, Khanty can put her organization in place and the planet'll never be rid of her. She'll be the single most powerful person in the quadrant."

"And you'll never hear the end of it from Mr. Toledano."

"Oh, I don't care about—Good God!"

Picard nearly jumped out of his skin when a reddish-gold life-form vaulted from behind the couch and landed on his shoulder. Then the alien announced, "MMrrrrrrewwwwww!" in his ear and put a paw on his nose.

"What—what is Mr. Data's *cat* doing in my ready room!"

Riker reached over and scratched the cat's neck. The amenable tabby arched in gratifying response and leaned into Picard's ear. "Don't you like cats, sir?"

"I can't imagine what an android needs with a cat, Mr. Riker!" He shouldered the liquid creature down onto his elbow, and somehow the cat melted onto his lap from there.

"What does anybody 'need' with cats, sir?" Riker tortured.

"Well, I *need* this one out of my Ready Room. Please return it to Mister Data." Handing the cat away to Riker, Picard grumbled, "I'd rather face Odette Khanty and all her Rogues."

"Mmm." Riker stroked the cat's ball-shaped head. "Worf says he's never seen a person whose private personality is so diametrically opposed to the public one. Ordinarily, there's *some* flicker of resemblance. She's like an old Earth union boss—self-insulating."

"Worf's never been a hypocrite," Picard told him evenly. "That's why he's sometimes been confused in his personal searches. It's why the Day of Honor bothers him. He doesn't always define honor the way other Klingons do. He tries very hard to fit into the Klingon mold, but every time he's come to a fork in the road, he's chosen the Federation path."

"I don't like this kind of enemy," Picard went on, his mind still on Odette Khanty. "I imagine it's even worse for Worf. He's used to someone he can challenge openly, honestly. With a bat'leth."

Riker nodded as he led the way into the nearest turbolift. "This is a lot more Mr. Toledano's kind of thing, all this espionage, subterfuge, spying, assassinations, all this local business—"

"It's just politics, Mr. Riker. So there's some politics going on. So what? Bringing down a criminal of this sort, with tentacles out to the Romulans and Cardassians . . . it's a good thing to do. What difference does it make how we're doing it? Certainly, being convinced to stay in the Federation isn't the worst thing that can happen to those people."

"No, sir," Riker agreed, "but it's tricky, this independence business. Do we or don't we? Should they or shouldn't they? Federation membership has its obligations, one being a long secession process."

"But Sindikash isn't a member that came in from outside," Picard pointed out. "There's a whole different set of procedures for colonial independence. Much harder ones."

"I don't know much about that," Riker admitted. "A planet we invested in and built decides, 'Well, we don't like this or that, so we're checking out.' Doesn't make sense."

"Like the Colonial United States," Picard said. "That didn't seem to make sense either, yet its successful independence helped sculpt the model for the galaxy as we now know it, and build the thriving civilization we now enjoy. I'm finding it difficult not to afford Sindikash the same chance."

As the lift opened and deposited them on Deck 10, Riker tilted his head. "That doesn't sound like you, sir."

"Doesn't it? What Sindikash wants to do is just what the Colonies did. Seize someone else's investment."

"But, sir, the Colonies weren't being represented. Britain was a caste system. What level you were born to was everything. And what about the people on Sindikash who want to remain in the Federation? They're our citizens, and their rights can't be abrogated simply by a planet's threat to secede."

"They can always leave the planet. That's what Mrs. Khanty would say. That's what the patriots of the Colonies said. Now, what's the problem with it?"

Riker smiled. "Quizzing me, sir?"

"Why not?"

"Well, given Mrs. Khanty's type of action, I'd say she would pass a one-hundred-percent departure tax."

The doors to Ten Forward opened. Picard scanned the empty room.

"And where is Mr. Toledano, anyway?" he asked, irritated.

"He's taking a shuttle ride, sir," Riker said.

"I beg your pardon?"

"He wanted to see the ship from the outside. So as soon as the Ferengi freighter passed along Worf's message, I sent Mr. Toledano on a nice, *long* tour."

"Oh, he's all right," Picard acceded, leading the way back

to the holodeck. "He's quite correct when it comes to the planet's effects on the sector if Mrs. Khanty entrenches herself." Riker frowned. "I can't help thinking that the people on that planet deserve the right to make a free and *uninfluenced* choice."

"They can't have one," Picard pointed out sternly. "They either get influenced by Mrs. Khanty or by us. Unless she leaves them alone, *we* don't dare."

The captain booted up Alexander's program, which materialized in its semifrozen state, with Grenadier Leonfeld, Midshipman Nightingale, and the *Justina*'s two deckhands moving at the pace of sick snails. Since he'd left, they hadn't moved an entire step, and yet there seemed to somehow be life in them, as though once called into being, like spirits in a seance, they couldn't be exorcised until their own mission was complete.

He gazed at them, troubled. "Odette Khanty is manipulating the people of Sindikash. The Federation has a right to countermanipulate."

"Aren't we using subterfuge to maneuver an outcome that should be a free choice?" Riker gestured toward the holodeck door. "So the British used cannons to do the same—what's the difference? I wonder . . . are we playing the part of the British?"

Picard tucked his chin. "Will, we're going after a criminal organization. That's the difference. A very big one." He looked at Grenadier Leonfeld, and his mind divided between worlds. "Find Alexander and have him come back here. I'd like to get on with this. We've got several hours before Worf arrives. I'd like to distract the boy."

"Right away, sir," Riker responded, and there was a clarity of purpose in his tone now, too. One final time he gazed at the pretty picture of the ship on Chesapeake Bay. "Was it a decisive battle, sir?"

"I think not," Picard said. "Sadly, it seems to be one of the hundreds of unnoticed skirmishes that took many men's lives and eventually contributed to a larger end. Odd, isn't it, how many footnotes it takes to make up a past . . ." He shook his head and balled his fists, and felt himself bristling.

"It's a big galaxy, Mr. Riker. How do our problems get so finely concentrated?"

Riker glanced sidelong at the old-world crew of the old-world ship, with all their old-world problems, and seemed, like Picard, to see a reflection of something much closer.

"Talent, sir," he said.

Chapter Thirteen

"Do you know where this Jeremiah Coverman lives?"

"A house beside a factory. He has a linen factory. He risked everything. His family rejected him when he came here. He was penniless. I sent him some silver to start his business."

"Then he should be happy to see you," Picard said as he crouched beside Sergeant Alexander Leonfeld. "Let's go down there."

"How shall we find the linen factory?" Midshipman Nightingale asked. "We're in uniform. We can hardly ask about."

"The town's scarcely two kilometers in diameter. We'll find it."

Bennett and the other oarsman, an impressed cobbler named Wollard, shuffled forward in the trees. "Sir," Bennett began, "me and Wollard 'ere, we ought to volunteer to go an' 'ave a look before you an' the young sirs go in there."

Picard rewarded him with a thready smile. "That's very gentlemanly, Mr. Bennett, but we'll all go. Better we stay together for now."

They'd walked half the night. More than that. And now they stood on a heavily treed ridge, looking down at a coastal village, where only a few candles glowed at this late hour. Just beyond the town, the small boatyard and the port could be identified by several masts sticking up into the moonlight.

"They must be asleep, sir," Wollard guessed.

"No, they're not asleep. Look," Picard pointed out. "There are lanterns lit at the boatyard. There's activity. I see people moving about."

"Fortifying," Leonfeld suggested. "In case we got through. Preparing to defend the yard."

"Then they don't know yet," Nightingale added.

"That could work in our favor," Picard said hopefully. "They'll be distracted, and they don't know anyone made it ashore. Let's hurry. And, Sergeant, you should leave that headgear behind. It'll be cumbersome and a little obvious."

Leonfeld nodded, ditched his tall yellow headpiece, and they moved out. They hustled together through the trees, making use of the darkness, and found their way to the narrow dirt streets. Picard was gratified to be quite right about the size of the town. There were only a handful of streets to be checked, a few of which were cobbled with rounded stones from the size of melons to the size of eggs. He recalled that many streets in the old eastern United States were paved with stones carried as ballast aboard ships. He warmed to the little town instantly.

Systematic reconnaissance paid off within a half hour. Three streets from the riverfront, they discovered a building with the right sign over the door.

"That's a factory?" Alexander ridiculed. "It's so small!"

Indeed, the word implied a massive complex to people of the 24th century, but here in 1777 a factory was something entirely different. The linen factory was a narrow three-story clapboard building, painted blue but weathered to gray, with a nicely carved business sign: COVERMAN TEXTILES.

Sergeant Leonfeld gazed at the sign with his cousin's name upon it and murmured, "Jeremiah . . ."

Alexander smiled in empathy for his relative, glad that the sergeant had found what he needed to see.

Picard, though, realized that the fact that Leonfeld's cousin's business was still here said precious little about whether or not the cousin was still alive. This could be the man's family running the business, or an entirely new owner who had kept the name.

"When last I heard from Jeremiah, he had employed four people," Leonfeld said. "I know it seems insignificant . . ."

"Perhaps to the landed aristocracy of Europe," Picard commented, annoyed.

Leonfeld cast him a crabby glare, but said nothing. Of course, the sergeant still believed he was speaking to a lieutenant of the Royal Navy. What would he have thought if he knew he was speaking to a captain of Starfleet?

They were hiding behind a wooden slat fence, watching men dash back and forth, carrying tools and boxes. The boxes probably held precious ammunition with which the fort would be defended. They thought there was a British ship coming in, but of course that wouldn't be happening now. These colonists had been victorious with their frontal assault, but didn't even know it yet. They were still afraid. Picard saw it in their faces. Afraid, defiant, dreading a battle while anxious to get it started.

"Perhaps we should go around back, sir," Nightingale offered. "After all . . ." He touched the facing of his blue uniform jacket.

Picard nodded. "Mr. Leonfeld, your recommendation?"

Leonfeld studied the cobbled street, the front of the linenworks, the house on the other side that they needed to get to, and the sporadic activity in the street. "The back. Yes. My cousin wrote that he lived in a house beside the factory . . ." He pointed to a house made of split logs, rather small, with two stories and square windows with painted shutters.

"Alexander," Picard murmured, taking the boy by the arm, "you stay close to me."

The boy looked at him, then turned longingly to the sergeant, who was obviously the person he really wanted to keep close to. However he made no protests, and the landing party moved out on Picard's signal.

Staying under cover of darkness and any structure that

would hide them, they picked their way clumsily around the back of the factory, stumbling several times in the darkness over packing barrels and mechanical parts, until they found the aft end of the log house.

There, they crouched and surveyed the house.

A small back window beside a clay chimney glowed with the light of two candles on tin sconces. So someone was awake.

But there was no noise of movement, talking.

"Mr. Leonfeld," Picard murmured, "look in that window. See if there is anything or anyone you recognize."

Leonfeld nodded, but couldn't find his voice. He handed his rifle to Nightingale, and picked his way to the window. Even at his height of nearly six feet, he had to stand on tiptoe to see into that small window. He pressed his fingers against the painted wooden sill and looked straight in, then left, then right.

"No one," he said. "No one at all . . . but candles burn within . . . and there is a pitcher and some papers on a table."

"Inside," Picard said. He made straight for a very narrow back door and gripped the latch.

The door opened hospitably before him, and the scent of a wood fire drew him inward, where he stood beneath a claustrophobic ceiling, scarcely tall enough to admit Sergeant Leonfeld. Until this moment, when the warmth of the crackling cobblestone fireplace and the sooty scent of burning logs coiled around him, Picard hadn't realized how chilled he'd become. Now his hands began to flex again and his arms and knees to ease their aches, and for a moment he was almost dizzy with the charming sensation.

The cabin was a single keeping room, with a narrow stairway to their left, leading most likely to sleeping quarters. An oval rag rug in the middle of the room was the only covering upon a worn wooden slat floor that had a few visible sags. The two candles stood in tin sconces with rubbed backings that reflected their glow forward from the exposed-log walls, casting a dim light upon the side of the room farthest from the fireplace.

The fireplace was also made of those ballast stones, soot-darkened from the cooking hearth, and laden with iron utensils hanging from hooks. Iron pots, molded muffin tins, and a rolling pin hung from one of the four ceiling beams. Near one of the two front windows was a trestle table, flanked by two simple benches made of half-logs and standing upon stumpy wooden legs. On the table near the pitcher were several pamphlets and papers. Over the nearest bench was spread a dull-colored quilt with star patterns. Picard smiled when he saw that.

Near the fire was a simple Welsh-type lambing chair and a small crooked tavern table, and on the other side of the room, the cool side, was a collection of grass baskets, a chopping block, and a barrel that might be a grain bin—

"Stand very still or die turning!"

Despite the sharp order, all five swung about toward the voice and found themselves staring down the barrel of a wide-muzzled pistol.

The pistol barrel protruded from the narrow stairway, in which there was only a blurred shadow of a man.

"What are you doing in this town?" the voice demanded. "Are you advance scouts?"

At the sound of the voice, with its decidedly English accent, Picard held his hands up cautiously. "We're survivors. Our ship ran aground. We only want safe haven until we can sort things out."

"There's no safe haven for you here. In this town, you'll be turned over to the Continental Army as prisoners of war."

"We're not here to participate in the war," Picard persisted. "We're looking for the owner of the linen factory. Jeremiah Coverman."

At the sound of the name, the gunman stepped out of the stairway shadow. He was a young man, perhaps twenty-five, medium height and muscular, and he possessed the same blue eyes as Alexander Leonfeld. The family resemblance was instantly recognizable, despite this man's much darker brown hair, more weathered complexion, and stockier build.

"What is it you want here?" Coverman asked, still leveling the pistol on Picard, as if understanding quite well that he was the officer of rank here. Evidently he knew something about the British military. He came into the room, and there was some movement in the stairwell behind him, but Picard couldn't yet see who else was there.

Without answering, Picard glanced around at Sergeant Leonfeld, who until now had been standing off to one side, near the wide cooking hearth.

Leonfeld was only staring, with a peculiar nostalgia gripping his features. As Picard looked at him, he choked up a voice. "Jeremiah?"

Coverman squinted into the candlelit dimness at the tall grenadier in the bright scarlet uniform coat with its white facings and brass buttons, and for the first time he saw something other than the clothing.

The pistol wavered, then finally came down.

Jeremiah Coverman narrowed his eyes again, crossed the line over to believing what he saw, and rasped, "Sa—"

Leonfeld dropped his rifle onto a bench, Coverman shoved his pistol onto the table, and the cousins came together in a long-overdue embrace. They seemed truly shocked to see each other, as if each had thought the other dead or forever lost.

"Sandy!" Coverman finally choked out the rest of the name.

After a moment Sergeant Leonfeld was laughing as he hugged his cousin, and Jeremiah Coverman simply gasped, "My God! My God! Oh, God, dear God!"

His enthusiasm was so heartrending that Picard half expected the roof to part and an answer to be delivered from on high.

Grinning happily, Alexander sidled to Picard's side during this distraction, and uttered, "Is this another relative of mine?"

Glancing down at the boy with a wistful grin of his own, Picard simply said, "Seems so."

Evidently, the two cousins were not the only ones in the room just discovering long-lost relations. The boy seemed overwhelmed by these human relations suddenly popping up in a life in which human things had seemed the more elusive and Klingon things the most important.

"My God . . . Sandy, Sandy . . . Sandy!" Jeremiah finally allowed his cousin to pull him back so they could get a good look at each other. "When—did you get taller? Look at you! My heaven, look at your hair! It's so light! And you actually fill out that jacket! You never filled out a piece of clothing in all our lives!"

"You always filled yours out mightily well," the rechristened Sandy chuckled, thumping his cousin's middle, "and now you've worked it off!"

"Starved it off, more like. My God . . . this is unthinkable! What are you doing here? Why didn't you write that you were coming?"

"I attempted to do so, but the ship upon which my letter traveled evidently was attacked and sunk. Your little war."

"Yes, yes . . ." Coverman pulled away another step, though he kept one hand clasped tightly on Sandy's elbow, and leaned toward the narrow stairway. "Amy!" he called on a laugh. "Amy, come down! It's all right! This is our Sandy! Can you believe it?"

A teenaged girl came peeking from the stairwell, her brown hair twisted up under a lace cap, and she was dressed in a day dress even though this was the middle of the night. Apparently the town had indeed been expecting trouble on the water tonight. Jeremiah, Picard noticed now, was also dressed, despite the hour, in a simple linen shirt with long full sleeves, a brown vest, and gray breeches.

Coverman caught the teenaged girl's hand and pulled her into the room. "This is Amy," he said, beaming. "My wife."

Picard almost bolted a protest—the girl could hardly be fifteen years old.

"Sandy . . . not really?" Amy Coverman's voice was very soft, far more demure than any female Picard had ever known. She offered her hand to her husband's cousin. "Mr. Leonfeld, I'm deeply glad you've come here!"

"Madam." Sandy took her hand and bowed at the waist, morphing instantly into that elegant aristocrat who was never far beneath the surface. "My dear cousin," he added as he looked at her pale young face. "I see, Jeremiah, you've transgressed into child-stealing."

Jeremiah smiled at his very young wife. "Our marriage

was arranged by the pastor of our chapel. We were married when Amy turned fourteen. And so lucky a man as I never walked in less than Heaven."

The girl smiled back, blushing in the candlelight, and Picard could hardly deny the adoration that had evidently survived the wearing away of girlish infatuation.

At the stairs another person appeared, a second woman of thirty or more, pulling behind her a child who seemed, by Picard's faulty reckoning, to be about four years old. The woman cautiously kept the child, a boy, behind her aproned skirts, but he peeked out at the strangers.

"Pardon me," Amy Coverman said. "Aunt Mercy, it's all right to come down. Gentlemen, may I present my mother's second sister, Mercy Starrett, and her son, Seth Starrett."

"Madam," Picard offered.

"Sir," the other woman said. She was very plump and nervous, wide-eyed at the sight of the strange men, and hid her child behind her skirts even as she entered the room.

"Have you eaten?" Jeremiah Coverman suddenly asked, pumping Sandy Leonfeld's arm. "How did you get here? Where is your regiment? I can hardly get over that uniform! Cursed if you don't look like a proper British tyrant in it! And who are these other men?"

"Oh—I beg your pardon." Leonfeld stepped back and motioned to Picard and the others. "This is Lieutenant Picard of Her Majesty's Fighting Ship *Justina,* Midshipman Nightingale, Seamen Bennett and Wollard, and Ship's Swab Alexander."

Scowling, Alexander didn't seem to care much for that particular title, and glanced at Picard in something like self-consciousness. Picard wasn't sure if the name had insulted the boy, or if the boy was bothered by having Sandy Leonfeld be the one to call him that. Nothing to be done about it.

Coverman scanned them, but something else was on his mind. "Where is the ship?" he asked.

Leonfeld started to answer, then thought better and turned to Picard, allowing an officer of the Royal Navy ship's command to speak for it.

Picard responded with an inward shrug. "I'm afraid our frigate is aground in the Bay and has fallen to colonials."

"Has it, now! Think of that!" Coverman turned to his wife. "Amy, think of it!" He swung around again. "How on earth did you escape?"

"We were on the land when the final attack came," Picard said.

"What exceptional luck!" Jeremiah gasped with a nervous, overwhelmed shudder.

Sandy Leonfeld patted his cousin warmly on the shoulder, and turned to look at Picard and the other displaced crew of the lost British ship. "You see? I told you we would find a Loyalist haven in this nest of rebellion!"

At once Jeremiah Coverman's smile fell away and a pasty fear took over his rosy expression. "Well, yes, you may have haven here."

He ducked under his cousin's arm, hurried first to one front window and drew shut the calico curtains, then crossed the closed front door and also drew together the curtains on the other front window.

"Yes—you could be safe here for a time, but . . . Delaware Station is a stronghold of patriots. Not like New York or Philadelphia, where there are forty or more percent of those still loyal to King George. You would be safer there, if you must stay. Loyalists are poorly tolerated here, especially among those who work at the boatyard, which are many. Have a care what you say and to whom you say it. How we can get you back upon a British vessel, I'm sure I've no idea . . . certainly, we must find that way, or all is lost." He ran a finger through the air to illustrate the clothes they were wearing. "Better you not be seen in your uniforms—I shall give you other livery. Oh, and you must be hungry! Amy, Mercy . . . please."

He motioned to the two women. Amy Coverman turned and hurried back upstairs, and Mercy put her child by the fire and hurried to a wooden cabinet with cut metal doors, from which she extracted loaves of bread, a deep tin with a pie-crust topping, and a round whey-colored mound that might be cheese. She took those to the trestle table and set them beside the salt-glazed pitcher that was already there. Then she went after several pewter tankards on a shelf.

"Please," Jeremiah said, and Picard noted that the cousin was suddenly nervous.

Picard empathized with the poor man, a Crown Loyalist living in a rebel port, now with a houseful of escaped British sailors, and even two officers, whom he felt a familial obligation to hide. This surely put Jeremiah Coverman in tricky straits.

"Please, sit down," Jeremiah repeated, taking Sandy by the elbow and gazing briefly at him with a sad warmth. "Let me give you a few moments of comfort before the difficulties ensue."

"Difficulties?" Sandy eyed his cousin, but stepped to the table and lowered himself onto the bench. He was tentatively joined by the two sailors, by Mr. Nightingale, and finally by Alexander and Picard.

Picard found himself watching the two cousins, especially Coverman. For a man caught in a strange country in which he was an enemy, Sandy Leonfeld was strangely relaxed. On the other hand, Jeremiah Covernman drew his brows, pressed a hand to his lips, tried to think, and each decision seemed to come at a price, even as simple as pouring ale from that pitcher into Sandy's tankard. And strong-smelling stuff it was, too—

What was this? A poke at his thigh. Picard looked automatically to his side. Alexander was knuckling him in the leg. The boy's eyes were wide, and he seemed aware of something Picard had missed.

"Something?" he asked, figuring matters were as well handled with honesty, but he asked it low, as the clatter of pewter plates and the murmuring of the women overrode his utterance.

Alexander didn't answer, but nodded twice, vigorously, and looked at Jeremiah.

The cousin's eyes were tight with concern as he oversaw their spare meal. What did Alexander see there, and what was Picard missing? A man frightened for his cousin's well-being? Even survival, probably. These were hot times. Of those in this cabin, only Picard and the boy knew that

Sandy would indeed survive the war to pass his chronicles along to future generations, or that his legacy would indeed reach so far, or that there would someday be such a telescope as this with which to gaze back.

Jeremiah was just now moving the stack of pamphlets aside to make room for Sandy's plate, and seemed to feel awkward about doing so, so much that Sandy noticed the pamphlets and plucked one off the top of the stack just before his cousin had a chance to turn away.

"What's this?" the sergeant asked. "Do they indeed possess literature in the Colonies? I hadn't thought so." He smiled, and looked at the pamphlet, not noticing his cousin's suddenly blanched face.

Then Sandy laughed spontaneously.

"'Common Sense'! I've heard of this. Thomas Paine, yes—I recall when that slackard left England. And good riddance as well. A failure and a scoundrel and troublemaker, that one. I've heard of his rantings since he came here. He's bent upon success here which he could not legitimately achieve in England. He wants it by wresting away the possessions by rebellion that he could not acquire by merit. He's worse than a rebel. He's an Englishman turned traitor."

And Sandy laughed again, this time looking up at Jeremiah and smiling. He gave the pamphlet a little shake.

"Why do you have this?" he asked.

Chapter Fourteen

"OH, NO . . ."

The small cabin turned suddenly chilly.

"You cannot be one of these creatures," Sandy Leonfeld declared to his cousin.

Flinty resentment surged through Jeremiah Coverman's contriteness. "Can't I?"

Caught fast by curiosity, Picard watched both men very carefully, and noted that Alexander was rapt as a hawk on prey.

Sandy Leonfeld looked like a man with the stuffing kicked out of him. His shoulders sagged, his proud chest caved in, his chin sank. His whole uniform seemed suddenly soggy.

He moaned upward from a sickened heart. Over and over he warbled, "No . . . no . . . no . . ."

He shook his head and blinked repeatedly at the pamphlet in his hands, then looked up.

"You're a British citizen," he uttered on a breath. "The Crown, Jeremiah . . . the Crown is everything!"

"The Crown is *nothing,"* Jeremiah countered with sudden abrasion, as if he had just taken the disagreement as an insult.

The two cousins, so lately reunited in great joy, stared at each other astringently.

Pity gripped Picard as he saw that Sandy Leonfeld was a man watching a precious thing die. Great loss shone upon his young face, in lines as purely etched as ancient rivers gouging the surface of a planet. His eyes disappeared in a shadow beneath his thick blond hair as he lowered his head and mourned.

That pain was mirrored fully in Jeremiah Coverman, and now threatened to be the only thing left the two had in common. Perhaps shame and certainly sorrow limned his face as well, but unlike his cousin he did not lower his eyes. He evidently had no intention of making excuses. Now Picard understood why the communication between the cousins had eventually ceased—Jeremiah hadn't wanted to tell Sandy what was happening in this household, in his mind and heart.

No—not shame. Picard looked again for it, expected it, but found none in Jeremiah's demeanor. Resentment, yes, but no embarrassment for this turn he had taken.

Sandy Leonfeld battled his very physical reaction to this news, and found the strength to square his shoulders. "The divine right of kings is beyond refute," he simmered. "A person *can* be born better than others. All blood is not alike. These Colonial ideas of equality are awkward, and their declarations are truant."

Though bread and cheese stood guard on the trestle, no one touched it. The two deckhands and the "ship's boy" waited for their superiors to begin, and the superiors were busy.

"Jeremiah, you deceive yourself," Sandy blazed. "You are not one of these rabblers. The Crown and the European system has given you everything. It set these Colonies into business. Gave you land, and the tools to work it. Provided you trade and market, protected you, sent you food and tea—we have *built* you. If this shabby, backward place were to somehow become a country, it would only be by the grace of your country and your King. And now you, an aristocrat, will spit in his face?"

Jeremiah's face turned rosy with emotion and he shifted as if aware of all the eyes, all the judgments, upon him. "I cannot be Tory any longer," he said simply. "The class system does not work in the New World."

"Because malcontents cannot work it!" Sandy shot back. And he stood very straight.

Picard deliberately said nothing. He was watching the two men, but also watching Alexander, who had stepped forward in rapt attention to what was happening between his ancestors. The complexities of human history, so often simplistic in the minds of spacefaring races, was coming to light for the boy.

And for his captain, guilty sometimes of the same charge.

Before Jeremiah could respond, someone knocked on the front door.

"Please, stand away." Jeremiah became suddenly nervous, and his wife crowded him as they both went to the door.

He opened it, and luckily its method of opening prevented anyone standing outside from seeing the trestle table and those who sat or stood around it. Picard motioned for the men to remain quiet and still.

"Thank you, Angus," Jeremiah said, and immediately closed the door again. Whoever had been there had said nothing at all.

As Jeremiah closed and latched the door again, he now held a piece of cloth, rolled and folded. He turned to his wife, and together they opened the tiny package. Inside, Picard could see a message scrawled on the cloth, and a large hand-forged square-headed nail.

Jeremiah glanced at Picard. "It's from Elder Nethers. He owns the nailery."

"Ah!" Sandy impugned. "Communicating with the elite, are we? Let us by all means sup with the nailer, the chandler, the cooper, the cobbler, and let us not snub the butcher, else we starve."

Jeremiah looked up sharply. "Have a care, Sandy."

"Cousin," Amy Coverman chided softly. "You insult us."

Glowering at her, Sandy responded, "You insult yourselves, madam."

"What does the note say?" Picard asked, hoping to scope out a plan of action that didn't end in these two men having a duel under some crooked tree.

Jeremiah almost answered, then suddenly looked at Sandy. Picard noticed with regret Jeremiah's abrupt realization that he might not be able to trust one of the dearest people to his heart in the world.

In that terrible instant, he crossed the line into distrust. He and Sandy became enemies.

And a sad thing it was to witness.

Jeremiah shielded his sorrow in the act of folding the note and stuffing it into his waistcoat; then he stepped to the mantel over the fireplace and placed the forged nail into a tin box with several others of its kind. Clearly, there had been messages before from the nailery.

Anxiety crawled through despair in Jeremiah's eyes as he turned with resolve to Sandy once again.

"I am a patriot," he quietly proclaimed. "We are decent people who want charge of our possessions."

"Decent?" Sandy shook his head. "Are your Committees of Safety decent when they arrest loyal British citizens? Tar and feather them? Seize their property because they fail to embrace your selfish rebel causes? Send them to prison? For people who speak of rights and freedoms, you suspend those for any who disagree with your politics. Have a care yourselves, Jeremiah, for frivolity is devil's play. Beware burning too many candles. The whim of the day is a dangerous tool with which to govern."

"Whim?" Jeremiah's tone turned abrasive for the first time. "Who exactly are you to come here with your powdered wigs and tell us what to do with the fruits of our pursuits?"

Sandy Leonfeld had been standing with one shoulder toward his cousin, as if attempting to mentally stalk away from the proceedings, but now he turned fully to face Jeremiah Coverman, and his shoulders drew slightly back.

His eyes burned as he made his cold announcement. "We are your betters."

Tension reached critical mass in the small cabin, braced passively by the fire snapping crisply in the hearth.

The sailors remained silent, riveted by the friction between the cousins, so clearly defining the little, sparking war that now embraced two continents.

"Everyone is better than someone," Jeremiah allowed. "I cannot deny others the chance to acquire betterment."

"One cannot 'acquire' the status of a gentleman," the sergeant clarified. "One must be born to that status. Officers and gentlemen have run the British government and military since ancient times, and that is why Britain has survived. Tradition must be respected, else we are no longer civilized. Look at France! Where would that cesspool of peasants be if not for the aristocracy? Should the elite crumble, Europe would go to pot. The class system in the military is the only reason the lowest soldier can eat. So it is in all of society. The system is run on our honor. While we are out here, thousands of miles from our king, we still owe loyalty to him. We owe loyalty to the system that feeds us. If it falls, we fall."

"You're living an illusion," Jeremiah told him quietly. "You've simply never seen any other way."

"Oh?" Sandy's eyebrow went up like a rising barometer. "Do you know you're insulting me now?"

"I'm insulting myself, then," Jeremiah said, "for mine is high birth as well."

Sandy Leonfeld's eyes narrowed, and his shoulders squared once again upon that narrow figure.

With great luster he said, "Not as high as *mine.* I am a peer of the realm. My descendants will be dukes and princes, lords, barons, and kings."

Picard leaned toward Alexander. "And Klingons," he murmured.

"Jeremiah, be reasonable!" the sergeant pleaded. "Do you honestly believe this clatter of colonies is a nation? Do you think you can survive without selling yourself to another foreign power? There is a king in your future, America, for that is where the power lives, and you need power to survive against power. Soon or late, the colonies will make deals with kings. If you're successful in breaking from Britain, I hope you enjoy being a Spaniard or a Dutchman. Or, God forbid, French! Independence! What a lie!"

He stalked away from Jeremiah, putting what precious little distance between them this cabin's keeping room allowed. As he paused near the fireplace, glaring into the fire with menacing eyes, he cast a single glance at Picard, noted what had just been said, but decided not to apologize. The sergeant seemed as baneful as he was appalled, and the level of his conviction was clearly met by the conviction in Jeremiah Coverman's face, and those of the two women.

He placed his hands on his hips and glared around at the cabin and its humble accoutrements; certainly, he was measuring it up with the splendor of his life, and Jeremiah's former life, as the aristocracy of Britain and Austria. Surely this place was humbled by the past of both these young men, and all that was reflected, down to the sconces, in Sandy Leonfeld's contemptuous survey.

"Freeze program." Picard waited for the computer to slow the holoprogram, but it didn't happen. Instead, all the people in the room turned to look at him and try to figure out what he was talking about.

"I beg your pardon, lieutenant?" Jeremiah asked.

Aunt Mercy craned about as if expecting spirits to come out of the walls.

"Computer, I *said,* freeze the program," Picard repeated.

Finally the holoprogram slowed to a stop.

He turned to the boy.

"Why did you stop it?" Alexander asked, his adolescent fists balling with attempted manliness. "It was just getting good!"

"Alexander, how did you know?" Picard wondered. "Before Jeremiah said anything, you realized he was no longer loyal to the Crown, didn't you?"

"Yes." The boy looked at him, his face crumpled with dissatisfaction and disappointment. He thought back, and said, "Jeremiah was acting like a kid who was afraid to say what he'd done. He just acted sort of . . . ungood."

As the corner of his mouth came up involuntarily, Picard smiled ruefully and repeated, "Ungood. Shakespeare couldn't have said it better. And what do you think was 'ungood' about his new beliefs?"

"He wanted to keep them a secret. He knew Sandy wouldn't like it that Jeremiah has turned against everything they both used to stand for. They had loyalties. They made promises. Sandy's oath was made for life. Jeremiah went back on his oath. I don't think I like Jeremiah very much. And I think he knows he's wrong, or he would be prouder of himself. He wouldn't be trying to keep secrets."

"Mmm," Picard uttered again. "May have something there. With which of these men do you find yourself agreeing?"

Alexander speared him with a glare. "With the sergeant, of course!"

"Why, Alexander?"

The boy balked at the question, not because of its difficulty, but that there should be any question at all. "Jeremiah made a promise to the king! That has to mean something. Sandy's sticking with his promise. *That*'s honor."

"What about Jeremiah's honor? Remember, the Day of Honor holiday is meant to appreciate your enemy's hon—"

"He doesn't have any!" the boy said scornfully. "Or else, how could he turn his back on his whole family? His family raised him to be something, and they worked to give him things, and he swore an oath, and he's dumping all that so he can be a rebellion person." The boy leaned toward Picard and lowered his voice. "I think he changed so he could get that pretty wife. *She*'s American, you know."

Trying not to grin, Picard nodded.

Alexander's eyes widened in a parody of suggestiveness, and he nodded in agreement with himself.

"Mmm-hmm," Picard muttered. "I do know that, yes . . ."

"These colonists," Alexander went on, "none of them have any honor! How am I supposed to understand celebrating your enemy's honor when he doesn't have any to celebrate? This holiday doesn't make any sense."

He dumped himself down like a sack on the bench, next to the slowly turning form of Midshipman Nightingale.

"What makes you say they have none at all?" Picard persisted.

Alexander fanned his arms. "Why else would they attack a ship that's stranded? That's not honorable at all! It's what cowards do!"

Picard tipped his head. "Actually, I thought it wasn't a bad tactic at all."

The boy hurled him a glowering look. "You'd do that?"

"If I had to, yes."

Astounded by the lack of shame in Picard's voice and his studied casualness at such an idea, Alexander pushed off the bench and stalked the room, patently avoiding the semistill figure of Jeremiah Coverman.

At the pie cabinet, he placed his hands on his hips and shook his head. "I never thought we were that kind of people!"

The purity of the boy's heart rang and rang, and Picard began to realize that somehow, despite Alexander's jostled upbringing and his life on board the starship—questionable at best for any growing child—he was turning out to be a young man of principle.

Feeling something shine in his chest from this revelation, Picard moved toward the boy.

"Alexander," he asked, "what's really wrong with you?"

The boy didn't look at him this time, but other things about his demeanor changed. His posture declared that this had gone beyond a history lesson, beyond a tradition, and, in fact, beyond a rite of passage. A certain fundamentality had taken hold.

"Oh, I see . . ." Picard circled around in front of him without crowding him. "It's your father and Mr. Grant, isn't it?"

Alexander kicked the leg of a spinning wheel that had been tucked into a corner. "Don't talk to me about my father! I don't want to talk about him."

"Why not?"

"Because I don't. And it's none of your business if I don't."

"Now, really," Picard said. "Who's being dishonorable now?"

Fuming, the boy toed the spinning wheel, but didn't kick it this time. He gnashed and grieved, spun around as if to challenge, then recoiled, and finally chafed out his thoughts.

"He's letting Uncle Ross down. And his life is in danger! You can't pretend it's not, because I know what's been happening on Sindikash."

"Are you worried that your father has lost his honor?" Picard asked. "It's his sense of honor that prevents him from lying, you know."

"What honor? If he knows Mrs. Khanty did bad things, why would he throw away a chance to lock her up? If he knows she's guilty, why can't he use what he knows to keep her from hurting more people? Maybe the person she hurts next will be Grant!"

Picard drew a troubled breath, balking at the boy's relentless logic. "Things are complex," he attempted. "Adult things."

Like a prosecutor in court, Alexander shot back, "If he saw her do these things, he'd use his phaser, wouldn't he?"

Taken by surprise, Picard admitted, "Well . . . I would hope so, yes."

Alexander fanned his arms. "Then I don't understand this! He won't lie, but he wouldn't *really* be lying, because he'd be making the truth happen. Instead, he's making Uncle Ross look like a liar. It's not fair."

"Unfortunately," Picard sighed, "'fairness' isn't all it's cracked up to be."

"He should come up with a way to support Grant," Alexander went on. "He should *make* it work. It's not honorable to just *say* you're honorable. I don't like my father very much right now."

The boy half-turned away from Picard, and fell starkly silent. That mouths-of-babes thing rose again as Alexander made perfect sense. What good was it to stand on thin honor while the platform of justice collapses beneath? None at all.

But how could he explain to Alexander the dishonor of

perjury, even to bring in a criminal? He already knew that simply explaining rarely did the trick for a child.

As Picard watched, Worf's image as a parent, a warrior, and a starship officer tarnished in his son's eyes.

Picard frowned. Perhaps he should have better minded the boy's sensitivities, protected him from what was happening on the planet. Alexander shouldn't have to bear the fallout of Worf's mission and its personal repercussions.

This was one of the difficulties of shipboard life. Alexander's friendship with Grant could compromise events. Yet, throughout history—from the first rowed boats, to sails, to starships—no one had found a way for a crew, however dapper, to keep from becoming a family. Nor had any but the stiffest Blighs expected otherwise.

These lessons were getting awfully big for one young boy to absorb. Even more troubling was his own rising doubt. He'd always found it easy to look down his nose at the simpler past, but he was finding that these times were not so simple at all. These were the times in which the laws he took for granted had been forged by fire, and he luxuriated in his loft built of others' great trials. They had stood the test, and he reaped the rewards.

Now Worf was going through the same thing—looking down from the platform of his honor, for which Ross Grant would pay the price.

Picard started wondering just who was getting the biggest lesson out of all this.

"You know what the colonies eventually became, don't you?" Picard asked, framing his question carefully.

"The United States of America," Alexander grumbled back, refusing to look up. "I know, I know. And later they brought the whole world together and started exploring and the Vulcans met 'em and they became the Federation." Now he did look up. "So what? How does that change the fact that *he* went back on his promise?"

He pointed fiercely at Jeremiah Coverman, which seemed somehow cruel, since Jeremiah was down to slow motion and couldn't speak for himself. Fostering a clear case of hero worship, Alexander went to stand beside his *favorite* relative—Sandy Leonfeld.

Together, spanning centuries, the two Alexanders made quite a figure as Picard gazed at them. Somehow the boy was less a boy now.

"I'm sorry about this," the captain said slowly. "I've failed to help you understand that honor is not so simple a thing. That was *my* mission."

"I'm tired of missions," Alexander rebuffed him, folding his arms. He stepped elbow to elbow with the sergeant, even though his elbow wasn't quite high enough yet. "Sandy didn't go against his family and government. He's an officer. He's a born gentleman. Klingons have the same thing. You can be born into a powerful family. *I* was! We're the same, him and me. Me and him. Him and I."

"Yes, but—"

"He didn't go into the British Grenadiers because it was that or starve!" the boy went on. "A lot of soldiers joined because of that, you know. I checked."

"When did you check?"

"When Mr. Riker came in. I didn't eat lunch. I went and looked in the historical banks about this time period."

Hmm—one step in the right direction, at least. Looking for his own answers.

"Your father was born into a powerful family, yes," Picard said, "but there are limitations of all kinds. Your father is trying to choose between his honor, Mr. Grant's safety, and the influence of Mrs. Khanty on the planet. It's not easy, and not as simple as you may think."

"It's simple," Alexander countered. "He's chickening out. And I don't know why. If that's Klingon honor, then I don't want it. I think I'd rather stay here and be a grenadier."

Picard smiled. "You can't stay here. It's a holoprogram."

"Well, there must be some planet somewhere with a Royal Marine unit I can join!"

In a moment of complete insanity, Picard almost turned to Mr. Nightingale and the seamen and told them they could resume eating. These people around them, still alive with minimal movement, were not the same cold, flat figures conjured up by the holodeck's amusement programs, like characters in some story. These were real people who had lived and died, who had real passions and grieved real losses, no less than he and the boy. They had simply done all that in a different blink of time. On the cosmic scale, he felt very close to them.

Obviously, tragically, Alexander did, too.

"Well," Picard began, "why don't we play all this out, and make our judgments later? After all, there are a few sides we have yet to hear. Shall we?"

Alexander hung his head, but his eyes still peered up at his captain. "I guess."

"Computer," Picard snatched at the moment, "resume program."

"I can no longer bear this!" Sandy Leonfeld's voice filled the cabin. He chopped a hand between himself and his cousin and made for the front door, clearly of no mind to remain in this den any longer.

"Sandy!" Frightened, Jeremiah rushed forward and caught the sergeant before Sandy's hand touched the iron latch. He took Sandy by the arms with the same urgent familiarity they had shown to one another moments ago, when things were so different, though little of that was returned from the grenadier. "Please . . . you must not go out."

"And why not?" Sandy gnashed. "Am I not in a clutch of my enemies? What safety does this place afford loyal Britons? Why should I not take my leave of you?"

Jeremiah pulled him away from the door. "Because you'll be hanged."

Sandy twitched, ready to shoot him an angry response, but what could he say?

Imploring with his eyes, Jeremiah waited until Sandy stopped pushing against his grip. "The message from the nailery . . . your ship is being towed upriver to the boatyard, where it will be converted for use by the patriots. Those officers and seamen still alive are imprisoned in the public stable. If you're caught, it'll be assumed you're attempting escape. You'll be executed as spies. Please—now, please. We disagree, yes . . . but I couldn't bear it if you were killed."

A crushing emotion rose between them. Despite his attempt at indignation, Sandy Leonfeld was clearly very upset. This was a terrible inner blow, not just a rift in philosophy. These things were deeply ingrained in his heart, and his heart was breaking.

"Sergeant," Picard interrupted, taking Sandy's elbow, "why don't we sit down and have something to eat?"

"I would retch," Sandy muttered.

"Please," Amy Coverman came to life, fluttering around and pouring cider into the tankards. "I shall have no one hungering in my home."

"Thank you," Picard said as he took a seat, surmising from their hesitation that the midshipman and deckhands would probably not eat until he did. He looked up as his tankard was filled, and spoke to Sandy. "Sergeant?"

Responding only with the barest attention he must give to a superior officer, Sandy Leonfeld lowered himself as non-committally as possible to the edge of the bench nearest him. He did not face the table fully, but sat on the end of the bench. Nor did he eat.

"Go ahead, gentlemen," Picard ordered. "We must keep our strength up. Alexander, eat something."

"I don't want anything."

Picard tucked his chin and gave the boy that look all children understand. "Regardless."

Pouting at full warp, Alexander flung himself onto the bench and ripped off a chunk of cheese, then smelled it and grimaced, determined not to have a good time.

The cheese was moldy, the cider was stale, the bread was crusty, and Picard began to regret the damned accuracy of the holodeck as he realized he wasn't hungry, but had just committed himself to setting an example. He tentatively bit into the bread, expecting to get the juicy end of a weevil, when abruptly the holodeck entryway opened again.

He looked up. "Freeze program," he said, but the computer didn't respond. Once again everyone around him blinked in confusion, and then all Klingon broke loose.

Worf walked through the entryway into the keeping room of the cabin, with First Officer Riker close behind.

"Computer, freeze the program," Picard repeated more firmly, but not soon enough.

Striding freely under a ceiling so low that his brow ridge almost scratched it, Worf presented a vision so monstrous that Amy Coverman screamed at the sight. Jeremiah jumped to protect his wife as the holodeck program twisted itself into knots, trying to compute the psychology of 1777 American colonists reacting to a Klingon.

"Demon!" Amy's aunt flew around the table, passed the fireplace, and scooped up the kettle of soup from the hook—luckily not directly over the fire—wheeled back, and creamed Worf directly in the face with the pot.

Barley soup splashed across Worf's entire head and cascaded down his shoulders to drench the front of his Rogue uniform. His mouth had been open, about to speak, and now came down upon a sprig of greenery lingering on a lip. Riker sidestepped just in time to avoid the splash.

"Great God above!" Jeremiah intoned.

Sandy Leonfeld vaulted toward his rifle and drew it to his shoulder, aimed and—

"No, no!" Picard plunged across the table like some kind of wild athlete, just gracefully enough to slam the rifle off its aim with the palm of his hand.

Then the grace played out, and he landed on top of the plate of bread, with his face in the cheese.

He lifted his head enough to shout out, "I said, freeze program, blast it all!"

The people in the cabin froze in position at last.

"Blast!" Picard rolled over and squeezed between Wollard and Alexander. "Hang this archaic technology!"

Someone caught his elbow and kept him from tripping over the bench, and he looked up to see that it was Riker.

Worf stood in the middle of the room, dripping, his arms slightly fanned outward, his uniform drenched; he smelled of barley. He looked around at the setting. "What is *this?*

This is Earth! The Day of Honor is a Klingon experience! And why did this relic strike me with a tub of stink!"

Stifling a grin, Picard stepped toward him, wiping cheese off his face. "I believe you've been promoted to the supernatural, Mr. Worf. This is an old style program. You have to be listed as a participant at the beginning or the computer doesn't know what to do with you. If we had any doubts that the safeties aren't functioning, we know it for certain now."

"I was wondering why you deflected that rifle," Riker mentioned. "Are you sure you want to keep this up?"

"Captain!" Worf interrupted. "What is all this!"

Riker smiled, and his eyes twinkled with mischief. "It's the American Revolutionary War. The captain lost a ship. Didn't you, sir?"

"This was my idea," Alexander said, stepping forward into his father's sphere of disgust.

Worf slapped his wet hands at the slowed figure of Mercy. "But this is supposed to be a lesson in Klingon culture! Not an excursion into witchcraft!"

"It's supposed to be a lesson in honor," Picard pointed out, "Strange how it's working out, though—"

"It was *my* idea!" Alexander repeated. "I got to pick the way the Day of Honor was taught to me, and I picked my ancestor's journal from Earth. I'm part-human, too, you know." He cocked a hip, folded his arms, and raised his chin. "And I'm figuring out a few things about honor that I don't think *you* know."

Worf dripped and stared. He looked over Alexander's head to Picard. "Captain! What are you teaching him?"

"I'm not *teaching* him," Picard said. "I'm guiding him. These people you see around us are doing the teaching. He's coming to his own conclusions. Isn't that the idea? Of course, we're not finished—"

"And we're going to finish." Alexander came up on his toes, to be noticed between the two men. He ignored Picard, and spoke directly to his father. "I'm going to stay here with Sandy until I hear everything he's got to say. You don't have any business telling me how to learn about honor."

Not liking the sudden discord that he felt was his fault,

Picard stepped to the boy's side. "Alexander, that's enough."

"What are you talking about?" Worf demanded, glowering down at his son.

Alexander tightened his folded arms. "You say you have honor, but you won't face up to Mrs. Khanty. You're throwing away a chance to win. You won't stick up for Uncle Ross."

Stunned, Worf wiped the soup from his face and glared at Picard again. "Sir! How did he find out about that?"

"Because I'm old enough to know," Alexander said, insisting that the conversation remain focused on him instead of going over his head between the two adults. "You won't say that you saw what Ross saw, even if it saves his life and catches that Mrs. Khanty."

Facing his son's disdain, Worf was kicked in the heart as no challenge from any bruising enemy ever could.

Picard's own chest tightened with empathy and the wish that he could spare Worf this torture. What could he say—what could any parent say—that would not sound shallow, empty? He was endangering a real, living, precious person so an ethereal concept could retain its integrity.

"Alexander," he began with effort, "I will not lie."

"You mean you won't embarrass yourself," the boy kicked back. "You know she's wrong, don't you? And you won't do one thing to save a whole planet."

"I told you," Worf steamed, watching his son's respect for him dissolve before his very eyes. How could he snatch it back? "I refuse to lie."

"You're already lying!" the boy countered, unfolding his arms as if preparing to wrestle. "Your whole mission was a lie! You were never just hiding out on Sindikash like you told them! Isn't that a lie? You're not a Rogue! Isn't *that* a lie? Your whole existence there was lie after lie. Do you think you have to say words to be lying?"

Riker leaned past the captain and plucked at the holocheese. "He's right about that, Worf. Can't deny it."

"Mr. Riker," Picard muttered. "You're not helping . . ."

"Sorry, sir."

Worf ignored them, smoldering in the confusion of what to do. Here he was, this huge warrior, nearly pathetic and sad with this fundamental loss, which no battle or angry demonstration could mend. He could not simply order his son to respect him. What did parents do in these moments?

"Alexander," he attempted, hoping to reinstate something, "you should not be speaking to me this way."

Picard held up a quieting hand. "The boy has a good point, Mr. Worf. Any covert mission is by nature a lie. We all lie at some time or another, to protect or spare others. Anyone who says he never lies is lying as he says it."

"That's not the point!" Alexander spoke up again. He squared off before his father. "If you can protect Grant by telling something you know is true, even if you didn't see it, why won't you do that? How is it honorable to do one right thing and let a bigger wrong thing happen? You think it's honor to let people die because you won't say one thing? How important can it be? Grant's gonna die because you won't tell a fib. Will your tongue snap off if you keep up the masquerade a little longer? That's pretty simpleminded honor, I think. Either you can press yourself to the limit or you can't! There's more to being a warrior than war!"

Worf stared in raw astonishment at his son, who had been only a boy, in the truest sense, when he left. Now there was something else here.

Picard found himself staring, too. Was this Alexander? Was this a *child?*

He flinched involuntarily when Worf swung toward him. "Is this how you teach him? By not explaining the difference between a covert mission and perjury? Captain, I must protest—"

"Don't talk to the captain! Talk to *me.*" Alexander gave his father a little push on the belt to get his attention again. "You'd shoot Mrs. Khanty if you saw her doing something bad, wouldn't you? So what's the difference? Are you going to stick up for Ross or aren't you?"

"All right, all right, belay this!" Picard pushed between them. "Mr. Riker, I want Worf, Dr. Crusher, Mr. Data, and yourself in the briefing room in fifteen minutes. Alexander, go somewhere and gain control over yourself until I call for you. We'll continue the Revolutionary War shortly. All hands, dismissed. Computer, store the program at this stage and end it until further notice. Don't look at me that way, Mr. Worf. I said you were dismissed. Go wipe off."

"All right, Mr. Worf, say what you have to say."

"I am deeply disturbed that Alexander yelled at me, sir."

"I mean about Sindikash, Lieutenant."

"Oh . . . yes." Worf fought inwardly to bury his frustration with his son and the captain, and forced himself to concentrate on his mission.

He sat stiffly in the briefing room, directly opposite the captain, who was at the far end of the long table. At Worf's right, Will Riker sat quietly. To Worf's left sat Dr. Beverly Crusher; standing near the large viewport, Commissioner Toledano twisted and twitched, his arms in constant movement and his hands repeatedly clenching.

Worf twitched uneasily. Strange how out of place he felt among these people and on this ship. Like coming from the mountains to the flatlands and feeling as if he were about to fall off.

He drew a breath and plunged into his summary.

"The freighter, piloted by myself and the other Rogues, was supposed to be 'caught' on the border of Romulan space, in order to frame the lieutenant governor. When we circumvented Mrs. Khanty's plan, she no longer trusted the Rogues to sacrifice themselves for her, and was forced to take events into her own hands. The only one she trusted was me, after I 'saved' the freighter from Starfleet capture with her Rogues aboard, which would have compromised her. So she put me on guard outside the suite, but evidently still did not trust me quite enough to ask me to assassinate the governor."

"Good thing she didn't," Dr. Crusher's fluid voice broke in. "You'd have blown your cover by refusing."

"Very likely," Worf agreed. "She needed public opinion

to swing back to her, and to make that happen, she assassinated her husband. However, Grant witnessed her action, and he informed the doctors that there was some sort of toxin involved, which was confirmed. Now Mrs. Khanty is accusing Grant of being the assassin. However, he could easily have kept quiet and not claimed he was in the suite at all. The doctors and Lieutenant Stoner of the City Police all quietly agree that Grant needn't have spoken up about the toxin if he had been the assassin. However, he sacrificed himself on the slim chance of saving the governor's life."

"Yes, I see the line of logic," the captain agreed. "He could easily have protected himself. What's happened since then?"

"I told you, sir," Worf said abrasively, "Mrs. Khanty has claimed that Grant's presence in the suite and my exposure as a Starfleet officer amounts to a confession. Federation personnel were in the room when they weren't supposed to be there, and the governor was poisoned. She says any reasonable person would conclude the obvious."

Picard frowned and rubbed his eyes. "That's not what we had in mind, is it?"

"I'll say it's not!" Commissioner Toledano spoke up suddenly, spreading his hands in frustration. "None of you have taken this mission seriously enough from the very beginning!"

Was the room fogging up? Worf squinted to see through his anger. He planted his hands on the slick black table and leaned forward. "We have risked our lives!"

Toledano pressed his legs against the table on his side. "*That* is expected of you!"

The blood of shame rose and made Worf's face hot. He gritted his teeth and responded with a blistering silence.

"That big mouth on Grant's face is going to work in Khanty's favor," Toledano stormed on, giving no quarter to the official decorum of the starship's briefing room or the presence of most of her senior officers. "If we continue our efforts, she'll say we killed her husband and now we're trying to frame her. She'll say Grant didn't get out in time and now he's trying to cast blame on her. She'll say she wanted no animosity with the Federation, but we insisted on interfering. Damn it! She's been spoon-feeding that corpse for weeks now, stoking public sympathy and waiting for an opportunity, and we handed it to her! Attempts to keep Sindikash in the Federation have completely backfired now. She might've lost the election before; now she certainly won't. You've handed everything to her."

"Commissioner," the captain began, "the decision to interfere was made by you and the Federation Council, not by Worf or Grant. Sindikash was a Federation colony with nearly fifty percent of its people still considering themselves citizens. The whole situation could've been handled more diplomatically, without extreme action. Much like the British who decided to flex their muscle and thereby pushed the American colonies away by power of resentment, this attempt at influence may well have cost us Sindikash."

"We're not the ones who made the mistake," Toledano said. He swung back to Worf. "That whole planet will have to suffer because you and Grant botched this mission!"

"Botched?" Worf erupted. The sides of his chair were getting tight. His boots didn't fit any more. His hair was boiling—

Straightening in his chair, Will Riker spoke very sharply. "Mr. Toledano, you're addressing a senior officer of a starship, and I'd advise you to do it with some respect."

Toledano twisted toward him, unintimidated, and pointed at Worf. "When he deserves it, I'll give it."

"Missions do sometimes fail, gentlemen," Captain Picard commented. "Ships are lost, people die, civilizations collapse . . . some turnings of the cogs can't be stopped, Commissioner. We can't always stem a tide the size of a planet. The people of Sindikash will pay for their gullibility. After a great deal of suffering and loss, they'll have to recover for themselves. Mr. Worf, I assume you haven't changed your mind about your official statement."

"I cannot say I saw something that I did not see," Worf

repeated. The words scratched his throat. He thought of Alexander again.

"That's fine, you keep your Klingon integrity." Toledano's whole body tightened in anguish. "And Odette Khanty's criminal organization gets control of the planet and a fifth of the sector. You'll be an honest man, and millions of lives will be destroyed. Good decision."

"Mrs. Khanty will act freely now," Data spoke up. "Certainly she knows there will be no act of direct force from the Federation."

Picard seemed annoyed at the confirmation of what they all knew, and he looked at Worf again. "What do you think is happening now to Mr. Grant?"

"No amount of protective custody will protect him on that planet," Worf said with contempt. "She'll find a way to put him on trial, or have him murdered and blame it on me. His only hope is Lieutenant Stoner, whom I believe is not corrupt. I can only hope Stoner will buy me time."

"Time for what?" Toledano interrupted.

"To go back and rescue my partner, Commissioner." Hadn't it been perfectly clear?

"You can forget about that. Just forget it. Forget you ever said it. I'm going to contact Starfleet Command and have a professional recon team sent in for Mr. Grant. You just stay out of this from now on. They'll get him out and that'll be that."

"That could take days."

"So what? You said he's in the hands of a noncorrupt policeman, didn't you? Do you believe it or not? After all, you *said* it, didn't you? So you sure must *believe* it!"

"That's enough, Commissioner," Picard steamed.

"No, it's not anywhere near enough. Mr. Worf, Captain Picard has command over you on this starship and on any mission sanctioned by Starfleet Command or the Federation Council, but as of this second, any further actions by you on or about Sindikash are not, and I mean *not,* sanctioned. Stay away from that planet. It's out of your hands. Got it?"

Toledano didn't have the bulk, the might, or the prowess

to challenge a trained mountain like Worf, but he certainly did wield the biggest weapon of all—authority. Any other Klingon would have peeled the commissioner's face and eaten the leavings, but Worf was indeed a Starfleet officer, which canceled all bets.

The commissioner pushed himself away from the table. "Just stay out of it," he concluded. "All of you, just stay out of it."

With that, the man who had at first been so affable and well-intended now left the briefing room with the lowest perceptions of persons he had once respected. Worf felt the loss keenly, and especially for the captain, who would bear the brunt of this.

First Grant, and now the captain would pay for Worf's honor. He wasn't used to that. Hadn't expected it.

"Well . . ." Captain Picard gazed at the door panels as they softly closed behind the commissioner, leaving the command crew uneasy with each other. "That could've gone better."

"You were right, Jean-Luc," Beverly Crusher reassured him. "Missions do fail now and then."

"I don't have to like it, Doctor. Well, Mr. Worf, now that you're back aboard, do you want me to stop being Alexander's mentor?"

Sweating like a jungle rain, Worf struggled between his responsibility as a father and the request he had made of his captain. There was some honor involved here, too, and a respect for his captain which he would be troubled to compromise.

"No, sir," he ultimately said, and nearly choked. "I gave you the right. I will not rescind it."

Because of his honor, as he saw it, Worf had to go back to the planet, therefore he had to leave Alexander's rite of passage into honor where he had put it in the first place. With Captain Picard.

The captain was watching him.

"I'll try to find some way to make him understand," Picard reassured him. "You're sure about this, Mr. Worf?"

"Yes, sir, very sure." Worf stood up. "I will not be here to take over with Alexander."

"Why not?"

"Because I must ask you to allow me to return to Sindikash to rescue Grant."

Picard looked at him and folded his hands in mock-passivity. *"Allow* you? I'm afraid not, Mister Worf. I can't give you *permission* to go on a rescue mission for someone who is in legal custody and not a Starfleet crewman. There is no way I can *authorize* such an expedition . . ."

"I understand, sir," Worf said tightly.

Was he reading the captain's tone correctly, with its oddly emphasized words? He would soon know.

Tenatively, he added, "Then I will not *ask* you, of course, sir."

"Good," the captain said, his eyes twinkling. "And don't ask Mr. Riker to go with you. I would not grant *him* permission either."

At Worf's side, Riker smiled.

Hope sprung high inside Worf's chest.

"Yes, sir," he said. "I would like to avoid asking Mr. Data as well."

Slowly Picard stood up and gestured at their resident android. "Agreed. Too much trouble. In any event, his appearance would be too difficult to explain. You'd have to put some kind of makeup on him so he would appear human."

Worf nodded somberly.

"And, of course, if you asked Dr. Crusher, that would be unacceptable as well."

"Well, I don't know about any of them," Riker said. "But I have no intention of going on any rescue missions. I'm going to lie down in my cabin for the next twenty hours or so, and leave orders that nobody disturb me. Mr. Data's going to do the same. He's having his first headache."

Data stood up, tipped his head in confusion, and said, "I beg your pardon, sir?"

Riker took Data's arm. "It's terrible. I can see the pain in your eyes. You'll need lots of rest. Right, Dr. Crusher?"

"Oh, lots," Crusher said, taking Data's other elbow. "At

least twenty hours. I'll stay with him the whole time and press a cool cloth to his brow. Come on, Data."

"Are we going somewhere?" the android asked innocently.

"Oh, yes," Riker told him, and grinned at Worf. "You have an appointment at the beauty shop."

Chapter Fifteen

"COMPUTER, REVERSE PROGRAM thirty seconds and resume."

Jean-Luc Picard nudged Alexander back into his place at the trestle table in Jeremiah Coverman's keeping room. Around them, the characters reversed like an old newsreel to a point before Worf had entered, and Picard sat down just as the scenario started moving again and the characters groaned to life.

"Alexander, don't pout," he murmured just as the characters took a reanimating breath.

"I've got a right," the boy shot back.

"Not on my time, you don't."

"Lieutenant Picard?" Nightingale asked. "Is something wrong, sir?"

"Nothing at all, Midshipman," Picard said, and turned. "Mr. Coverman, what affected you most in your new way of thinking?"

All eyes struck Picard like whips. He had dared to keep the flames of dissent burning. But he wanted to know, and turning away from a problem did nothing but cause it to fester.

To ease the dare, he handed the sergeant a chunk of bread and some cheese, causing Sandy to begin eating whether he liked it or not, because he couldn't disobey an order.

Sometimes rank could be an advantage.

Jeremiah sighed, but there was no vice left in him. He had plainly thought all this through for months, possibly years, and done his emotional wrestling long since. He seemed also to have anticipated this confrontation with his family, though Picard suspected he hadn't wanted to have it with Sandy.

He took the pitcher from Amy and poured Mr. Nightingale's drink.

"The class system doesn't work here. There is unthinkable mobility. The poor can become wealthy in mere months. The wealthy can lose fortunes even faster. Many live on the frontier. We are *months* away from Britain. Our remoteness reduces the edicts of the king to the baying of hounds in the distance. We scarcely hear it. No one cares to listen. The elite of Europe—Sandy, I'm sorry. For the elite, who have never set foot here and think of this place as a manure-filled backwater to be telling us what to do . . . it becomes untenable after a short time. British tariffs choke us, we are required to use their currency and none other, we are patently tried and convicted, treason is undefined—we may not even speak out against the Crown's policies, lest we risk our very lives. Is that freedom?"

No one made any response, but Picard suspected there were a half dozen different responses running under the table, each riding on some condition or other. No, yes, maybe, only if—

Jeremiah put the pitcher down on the table and sat opposite his cousin. He laid out a hand and implored, "Sandy, please try to understand. Even you must have trouble defending the abuses of the monarchy. You defend the Magna Carta, do you not? This is the next step of granting rights to everyone. This rebellion asks, 'Why do we need a king at all? Why does the gentry need the aristocracy?' "

Sandy swallowed the whole lump of breath that was in his

mouth and buried his response in a slug of cider. His eyes never left his cousin's.

"What's that?" Alexander asked, and his voice broke Picard's thoughts. "Magna something."

Stepping back into an element he found more comfortable, Picard answered, "In the early 1500's, King John I was forced to sign the Magna Carta because he was a bad king. It lessened the power of the Crown and shared it with the nobility. The power of the king was no longer absolute."

"And he was a bad king," Jeremiah picked up, "because he was king by blood and not by merit." He looked again at his cousin, evidently finding his stride with his convictions. "Why should anyone be born into power over another? If the government should have say over a man's life, that man should have say over the government. Government is a necessity, but we should accept that it is always excessive and inefficient by its very nature, and should be strictly limited, else we lose control."

Amy Coverman nodded as she placed a bowl of fruit on the table, but she said nothing. Picard looked at her, expecting her to speak up, as the women did in his own time, but obviously this was a discussion for the men. Yet, she didn't seem to disagree with a single one of her husband's words, for she nodded and beamed proudly.

"We pay taxes here," Jeremiah continued, and looked at Picard suddenly, "but no one speaks for us in the British Parliament. Since the Magna Carta, the Crown has shared power with the Houses of Lords and Commons, but no one represents us in the colonies. We are less than commoners here. Men born to their titles are running our lives. We understand the need for taxation, but who goes with our portion to speak for us in Parliament? No one. Our voice is mute. We have no lords here, because no one is 'born higher' than anyone else. Some colonists have been here for centuries. Amy's family, for instance, since Plymouth!" He motioned to his shy wife. "She is an American, not an Englishwoman at all. Yet England would have rule over her. Yet England tells her, 'Lowborn you are and lowborn you will remain, for you have no birthright. You will have a meager existence and then die, because that is what God wants, because the king's right is divine. Accept your place and harbor no ambition.' "

Picard glanced up as Mercy came down the stairs with a pile of folded clothing in her arms. He hadn't even noticed that she'd gone up there, but apparently these were the disguises he and the sailors would wear to keep from being hanged as "spies."

"For the first time," Jeremiah went on, "average men are demanding that no one have arbitrary power. All government power should be answerable to those whom it governs. How can such a thought be forever so foreign to humanity?"

"Only a thousand years or so, Mr. Coverman," Picard pointed out. "A very brief period, once you have a more cosmic perspective."

"But troubling, Lieutenant, troubling. Power should flow from the people on up, not from God to the king and on down."

"God ordains who should rule," Sandy rasped, putting down the bread for which he had no appetite. "There *is* divine right of kings. God blesses the highborn with their place in society."

"Then God has a jester's humor," Jeremiah challenged, "given the shabby judgment of those who call themselves the 'blessed.' "

Sandy looked sharply at him and for a moment seemed about to explode again. Instead, he spoke rather quietly, like a storm rumbling on the horizon.

"This is a waste of breath," he told his cousin. "You can't possibly win a war against the might of Britain. The Colonial militia will be slaughtered. You have no navy . . . what will you do, my dear cousin, when this is over and you are still British? Will you travel into the western wilderness where you cannot be found? Drag these women and this child even farther from civilization until you all die where there are no roads?"

Jeremiah looked with deep regret at his young wife, then

drew a long breath. "No," he said. "Win or lose, I shall not leave Delaware."

"Then do you realize," Sandy asked, his voice finally softening, "that you *will* be executed for treason?"

As Amy Coverman came around the table and took her husband's hand to steady him, Jeremiah beamed at her, then nodded at Sandy. "Yes. I know."

Picard looked at Alexander. The boy had stopped eating too, and was staring at Jeremiah with new realizations. Jeremiah was no scoundrel. All he wanted was possession of his own life.

Beset with confusion, Alexander looked hard at his other cousin, and the hero worship for Sandy Leonfeld got sudden competition.

"Someone will remember," Amy Coverman finished on her husband's behalf.

With those three words, the young wife told her whole story. She believed in her husband, and she was ready to sacrifice him and herself for their beliefs and the future of others yet unknown.

Picard knew he was living with the fruits of their courage. He looked to his side.

Alexander gaped at her, absorbing the depths of her convictions. He glanced at Picard, and tucked his shoulders with shame for what he had said earlier.

"If you persist with these loyalties," Sandy said poignantly to Jeremiah, "then one of us will have to kill the other eventually. I am an officer and a gentleman. I've sworn an oath. I will not betray it."

Jeremiah gazed at him. "You would turn me in?"

"I would have to," Sandy said. "It is my sworn duty."

Not as surprised as Picard would have expected him to be, Jeremiah offered only a shrug. "So be it. I have a duty as well, yet I will compromise mine to make sure you survive. I know how you think, and I hold no malice toward you for it. You have sanctuary here, all of you, until we can find a way to return you to England."

The words caused a great deal of trouble in Sandy

Leonfeld's face, washing away the defiance to some degree. Clearly, he was disturbed that his cousin would protect him, when he had just declared refusal to do the same for Jeremiah.

"What if we can't go back, sir?" Seaman Wollard asked, his food still in his mouth. "If there's no ship—"

Picard looked up, noting the "sir" and knowing that meant him.

"Then we'll find safety in one of the larger cities, Seaman," Picard told him. "Philadelphia or New York."

"We should steal *Justina* back!" Seaman Bennett declared. "We can free the captain and the others!"

"You'll be killed instantly," Jeremiah said. "They're under guard of the Colonial militia. Men who hunt squirrels and foxes. They can kill two of you with one shot."

Picard wondered what Jeremiah really thought—whether the former Briton would allow such action to occur, now that he was loyal to independence. A man's devotion could be stretched only so far.

He thought suddenly of Worf, torn between devotion to his honor and to Grant, devotion to a principle and to a better end to a problem that could affect millions of lives. Odette Khanty seemed like small potatoes on the scale of galactic politics, just part of the muscle-stretching that had gone on in governments for thousands of years, but for most of those thousands of years, there generally weren't lives and lifestyles at stake on the kind of scale as nowadays faced the Federation.

But was that true? He wondered, as he looked at Jeremiah and his wife. These people's struggle seemed almost silly, insignificant, even annoying if Sandy Leonfeld were consulted. Sandy was right—no one thought the colonies could win. In fact, they probably couldn't have, if Britain's willpower hadn't been slackened by preoccupation with France and by selective British blunders at running a war so far and so much time away from their center of command.

Yet, despite its humility, this upstart militia attempt had become the foundation for the most encompassing law and justice in the galaxy. His mind reeled with the breadth of scope of these words, spoken in these small houses, during these long-faded days, and he charged himself never again to forget.

"I must go for a little," Jeremiah said, standing up. "Mercy has your clothing. Your uniforms will be hidden here. With common clothing, you shall be able to walk among the villagers, but be wary, all of you. This is a close community, and strangers can be easily noticed. Stay quiet, go out with greatest caution, and I beg you, do not approach the stable. If you care to go off to Philadelphia or New York, I have no power to stop you. That is for the lieutenant to decide, as your commanding officer."

The men stripped out of their uniform jackets and handed them to Amy Coverman and Aunt Mercy. Picard noted with some concern that Sandy Leonfeld resisted the longest, and it took Amy's plaintive gaze to get his scarlet coat off his shoulders. His being a gentleman came in handy, as he broke down under Amy's comely insistence.

Jeremiah watched the change of officers and soldiers to common townsmen, then reluctantly went to his front door and left. Amy latched the door behind him, then she and Mercy carried the men's uniforms up the narrow stairs.

Except for the little child drowsing at the hearth, Picard and the men were alone for the first time since coming here.

"This is unacceptable!" Midshipman Nightingale seethed. "We're in an enemy camp!" He appealed first to the seamen, who only stared at him, then turned to Picard. "Sir!"

"We'll look around," Picard said evenly. "There will be absolutely no action until and unless I order it. Is that clear?"

The two sailors instantly responded, "Aye, aye, sir."

But the two officers had said nothing, and Picard wasn't opening that door without confirmation of his authority, despite the conditions.

"Mr. Leonfeld?" he prodded. "Mr. Nightingale? Is it clear?"

All eyes shifted to the grenadier. Sandy's golden hair twinkled like stars in the firelight. "Clear, sir," he moped finally.

On that cue, young Edward Nightingale echoed, "Aye, sir."

Picard stood up and indulged in a surge of reckless excitement.

"I'll hold you to it. Because we're going to recapture our ship."

If I were an American, as I am an Englishman, while a foreign troop was landed in my country, I never would lay down my arms—never—never—never!

William Pitt, Earl of Chatham

Chapter Sixteen

"Make fast two!"

"Make fast two, aye!"

"Take up three! Make fast one!"

"Aye, sir! One's fast!"

"Let out four!"

"Four, out!"

"Line three, wake up, man! Take up that line!"

A grind of wood against a dock . . . the slap of water somewhere below . . . the creak of broken yards.

Itchy.

The wool breeches felt as if they had chunks of wood floating in the weave. The cotton shirt lay stiff against Picard's neck and shoulders, beneath a rather loosely fitted linen waistcoat.

He wanted to scratch, but in an impolite place. And he was hurrying along a public street. And there were women.

In fact, it seemed the whole town had turned out at the docks to rejoice at the tying-up of His Majesty's Ship *Justina.*

And a pathetic sight it was. Now, in the dimness of

predawn, Picard could see just how much damage had been sustained by the frigate, such as he had not been able to see at night from a distance. The ship and crew had evidently put up more of a fight than he had been able to measure from the shoreline, for she was brought in with canister-shredded sails hanging torn from smashed yards broken in two or three places, and part of the bow stove in from a cannon ball. Luckily, above the waterline.

Justina was by far the largest ship in this demure marina, including the boats being worked on or converted in the boatyard. All around were craft the size of the spider catchers, as well as utilitarian fishing craft and loading barges. This was a small port, but a working and busy one.

At his right side, Alexander pressed close to Sandy Leonfeld. To his left, Mr. Nightingale and the two deck-hands crowded the wooden fence that funneled down to the two narrow docks. No one said anything as they watched their ship nudge up to the dock, crewed by colonists in common clothing and a half dozen blue-jacketed Delaware Light Infantry militiamen. And their long-barreled rifles. And flintlock pistols. And the cannons on board the ship.

Those uniformed men, and the ones waiting on the shore, Picard guessed, must be of the battalion authorized by the Delaware Committee of Safety, which Sandy had mentioned. Picard had harbored disparagements about them, about how he was of an advanced era and could have vaporized them without a thought if he had a single phaser, but now he looked at them, saw the familiarity with which they handled those long guns, and the strapping, survival build of their bodies. These were neither the coddled aristocracy who lived above the streets of Europe nor the emaciated masses who starved below. These were strong, hardened, frontier-taming Americans, who had taken this wild young seacoast and whipped it into a burgeoning civilization, and who, Picard knew, would do much more in the decades to come.

Take back the ship. It had seemed a bold and simple statement when he'd said it quickly, but now, as he looked down at the forbidding size and complications of the frigate, and the damage they would have to deal with, and the men guarding it, the concept took on afflictions.

And he was curious that the computer hadn't made somebody stop him. This was a holoprogram, of course, not just a book or a play, There were interactive elements. Yet this particular program was also history—real events that had to happen a certain way. He could go back and win Trafalgar for the French if he wanted to, but that couldn't happen in this kind of program. Certain things had to happen. The *Justina* had to be overtaken. Jeremiah and Sandy had to be reunited. Jeremiah had to have changed his loyalties. The program would naturally steer Picard and Alexander in certain directions, or keep them from doing something that absolutely did not occur, like killing Jeremiah or burning the town.

But how far could he push it?

Retaking the ship . . . had it really happened? Was he taking the place of an officer who had orchestrated it? Would they succeed?

Or did the computer even know? Sandy Leonfeld's journals hadn't been this detailed, of course. The essence of conversations had been noted, but not the actual lines. Yet the computer, with its vast billions of bits of data, had reached into history and reconstructed all this. And eyewitness tests with contemporary events had proven time and again that the holodeck computers did their jobs remarkably well. There was good reason to believe just as excellent a job would be done with the past.

So, could he save the ship? Or would he be thwarted? And would this clumsy old program accidentally slice his head off with a slashing headsail sheet?

Whatever the chances, he suspected this program would give him the chance to manipulate events. So be it. He would deal with the risk. Right now he felt like saving something.

"They got their own crew on board," Wollard commented with bald disgust from Picard's side. "On *our* ship!"

"Bloody rebel colonists on a British ship!" Bennett echoed with the same invective, his teeth pressed together.

"Keep quiet, both of you," Picard said. He glanced at the militia soldiers who stood barely paces down the dock from them. "If we're found out, we'll be shot."

"Sir, look!" Wollard gasped, and pointed.

Picard—and all—looked down the fence, beyond three women in Quakerlike dress.

"It's Mr. Pennington!" Nightingale uttered, remembering to hold his voice down, and he stepped away from the fence.

Reaching out quickly, Picard snatched the young officer's arm, then crossed by him. "Wait! I'll speak to him. All of you stay here."

"I'll go with you!" Alexander spoke up, and hurried forward.

Picard almost stopped him, then remembered the reason he was here at all. "Yes, all right."

He stepped away from the small fence and felt the eyes of the men follow him down the wharf. Pennington stood grimly watching the ship being tied to the dock. He was still in uniform and his injured right arm was in a crude sling.

Just before Picard would have reached Pennington's side, Pennington noticed his approach and blinked in shock.

"Mr. Picard!" he choked out. Then he suddenly noticed that Picard was out of uniform, and glanced about almost frantically.

"Mr. Pennington," Picard responded, "are you well, sir?"

"Yes, I'm reasonably well, but how is it that you're here? Have you been captured?" Pennington's voice barely went over a whisper, and he was supremely aware of the people victoriously crowding the dock to watch the big ship being brought in, and of the armed guards.

"We came in under cover of night," Picard explained. "Sergeant Leonfeld has a relative living in the town. We took refuge there. Are you under guard, sir?"

"No, I'm paroled. The crew has been imprisoned, but the officers are on our own recognizance, allowed to walk about if we swear on our honor not to leave the town or take any aggressive actions."

"How many officers are here?"

"Myself, Fourth Lieutenant Frost, Engineer Rollins, and Midshipman Parks."

A chill ran down Picard's arm. "Captain Sobel?"

Pushing up behind him, Alexander peeked around at Pennington. "What about the captain?"

Sympathy crossed Mr. Pennington's face, such as Picard had never witnessed from this man aboard the ship. The first officer looked down at Alexander, then back up. "I'm sorry to report that the captain died as we were rowed in. Rather slowly and grotesquely, I'm pained to say . . . . We lost many men, including the second lieutenant. Nearly a third of the crew, and seven marines, including Marine Captain Newton, who took a ball through the eye. They fought so valiantly, too . . ."

"I know, sir," Picard said gently. "We saw it all."

"Of course, that makes you the ranking nonparoled officer, Picard," Pennington told him. "Any decisions and actions on land or on the ship will be yours to make now."

"I see . . . yes, of course."

Together they watched as the last lines were belayed securely to the dock and the bulky British prize became a spoil of war, her masts dominating the dockscape, her cracked yards draping rags of sail that fluttered fitfully in the Delaware River breeze.

"Do you have the entire landing party with you?" Pennington asked, taking Picard's arm urgently.

"Yes, all accounted for, sir."

Pennington glanced down the dock, saw Nightingale and the two deckhands and Sandy. "Six of you . . . not enough."

"To do what, sir?"

"To take the ship back, of course."

Alexander bolted forward. "There are only six of us, but with all the officers walking around in the open, we could break the crew out of jail! Let's do it!" He pulled at Picard's sleeve. "You said we could *do* it! Mr. Pennington could lead us!"

Pennington's sympathy extended once again as he gazed

down upon the face of hope and defiance. "I couldn't possibly participate, swab."

Instantly shot down, Alexander frowned. "Why not?"

The naval officer dropped a hand on the boy's shoulder. "Because, my boy, I've given my word of honor. I promised not to fight. To break that trust would be second only to treason."

Alexander looked up into the first officer's eyes and tried to speak, but couldn't.

Pennington, who had until now seemed so hardened a seafarer and so stiff an officer, softened into an uncle figure. He saw the trouble in the boy's face, and took time to assuage it.

"The reason we hold to our honor," he said, "is what war would become if we didn't. If I could not be trusted to be paroled, they would no longer parole anyone, and all soldiers captured would be shot, or die in some stinking camp. I give my word to my enemy, and sometime in the future, when he gives his word to me, I will have reason to expect him to keep it."

The boy gazed up at this man whom he clearly admired, and his confusion deepened, just as it was deepening toward Sandy Leonfeld, and Jeremiah Coverman, and his own father.

"But . . . it's war," he protested. "Shouldn't you do anything you can, anything you have to . . . to win?"

Pennington smiled through his pain. "I would sacrifice my life, or any officer's—indeed, the entire crew—rather than break my parole. The cost to everyone of breaking my word is too great to live with. Rules of civility give us our society. There are some things we shall never do, no matter the circumstance. Where there are no rules, in warfare or peace, life becomes chaos. You say it's war . . . yes, of course it is. Exactly my point. Warfare without rules becomes barbarism."

Gazing at Pennington in a comradelike admiration, Picard was glad to see the doubts and troubles in Alexander's eyes. No answer was crystal clear in times like these, and the boy was looking for clarity where he would never find it. The confusion was a good thing.

Pennington patted Alexander once more on the shoulder, and turned. "Picard," he said, "listen to me now—"

"Sir?"

"In case this arm proves fatal, you must report your activities to Mr. Frost. He won't be able to participate, since he's on his honor as well, but he should be informed. He'll be the ranking officer among the prisoners. He's now third lieutenant, and you are now second lieutenant."

"Begging pardon, sir," Picard pointed out, "but if the captain is dead, you're now the captain. I'm now first officer, and Mr. Frost is second."

Pennington eyed him sadly. He evidently knew all that, but had been unable to actually vocalize it.

"Yes," he said reluctantly. "It's very hard for me . . . the captain and all. I've been his first lieutenant since . . ."

He lowered his eyes, pressed his lips tight, rubbed his sore arm, and worked to regain control. A few moments later he summoned the will to continue.

"In any case, Picard, we are the Royal Navy, and we must maintain discipline or we're lost. If I should die, be sure you look after the men. They've done their duty, and they deserve to be treated accordingly."

Picard paused for a moment of admiration for this wounded officer. The injury seemed minor for a man of the twenty-fourth century, but in 1777, not so. These people had no anesthetics, no antibiotics, and they didn't know how wounds got infected, how fever came, or why people died. Families would have six, eight, ten children, some eighteen or twenty children, in hopes that three or four would survive to adulthood and care for each other and their aging parents.

And Mr. Pennington was displaying officer thinking, not worrying about himself, though he might yet face a slow, unpleasant death. He was concerned about how his crew would fare without him.

"You shouldn't be out in the open," Pennington advised. "Go back to your sanctuary and make your plans. Whatever you do, keep control of Seaman Wollard and Gunner Bennett. You know how independent-minded sailing men can be."

"Mmm . . . yes, I do. Take care of yourself, sir."

"Thank you, Picard. Be extremely careful. This circumstance is not good."

"Agreed, sir. Come on, Alexander, quickly."

"Thank God! Where've you been?"

Jeremiah Coverman rushed to them as the gaggle of *Justina*'s crew piled in his narrow front door.

"We wanted to see the ship," Picard explained.

"It's right there at the dock!" Alexander piped in. "It looks a lot bigger than it did from the deck!"

Picard dropped a quieting hand on the boy's shoulder. Alexander glanced at him, and shut up.

"Please, all of you come back in immediately." Jeremiah fanned them into the warm room, glanced out the door, then closed it.

Amy and Mercy were both here, and Mercy's child was now asleep on a blanket near the fire, completely oblivious to the shufflings of the adults. The cabin possessed a bucolic peace that was entirely false.

"My heavens, I thought the worst," Jeremiah gasped, actually out of breath with worry as he turned and reached for Sandy, then abruptly drew back at Sandy's hard expression.

Empathy creased Picard's brow, for Jeremiah was hurt by that hardness. Hurt, yet not ashamed. Somehow that came across in spite of everything.

Picard turned to Nightingale, Wollard and Bennett. "Sit down, gentlemen. Stay quiet."

"Yes, sir," Nightingale responded, and herded the seamen to the table.

Before Picard could even turn back to Jeremiah and Sandy, the door crashed open suddenly, knocking Sandy back a step. A red-haired colonist tumbled in and caught himself on the back of the lambing chair, gasping and clearly in pain. If he'd been standing straight, Picard would figure his height to be just between Sandy and Jeremiah, and he was a lean fellow in his thirties, though at the moment he seemed to feel a hundred years old.

"Patrick!" Jeremiah plunged in to support the newcomer

before he fell over. "Amy, bring water! Good Lord, what happened?"

As Mercy rushed to close the door, Jeremiah and Picard helped the man to the bench beside Edward Nightingale, and Jeremiah stood beside the fellow in such a manner that allowed the exhausted, injured man to lean against him.

"Patrick, what happened to you?" Jeremiah asked again.

"My horse . . . shot out from under me . . . took a ghastly fall."

The man bent forward briefly and shuddered for breath.

"Who is this person?" Sandy asked, somewhat snappishly, as if he had some right to demand anything in another man's home.

Jeremiah shot him a reproving look. "This is Patrick O'Heyne. The man who changed my life." He looked down now at the exhausted visitor. "He's also my dearest friend. Patrick, who shot your horse?"

"Royal Marines!" Patrick O'Heyne grasped Jeremiah by the arm, his words clipped by a clear American accent, without a trace of Jeremiah's lingering British. "There's been a landing! Another Royal Navy ship . . . the bayside sh—"

He coughed suddenly and crumpled against the edge of the table. Amy Coverman supplied a tin cup of water, which O'Heyne gulped down. Then the gentle young girl pressed a moist cloth to a patch of blood on the side of O'Heyne's head.

"Patrick, you're hurt," Jeremiah said solicitously. "You should lie down."

"No time. The ship must've been waiting to rendezvous with the *Justina.* When the frigate failed to appear, they landed a company of redcoats five miles south of our shore. Grenadiers. I was barely ahead of them the whole way! They'll be here any time—we must get word to Colonel Fox to bring the militia. He's billeted three miles northeast of the mill tributary—"

A sudden grip of pain cut him off again, but there was already a flurry of movement in the room.

"I'll go!" Mercy snatched a wool shawl from a hook and flung it around herself.

"Mercy!" Jeremiah snapped. "Nonsense! I would be no gentleman to let you go!"

"You stay and defend our town!" the woman insisted. Don't you worry about me. I've got my guardian angel, and I'm out this door after the Dover Light Infantry!"

And she was gone, the clap of the door as her send-off. Picard got the idea she'd have happily cracked the elbow of anyone who tried to stop her.

Jeremiah helped Patrick O'Heyne get a more controlled drink of water, and looked at his wife. "Amy, take the baby upstairs. Stay in the back of the house, in case balls fly."

"I will, Jeremiah," the girl said, and moved to comply.

As the hem of her skirt licked the stairway corner and she was gone, leaving only men in the keeping room, her husband's friend looked around with clearing eyes at Picard and Sandy, and at the sailors sitting near him, who all wore nondescript clothing of ordinary colonists.

He didn't seem to buy that entirely.

"I don't know these gentlemen," he said, suddenly cautious.

Picard found O'Heyne's instincts impressive, especially since he was seeing these strangers in the home of his best friend and should have trusted that. Yet, he knew better. Interesting.

Perhaps these were suspicious times.

Jeremiah locked eyes briefly with Sandy, and luckily Sandy decided on forbearance.

"This is Sandy Leonfeld, my cousin from Austria," Jeremiah said tensely. "And his traveling companions, Mr. Picard, Mr. Nightingale, Mr. Wollard, Mr. Bennett, and . . . Mr. Picard's son."

"Alexander," the boy spoke up, demanding to have a name if everybody else was going to.

A strained glance passed between Picard and the boy, then nothing more was made of it, especially since they were interrupted by Amy's reappearance; she, too, was now wearing a heavy wool knitted shawl that drowned her shoulders and went almost to her knees.

"What's this?" Jeremiah asked.

"I shall ring the bell for the minutemen. They must man the picket line."

Her husband protested. "But I'm just going."

"You stay with Patrick and make your plans," the brave teenager insisted. "I can certainly ring a chapel bell, can't I? After all, it's my town, too."

And she dashed out the front door, allowing for no protests.

"Wonderful family," Patrick O'Heyne said. Then he suddenly shivered and pressed a hand to his forehead.

"Are you all right, Patrick?" Jeremiah asked.

O'Heyne offered him a smile. "Recovering. I've bruised my hip notably . . . a knee, my shoulder, and I wisely stopped my fall by striking a tree with my ribs."

"And your head is bleeding, Mr. O'Heyne," Picard pointed out.

The redheaded man looked up with something like gratitude. "Is it? Well, it's only my head. If the redcoats take the Station, I won't have long need of it."

Evidently, Picard's British accent was common enough among patriots, for O'Heyne took no particular note.

Picard said passively, "Then you'd better learn to think from your knee, because the British are fiercely organized warriors."

He truly meant nothing but to voice his admiration for the action he saw on board the *Justina,* but Patrick O'Heyne noted something else about those words, and about all these strangers in the room.

O'Heyne blinked around at the disguised seamen, then finally back around to Sandy, then back to Picard. "Sir . . . how come you to be here? And how do you know Jeremiah?"

"Patrick," Jeremiah uttered. "Please . . . things are somewhat complicated this morning."

Brushing his tousled red hair out of his eyes, O'Heyne scanned Picard and Sandy, evidently taking them for being the ones in charge, since they were standing and the others seated. He gestured at Sandy, but looked at Jeremiah. "Your cousin?"

"Yes," Jeremiah confirmed. "Yes, he's my cousin. We grew up together."

"Well, then." O'Heyne looked at Picard and Sandy. "I'm glad these are your relatives, Jeremiah, else we would have some tension here, I think, wouldn't we?"

He coughed briefly, winced, then surveyed Wollard, Bennett, Nightingale, and Alexander with a keen and experienced eye. After a moment of sheepish, tense glances from those men back to him, O'Heyne looked once again at Sandy and Picard.

"The *Justina?"* he asked.

"Yes," Picard flatly answered.

"The warping party?"

"Yes."

"And you are an officer?"

"Yes. Mr. Leonfeld is sergeant of the grenadiers."

He didn't mention that the captain of the marines was dead now, giving Sandy that rank. He just didn't want to get into it, or offer Sandy a rank technically higher than his own. Not yet, anyway.

"Mmm . . ." O'Heyne stood up, pondering the problem. After a moment he said, "Jeremiah, you're not thinking. Don't you know what you've done to these men by taking them out of their uniforms? If they're discovered out of uniform by the Dover Infantry and found to be British, they won't simply be impounded as prisoners of war. They'll be hanged as spies. Like criminals. That's certainly no way for a soldier to die, is it? In the enemy's clothing?"

Jeremiah stared at him, then looked at the simple breeches, shirts, and jackets he had supplied his guests.

"Oh, my . . . I didn't think of that," he said, his face suddenly flushed.

"Gentlemen," O'Heyne addressed, "if you know what's good for you, you'll put your uniforms back on and go out and get killed. Otherwise, you'll go out there and pretend to be colonists until a chance comes to turn yourselves over to the King's men. I put you on your honor not to shoot anyone in the back, or without identifying yourselves."

Sandy Leonfeld puffed up with noble insult. "No man

here will shoot anyone in the back, sir. We are not brutes, you know."

"I know," O'Heyne said. "I've been to England." He paused, surveyed all the men, and added, "We're not that different."

Quite unexpectedly, he reached out a welcoming hand to the sergeant, whom he now knew to be his sworn enemy.

Sandy did not comply right away, but took several strained seconds before he accepted the gesture. Beside O'Heyne, Jeremiah quaked with relief.

Picard tucked back a smile as he appreciated the sight of the two powerful young adversaries, each well-armed with conviction, standing only a pace from each other, neither really knowing what to do next to keep the situation from exploding.

At once, Sandy stepped back and narrowed his eyes as if something had struck him. He pointed with discovery at Jeremiah's friend. "Patrick O'Heyne . . ."

"Yes?"

"Patrick Harper O'Heyne? Of the Liverpool-New York Convoy Company?"

"Yes, thank you. My brother and myself."

"Sir, we—" Sandy said on a gasp, "we have met before!"

Alexander stepped up to Picard's side, overcome by his surprise. "You two know each other?"

"Evidently," O'Heyne said. "Where might that meeting have happened, Mr. Leonfeld?"

The color rose in Sandy's face. "At . . . the court of King George, sir."

"Oh—you must mean the Royal birthday banquet."

"I'm . . . I must mean that, sir."

O'Heyne smiled. "Well, in that case, it's mighty pleasant to meet again, Mr. Leonfeld. I'm sorry for the circumstances—"

He swayed with the dizziness brought on by his head wound, caught himself on the edge of the table, and Jeremiah reached out and clasped his arm to steady him, and Picard caught the other one.

"Patrick, you really ought to rest."

"We'll have eternity to rest soon enough, Jeremiah." O'Heyne regained control through some effort, gave his friend a not-very-convincing pat of comfort. Then, favoring his injured knee and hip, he stepped to a cabinet on the wall and opened it with the familiarity of one who indeed nearly lived here.

From the cabinet he drew four American muzzle-loading rifles, powder horns, bullet pouches and ramrods, and relayed two of the rifles to Jeremiah.

Then he turned to Sandy and Picard. "Do I have your word of honor that, until the redcoats breach our picket line, you'll take no action against any patriot who is honorably fighting for his cause?"

Sandy visibly shuddered, and Midshipman Nightingale's eyes were wide as eggs. The two seamen stood up, and turmoil showed clearly in their faces, but, being seamen, they would follow the word of their commanding officer—who was now First Lieutenant Picard.

Suddenly everyone was looking at him.

For the sake of gamesmanship, he said, "Agreed."

He signed the other men up with a stern glance, and noted that they didn't like his compliance.

"However, Mr. O'Heyne," he said, "we are still men of the Royal Navy. There will come a moment when that will play itself out. Until then, we will not take any dishonorable action against anyone who does not know our identity. Fair enough?"

"Does that include us?" O'Heyne said with a canny smile, and handed Picard an American musket. "In that case, unless you mean to slaughter us here and now, Jeremiah and I have a town to defend. In all fairness, it's no less than you would do. I invite you to come with us and see what we're all about."

Limping toward the door, he opened it for Jeremiah, whose lingering gaze on Sandy was simply heartwrenching. O'Heyne gave him time, but finally, torn and tortured, Jeremiah hurried out the door.

O'Heyne made good on his belief of Picard's promise, and dared turn his back to the Royal Navy men as he, too, went out of the cabin.

Picard looked down at the American rifle in his hands and luxuriated in the balance and weight of the classic weapon. Beautiful! Imagine actually firing it!

He turned a glinting eye to his crew.

"Well, men?" he prodded.

"I'm uneasy with our duty, sir," Sandy said, "being in the company of colonists and even protected by them . . . trusted by them . . ."

"Nonsense!" Midshipman Nightingale said. "There's a skirmish coming! We can't stand by, sir!"

"We can do terrible damage from this side of the line," Bennett spoke up. "I'm a gunner!"

"Not without orders, you won't," Picard pointed out. "We made an agreement."

"You made it," Bennett shot back.

Picard reached out with all the piled-up frustration of both his man-of-war and his starship, and grasped Bennett by the black neckerchief the sailor wore.

"I *am* you, seaman," he clarified. "Don't forget it."

Bennett leaned back, sneered, but did not dare react physically to his senior officer.

Sandy put out a hand. "And I refuse to fire at any man's blind side, even my enemy's. Nor will I fire at any man of King George's military under any condition."

Throwing Bennett off and gripping the American rifle in both hands, Picard looked at him. "Where does that put you, Sergeant?"

Sandy Leonfeld paused, a dozen emotions passing through his eyes. For the first time Picard saw flaming doubt rise, and the shield of aristocratic superiority grow thinner.

Picard didn't wait for an answer. He stepped to a corner and scooped up Sandy's British-issue rifle and handed it to him, then turned to grasp Alexander by one arm.

"Oh, what the devil," he said. "Let's go out and see what happens. After all, we've been invited."

Chapter Seventeen

"DATA, YOU ALMOST READY?"

"Yes, sir. The shuttlecraft is hidden in the emission blind of an orbital processing station, and the helm is on automatic hover outside of orbit range. All broadcast systems are heavy-duty to avoid overload, and satellite connections are tied in and operating."

"Good. Doctor? Ready?"

"Ready. Listening devices sewn into my cuffs—right here in the lace—"

"Perfect. I can barely see them."

"And here's the camera."

"That's huge."

"It's the width of two human hairs."

"But it's visible, is what I mean."

Worf listened to the conversation between Riker, Data, and Beverly Crusher, and had to shudder down a distasteful fit of nerves about this whole mission. He was determined to get Grant, but the captain's idea of taking shipmates along did not sit well. Four persons could not hide as well as one, could not effect stealth, and quadrupled the risks for great loss. These people's lives were in his hands, and their deaths would be on his conscience.

Still, he was also deeply moved by their willingness to go after a Federation operative whom they didn't even know and whose cover had been blown. Many would consider that too much risk for very little gain, and they would be right. All talk of operatives, partners, missions, and official business was thinning out. They were now doing all this just to get his friend back.

He wanted to thank them, to turn warmly and display his gratitude for their devotion. Somehow that desire kept turning inward each time it began to surface. How much could one man bottle up?

"Sir," he turned to Riker, disturbed by what he had heard the first officer say to the doctor. "You also have audio and video devices on—you must both have them on your persons. I know how Ugulan thinks."

Riker smiled reassuringly. "I've got mine. Right here." He plucked at a button on his Sindikash city-style buffalo-hide jacket. "And here's the audio." He pointed at a fingernail, which had a thin layer of gloss upon it. Virtually invisible.

Beverly Crusher palmed her red hair back and tied it out of the way. "I hope this goes the way you plan, Worf. Khanty had enough spies everywhere that she knew where two unidentified witnesses were. What are the chances she'll know we're coming?"

"Pretty darned good," Riker filled in.

Worf sighed. "This is too dangerous."

Riker gripped his arm. "Don't worry. It'll just distract you."

"The situation is deadly. We can die."

"Decision's been made."

Feeling his bones rumble, Worf knew Riker was forcing him to shift back into obey-the-order mode just long enough to get him to stop hesitating.

"Aye, sir," he complied, irritated.

"Data?" Riker strode away from Worf, somehow moving casually despite the cramped quarters of the shuttlecraft cockpit.

"Ready to beam down anytime you wish, sir," the android said, and looked up. "Coordinates are set for the central government compound, outside the holding cell area."

"Did you try to beam us directly into the cell?"

"I found those coordinates, sir, but we have no way of knowing which specific cell Mr. Grant is in. Also, the cells have scrambler shields around them. We might materialize, but without most of our extremities."

"Well, I'd like to keep my extremities. So we'll just break in. Let me have a look at you, Data."

Data came to his feet and turned to face them. He wore a dark gray double-breasted vest that was made of corduroy, a drover's yellow embroidered bandana, like the kind Sindikash wives and sweethearts made for their men before the annual bison drive, and a simple brown shirt and trousers. The most remarkable change, however, was to his skin and eyes. A prosthetic covering had been fitted to his face and hands, so hair-thin and sensitive that it was completely indistinguishable from real human skin. He even looked a little tan. His amber eyes were now blue. His lips had some color for a change, and he had eyebrows.

"You look like my little brother," Riker said with a grin of satisfaction.

"I rather enjoy the appearance," Data mentioned. "Except that the prosthetic loses its integrity with time and begins to shrink."

"Not a bad way to lose weight. Worf, you ready to do this?"

"No, sir."

"Good. Let's beam down."

"Oh, my God . . ."

Beverly Crusher was a physician, and not easy to shock. Worf knew she was being shocked not by the sight of a mutilated human form, but by the thoughts of what had mutilated that form and who could have done it.

Before them, in the cell surrounded by stone walls and with crisscrossed metal grids in front, Ross Grant's body hung from a mattress cord tied to a light fixture. He was as still as drying meat. His head was tilted slightly to one side, his scorched hands splayed in the final muscle spasm and frozen that way.

Crusher pushed past Worf, who could no longer make himself move, though adrenaline still ran hot in him from their breaking into the jail. Fortunately, jails were arranged to keep people from breaking out, not the other way around.

Behind Worf, Riker scanned quickly for recording devices. "Nothing here," he said. His voice cracked. "We can talk."

The doctor was already running her medical scanner along Grant's body, and somehow the sight of that jarred Worf into movement. He wrapped his arms around Grant and took the weight off the cord around the neck until Crusher untied the cord.

Worf lowered Grant's body to the cool floor, then stood back to absorb what he saw before him. What could he say to Alexander? How could he tell his son that he had let this happen?

Grant had been stripped down to his undershirt and trousers. The trousers were slashed to the knees, exposing his legs. His arms had been slashed, too, as if the skin were fabric.

The slash wounds had been allowed to bleed freely until the blood caked on his body and clothing, then later cauterized. There were burns. Deep burns that still smoldered. Some of the wounds were coagulated. Others were still moist. This had gone on for hours upon hours.

Of the freshest wounds were the two that had gouged out Grant's gentle eyes.

The pain in Crusher's face as she examined the body was enough to smash the strongest constitution. She wasn't telling Worf anything, but she knew.

And from her expression and the condition of the body, Worf knew, too. Grant had not died of the wounds. Not even the eyes. From the swollen smear that ringed his neck, they had finished him slowly, drawing him gradually upward instead of putting him high and kicking something out from under him. There had been no quick snap of the neck. There had been no hint of mercy.

"Time of death," Crusher struggled, "about two hours ago. Maybe a little longer. Some of these cut wounds have been cauterized, as if they didn't want him to bleed to death or lose consciousness too soon. Both feet are broken . . . his clavicle is cracked. There's no brain damage. His groin is badly burned. So are his fingers and toes. Cause of death . . . asphyxiation."

She glanced up at Worf's narrowed eyes.

He felt her gaze, her pity. His arms and legs were suddenly double their normal weight. A thousand bitter emotions piled upon him, coupled with the burden he now put upon his shipmates, for they wanted to give him comfort, and he would have none. Of all the challenges he had ever faced and stemmed in his life of struggle for identity and cause, never before had he been so completely afraid as he was of this—facing his twelve-year-old son.

He stared at the swollen body of Ross Grant. What had the last hour been like? Had Grant waited for him to come? Had he found sustaining courage in the faith that Worf would show up in time?

"They had to kill him," Worf ground out. His voice was rough as sandpaper. "He would not die from their torture. He made them kill him. He was more courageous than I ever . . . imagined."

"Worf, I'm so very sorry," Crusher murmured. Her medical distance suffered as she accepted that horrible punishment of not being able to do anything for her patient.

Worf shook himself to movement. His cold fingers dug into the hem of Grant's T-shirt. In a fit of anger, he tore the hem open, fished through the fabric, and drew out a single thread with a tiny bead tied to one end. It looked like all the other threads in Grant's clothing, except that on close examination there was a faint satin sheen.

"Grant organized all his findings and committed them to this metallic thread. He coordinated dates and facts, statements, shipping orders and times, signatures on bills of lading and manifests, locations of various Rogues at key moments before, during, and after suspicious incidents, and a thousand bits of circumstantial evidence against Mrs. Khanty."

They all looked at the single foot-long thread as if it were about to sing.

"He was no fighter," Worf went on tightly. "He was no soldier. He had never trained to resist torture. Yet here this is in my hands. He never gave it up. He knew I would retrieve it. He expected . . . me . . . to come back."

Riker stepped to him. "Worf, don't do this. This isn't your fault. It's Odette Khanty's fault. Don't get that mixed up."

His innards shriveling, Worf bottled up a need to spit in Riker's face and drive those words back. Not his fault?

"He died because of me. I kept my honor, but he paid the price."

Shuddering, Worf gazed down at the body of his brave, dead friend, and his heart snagged.

He stuffed the critical thread into Beverly Crusher's hands, and noted peripherally that she quickly fed it into her tied-back hair. Once that was done, Worf plowed between Riker and Crusher and out of the cell.

"Worf!" Riker called after him, but the warning had no effect.

Five seconds later Worf was back, with a terrorized Burkal City police lieutenant in his claws. He drove the policeman before him into the cell and bent the man over Grant's body.

"Dead!" Worf roared.

"I know . . . I know he's dead," the policeman quivered.

"Why was he still hanging there so long after he died?"

"There's—there's an investigation underway—"

"You mean there's a cover-up being developed! Who did this to him!"

Barely able to move his head because of Worf's unkind grip on the base of his neck, the policeman glanced at Riker and Crusher. "He did it to himself."

"He inflicted these burns on himself?" Crusher shot back. "He gouged out his own eyes? You've got to be kidding!"

"I—I—he did it to himself. That's what's on the report. He hanged himself."

"You tell the *truth!"* Worf shrieked in the policeman's ear, reaching his breaking-somebody's-neck point.

"It's—look—" The policeman raised his hands and winced. "Look, it's suicide. It's in the report."

"What about all these wounds!"

"They're . . ." The policeman grimaced. ". . . self-inflicted."

"Curse you!" Worf shook the man violently.

"Worf, let go of him." Riker stepped forward and took the rattled policeman away from Worf.

He must have seen something that Worf, through his rage, could not see. As the policeman looked at the body, then up again, Worf found it in himself to notice that there were tears in the man's eyes.

The officer's voice was thin and miserable. "I can only tell you . . . what's in the report. Sorry."

"Where is Lieutenant Stoner?" Worf demanded.

The policeman sighed hard. "They say he didn't show up for work this morning."

Then the man shrugged.

"When the truth comes out," Worf threatened, "I will see you again."

Obviously more afraid of something else than he was of Worf, the policeman looked at him firmly now and with great sympathy. "If I were you, I'd worry about seeing morning."

He reached into his pocket and pulled out a plum-sized device that was flashing a blue and red pattern of lights. Worf recognized it—the policeman had notified the Rogues. Understanding boiled through the anger. The policeman had no choice.

"Sorry," the man said again. "I got four kids."

"Get out!" Worf thundered.

"Going." The policeman veered for the cell door, hurried down the narrow stone corridor, and disappeared.

"Poor guy," Riker uttered.

Though there was no charity in Worf's heart, he felt for the first time Grant's intense passion to cure this planet for the sake of its people, and not just for the integrity of the Federation as a whole. His knees and elbows trembled with the strain of containing his rage.

Contain it? Why!

He swung about and rammed his fist into the wall.

The wall cracked. Plaster clattered to the cold floor.

Riker eyed him sympathetically. "Don't do that again. You'll hurt yourself."

"I will hurt *someone!*"

From the corridor outside the cell, a voice was there to answer.

"Hurt *me.*"

The Starfleet team swung full about and found themselves staring down the phasers of Ugulan, Goric, Tyro, Mortash, and four other Rogues whose names Worf had never bothered to learn.

Ugulan stood in the forefront, with an expression of bizarre pleasure on his harsh face. He was getting revenge on Worf, and he liked that. Simple pleasures.

"Search them," he snarled, drawing each word out twice as long as it needed to be.

Mortified at the arrival of dishonorable Klingons in the presence of his Starfleet crewmates, Worf shuddered and bottled up a surge of insane rage. He hadn't anticipated this reaction—his stomach heaved as Riker, Crusher, and Data were forced to look into the faces of these bottom feeders. It was one thing to face them alone, but this—

Not yet . . . not yet . . .

Tyro, Mortash, Goric, and one other came forward, dividing among the four Starfleeters. They each pulled out a scanning device, far more advanced than most technology on Sindikash, and within seconds they had possession of Crusher's recording devices—both of them—and Riker's audio fingernail. Another few seconds' searching gave up Riker's video button.

At the same time, Mortash began locating and scooping up their hidden palm phasers. "Starfleet issue," he said.

"Naturally," Ugulan agreed. He stepped to Riker and surveyed him up and down. "Who are you?"

Riker lifted his chin and met Ugulan's glower with an aloof courage. "Kirk. James Kirk."

Ugulan sneered. "Starfleet?"

"Iowa Regional Militia."

Confused, Ugulan was interrupted as the recording

equipment Riker and Crusher had carried was gathered by the Rogues and handed over to him. He immediately rumbled up to Data and surveyed his face disapprovingly.

"What about this one?"

"Nothing on that one," Tyro said, clearly perplexed. "Why would those two have something and this one have nothing?"

"Is he stupid?" Ugulan suggested, pushing his face close to Data's. "Or is he here for something else? Well, skinny?"

Data glanced at Worf and tried to lean away from Ugulan, but said nothing.

"Where are you going?" Ugulan's hand flashed to Data's throat and dragged him closer. "You can go exactly nowhere. To make sure you go nowhere, I think you need a leash."

He backed Data up against the wall. At the same instant, Tyro and two other Rogues shoved their phasers into Riker's ribs and crammed both him and Crusher against the cell's forward grid.

Worf raised both his arms at the same time, in two directions. He drove his elbow into Mortash's chin and his other fist into another Klingon's teeth.

They both went down, but three more Rogues were on him, then suddenly a fourth. A fifth.

And he was held. They wasted no time with him, but instantly pressed him to the cell grid and tied his hands far out at his sides. He strained and yanked, but they had him.

And they had Riker and Crusher pinned on the other side of the front grid. He knew what was happening—they were being positioned as an audience.

Ugulan humphed in satisfaction and turned again to Data, then made a sharp gesture that brought Mortash and Goric to his sides, with a cord.

This cord was braided, and evidently this time they didn't care whether appearances implied that the rope had come from somewhere inside the cell. Their confidence was peaking. They believed they couldn't be caught, for their only real threats were now at their phaserpoints.

Ugulan tugged at Data's neckerchief until it came off. He stuffed it into his belt. Mortash and Goric clasped Data's arms while Ugulan slipped a noose around Data's neck, then tossed the other end through the metal ceiling grid.

"No!" Crusher shouted. She tried to bolt forward, and endured a fierce throttling until she fell back. Riker tried to protect her, and fielded a vicious slug.

Worf quaked and wanted to roar, but he knew that would only encourage Ugulan. He could only watch, as he was meant to, as the noose tightened around Data's throat. Data slipped backward, tripped over the cot, and fell. The force of his fall constricted his throat and he clawed at the cord, his mouth going wide on a gasp. He tried to get his legs back under him, but tripped again, and now Ugulan himself enjoyed heaving back on the tied end of the rope.

"Not again!" Riker shouted. "Isn't Grant enough for you in one day? You can't do that to him!"

"No?" Ugulan shook his head. "Are you sure? Is it 'inhuman'?"

He heaved harder. Data's feet toed at the floor as he was hoisted beyond reach. He kicked frantically, trying to knock Ugulan away from the rope, but there was no doing it.

His kicking made his body jerk back and forth in a corkscrew motion. His fingers dug at the cord around his neck. He expelled breath after breath, but could suck none in.

"See what happens to someone who fails to gain our trust?" Ugulan said. "All of you will follow Skinny, and we will have more entertainment with each of you until we get to the traitor."

Worf gritted his teeth and felt his lips peel back at Ugulan's glance.

Halfway to the ceiling now, Data kicked more frantically, forcing Mortash and Goric to step away from the flailing boots. Data's throat gurgled and gagged, and the terrible sounds washed through the cell, torturing his shipmates and delighting the Rogues.

Disgusted, Worf took in a shiver of shame that they were so completely enjoying themselves, and understood that this was part of the reason they stayed with Odette Khanty. Not just the power or the promise of influence, but the bloodlust.

Hideous. Inexcusable. His sudden distaste surprised him, for it extended not just to these particular bandits, but to all Klingons, for it was giving in to their Klingon nature that made them so sadistic. Suddenly he wanted nothing to do with them. He wanted nothing in common with them. He did not want even to look like them.

And he wanted to rush back to the ship and yank Alexander out of that Day of Honor ritual. His shame itched all over his body.

He realized his eyes were fixed on Data again—just in the last second. Just in time to hear Data gag out one whimpering gasp and see him finally fall limp. His eyes lost focus, and glazed over.

"Oh, no . . . oh, no," Beverly Crusher moaned, and sank to her knees.

Riker drove his shoulder into Tyro's chest, but was hammered back by Mortash's enormous fists. When Riker recovered and looked slowly up again, his lip was bleeding, and his cheekbone bore a purpling bruise.

Worf lashed out a foot at Ugulan, but the Rogue easily sidestepped. Ugulan teased him with a laugh, and pointed at Data's sagging body.

"The other one took longer," he crowed, swinging his gesture around to where Grant's sorry corpse lay on the floor. "This one is even more of a child, to go so fast. This one's not drooling. I like it when they drool."

"Pig!" Worf snarled. "Coward!"

"Yes," Ugulan said. He turned to Riker and Crusher, as if trying to choose who would be next.

Breath came and went in heaves from Worf's chest. Had he timed things wrong? Had he miscalculated? A few minutes would be critical.

Seconds began to tick by as Ugulan measured Riker and Crusher on his enjoyment meter. Would a woman be more fun to torture? Or would it be more fun to watch a woman's reaction as a handsome man like Riker was tortured?

Worf knew he was meant to see the deaths of all his friends before he, too, would have his skin peeled off.

Before Ugulan could make his choice, a commotion at the

end of the dark corridor drew the attention of all, and in strode Odette Khanty with two more Rogues in attendance.

That made . . . ten.

Mrs. Khanty strode into the cell as easily as a woman entering church. She wore a salmon-colored business suit with a Sindikash embroidered silk scarf at her collar, and she looked entirely out of place among the rampart of Rogues around her. On her arm was a black armband with a noticeable purple orchid—a real one—affixed to it, and she wore a polite black velvet hat with a lace swirl of some kind. Mourning garb. Just enough to remind everyone who saw her.

Without saying a word, she opened a hand, palm up. Ugulan delivered the tiny listening and video devices to her and she looked at them with a skilled eye. "This is the best Starfleet could do?" She looked up at Worf. "These are the people you're loyal to, and they couldn't do better than this? I've seen this kind of thing on Cardassian smugglers."

She handed the tiny pile over to one of the Rogues, then snapped her fingers. Another Rogue handed her a metal stick, about a meter long with a bulbous handle, and she pressed a switch with her thumb. She didn't look at Worf, but she moved toward him.

"All of you, pay attention," she said. "so nobody will ever do this to me again. I want—"

She paused, noticing Data's pathetic body hanging from the cord.

"That's not the same one," she said.

"No," Ugulan told her. "Grant is behind you."

She looked around, saw Grant's body on the floor, and seemed satisfied just that easily.

Once again she looked at the metallic stick.

"This is a *T'kalla* prod," she said. "It's stronger than a cattle prod. From Alak IV. We use it on our bison because buffalo fur is so thick. Almost as thick as your hide, Worf."

Abruptly, she swung the stick around and thrust it into Worf's rib cage.

Electrical shock ripped through his body, choking out a grunt and crackling through the metal grid behind him.

And his brain began to fry.

Chapter Eighteen

EVEN WHEN MRS. KHANTY took the stick away, the electricity snapped and sizzled through Worf another two or three eternities.

He coughed and fought, but only when he shuddered down the last surge and his gasping steadied did Mrs. Khanty speak again.

"Now pay attention" she said, glancing around at the ten Rogues. "The parts of his body will never be found. You think you have imagination? Think you're scary? Wait until you see what I do with this man."

Now she turned to Worf again.

"The election is tomorrow, you know. Your plan backfired. People on this pissant planet are believing that it was a Starfleet plot to kill my husband. Before this, I stood a chance of losing the election. If that happened, my empire would collapse. But, thanks to you and your dead friend over there, I'm going to sweep it. My polls are higher than ever. Everything you wanted to stop is going to happen. All because you betrayed me."

"I never betrayed you," Worf choked. "You never deserved my loyalty. You never had it. You showed no loyalty to anyone. Not the people, not the children, not even your husband."

She twisted the handle of the buffalo prod, and the instrument began a faint hum. She had powered it up.

She reached out and poked him again with the prod. *Dzzzzt—*

Electricity bolted through Worf even more jarringly than before, and sent him crashing against the grid. Mrs. Khanty watched and waited for the snapping and sizzling to die down, until Worf was groaning and gasping.

As he gasped, she said, "My husband was a patsy. He couldn't make a decision. He was a wind sock. Whatever the day demanded. His goals were a mile wide and an inch deep. I was the only one who had a vision."

"You . . . had . . . ambition," Worf coughed, "not vision."

She clicked the buffalo prod up another grade until the rod hummed angrily, then zapped him again, this time in the hollow of his shoulder.

Dzzzzzzaaat—

The surge was blinding. He stiffened in agony, and his entire side went numb. When she drew the prod back, Worf sagged and began twitching uncontrollably. In his periphery he saw Riker and Crusher gazing at him with tortured eyes, and he hoped they would keep quiet. He knew what he was absorbing, and knew their human frames would be blown to rags with very little of this.

Looking at the Rogues again, she said, "There's got to be buffalo pee in the water on this colony. I dress like Bo-Peep and tell them there's no evidence, and they think it's the same as saying I didn't do anything. And thanks to Worf, no matter how much I control, no matter who I kill for the next ten years, I'll be able to blame it on Starfleet. Not everybody's as hard to kill as my husband. It took two tries to finally get rid of him."

Beverly Crusher peered around Mortash's considerable shoulder. "You mean you're the one who attempted to kill your husband the first time?"

"With my own lily-white hands," Khanty said. "Only he

didn't have the common courtesy to die. I finally had to finish him, and Worf and Grant were very polite to take the blame. And these colonial yokels will swallow it. I don't know what to do to thank you, Worf. So I'll kill you."

"Betrayer," Worf rasped. "Conscience does not confuse you. You are a public hack. Any lie that advances you is fair play. Simple justice never impedes you. How long can you keep control that way? You can not even control me. Remember, you do not have *my* Oath of Sto'Vokor.

"These people . . ." Worf continued, "trusted you . . . you could have helped build a . . . fine community . . . here."

"Here? You think I'm spending the rest of my life with manure on my shoes? This dump is a stepping-stone."

Mrs. Khanty clicked the buffalo prod up another setting. Then another, until it hummed and actually sparked. Another click or two and it would easily become a shuttlecraft prod.

"I've ordered thousands of deaths, but I've only done two with my own hands. My husband, and now you."

She turned to Worf and moved closer, as if sizing him up. Even the Rogues were tight with nervousness and empathy. Ugulan had stepped away—well away.

Interesting way to die. Prodded to death. What would that look like on his service record?

She surveyed him as if trying to decide which part of his body would be more fun to poke with that heartless device, and he knew she was giving him time to think about what was coming. Him, and the Rogues.

She raised the prod, and stepped back to give herself room to use it—

"Wait!" Riker called.

Mrs. Khanty looked at him. "Wait for what?"

The first officer made a motion at the wall-mounted observation screen just outside the cell. "You might want to turn that on."

"That will do you no good!" Ugulan shouted. "That one is a security display monitor, not a recording monitor, fool."

"Why don't you see if there's anything to display?" Riker suggested.

Crusher gave Khanty a thick woman-to-woman look and added, "I think there is."

Khanty's expression lost its smugness. She gestured to Goric. "Turn it on."

Ugulan swung to her. "That monitor cannot possibly record anything you've said. It has no way of doing that!"

"Turn it on!" Khanty roared.

Goric plowed out of the cell. Every body in the place was tense now, sensing complication. Goric pounded the monitor control until it came on.

A fritzing picture jumped to life, fielding some interference, and struggled to clarify itself. The sound crackled, then settled into a voice.

"There's got to be buffalo pee in the water on this colony. I dress like Bo-Peep and tell them there's no evidence, and they think it's the same as saying I didn't do anything. And thanks to Worf, no matter how much I control, no matter who I kill for the next ten years, I'll be able to blame it on Starfleet. Not everybody's as hard to kill as my husband. It took two tries to finally get rid of him."

"You mean you're the one who attempted to kill your husband the first time?"

"With my own lily-white hands. Only he didn't have the common courtesy to die. I finally had to finish him, and Worf and Grant were very polite to take the blame. And these colonial yokels will swallow it. I don't know what to do to thank you, Worf. So I'll kill you."

The picture fritzed again, shifted, and settled again, this time on a close-up of Mrs. Khanty as she turned to Worf.

"I've ordered thousands of deaths, but I've only done two with my own hands. My husband, and now you."

The Rogues stared and stared, utterly stunned and no doubt running over in their minds how this could possibly be happening.

"It is being broadcast colonywide," Worf shuddered out. "All the airwaves have been pirated. The whole planet has been watching you."

"How!" Khanty shrieked. "It's a trick! This is a trick! How could this happen!"

Abruptly, a hand clamped on her wrist and held her in place. She automatically tried to wrench away, but she was held as tightly as Worf was to the grid. She looked up, and sucked in a hard breath. She was staring up into Data's bright, living eyes and his pain-free face.

"You are being most discourteous, madam," Data said blandly. "Perhaps a pause to regain composure would serve us all."

The Rogues gawked in shock, unable even to swing their phasers around before Mrs. Khanty reacted.

She howled and twisted the buffalo prod upward toward Data's face.

Though he was still hanging and without leverage, he managed to crank his face away from her just as the prod veered toward his eyes. The prod struck his vest lapel, zapped brightly, and set the vest instantly on fire in a hail of sparks. The fabric enjoyed burning, and flames quickly swept the front of Data's clothing. Still, he did not let go of Odette Khanty's wrist.

Terrorized, the woman transferred the rod to her other hand and swung it wildly, striking Tyro with a numbing jolt of electricity and setting him on fire, too. He slammed backward, numb and convulsing. He tumbled into two other Rogues, who also rolled into flames and scrambled away, trying to put out their clothing.

Riker blew into action, pulling from his belt a simple shielded stunner, unscannable, and driving it into Mortash's sternum. The big Klingon stared at his body, looked at Riker, and clawed at the air. Riker instantly took possession of Mortash's phaser and started dropping Rogues when he could get a clear shot.

Unfortunately, that wasn't easy. The small cell burst into a flurry of movement. Under cover of that movement, Crusher pulled out a medical injection device—smaller than the usual sickbay version—and lanced another Rogue in the throat. He knocked her to the ground, then dropped like a sandbag, unconscious. As another Rogue sprung after

Riker, Crusher got that one, too, with an injection directly in the face.

How many was that? Worf tried to clear his head. How many Rogues were left standing?

Data raised his other hand and tried to pat out the flames on his clothing. The heat was becoming intense enough for Worf to feel it several steps away, and Data wouldn't be able to see through the fire, which might also damage the delicate camera mechanisms in his eyes.

The prosthetic sheath on his face was now melting, his human disguise curling like parchment, revealing the golden android skin beneath. His special contact lenses were fading, spreading wide and losing their integrity, revealing his catlike amber eyes. Those eyes sta ed down at Odette Khanty.

Mrs. Khanty struggled insanely, but now looked up at the creature holding her wrist in his iron clamp and saw the corpse becoming a wraith. She pulled back and screamed out her horror.

At the metal grid, Worf yanked and strained, but could not break the cords that bound his wrists. "Data!" he shouted.

Data slapped at his clothing, and decided to sacrifice his grip on Odette Khanty long enough to reach up and rip the noose off his neck. He dropped to the ground, distracted for a fraction of a second.

During that instant, Odette Khanty swung her buffalo prod in a great arc, snapping and setting fire to another Rogue, and Crusher's lace sleeve, then bolting for the corridor. She slammed into the opposite wall, just under the monitor.

"Here? You think I'm spending the rest of my life with manure on my shoes? This dump is a stepping-stone."

She swung the prod upward and smashed the viewscreen. Sparks erupted in a violent display that blanketed half the corridor, and in that fog of fireworks, she disappeared.

"Data!" Worf howled again, this time over the whine of Riker's careful phaser shot.

"Coming," Data said evenly. Plowing over the fallen

Rogues, he snapped Worf's braided bonds as if they were shoelaces.

As Worf struggled to regain control over his numb legs, Data whirled on the remaining Rogues and drove two of them into the back wall, one with each hand, hard enough that they both collapsed with head injuries. Data's violence could be very precise.

Then he turned to the last Rogue standing—Ugulan. Ugulan's notable obstinancy ran out as he gaped into the shredded face of a powerful wraith whose clothing still smoldered, embroiling Data in a monstrous shroud. Every move he made threw off a tendril of smoke, as if he were a wizard casting spells.

Ugulan didn't even try. He spun around and headed for the cell entrance.

In his panic he forgot that Worf was standing there.

Worf reached out as Ugulan tried to pass him by. For an instant they simply stared at each other, until Worf's fury peaked.

He skewered Ugulan with a long, cold glare, gritted his teeth, and roared, "It is a good day to die!"

His right fist drew back and flew forward in a short, hard punch to Ugulan's rib cage. Never had Worf thrown such a punch in his entire life. Never had he felt such rage driving his actions. His fist struck Ugulan's sternum, cracking the bone, then his other fist drove into the other Klingon's chest. Before Worf's eyes, Ugulan's body collpased. Living or dead, Worf did not know. Either way, his soul was doomed.

Dizzy and wheezing, Worf spun twice to make sure all the Rogues were down or gone, then looked around to where Riker was snuffing out the flames on Crusher's sleeve. "All of you stay here!" he shouted.

Data smoldered forward. "I will go with you—"

"No! This is for me alone!"

"You'd better run," Riker said. "She's getting away."

"She will not get away," Worf snarled back. "And I refuse to run."

Chapter Nineteen

DARKNESS STILL COMMANDED the port of Delaware Station, although the first pale periwinkle of coming day now showed itself above the black cutouts of trees, houses, and the boatyard. The details of *Justina*'s rigging jumped out against the velvety purple predawn sheen.

Amazing. All this in one night.

Behind them, the chapel bell rang and rang, and around them armed men poured out of cottages, inns, cabins, and rooming houses. Old, young—every manner of man came out with a rifle or flintlock pistol. Some seemed confused, then joined others who were following behind Picard, Alexander, Patrick O'Heyne, Jeremiah Coverman, and their men. The patriots seemed pathetically disorganized, but determined and of a single mind as they flocked to face the incoming redcoats.

"Cavalry? Artillery?" Jeremiah asked O'Heyne as they ran toward the south side of the town.

"No," O'Heyne said, struggling with his wounds. "They landed no artillery or horses that I saw. They have, by my estimate, about two hundred men on foot. And they do have sharpshooters, I'm sorry to recall for the sake of my poor Whistler. I loved that horse . . ."

Caught in a moment of sorrow, O'Heyne didn't mind his wounds and tripped on a small wooden plank, skidding to one knee on the dirt road. Jeremiah, understandably, rushed to help him up, but so did Sandy, and that was enheartening. Picard helped O'Heyne over the discarded plank that had tripped him. "Perhaps go a little slower."

"Not tonight," O'Heyne said, bothering to knock back the ponytail loosely tied at the nape of his neck. "I'm all right. There's the barricade."

At the end of a stand of houses and shops, likely the edge of town as well, minutemen with rifles and townsfolk, including women, were building up a line of scrimmage made of sea barrels, crates, and a horse trough that had been spilled and moved into place. The barricade looked all too fragile, and would stop no one from rushing through, but Picard noted that it would provide fair cover for those shooting over it, which the flanking trees wouldn't.

"Hear them?" Jeremiah said abruptly, looking down the dark road. "Drums! They're nearly here!"

"Yes, marching snares," O'Heyne agreed. "Remarkable sound. Keeps the soldiers marching for hours and somehow their backs don't hurt when they're done. There's nothing like marching drums. You should hear the sound when they've got pipers along. They can go for days, and I find myself wanting to go with them."

Enjoying himself more than he should have been, Picard glanced at him. "Mr. O'Heyne, I think you're a bit crazy."

"I'd have to be, wouldn't I?"

That sound *was* stirring! The *clap-trrrrap-ap* of snares coming through the trees like approaching rattlesnakes, and the sounds of footsteps as the march drew close enough to be heard. Picard crouched behind the barrels with all the other men, with Alexander and Sandy to his left, and beyond Sandy were O'Heyne and Jeremiah. To Picard's right were Nightingale, Bennett, and Wollard. Nightingale and Bennett had two of Jeremiah's rifles, and Wollard seemed perfectly happy holding the ball pouches and powder horns. He seemed less warrior than just a clumsy, landed sailor at the moment. Bennett, on the other hand, seethed with frustration at Picard's agreement to take no action.

Alexander twisted around suddenly and looked back at the town's main business area. "I can't believe all those people came out because the bell rang! They came out in a minute, just like my teacher told me! And with their rifles and pistols! Look at them! I think it was *less* than a minute! They should be called half-a-minutemen!"

Picard gave him a conciliatory glance, then looked back at the town, where indeed people were scooting out of doorways, but then made a quieting motion. "Relax, Alexander. We're British, remember?"

"I know, I know." And the boy cast him a mischievous grin that made Picard think of Will Riker.

"Load your guns, gentlemen," Patrick O'Heyne said, and smiled. "And how's that for taking my life in my hands?"

How could he smile at a time like this?

"You must fight," Jeremiah added, leaning so Picard and Sandy could see him. "At least pretend. Shoot at the trees if you like. For all our sakes, while you wear these clothes you must behave as Yankees, or you'll be shot as traitors."

"Feel like one," Bennett grumbled, but Picard and Nightingale were the only ones to hear him.

"This rifle is different from the sergeant's," Alexander said, pointing at the musket Picard held.

"You've not seen an American musket before, swab?" Sandy asked, pressing an elbow into the crate in front of him.

Alexander shook his head. "It's longer than yours."

"Explain the difference to the boy, Sergeant," Picard said, seizing on the opportunity.

Sandy glanced at the woods nervously, measuring the nearness of the snares. "Mine is a British sea-service musket. It's shorter so I may more easily maneuver it among the ship's rigging. The butt is flat on the bottom, not crescent-shaped like this American gun. This way I can easily load it while the butt rests flat on the ship's deck. The barrel of mine is blackened and its ramrod is made of wood, to fend away corrosion from the salt sea and air."

"Never thought of that," Picard murmured, and smiled at Alexander. He handed his musket to Sandy. "Here, Sergeant. Show the boy how it's loaded."

Sandy blinked, dismayed, clearly wondering why Picard didn't just show the boy himself. Picard hoped Sandy wouldn't notice how closely a lieutenant of the Royal Navy was paying attention to the process.

"This is my powder horn," the sergeant began, pulling his equipment around. "This little thing is my powder measurer, this is my bullet pouch, with about fifty rounds remaining . . . the ramrod comes out so . . . the powder is measured . . . poured in the barrel, and keep a pinch to use for priming. Drop the ball inside . . . the ramrod goes down, a firm push, and out again. Gun up, pull back the cock, put the priming pinch on the pan, take aim, and fire. And hope your flint doesn't crack. Then do all again, and fire into the center of the smoke from your last shot, because you now cannot see. In the smoke of a dozen muskets, the enemy is but a ghost. Try it, boy."

"Oh—" Suddenly parental, Picard spoke up as Alexander took the musket. "I don't think that's wise."

"He's old enough," Sandy said defensively. "I began at the age of seven, sir."

"Great!" Alexander shouldered the long rifle and tested the weight. "I can do this."

A sad moment, perhaps, but it had to come sometime. It had come for Picard, and would for every young man who decided to serve.

Sandy leaned on the barrel before him and peered into the dimness. "Decisions come for us all."

"Is something wrong?" Alexander asked.

Glancing at his other side—at Patrick O'Heyne, as the Yankee businessman spoke quietly to Jeremiah—Sandy lowered his voice and spoke to Picard and Alexander.

"He left a thriving business in England and New York. How could a man do that? His schedules and methods of correspondence relay revolutionized Atlantic shipping. He was received at the British court! Why would he forsake all that to crawl in the dirt and risk his life?"

Picard prodded, "Must be a compelling reason."

"I cannot imagine," Sandy murmured.

Alexander made a face. "Neither can I."

"Why don't you ask him?" Picard suggested.

"Really?" The boy looked at him.

"That's what we're here for."

"Right!" The boy shimmied closer to Sandy. "Yes, ask him!"

"Very well!" Sandy twisted around to his other side. "Mr. O'Heyne—"

O'Heyne turned. "Mr. Leonfeld?"

"Yes, we have a question."

"I'm at your service."

"You're an educated, successful man of high standing, yet here you are holding a musket. Why would you fight with these common people when you could be safe and comfortable elsewhere?"

"Thank you for that, but I'm not of high birth at all," O'Heyne admitted openly. "My father was a Dublin pauper. He came to the colonies as a criminal."

"Criminal?" Alexander asked. "What kind?"

O'Heyne looked at the boy. "A murderer. Killed a landowner with a shovel to the side of the head. I don't know the situation, but the dead man's wife took pity on my father. Rather than go to prison, he was sent here. He began as a collier and gradually gained security. He made certain my brother and I were educated in the concerns of finance."

"And you built a business?" the boy pursued.

"My brother and I built it together, but the British impounded our business, both in Liverpool and New York, when I spoke up against the monarchy. We sacrificed it all. My brother is now a captain in the Fourth Continental Light Dragoons."

"You could have lived in riches in England, or even here," Sandy protested, "if you had simply run your business and not become involved in this dispute. Why on this earth would you give up everything, sir?"

O'Heyne's green eyes flickered. "For freedom, sir. Not to

worry. If I live, I'll build my fortune again. Wealth cannot be kept out of the hands of the industrious."

He paused briefly, leaned over the crates, and looked down the dim tree-lined road.

"In England, I've been treated with respect, but in a bastard-son manner. They'll have me for tea, but they don't *prefer* to have me. You gentlemen should walk among the English dressed as you are now and see what it's like. As colonists, you have no right to speak your mind. You'll be lower than the lowest East Ender. You'll be required to quarter soldiers of the British military, no matter what your loyalties are. Your goods are required to be sold through Britain, and you have no say in how these revenues are spent or—"

"But that," Picard said, "is how the protection of the colonies is paid for, Mr. O'Heyne. Your movement is wresting away a large and legitimate British investment."

"The investment of those living and working here isn't considered at all. The British have some legitimate claims, but not enough. This is a philosophical disagreement, not just two bullies striking at each other. It's an argument over the worth of a human being. How long should the class system last? How long does God want me to keep my station of birth? If I'd kept to my father's station, I'd be hitting you with a shovel. Now that I've achieved 'betterment,' even in your eyes, should my sons have to go back to the shovel? Or can we continue the pattern until all are 'better'?"

"I love to hear you talk, Patrick," Jeremiah said with a grateful smile. He seemed glad not to be holding up the platform by himself anymore.

"Thanks, Jeremiah," O'Heyne said with another grin. "You hear those drums, Mr. Leonfeld? Those soldiers are coming here to shoot me for wanting sway over my own destiny. Should I be shot for that? Who is it I've stolen from by making myself successful? What is it I've done? What should I be hanged for? What have I taken from my king or countrymen? We desire to determine our own fate. We'll rise or fall, right now. This country is so open, everyone is so busy surviving and building and being productive that no one has time to worry about who's born to what and who shall marry whom. I want to make sure it stays that way. I owe this little nation a great debt. Live or die, I think our message will survive us. Freedom has to start somewhere. That's why I'm here with a musket."

He seemed to know the speech by heart—or perhaps it *was* his heart speaking. He turned toward Sandy and Picard, relaxing as if those drums weren't rattling in the closing distance.

"If you're going to come here and shoot me, you'd better be *damned* sure you're right. You'd better be able to look me in the eye and tell me why you're doing it, and still be able to sleep at night. Can you?"

Both Sandy Leonfeld and Alexander seemed suddenly nauseated with their own self-doubt. Even Picard felt a niggling wonderment at his own convictions. How sure had he been, all those times in the past?

"If your beliefs are so strong," O'Heyne said, "you have your gun. Shoot us now."

Pale, Sandy Leonfeld looked as if the invitation had physically slapped him across the face and knocked him back.

Alexander stared at his worshiped cousin, baffled by the doubts he saw in Sandy's elegant young face.

"They're here," O'Heyne said then, peering through the night. "There they are."

Picard looked out through the dark road, expecting to catch a glimpse of ghostly figures hiding among the trees.

Instead, he was confronted by—

"They're all in rows!" Alexander burst out. "They're coming right at us in long lines! Why would they do something that stupid?"

"Because battle by ranks has won them war upon war for centuries," Picard recalled. "It hearkens back to the days of hand weapons. It doesn't take guns and artillery into consideration. Apparently something about it still works."

"It works," Wollard muttered, his voice dripping with contempt.

Still, there certainly was some shock in seeing rank after rank of redcoats blend out of the darkness on the road, each holding a rifle with the muzzle at a tilt slightly in front of his white crossbelt. Their scarlet jackets and white facings were cast nearly gray in the darkness, but a forgiving moon lanced the trees and frequently gave a strike of red in the picture, as if hinting of what was to come. As the Royal troops drew closer with each step, the moonlight began to catch the savage flicker of bayonets, which would do their work if the two masses, redcoat and rebel, came hand-to-hand.

Abruptly, a shot popped from the British ranks. None of the redcoats seemed startled, but the colonists all flinched.

The musketball whined in and buzzed away, well over their heads, and tore through an oak tree overhanging a house.

"Ranging shot," Picard uttered automatically.

"And they're within range," Alexander replied.

A voice shouted something unintelligible in the woods, and the marching ranks stopped abruptly, barely within sight.

"Heads down," Patrick O'Heyne warned.

Around them, on all sides, Yankee riflemen tucked themselves deeply behind trees and around corners of the cabins, and behind steps and in doorways. The fear was palpable. Of course, most of these were not regular soldiers. They were people defending their homes.

"Grenadiers, ready! First rank, kneel!" The voice in the darkness was muffled. "Present arms!"

Dark muzzles of British guns were eerily invisible in the night, making it appear as if the soldiers were pantomiming the aiming of guns, as boys might playact a battle.

A thunderous rocking volley erupted, and musketballs slammed into every barrel and crate, every building, and many human bodies, who now suffered the onslaught of the famous and formidable British military. Smoke from fifty muskets rolled into a single murderous fog, and the phantom guns took on a slamming reality. Picard crushed Alexander down, beginning to see in his mind all the wars that the British had waged and won, and how many in the coming years they would win with their dogged discipline and raw courage. As the terrible sound pounded in his head, he couldn't tell past from future at all.

Not quite a headlong fight yet. They were just shooting, as if to scrape off the icing of cowardice or weakness before the real men got at it.

But no one here ran away.

"First rank, reload! Second rank! Fire!"

Another roar, more musketballs splattered the barricade and pocked into human flesh. Injured and dying Yankees screamed and moaned. Two men beyond Jeremiah skidded hard into the dirt and lay slaughtered. Astonishing!

And the intimacy of it—phasers had eased all that, and before that the distance weapons of higher technology. With these gunpowder weapons, one had to get close enough to watch one's target die. As O'Heyne had said, better be sure.

Jeremiah checked the dead man nearest him, then scooped up the man's rifle and passed it to Picard.

"In case you must defend yourself," he said. "After all, they won't know who you are. Shoot if you must, for they surely will."

"Fire!" O'Heyne suddenly shouted, knowing something about timing this that eluded Picard.

SNAP—BOOM!

Musketfire from mere steps away nearly deafened him. The first and second ranks of the red mass now dissolved, every other man crumpling. Behind them was another wall of red. Behind that, another.

"Quick, maaaaarch!"

The drums started again, and the darkened menace surged forward with a stinking white cloud of gunsmoke rolling before them.

Not too far from the back of Picard's mind were the words *freeze program*. He primed himself to say them at an instant's notice, in case he or Alexander were immediately threatened. The holodeck could reverse itself or dissolve a holo-musketball, but it couldn't pull back the damage done. He toyed with the idea of stopping everything now, but this was what he and the boy had come for. If he stopped in the middle of this blistering attack, what would Alexander learn about honor? That these patriots stood up for each other's lives, and his father wouldn't?

Beside him a musket *crack-boomed* loudly. Alexander had just let fly his first deadly element. Had he aimed high? Or had the target of oncoming soldiers been too much for him to deny?

"Ow!" The boy bellowed. "Ow, that hurt! My shoulder! And it's burning my face!"

Picard saw the hot grains of powder stuck to the boy's cheeks, but made no move to brush them off. Alexander might as well learn here and now.

Around them, the Yankees took careful aim and fired. Musket volleys pocked the nightscape, creating a surreal dance of smoke, darkness, musket flashes, and patches of moonlight. River breeze made the musket smoke twist fitfully and seem to entangle, obscuring Picard's vision, and he possessed neither the training nor the experience for this.

He brought up his own rifle and tucked it into the hollow of his shoulder, aimed high, and pulled the trigger. The cock snapped down—*crack-boom!—hissss—*

His musket gasped fire like a dragon in the dark. The blast of priming powder in the pan stung his face. Acrid smoke and bits of powder grains burned his eyes. Nasty.

Among the British ranks, a man holding a sword high came strutting forward, waving the sword. "Forward! Forward!" he cried.

An officer. Captain, or colonel.

A Yankee stood up on the other side of Jeremiah, ignoring the danger of exposing himself, shouldered his long rifle, and took his time aiming. *Boom!* The rifle went off, and on the road the officer spun to his death. His sword clattered into the rifles of his own grenadiers.

"Rebel bastard!" Seaman Wollard roared. He swung around, aimed over Picard's head, and fired at the Yankee who had just shot the British officer.

The Yankee spun, stunned, and gaped at Wollard, then looked down at the sprawling gore that was now his rib cage, blinked up one more time, then slid to his knees. He was dead before he struck the ground. Picard knew the look.

"Sergeant!" he snapped.

But Sandy's rifle was already swinging about, and Wollard was blown into a disgusting mass. The concussion slammed the dying seaman a good ten feet back, and he lay twitching in the shadow of a porch.

"Thank you, sir," Sandy said. "I would've shot him anyway, but I cherish your approval. After all, he was your crew."

"We made an agreement," Picard confirmed, and fumbled to reload his rifle.

Above the heads of the oncoming British floated the King's colors, the flag of Great Britain emblazoned with the badge of that particular grenadier unit out there. The red-jacketed wraiths' faces were blackened with powder burns now, but they kept coming, unaffected by the sight of Yankee minutemen being mowed down in the town road as one might mow grass. Some grenadiers marching, and others were pausing to fire, then moving on forward. They were doing that by ranks, in disciplined shifts, and Picard found it stunning that such efficient destruction could be so messy.

Behind him, daring patriots were hurled backward and lay moaning in the thickening musket smoke that crippled aim from both sides. Musketballs plucked at the dirt street and snapped bark off trees.

Terror for Alexander knitted Picard's spine. If one of those hit him, there would be no time to hold the program.

"Keep firing!" O'Heyne shouted over the tangled howl of musketfire from the British.

Picard tipped his musket down in an effort to see what was happening, then brought it up quickly and fired, though he couldn't see a damned thing, not enough to avoid hitting those who were ironically his allies. The explosion came again, but this time there was no "kick."

Had he forgotten to put the ball in?

He glared at the pigheaded musket as if it was about to grow lips and answer him. Had it misfired?

Sandy Leonfeld leaned down in front of Picard and came up with a lead ball in his hand. "You tipped the barrel down, Lieutenant. The ball rolled out."

"Oh . . . thank you, Sergeant."

"Your servant, sir."

Picard fielded a perplexed glower from Sandy, intimating that the sergeant didn't understand why a naval officer wouldn't know to hold his gun up.

Jeremiah grasped O'Heyne's arm. "Patrick, we'll hold this line if we can. You hurry and meet Colonel Fox and tell him what's happening."

"I don't like that much," O'Heyne said.

"Like it or not, you'd better go. I can't explain the military approach those men are using, and I think it would be patently beyond the call of our agreement to ask any of these other gentlemen to do our reporting for us."

O'Heyne glanced through the pale trees at the fleeting phantoms of British soldiers, and reluctantly nodded. He threw an arm around Jeremiah and added, "Fall back if you must. Promise me, now. You have a wife to live for. I'll have to marry her if you die, and she's too young for me. Besides, you're not that good a soldier."

Jeremiah smiled, but before he could answer, a huge jarring boom burst out behind them!

Picard twisted to see what had happened. Out of the maddened night came a flock of soldiers armed with bayoneted rifles and wearing green jackets faced with red. The colonial militia—the Dover Light Infantry!

"Oh, how nice," Picard murmured. "Look at that."

"Can I stay now?" O'Heyne laughed.

Strangely romantic and compelling, the Dover Lights braced in the middle of the street, took aim, and fired as a unit without anyone shouting an order to them, unleashing a hideous punishment over the heads of Picard and the others. The British column hunched forward against the blistering attack, but did not break.

Now there was smoke on both sides of the barricade and it crippled the aim of both units. That didn't stop or even slow the crack of gunfire or the whine of musketballs. Picard looked up and saw bloody nothing. There was noise, though, lots of it—the boom of rifles, the sounds of gasping, screaming, vomiting, and the rattle of snare drums. Everything was muted, though. He was half deafened.

Jeremiah shouted cryptically, "We can't hold against them!"

"Maybe they'll let you be prisoners," Alexander coughed. "If you give up, they won't kill you. That's right, isn't it?"

"I've been supplying the Colonial militia," O'Heyne told him. "If Delaware Station is taken, I'll be hanged. If there's one thing the British hate, it's an uppity American who made some money in England. They'll take it out of my throat, I think."

On O'Heyne's last two words, a Dover infantryman rushed up and tried to go over the barricade between Picard and Alexander, and was met by a musketblast that twisted his head full about, though his body remained facing forward.

Alexander blinked right up into that terrible sight, the laid-open face, the stare of a remaining eye, until finally the man stumbled backward—was he still alive?—and dropped to his knees. The mass of gore wobbled, and fell forward on top of Alexander.

The boy yelled out his fear and kicked fiercely. Picard shoved the heavy body off the boy and thought about holding the program.

But he didn't say it.

"Sir!" On Picard's other side, Nightingale came to life and pointed at the British lines.

Picard, O'Heyne, Jeremiah, and the others all peeked through the barricade. The British, rather than being driven back by the appearance of the Dover Light Infantry, were rising from the bloodied dirt.

Another officer, or someone who had taken that role, waved a sword and screamed, "Chaaaaarge!"

And the invasion became a stampede. Hell cracked open. British soldiers plowed over the barricade to meet the Dover Infantry. Men from both sides fell in heaps, entangled enemy with enemy, and died in each other's embrace.

"Fall back!" Picard shouted.

He grabbed Alexander and rushed to his right, shoving

Nightingale before him, hoping the others would follow. They were just in the way now.

Suddenly he tripped over something and slammed to his knees. Before him, Edward Nightingale's neck had been torn open. Picard had tripped on the midshipman's paralyzed legs.

"Aw!" Alexander choked as if it had been his neck instead of the midshipman's.

Half of Nightingale's left shoulder was gone, too. The young man's eyes pleaded and his hand dug into Alexander's sleeve.

"He's still alive!" Alexander gasped. "We've got to save him!"

Picard put the muzzle of his long rifle to the midshipman's chest, careful to angle it so the ball wouldn't roll out. He pulled the trigger. The gun discharged, blew a hole in Nightingale's heart, and the young officer's beseeching eyes glazed over mercifully.

"I can't believe you did that!" Alexander choked.

"You came here to learn," Picard said coldly. "Now you're learning. Let's go."

With Seaman Bennett stumbling before them and Sandy and Jeremiah after—there was no sign of O'Heyne now—they dodged into the protection of a building. On the street behind them, a mass of uniformed men tangled. More and more redcoats surged out of the woods, though. The Dover Lights were being overwhelmed by sheer numbers.

Jeremiah scrambled out into the street and yanked the red jackets off two dead grenadiers. Somehow he made it back alive and shoved the bloodied jackets into Picard and Sandy's hands.

"Put these on," he said. "The agreement is satisfied. Do what you must. Thank you for being honorable men." He gripped Sandy's arm. "Thank you most sincerely."

And without waiting for a family farewell, Jeremiah plunged back out onto the street and into the fight. He disappeared in the pall of white smoke.

Sandy gazed after him sorrowfully.

"What'll we do now, sir?" Bennett choked out.

Picard paused, then raked on the jacket. It was too big,

but would serve to keep him from being shot by *both* sides. At least now only one side would shoot him.

"Defend the ship," he said. "The colonists will burn it before allowing it to be repossessed and used against them."

"How do you know?" Alexander asked.

"Because that's what I would do. The shipyard! Follow me!"

Chapter Twenty

THEY MADE IT TO THE DOCK ALIVE.

Behind them, patriots plunged through the streets, along with panicked residents, mostly women. Some of the women weren't panicking at all, but were busily reloading muskets and relaying them to nearby men.

Picard led his little band to the top of the wharf, leading out to where the *Justina* rested at the point of deepest water, for her draft was a good ten feet deeper than any other vessel here.

"What's holding us back, sir?" Bennett wanted to know when Picard paused.

"Looking for Committee of Safety guards," Picard answered. "Seems they've all gone to defend the town. All right, let's board and load."

There were only the four of them now, their shoes throbbing on the dock as they ran out to the gangplank and charged onto the ship. The *Justina* was eerily quiet, without another living soul on board. And yet there seemed to still be a pulse of life here, as if the beast were just in repose, waiting for its master to return.

So it was true . . . no ship was entirely inert. The life pulse of the shipwrights, the sailors, the officers remained on board somehow. She was alive.

"Is this your first action on this continent, Mr. Leonfeld?" Picard asked as they reached the main deck.

"Yes . . ."

"What do you think so far?"

Sandy tightened visibly. He sighed twice. "I cannot believe it can work for the mob to decide . . . yet how can I tell a man like Patrick O'Heyne to go and be a collier because he was born to a collier? To go back to his 'station' in life? And my dear, decent Jeremiah, whose heart I know as my own . . . . How can the right of kings be less than divine and still be sacred?"

"Perhaps power flows the other way in a better world, Sergeant," Picard said. "From the people to the government, instead of the other way round."

Sandy shook his head. "You are a confusing man, sir! And I am confused."

Picard nodded. "Congratulations."

In the town, shouts pierced the night, the voices of commanders barking instructions spared them from pressing the issue.

"Close up!"

"Wheel right!"

"Forward!"

"Fix bayonets!"

"Uh-oh," Picard uttered. "Mr. Bennett, arm phasers. Eh—instead of that, prepare a cannon to fire. We're going to make the dock impassable."

"Aye, sir!" Bennett sprang for a midships gun. "I'll use the foredeck gun, sir, beggin' your pardon. We'll get a good punch taking the dock at a bit of an angle."

"Very well. Help him, Sergeant."

"Yes, sir." Sandy put down his sea-issue rifle and hurried to assist.

As the skirmish escalated on the visible street beyond the wharf, Picard and Alexander crouched at the ship's rail, weapons aimed. Dim outlines of redcoats and patriots picked through bloodsoaked bodies cluttering the ground.

It took time to load and run out a cannon, and before Wollard and Sandy were finished, several armed townsmen appeared on the wharf, running toward the extended dock that would bring them out to the ship's T-shaped dock.

Picard raised his rifle and fired, but the unfamiliar weapon damned his aim, and shot downward and a foot to the left of the colonist he had sighted down. Fortunately, it did take out the dock plank the man was standing on, and the colonist fumbled and spun into the water. With a soaked rifle and heavy clothing, the floundering man was now paddling about uselessly, trying to find a way out of the water.

Alexander looked at the other colonists pounding down the dock. "Should I shoot?"

Picard glanced at the boy. "Do what you think is right."

The boy stared at him, then looked down at the long rifle in his hands. Unexpectedly, he lowered the gun, and looked up again. "They're only defending their say over their own lives. They just want to keep what they earn."

At first he seemed to be waiting for approval for his words, but when none was forthcoming, Alexander glowered fiercely as if making up his mind a second time, put his rifle down, and turned his back.

In that silent moment, the halyards flapped against the mast, the water patted the ship's planks, and the pop of riflefire pressed into the night, each percussion ticking off a second. A full minute went by, and still the boy did not turn.

"Mmm," Picard mumbled. "Progress." He gripped the nearest shroud and called, "How's that cannon, Wollard?"

"Ready, sir!"

Bennett's voice cracked on a grunt as he and Sandy put their shoulders to the lines. The loaded gun groaned out on its heavy truck. It took considerable strain, and all the leverage the blocks could offer for only two men to move that twelve-hundred-pound gun outboard through the gunport. Luckily, the gun carriage was weighted well, and the whole system of ropes and blocks were brilliantly arranged to do this, and the gun went out. Picard began to see why these ocean-going fighting ships, so much smaller than his starship, needed a crew almost as large.

He looked out at the approaching patriots. "Take aim on the dock and fire! Quickly!"

Bennett aimed the gun by shoving down a heavy stick that changed the elevation of the cannon's back end, then Sandy shoved in a wooden wedge to hold the cannon in place. Sandy already had a spark reddening on a linstock—some kind of fuse—and Bennett snatched the linstock and touched it to the base ring. He avoided the actual touchhole itself, Picard noticed.

The explosion was instantaneous, thrumming the whole side of the ship with its concussion. Below, the dock dissolved into splinters, dispensing a half dozen patriots into the water. Four of them came up sputtering. Two never came up at all.

The ship's two middle docklines now hung limp, tied to pilings that no longer had a dock. The two outer ones, however, bow and stern, were made off to other docks for stability, and held the ship to the boatyard. However, there was no longer a dock leading up to the side of the ship.

They were defensible now.

Scarcely had the thought of his success sunk in when a fleshy mass dropped before his eyes and clamped over his mouth, leaving only one nostril free so that he could barely breath. It was a human forearm, and he was caught! He pressed out one fitful "Mmmmmph!" as he was pulled backward off balance, and two more figures charged past him.

As he gripped the arm around his mouth and twisted around the other piece of meat that had coiled around his chest to keep him off balance, he watched the two invaders plunge up the maindeck toward the bow and attack Sandy and Bennett, and—horribly—he also saw Alexander charge the armed patriots!

The patriots had stripped off their jackets and shirts in order to swim effectively and climb the chains, and now their wet backs glistened in the first spark of morning light. Their shoulders flexed as they raised swords and brought them slashing down upon Bennett and Sandy. Sandy fell back and tumbled behind the foremast, then rolled to his feet and squared off to parry his opponent.

Bennett was less fortunate. The seaman took a shattering blow to the left cheekbone from the second patriot. Bennett bellowed his gutwrenching agony and dropped like a stone. As he lay on the deck, clawing at the destruction of his face, blood flowed freely from the wound, which continued to open as his skull lost its structural integrity.

And Alexander now reached the foredeck, snatched up the red-hot linstock, and took a mighty swing at the back of the man who had killed Bennett.

Picard dug his heels into the deck and heaved backward on the man holding him, squeezing part of his mouth out from behind the mighty forearm. "Hullllfff—"

Freeze program! Freeze program!

The arm tightened against his mouth. He tried to shove the words right out through his nostrils, but the computer evidently didn't understand the command.

Engulfed in the horror of his own lack of foresight, Picard watched as the linstock in Alexander's hands whipped down on the patriot's bare back and dealt the man a searing burn, which the man repaid instantly by a swirl of flesh and steel. The man's sword swiped toward Alexander. The boy ducked back and to one side, but the sword's point laid open the tip of one shoulder and slashed diagonally across his chest as the patriot bent his elbow at the wrong instant.

Picard roared against the strap of human forearm that clamped his mouth. He forced his jaws open, and sank his teeth into the nearest muscle.

A howl of pain blew against his ear and the arm came loose. He rammed an elbow back and drove it into the man's diaphragm, then clamped his hands into a rock and swung around, driving his makeshift club into the patriot's ear. Dizzied and breathless, the patriot staggered back and fell on top of the maindeck hatch.

"Freeze—oh, to hell with it!" Picard rushed to the foredeck and drove a shoulder into the patriot, who was about to finish Alexander with another sword swipe. Together, Picard and the patriot went sprawling.

The man was half his age, but Picard was twice as mad. He grasped the armed man by the neck, raised him up a bit, then slammed his head into the deck. The sword clattered from the man's numbed hand.

"Alexander!" Picard spun off his knees and scrambled to the boy, who was trying to sit up.

"I'm getting up!" Alexander insisted valiantly. "Don't stop the program! It's just a cut! That's all!"

Damn, the boy was quick! Before Picard could hold him down he cranked his legs under him, grasped the ship's rail, and hoisted himself up. The front of his shirt was soggy with plum-colored blood, and the same for the cut shoulder. One arm hung numb, but other than that he was looking out at the wharf.

"Look!"

British soldiers were swarming from the street onto the wharf, lined up just beautifully, and took stern aim at all the patriots on the docks.

"Cease fire!" a voice called from the docks. "Colonials, cease fire! Cease fire!"

Picard looked . . . it was Patrick O'Heyne, standing at about the middle of the main wharf, holding both hands up. His rifle lay on the wharf at his feet.

He was giving up, to spare the lives of the cornered patriots—people who had been led out here by the need to possess this ship.

The patriot sparring with Sandy backed off, and Sandy cautiously came around to Picard's side. "The boy is wounded, sir," he said.

"I know! What kind of swine attacks a child!"

"But, sir, it's *war,"* Sandy explained simply, and of course he was right.

The patriot who was still standing on the deck stepped well away from them and waved to O'Heyne, then put his sword down reluctantly. He was giving up.

Like so much of the Revolutionary War, this skirmish had been for nothing but the philosophical point struggling to have its meager voice heard. The frigate *Justina* was once again a Royal Navy ship.

* * *

The night was blessedly cool against his hot skin and the hairs on his neck that were still standing from the electrical jolts.

On his way to the main doors of the jail complex, Worf had stepped through a half dozen fires set by Odette Khanty as she tried to block him from following her. She had kicked her awkward business shoes off and set fire to them, too. She was probably running now.

Worf refused to run. He balled his fists and stalked, step upon step, as regulated as a parade. His boots made an authoritative *chunk* on the brick with stride. He began to concentrate on the sound, for it brought his mind slowly back from the effects of the buffalo prod.

Behind him, the jail building burned more and more excitedly as the fires began to spread to floor cloths and fabric-covered chairs, and anything else. Even in a jail, fire would find something to consume, even if only the paint on the walls.

He felt like the fire. Ready to burn and determined to avenge his friend's death.

He approached the balcony of the governor's mansion, as he saw the guards there and the dozen or more police vehicles rolling or hovering into the courtyard behind him, drowning the courtyard in scene lights. They were all coming to arrest Odette Khanty. He ignored them. He saw his target.

A good day to die.

The police officers flooded from their vehicles and hurried across the courtyard toward the balcony. Worf felt them closing behind him, but he refused to break into a run. It was as if he had a deflector shield around his body. None of them approached him or tried to stop him. Whether they recognized him from the broadcast or simply wanted to concentrate on the woman, he did not know or care.

Each bootstep drove into his aching head like a nail. He wished he had treated Grant with more respect. How impressive—the data thread had still been there. Grant never gave it up. He might've bought himself a more merciful death if he had, but the thread was still there. Hours upon hours of circumstantial evidence that, when combined with Data's recordings of Odette Khanty's own words, would damn the woman to where she belonged. Anything Data recorded was admissible in court. They had her.

Yet the loss . . . it nearly took him down with every step. The vision of Grant's body hanging there, ravaged, would not leave him alone.

Honor was not always being tough, he now knew. Bravery did not always define itself in raw strength. When strength—real strength—was required, Ross Grant had summoned it. Certainly, those hours must have been wretched persecution. Worf felt every minute of every hour now as he stalked his prey.

Anguish squeezed him hard. Action charged the courtyard as the police surrounded the mansion.

Worf climbed the brick stairs to the balcony and turned immediately to his right. He could still see her.

She was running along the wide balcony. Worf could not imagine where she thought she was going, but certainly a woman as clever as this one might have an escape plan or two worked out.

He didn't care. He would walk—not run—after her if he had to walk into black space on the stairway of his own rage.

Sirens and flashing lights from far off before him cast the mansion's balcony, and the form of Odette Khanty, in silhouette, as she pulled the iron chairs over into Worf's path. The police were blocking her way. She would not get off this balcony.

He saw her glancing back at him and fancied that she was terrified of him as she ran and he walked. He hoped she was.

She disappeared unexpectedly. Worf heard the slam of a door. When Worf reached that place, he realized he was looking at a utility closet of some kind.

He kicked the door in.

She slammed another one in front of him. He kicked that in, too. When the door smashed before him, he noticed the T'kalla prod lying on the floor, its LOW BATT sign blinking.

There was no one in this room.

He looked up. A wall-mounted ladder led through some kind of conduit.

He climbed it.

"You can't do this to me!" Her voice came down with a slight echo.

"Yes, I can," he said, climbing steadily into the dimness.

"I'll recover from this!"

"No, you will not."

"I've got influence in places you never heard of!"

"Not any more."

He had no idea where she was heading, but he would meet her there.

He continued to climb. The metal rungs were cold on his hands, and he realized his fingers were twitching with pain.

The sky opened up before him. Mrs. Khanty had apparently climbed out of the conduit, and now there was sky. Night sky. In his mind Worf saw the shuttlecraft hovering out in space, dutifully broadcasting over and over the self-immolating words of Odette Khanty in the cell.

The whole population would know, if they didn't already.

And the profit was interesting. He hadn't realized she had shot her husband in the first place.

There she was. As he climbed out of the conduit, he saw Odette Khanty at the edge of the roof. They were four stories high, all the way to the top of the mansion.

All around, the courtyard glowed with police lights and buzzed with activity. Below, people flocked to see what was happening.

All eyes were fixed on the edge wall of the roof, where Odette Khanty was trapped against the open air.

"Stay back," she said as Worf walked across the roof toward her.

There was a short wall framing the roof. She climbed up onto it, having some difficulty with her narrow skirt.

Worf stopped.

She crawled a few feet along the brick riser, then paused. She had nowhere to go.

"I'll throw myself off," she called on the wind that swept down.

"No," Worf countered. "You will not."

"You can't win here," she insisted. "I'll go down as a trapped heroine. The people here will think it was all a plot. A frame. They love me!"

Worf felt the wind tug at his hair and cool his face. "The time has passed for that. You have done ten thousand heinous things in your life, and Ross Grant cared about every one of them. I care only about two."

He stepped closer to her, close enough that he could easily have yanked her off the edge of the roof.

"One thing you should never have done," he said, "was kill my friend."

Baffled, Odette Khanty drew her brows together and peered at him as she remained there on her hands and knees, her black hat now missing and her stockings shredded by the brick.

"You came back for *that?"* she wondered. "For *him?"*

"Yes, for him." Worf raised his hand.

One push. Barely enough to feel against his skin, and she would be gone. Gone, quickly and abruptly, with only a few moments of terror, a free-fall, and a quick death.

"And the other?"

"Your death will release the Rogues from their Oath of Sto–vok–or. They would be able to recover what honor is left to them, and perhaps gain more."

"Wait," she cried, "I release them, they are freed of their oath!"

"Thank you. Will you now restore my friend to life?"

"Don't!" Khanty shouted as Worf reached for her.

He clasped her elbow as easily as plucking a flower, and dragged her away from the ledge.

Behind him, the conduit began burping policemen. One after another, they surged out onto the roof and formed a jagged half-circle around him and the woman. He knew they were there, but he did not look at them.

He looked only at her.

"Odette Khanty," he said, "by authority of Starfleet and the United Federation of Planets, I place you under arrest for murder, attempted murder, extortion, espionage, and treason. Be glad you are in my custody, and not the custody of those who 'love' you."

Chapter Twenty-One

THE DIRT OF THE TOWN was littered with spent balls, spilled powder, bits of torn fabric, smears of blood, lost ramrods, and severed limbs. Most of the dead had been removed to a clearing area at the churchyard, and the wounded had been taken somewhere to be treated or to complete their dying.

With trembling hands, Picard patched Alexander's shoulder and chest enough to let the bleeding clot, and thought more than once about stopping all this, but something in himself, and in the boy's eyes, kept him from uttering those words. There were times when safety wasn't all it was cracked up to be.

He, Alexander, and Sandy Leonfeld were removed from the *Justina* and a dockside crew of grenadiers had been put on board to secure the ship and then guard it. Now Picard and his remaining crew were being escorted to the British field headquarters.

It was Jeremiah Coverman's house.

The keeping room had been transformed into a military outpost. Amy Coverman was being forced to serve dinner to British officers, and at the trestle table sat an infantry captain with a heavy brown mustache and a thatch of graying hair. Picard stood before the man, with Sandy on one side of him and Alexander on the other.

The captain looked up at them and eyed the inappropriate, ill-fitting red coat on Picard. "Are you a lieutenant of the *Justina?*"

"Yes, sir. Picard, sir."

"I'm Captain Holmes."

"How do you do, sir."

"Well. Mr. Picard, I have new orders for you. The captain has authorized me to reestablish Mr. Pennington's status as senior officer of the *Justina* and confer upon him a field rank of captain. He and his crew are being released as we speak. Because the first and second lieutenants have been killed, you're now his first lieutenant. It will be his and your responsibility to return the ship to fighting condition and take a blockading position in Delaware Bay. You'll have the boatyard to use at your convenience."

"Yes, sir."

"Mr. Pennington has indicated that you've been conducting some espionage among the colonists, and are more familiar with the situation than he is."

"Yes, sir."

"Very well. Then confirm something for me. Corporal." Holmes looked at a guard who stood at the back entrance.

"Sir!" The guard opened the back door and waved.

Another guard came in, leading Jeremiah Coverman and Patrick O'Heyne. Behind them were two more guards.

"I believe these are the men who have been leading the colonialists, the minutemen, in Delaware Station. Can you confirm their role?"

Picard felt Sandy tense at his side. As British officers, they were expected to eagerly condemn the civilian rebel leaders, who were seen not as military equals, but as insurrectionists. Traitors.

They would be hanged.

"Captain, I am Patrick O'Heyne," Jeremiah's friend interrupted before Picard had to commit himself. "I've been organizing the minutemen in this area. You have no need to confirm beyond my word. No one else is responsible."

Jeremiah nudged forward, but Sandy reached out and pushed him back before he could speak up for part of the blame. Captain Holmes noticed the gesture, but didn't seem to know what to make of it.

"Captain," Sandy spoke up, bringing attention back to himself. "I am Sergeant Alexander Leonfeld, His Majesty's Grenadiers, H.M.S. *Justina.*"

"Sergeant?"

"Begging your pardon, sir," Picard interrupted, "but the sergeant is now captain of the marine unit. Both Captain Newton and his lieutenant were killed when the ship was taken."

Holmes looked at Sandy with new respect, even though that made no sense at all. That's the way it was, though. "Understood. You have some observations, Captain Leonfeld?"

"I do, sir. This has been a forthright battle. The colonists have lost in good military style and have behaved like soldiers. I suggest they be treated as such, whether infantrymen or civilians. That is how they see themselves and I've come to see them that way also."

"Really . . ."

"Yes, sir," Picard agreed. "The colonists here have treated our crew with utmost respect and properness. I find it my charge to see that the same decency is afforded to them. We are at war, but we are not savages."

"These are commoners, Picard," Holmes snapped. "If we choose to hang these two men, to slap the women in stocks, to ship out the children for a proper upbringing as the servants they are, then that will be my decision. Not yours, or Captain Leonfeld's."

Picard lowered his chin. "No, sir. These two men will not be hanged. They will be treated as officers. We do not hang officers who have done their duty, even if it is not duty to King George. We owe a certain respect to our enemy's gallantry or we lose our own, palling of victory."

"Sir, Britain made an investment," Sandy Leonfeld

pushed in, "but that investment was a gift. These people did not serve themselves up as chattel."

Holmes bolted to his feet. "You dare to speak to me that way! I've never been spoken to that way!"

"And while you're here," Picard surged on, "your men will respect the women, you will respect property, and you will treat these two gentlemen as you yourself would wish to be treated should you fall into enemy custody. I don't think that's asking too much, to keep our platform of decorum from crumbling beneath us. Any misconduct toward these people by uniformed men of the King would be irremediable. The world is dangerous, and we may someday find the obligations reversed."

Holmes' face turned red. "Who are you to dictate conduct to an officer of the King's Grenadiers!"

Picard's arms flexed at his sides. But before he could speak, Sandy Leonfeld spoke up "I am, sir, an officer of the King's Royal Navy who helped make it possible for you to successfully regain control of a British frigate, which was the goal of this entire maneuver. Your assignment is to protect and defend His Majesty's ships. Therefore, the entire maneuver is under the authority of the Royal Navy. And that, sir, is Mr. Pennington, and it is *me.*"

The two stared at each other and Holmes' face got nearly purple, but he finally leaned back a bit and lowered his brows.

"God's hair, that's a lot of gall," he commented. "Quite a hell of a lot of gall. Almost as much as these upstarts here." He waved his quill pen at Jeremiah and O'Heyne. "Hmmm . . . are you a barrister in civilian life, Mr. Leonfeld, by chance?"

He put down the quill and came out from behind the table, stalking Jeremiah and O'Heyne. When they didn't look away from his glare, he seemed to be noting something in their eyes that Picard and Sandy insisted was there.

"Hmm," he uttered again. "Can't have a dirty reputation for the King's uniform . . . tell you what, I'll confer with Mr. Pennington and his bidding will win the day. I'll leave it to him to decide whether or not these two are hanged in the morning."

"Thank you, sir!" Sandy heaved out, shuddering with relief.

"Don't thank me yet," Holmes said. "He may decide they should be *shot* in the morning instead. All right, my men are billeted in the linen factory next door. You men, round up your crew and restore them to the ship and get them working. We'll supply any further crewmen if you need muscle. Get moving before insult sets in and I become surly. And clean up this powder monkey. He's bleeding on my floor."

Without offering the captain the respect of a "Yes, sir," Picard put his hand on Alexander and ushered the boy out. Sandy followed them, and when the door closed behind them he sagged against the doorframe.

"Thank you for your help, Mr. Picard," he huffed. "Perhaps Jeremiah's life will be spared."

"If so, it was your doing," Picard said.

The next moment, the door opened again and two guards led Jeremiah and O'Heyne out onto the plank porch. Jeremiah instantly rushed to Sandy and the two clasped hands warmly.

"You're everything I knew you were," Jeremiah lauded. "Someday this will end and we'll be family again."

"I'll always be your family," Sandy told him warmly. "I swore an oath to the king and I'll honor it, but I know now that I'm not your better at all."

Jeremiah patted his hand. "Oh, in a few ways!"

"Don't worry," O'Heyne said, clapping Jeremiah on a shoulder. "England and the continent will be friends one way or the other, because we simply can't have this for long." He reached out to shake Picard's hand. "Thank you deeply."

"Quite welcome," Picard responded drably. "Fair weather, Mr. O'Heyne."

The guards took the two men away, and Sandy Leonfeld stared emotionally after them.

"You'd better go and inform Mr. Pennington," Picard told him. "The ship is ours. And the fate of your cousin and O'Heyne are in his hands."

"Yes," Sandy said. "Yes—thank you." He clasped Picard's hand, then Alexander's. "Thank you both!"

As he jogged off through the British military men now common in the brightening street, Alexander swung around to Picard.

"Wow!" the boy gushed. "I wonder if that really happened! I hope it did!"

"Well, the holodeck computer didn't stop me," Picard said on a sigh, "or contradict me either. So perhaps something like that *did* happen."

"Sandy really stood up to that captain! He actually defended Britain's enemies right to his face!"

"So he did. I liked what he said very much."

"Do you think Mr. Pennington'll let Jeremiah and Mr. O'Heyne live?"

"Mr. Pennington's a compassionate and decent man. He doesn't strike me as vindictive. And if war dictates otherwise . . . well, there are worse ways for a patriot to die."

"Do you really think that? That there are good and bad ways to die?"

"Yes, and things very much worth dying for. You've heard these men, these colonists saying what they're about, and you've seen dauntless behavior from the British as well. Higher civilization is emerging here. It's bringing a higher morality with it. The old system of monarchy saw humanity through primitive times with great success, but with progress is coming the morality of individualism. It's given us all we possess in our time, and we'd better nurture it, or we'll lose everything."

Alexander looked around at the morning scene—the early American town, masts stemming over the rooftops, the quaintly costumed people trying to get through this difficult day after a difficult night, and redcoat guards leading groups of Dover Infantrymen to the guardhouse.

"I think I get it now," he said.

Picard couldn't manage a smile. "I think I do, too."

"What do you mean?"

"I mean that people have the right to make a decision,

good or bad. How closely should anyone else hold the lens? And at what cost? Now, let's get you to the sickbay. The real one. And I'd better make a will, because when your father finds you've been wounded, he's going to relieve me of some important cerebral matter, I think."

He paused, and gazed over the houses at the masts of the *Justina.* He let the Delaware River breeze brush his face as he memorized the masts and rigging, so he also would never forget.

"Computer," he said, "end program."

Chapter Twenty-Two

"AND NEVER COME WITHIN A BOATHOOK's length of the captain unless you have a good reason. Remember that, Number One."

"Oh, I will, sir. How long a boathook?"

Picard led Will Riker into the ready room off the bridge and headed for his desk, but never got a chance to sit down.

The door slid open without the courtesy of an entry request, and a gargantuan fit of fury plowed in.

"My son has been wounded in the Revolutionary War!"

The walls rattled. The desk buzzed. Riker backed off a good four feet.

"Yes," Picard responded, and continued getting behind his desk. He didn't sit down. No sense dying in a chair. "Yes, Mr. Worf, I know. I'm very sorry about that. I understand I was supposed to protect him, and you left him on the *Enterprise* for safety—"

Worf's brow came down. "I am proud of his wound!"

With a blink, Picard asked, "You are? Oh—of course you are."

Stepping closer, Worf demanded, "Captain, I must know if the scar will be an honorable one."

"Oh, yes," Picard assured him. "He fought valiantly to protect our ship. I was hard-pressed to tell him from the actual soldiers."

Worf fell silent for a moment, absorbing all this, all the parental worries about a wounded child crashing up against the Klingon sensibilities about where this fit on the honor scale of injuries.

Yet there were other things playing in those nut-dark eyes, things more complicated, more tortuous.

Before either spoke again, the door opened a second time without a chime for permission, and Alexander charged in at full tilt, almost slamming into the captain's desk.

"Father!" the boy blurted.

Worf worked to control himself, and did about as well as any overheating steam engine. "The Captain has informed me that your wound was an honorable one."

"Mr. Worf," Picard broke in, "I'm glad you came. I'm logging a commendation for you—or, rather, I would be, if your 'mission' had been authorized. On a more pratical note, I have blocked the reprimand that will no doubt be forthcoming from Commissioner Toledano—"

"Captain," Worf interrupted, "I cannot accept any commendations, or any other consideration, for this particular mission.

Picard eyed him. "Because of . . ."

"Yes, sir." Worf lowered his voice a little. "I do not suffer about my decision, Captain, but I must not gain from it. To honor me in any way would be an insult . . . to Grant's memory."

Startled, Alexander looked up at his father. "What does that mean? What are you talking about?"

A chilly tension blanketed the ready room as both Picard and Riker realized just then that Alexander hadn't been told what had happened on the planet. Worf did not shirk the moment. He looked at his son and said, "Alexander . . . I was not strong enough or fast enough to rescue Grant."

Father and son stood barely beyond arms' length from

each other. Between them the terrible meaning of Worf's words festered and cried.

"He's dead?" Alexander's voice was thin, tiny.

Picard buried a shuddering desire to interfere. His custodial feelings toward the boy were supposed to be released now, yet he couldn't retire them. He wanted somehow to soothe Alexander, and hold the program long enough to explain how such things could happen.

But life was no holoprogram, and there would be no pauses to think things out. There would be no scrolling back to save Grant's life.

"He died," Worf said slowly, "before I could get to him. I failed him, Alexander . . . I failed you."

Grief twisted Alexander's face. He averted his eyes from everyone for a long minute, working valiantly to keep control. Alexander kept staring at the carpet, nodded at some thought or other with which he grappled, then finally looked up. He couldn't look in his father's eyes, but stared instead at his father's uniform.

"Some things are worth dying for," he rasped.

At the boy's generous words, Worf twitched, squinted, and fixed a perplexed look on his son. His lips parted, but nothing came out. What his son said was something all Klingons knew, but until now Worf had never known if his child believed it in his heart.

Tight-lipped, Alexander stepped back a pace or two, so he could face his father without seeming to look up so sharply. His voice was thready, full of effort.

"The Day of Honor is meant to help us understand that our enemy might have honor, right?"

Worf forced his voice up. "Yes . . ."

"Mrs. Khanty didn't understand that. She didn't think her enemy had any honor, but she was the one who didn't have any. So she underestimated you. I don't know if what you did was right, but I know honor isn't simple. Sometimes it means both sides might be partly right, and you've got to figure that out before you go killing people."

The room fell silent. All three men were riveted by the echo of a child's words. And the same pride.

Alexander's gaze rose to his father's face, never flinched, never wavered.

"I still don't know what honor is," the boy said, "but I know it's *why* you fight, not *how* you fight."

Speechless, Worf stared down at his son. Then he looked up at Picard, and his expression changed. Anger still lingered, but there was something more—as if he thought that perhaps Picard did far more than had been expected.

"If it's all right," Alexander said, "I have to talk to the captain for a minute."

Perplexed by his son's command of the moment, Worf squeezed the tension out of his hands, nodded, and said, "Very well. Captain . . . thank you."

Satisfied, Picard nodded back. "My pleasure, Mr. Worf." Given the price paid, Worf guarded his reaction and left the ready room.

After the door panels closed and Worf was gone, Riker asked, "Do you want me to leave, too, Alexander?"

"No, you don't have to." Alexander came forward to the desk and looked at Picard. "I checked on some things."

"Oh? Things like what?"

"Like whether or not Mr. Nightingale died that night. He did. And the name of the British colonel. And Patrick O'Heyne really did have a business in London and New York. And Mr. Pennington wrote some articles and letters that were published, so the computer was probably using his own words when he was talking to me. A lot of what we saw really did happen."

"That's good work," Picard told him. "Did you also check as to the fates of Jeremiah and Sandy?"

"No . . . I thought about it, but I decided not to."

"Why not? You have the rest of the journals, don't you?"

"My relatives have them. I can get them."

Picard leaned forward suddenly. "Just a minute—you're not thinking about using a holoprogram again, are you?"

The boy nodded. "Yes, I want to go back. But . . . I think I'll wait until next year's Day of Honor to see the rest. And if it's all right with you," he added, steeling himself, "I think I'll go with my father next time."

Behind the boy, Riker's blue eyes gleamed and he smiled.

"It's quite all right with me," Picard said. "A most honorable decision. Dismissed, swab."

"Thank you, sir."

Like a proper sailing man, Alexander came to attention, turned on a heel, and strode out of the ready room.

Picard leaned back and grinned at Riker. "Hmm . . . what do you know about that? Perhaps I wouldn't do such a bad job of raising a child after all."

Riker chuckled. "Well, sir, I have to admit—"

The door flashed open again. Wasn't anybody using the damned door chimes anymore?

"Captain Picard!"

"Ah, Mr. Toledano . . . good evening."

"You are going to be the captain of a mule train when the Federation Council gets done with you! You handed Odette Khanty over to the planetary law enforcement!"

"Yes, I did. And she's been charged with assassinating her husband, along with a long trail of other corruptions. Mr. Data's recordings are admissible as evidence and—"

"With her present on the planet, the election could still be held! It was held today!"

"And the lieutenant governor won," Riker supplied. "He's now planetary governor."

Toledano rounded on him. "And they also voted to secede from the Federation!" He whirled back to Picard. "We've lost the planet because of your damned defiance!"

Picard kept his voice controlled and relaxed. "Think what you will, Commissioner, but I refused to put myself in the position of the British."

"The *what?*"

"Sindikash has the right to set its own course. Independence was once a concept to be warred over, but I see it as the right of any colony that can prove itself self-reliant and stable. There'll be a muscle-stretching period, a generation or two of struggle, hunger, weakness, and, if they survive, they'll probably join forces with us again someday."

"Assuming they don't self-immolate! The whole area will be unstable for decades! How many colonies flare briefly, only to be snuffed out in power struggles? The toll is always high—"

"And the story disastrous and the songs very sad," Picard filled in, "but that is part of political autonomy. It's up to them, Commissioner, not us. In all conscience, I can't deny the people of Sindikash the same advantage of hindsight with which I look upon the early United States."

Toledano put a pointed finger on the edge of Picard's desk, tried to think of something more to say, then decided he'd be better off saying it to the Federation Council. He stalked out.

Riker let out a long breath, and sat down. "What a week, sir."

"On two fronts," Picard agreed. He leaned back and crossed his legs. "I've got a peculiar taste for a rum toddy tonight. Isn't that odd? Care to join me?"

Riker tipped his head. "Are you worried, sir?"

Picard raised and dropped one shoulder. "It'll be a black mark on my record. There'll be people who want my head on a pike. Sindikash voted for independence, but its new governor wants a relationship with the Federation. The Council can work with that, don't you think?"

"Yes, sir, I do think that."

"As for me . . . if I lose the ship, well, nothing lasts forever. Maybe I'll never get an admiralty, but I'll be able to sleep at night. So we made a value judgment—if not us, then who? And don't forget, if you look at history, it's simply not believable that the United States actually won the Revolutionary War. So keep up hope, Mr. Riker. Save the galaxy a couple of times, you get some friends in key circles."

Picard puffed up and raised his chin.

"After all," he declared, "we're not brutes, you know."

Turn the page for an excerpt from Book Two of *Star Trek: Day of Honor. . . .*

Sisko's luck held for four of the five hours he'd allotted himself for sleep. His dreams roiled uneasily with cloaked Klingon vessels that turned out to be Cardassian warships hurling comets at the *Defiant.* When Odo's gravelly voice condensed out of one thunderous collision, Sisko at first burrowed deeper into his pillow and tried to ignore it.

"Captain Sisko, report to the bridge," Odo repeated impatiently. "There's a Cardassian vessel entering this system."

"Damn!" Sisko rolled out of his bunk, still feeling trapped in the remnants of his nightmare. He yanked on his pullover and stamped into uniform pants and boots. "Have the Klingons done anything to it yet?"

"No, but they may just be biding their time. The Cardassian ship is still out of weapons range."

"I'm on my way." He grabbed his uniform jacket but didn't bother to sling it on, heading for the door instead. Worf met him in the narrow corridor bisecting the crew's quarters, looking much more alert than Sisko felt. They strode into the turbolift and told it "Bridge!" in curt unison. The lift hummed upward while Sisko shrugged into his jacket.

"Any news from the away team?" he asked his tactical officer.

Worf slanted him a wary glance. "How were you aware that I had the away team's secure channel routed to my cabin?"

"Just a guess. What have you heard?"

"Little of promise," the Klingon said somberly. "Doctor Bashir was discovered to be missing after Commander Dax last spoke with us. They have a fix on his combadge and are looking for him now, but Dax estimates it could take several hours to reach his presumed location."

"How did he get lost?"

"Unclear, sir. Major Kira believes he might have been kidnapped by the same group holding the *Victoria Adams*'s crew."

"Lovely." Sisko scrubbed a hand across his face, wondering what else could possibly go wrong on this mission. The turbolift doors hissed open before he could ask further questions.

Odo turned to face them from his watchful stance beside the command chair. As far as Sisko knew, the Changeling never did sit there, even when he was left in command of the *Defiant*'s bridge.

"The Cardassian ship is preparing to enter the far end of the cometary belt," Odo said, for once passing information along with Starfleet succinctness. Sisko glanced up at the viewscreen, but Farabaugh's computer model had been replaced by a real-time image of Armageddon against a comet-hazed starfield. A blinking red cursor now marked the position of the cloaked Klingon vessel, in what looked like a geostationary orbit above the comet-scarred main continent. "Mr. Thornton is constructing an approximate sensor image of the Cardassian vessel, using preliminary data from our long-range scans."

"Good." Sisko sat and gave an approving nod to the dark-haired engineering tech who'd replaced Farabaugh at the science console. "Put it on screen when ready."

"Aye, sir. Convergent resolution coming up now."

The viewscreen abruptly distorted, shrinking Armageddon to a distant dust-stained globe in the upper corner, while a steady twinkle in the background enlarged into a massive battle-armored ship, many times larger than the *Defiant*. Sisko whistled when he saw its familiar military markings. "Looks like we have some very official Cardassian visitors," he remarked.

"My data banks identify this ship as the Cardassian battle cruiser *Olxinder,*" Odo said from his weapons console. "Commanded by our friend Gul Hidret."

"Why am I not surprised?" Sisko leaned back in his chair, frowning as he watched the Cardassian ship enter the comet field. Unlike the Klingons, they took no evasive action, nor did they appear to slow and angle their shields to deflect the comets they encountered. Sisko wondered if Hidret understood the danger he was in—unlike the small *Defiant* and equally small Jfolokh-class Klingon vessel, the *Olxinder* was practically guaranteed to get itself slammed with comets at the speed it was traveling. A moment later, the blue-white flare of phasers across the viewscreen answered his question. Gul Hidret was dealing with the comets with characteristic Cardassian arrogance, by summarily shattering to pieces every large fragment in his battle cruiser's path. Sisko supposed the ship's heavy armor could take care of the rest.

"For someone who was worried about Klingon aggression, he's not exactly trying to sneak in, is he?" Odo commented.

"No," Worf agreed. "I thought Gul Hidret did not believe us when we said there were no Klingons here."

Sisko shook his head. "Commander, I've found that what Cardassians say they believe and what they truly believe have about as much in common as Ferengi prices do with the true value of an object." He watched the *Olxinder* execute a gracelessly efficient turn, its corona of phaser fire leaving an afterglow of superheated gases in its wake.

"But then why come? He must know he cannot locate either of us while we are cloaked," Worf pointed out. "Why would Hidret make himself such a tempting target for attack?"

"Perhaps to provoke us into it," Sisko said.

Odo snorted. "More likely to provoke the Klingons into it."

"Thus giving the Cardassians all the excuse they need to start a war," Sisko finished grimly.

"The Klingons have just opened a hailing frequency to the Cardassian battleship, Captain," Thornton said, glancing over his shoulder. "It's on an open channel."

Sisko exchanged puzzled looks with Worf and Odo. The

last thing he'd expected the Klingons to do was talk first and shoot later. "Put it on the main screen, split channel."

"Aye, sir." The phaser-wreathed glow of the *Olxinder* vanished, turning instead into Gul Hidret's furrowed visage on one side and an even more familiar Klingon face on the other. It wasn't the magnificent mane of gray hair or the broad brow that jogged Sisko's memory so much as the surprising glint of humor in those crinkled eyes. He snapped his teeth closed on a surprised curse. What in God's name was Curzon Dax's old drinking buddy doing out in the middle of the Cardassian demilitarized zone?

"Ah, Hidret," Kor purred in the same tone of pleasant reminiscence he might have used to greet an old lover. "What a joy it is to see your face and recall once more the delightful memory of how I demolished your last battle cruiser. How nice of the Cardassian High Command to give you another."

"It pleases me, too, Dahar Master Kor, to see that your legendary drunken stupors have not cost you *all* of your titles and privileges in the Klingon Empire," Hidret shot back with equally venomous politeness. The old gul's lined face was rigid with some fierce emotion, but Sisko couldn't tell whether it was fury or satisfaction. "Although they have obviously condemned you to manning an obscure post in an unimportant system."

"How unimportant can it be, when a Cardassian ship as magnificent as yours drops by to pay a visit?" Kor retorted. "Although it is a Klingon tradition to welcome visitors, I'm afraid you might not like my particular brand of hospitality."

Hidret raised his brows in mock incredulity. "Are you telling me I have to leave? And here I thought you would welcome my help in evacuating the planet."

"What?" All traces of humor evaporated from Kor's eyes, giving Sisko a glimpse of the formidable warrior Jadzia Dax had once been willing to risk her life for. "What are you talking about?"

A little more satisfaction leaked out around the edges of Hidret's inscrutable expression. "Aren't there Klingons stranded down on that planet, being bombarded by comets? I came to help you rescue them."

Sisko exchanged startled glances with O'Brien and Worf.

"I thought Hidret suspected those exiles of being planted, to give the Klingons an excuse to claim the planet."

Worf snorted. "More Cardassian lies."

"More Cardassian lies!" Kor echoed, his voice a bubbling growl. "I don't know where you got that information, but it's wrong. No one here needs to be rescued."

"You're telling me there are no Klingons on that planet?"

The Dahar Master bared his stained and shattered teeth. "I'm telling you that *no one needs to be rescued.* The Klingons on this planet have chosen their fate, and it is my duty as a Dahar Master to make sure that no one interferes with it. It is a matter of Honor."

Hidret pointed an accusing finger at the viewscreen. "And you can make no allowances for the Cardassians who are dying of ptarvo fever, and need the drug that only this planet can provide?"

Kor snorted. "Bring me a Cardassian dying of ptarvo fever, and I'll be glad to let him beam down to Cha'Xirrac to be cured. In the meantime, old enemy, the only allowance I will make is to let you turn tail and run before I start firing."

"But—"

"But *nothing!"* The Klingon's sudden eruption into a roar made even Sisko start. "And if you ask one more question, your answer is going to be a photon torpedo!"

Gul Hidret snorted in apparent disgust, but the triumphant glint in his eyes made Sisko's stomach roil in apprehension. He was starting to suspect why the old Cardassian had engineered this unlikely confrontation. "From you or from your ally?"

"Ally?" Kor demanded.

"The cloaked Starfleet vessel we spoke to several hours ago. Her transmission originated from within this system."

"You spoke to a cloaked Starfleet vessel?" Kor's eyes narrowed. "That means the *Defiant* is here."

"And they didn't even bother to inform you?" Gul Hidret showed his own teeth in a maliciously triumphant smile. "How rude of them—" A photon torpedo explosion slammed across the open channel, and the Cardassian's smile vanished. "All right, I'm leaving, damn you! Stop shooting!"

Hidret's side of the connection sizzled and went black,

but Kor's scowling face didn't vanish with it. "I know you're listening in on this, Benjamin Sisko. If not, then Dax probably is. Take my advice, both of you, and follow that old Cardassian fool out of this system. If you don't, I'm afraid I will be Honor-bound to hunt you down and kill you."

Look for STAR TREK Fiction from Pocket Books

Star Trek®: The Original Series

Star Trek: The Motion Picture • Gene Roddenberry
Star Trek II: The Wrath of Khan • Vonda N. McIntyre
Star Trek III: The Search for Spock • Vonda N. McIntyre
Star Trek IV: The Voyage Home • Vonda N. McIntyre
Star Trek V: The Final Frontier • J. M. Dillard
Star Trek VI: The Undiscovered Country • J. M. Dillard
Star Trek VII: Generations • J. M. Dillard
Enterprise: The First Adventure • Vonda N. McIntyre
Final Frontier • Diane Carey
Strangers from the Sky • Margaret Wander Bonanno
Spock's World • Diane Duane
The Lost Years • J. M. Dillard
Probe • Margaret Wander Bonanno
Prime Directive • Judith and Garfield Reeves-Stevens
Best Destiny • Diane Carey
Shadows on the Sun • Michael Jan Friedman
Sarek • A. C. Crispin
Federation • Judith and Garfield Reeves-Stevens
The Ashes of Eden • William Shatner & Judith and Garfield Reeves-Stevens
The Return • William Shatner & Judith and Garfield Reeves-Stevens

#1 *Star Trek: The Motion Picture* • Gene Roddenberry
#2 *The Entropy Effect* • Vonda N. McIntyre
#3 *The Klingon Gambit* • Robert E. Vardeman
#4 *The Covenant of the Crown* • Howard Weinstein
#5 *The Prometheus Design* • Sondra Marshak & Myrna Culbreath
#6 *The Abode of Life* • Lee Correy
#7 *Star Trek II: The Wrath of Khan* • Vonda N. McIntyre
#8 *Black Fire* • Sonni Cooper
#9 *Triangle* • Sondra Marshak & Myrna Culbreath
#10 *Web of the Romulans* • M. S. Murdock
#11 *Yesterday's Son* • A. C. Crispin
#12 *Mutiny on the Enterprise* • Robert E. Vardeman
#13 *The Wounded Sky* • Diane Duane
#14 *The Trellisane Confrontation* • David Dvorkin

#15 *Corona* • Greg Bear
#16 *The Final Reflection* • John M. Ford
#17 *Star Trek III: The Search for Spock* • Vonda N. McIntyre
#18 *My Enemy, My Ally* • Diane Duane
#19 *The Tears of the Singers* • Melinda Snodgrass
#20 *The Vulcan Academy Murders* • Jean Lorrah
#21 *Uhura's Song* • Janet Kagan
#22 *Shadow Lord* • Laurence Yep
#23 *Ishmael* • Barbara Hambly
#24 *Killing Time* • Della Van Hise
#25 *Dwellers in the Crucible* • Margaret Wander Bonanno
#26 *Pawns and Symbols* • Majiliss Larson
#27 *Mindshadow* • J. M. Dillard
#28 *Crisis on Centaurus* • Brad Ferguson
#29 *Dreadnought!* • Diane Carey
#30 *Demons* • J. M. Dillard
#31 *Battlestations!* • Diane Carey
#32 *Chain of Attack* • Gene DeWeese
#33 *Deep Domain* • Howard Weinstein
#34 *Dreams of the Raven* • Carmen Carter
#35 *The Romulan Way* • Diane Duane & Peter Morwood
#36 *How Much for Just the Planet?* • John M. Ford
#37 *Bloodthirst* • J. M. Dillard
#38 *The IDIC Epidemic* • Jean Lorrah
#39 *Time for Yesterday* • A. C. Crispin
#40 *Timetrap* • David Dvorkin
#41 *The Three-Minute Universe* • Barbara Paul
#42 *Memory Prime* • Judith and Garfield Reeves-Stevens
#43 *The Final Nexus* • Gene DeWeese
#44 *Vulcan's Glory* • D. C. Fontana
#45 *Double, Double* • Michael Jan Friedman
#46 *The Cry of the Onlies* • Judy Klass
#47 *The Kobayashi Maru* • Julia Ecklar
#48 *Rules of Engagement* • Peter Morwood
#49 *The Pandora Principle* • Carolyn Clowes
#50 *Doctor's Orders* • Diane Duane
#51 *Enemy Unseen* • V. E. Mitchell
#52 *Home Is the Hunter* • Dana Kramer Rolls
#53 *Ghost-Walker* • Barbara Hambly
#54 *A Flag Full of Stars* • Brad Ferguson
#55 *Renegade* • Gene DeWeese
#56 *Legacy* • Michael Jan Friedman
#57 *The Rift* • Peter David

#58 *Face of Fire* • Michael Jan Friedman
#59 *The Disinherited* • Peter David
#60 *Ice Trap* • L. A. Graf
#61 *Sanctuary* • John Vornholt
#62 *Death Count* • L. A. Graf
#63 *Shell Game* • Melissa Crandall
#64 *The Starship Trap* • Mel Gilden
#65 *Windows on a Lost World* • V. E. Mitchell
#66 *From the Depths* • Victor Milan
#67 *The Great Starship Race* • Diane Carey
#68 *Firestorm* • L. A. Graf
#69 *The Patrian Transgression* • Simon Hawke
#70 *Traitor Winds* • L. A. Graf
#71 *Crossroad* • Barbara Hambly
#72 *The Better Man* • Howard Weinstein
#73 *Recovery* • J. M. Dillard
#74 *The Fearful Summons* • Denny Martin Flynn
#75 *First Frontier* • Diane Carey & Dr. James I. Kirkland
#76 *The Captain's Daughter* • Peter David
#77 *Twilight's End* • Jerry Oltion
#78 *The Rings of Tautee* • Dean W. Smith & Kristine K. Rusch
#79 *Invasion #1: First Strike* • Diane Carey
#80 *The Joy Machine* • James Gunn
#81 *Mudd in Your Eye* • Jerry Oltion

Star Trek: The Next Generation®

Encounter at Farpoint • David Gerrold
Unification • Jeri Taylor
Relics • Michael Jan Friedman
Descent • Diane Carey
All Good Things • Michael Jan Friedman
Star Trek: Klingon • Dean W. Smith & Kristine K. Rusch
Star Trek VII: Generations • J. M. Dillard
Metamorphosis • Jean Lorrah
Vendetta • Peter David
Reunion • Michael Jan Friedman
Imzadi • Peter David
The Devil's Heart • Carmen Carter
Dark Mirror • Diane Duane
Q-Squared • Peter David
Crossover • Michael Jan Friedman
Kahless • John Vornholt

#1 *Ghost Ship* • Diane Carey
#2 *The Peacekeepers* • Gene DeWeese
#3 *The Children of Hamlin* • Carnen Carter
#4 *Survivors* • Jean Lorrah
#5 *Strike Zone* • Peter David
#6 *Power Hungry* • Howard Weinstein
#7 *Masks* • John Vornholt
#8 *The Captains' Honor* • David and Daniel Dvorkin
#9 *A Call to Darkness* • Michael Jan Friedman
#10 *A Rock and a Hard Place* • Peter David
#11 *Gulliver's Fugitives* • Keith Sharee
#12 *Doomsday World* • David, Carter, Friedman & Greenberg
#13 *The Eyes of the Beholders* • A. C. Crispin
#14 *Exiles* • Howard Weinstein
#15 *Fortune's Light* • Michael Jan Friedman
#16 *Contamination* • John Vornholt
#17 *Boogeymen* • Mel Gilden
#18 *Q-in-Law* • Peter David
#19 *Perchance to Dream* • Howard Weinstein
#20 *Spartacus* • T. L. Mancour
#21 *Chains of Command* • W. A. McCay & E. L. Flood
#22 *Imbalance* • V. E. Mitchell
#23 *War Drums* • John Vornholt
#24 *Nightshade* • Laurell K. Hamilton

#25 *Grounded* • David Bischoff
#26 *The Romulan Prize* • Simon Hawke
#27 *Guises of the Mind* • Rebecca Neason
#28 *Here There Be Dragons* • John Peel
#29 *Sins of Commission* • Susan Wright
#30 *Debtors' Planet* • W. R. Thompson
#31 *Foreign Foes* • David Galanter & Greg Brodeur
#32 *Requiem* • Michael Jan Friedman & Kevin Ryan
#33 *Balance of Power* • Dafydd ab Hugh
#34 *Blaze of Glory* • Simon Hawke
#35 *The Romulan Stratagem* • Robert Greenberger
#36 *Into the Nebula* • Gene DeWeese
#37 *The Last Stand* • Brad Ferguson
#38 *Dragon's Honor* • Kij Johnson & Greg Cox
#39 *Rogue Saucer* • John Vornholt
#40 *Possession* • J. M. Dillard & Kathleen O'Malley
#41 *Invasion #2: The Soldiers of Fear* • Dean W. Smith & Kristine K. Rusch
#42 *Infiltrator* • W. R. Thompson
#43 *A Fury Scorned* • Pam Sargent & George Zebrowski
#44 *Death of Princes* • John Peel
#45 *Intellivore* • Diane Duane

Star Trek: Deep Space Nine®

The Search • Diane Carey
Warped • K. W. Jeter
The Way of the Warrior • Diane Carey
Star Trek: Klingon • Dean W. Smith & Kristine K. Rusch

#1 *Emissary* • J. M. Dillard
#2 *The Siege* • Peter David
#3 *Bloodletter* • K. W. Jeter
#4 *The Big Game* • Sandy Schofield
#5 *Fallen Heroes* • Dafydd ab Hugh
#6 *Betrayal* • Lois Tilton
#7 *Warchild* • Esther Friesner
#8 *Antimatter* • John Vornholt
#9 *Proud Helios* • Melissa Scott
#10 *Valhalla* • Nathan Archer
#11 *Devil in the Sky* • Greg Cox & John Greggory Betancourt
#12 *The Laertian Gamble* • Robert Sheckley
#13 *Station Rage* • Diane Carey
#14 *The Long Night* • Dean W. Smith & Kristine K. Rusch
#15 *Objective: Bajor* • John Peel
#16 *Invasion #3: Time's Enemy* • L. A. Graf
#17 *The Heart of the Warrior* • John Greggory Betancourt
#18 *Saratoga* • Michael Jan Friedman
#19 *The Tempest* • Susan Wright

Star Trek: Voyager®

Flashback • Diane Carey

#1 *Caretaker* • L. A. Graf
#2 *The Escape* • Dean W. Smith & Kristine K. Rusch
#3 *Ragnarok* • Nathan Archer
#4 *Violations* • Susan Wright
#5 *Incident at Arbuk* • John Greggory Betancourt
#6 *The Murdered Sun* • Christie Golden
#7 *Ghost of a Chance* • Mark A. Garland & Charles G. McGraw
#8 *Cybersong* • S. N. Lewitt
#9 *Invasion #4: The Final Fury* • Dafydd ab Hugh
#10 *Bless the Beasts* • Karen Haber
#11 *The Garden* • Melissa Scott
#12 *Chrysalis* • David Wilson

Star Trek®: New Frontier

#1 *House of Cards* • Peter David
#2 *Into the Void* • Peter David
#3 *The Two-Front War* • Peter David
#4 *End Game* • Peter David

Star Trek®: Day of Honor

Book 1 *Ancient Blood* • Diane Carey
Book 2 *Armageddon Sky* • L. A. Graf
Book 3 *Her Klingon Soul* • Michael Jan Friedman
Book 4 *Treaty's Law* • Dean W. Smith & Kristine K. Rusch